THE UNRULY

USA TODAY BESTSELLING AUTHOR

K WEBSTER

Content Warning

Please be warned that this story contains incestuous relationships, sexual assault, rape, physical violence, murder, forced marriage, captivity, blood/graphic explanations, childbirth death, and other scenes or themes that could be triggering to some readers. This book is much darker than *The Untamed*. Read with caution.

They took everything from us.
Our home. Our family. Our freedom.

We've been forced on a trip from hell with people we hate.
With each step we take, we lose hope of ever making our
way back home again.
These people have a wicked agenda.
We are their prey.

They're brutal and cold.
Every person in their group has twisted delusions.
I need my other brothers to rescue us and release us from
our prison.

As time quickly passes, I realize no one is coming for us.
The only way we'll escape is if we save ourselves.

I'll have to be smart and calculating.
The timing needs to be just right.

When we make our great escape, I'll finally be at liberty to
explore the feelings I have for my brothers. Love, so pure
and innocent, can't be a bad thing.

Desperate. Starved. Agonizing. Desire.

The way I ache for my siblings doesn't feel wrong.
I can no longer fight against these forbidden cravings.

We'll love in secret and hope our parents don't find out.
Because, if they do discover what we've done, it could
mean banishment, *or worse.*

Whatever happens, we'll figure it out. We're in this
together.
Nothing will keep us apart ever again.

Our love is untamed.
And we are the unruly.

****The Unruly, the sequel to The Untamed, is a second
generation forbidden romance in the Wild World taking
place on the timeline after The Wild and The Free. While
it's not necessary to have read the other two books, please
note these characters are the children of Daddy Reed from
The Wild. You'll see all of the characters from The Wild
and The Free in The Untamed and The Unruly. Please
read trigger warnings before proceeding.****

63 REED
40 DEVON

22 ROWDY
19 RONAN
18 RYDER
17 RAEGAN
14 DESTINY
5 DAKOTA
63 DECLAN
1 DAWSON

The Jamison Family

REED   DEVON

ROWDY   RONAN   RYDER   RAEGAN

DESTINY   DAKOTA   DECLAN   DAWSON

WILD WORLD

BY K WEBSTER

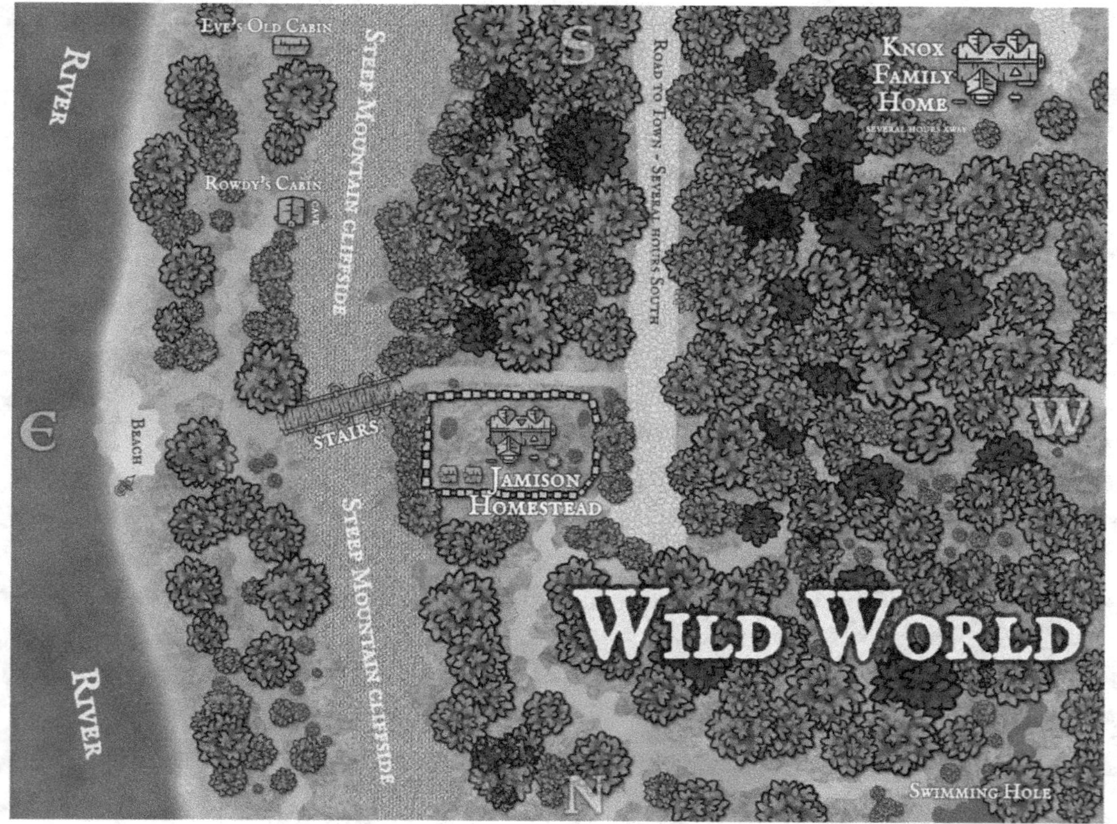

WILD WORLD
RIVER
RIVER
EVE'S OLD CABIN
ROWDY'S CABIN
CAVE
STEEP MOUNTAIN CLIFFSIDE
STEEP MOUNTAIN CLIFFSIDE
STAIRS
BEACH
JAMISON HOMESTEAD
ROAD TO TOWN - SEVERAL HOURS SOUTH
KNOX FAMILY HOME -
SEVERAL HOURS AWAY
SWIMMING HOLE
S
N
E
W

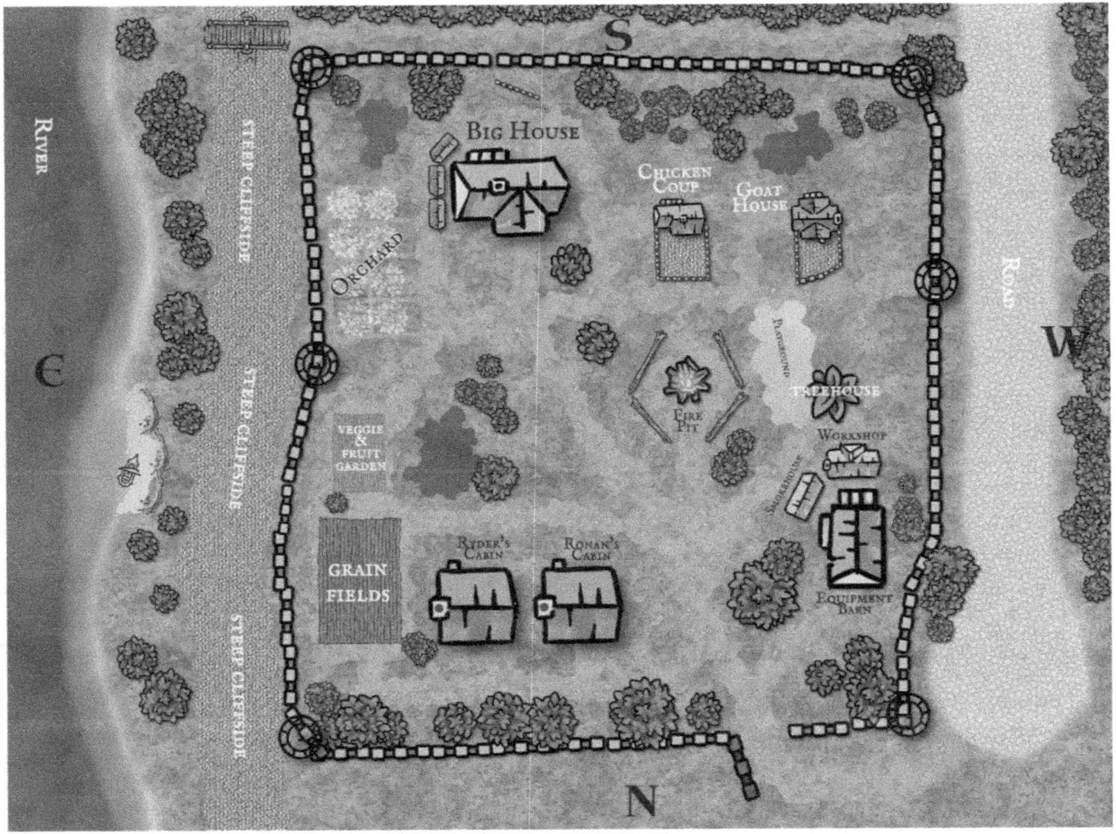

ROAD

WORKSHOP

TREEHOUSE

EQUIPMENT BARN

SMOKEHOUSE

PLAYGROUND

GOAT HOUSE

CHICKEN COOP

FIRE PIT

BIG HOUSE

ROMAN'S CABIN

RYDER'S CABIN

ORCHARD

VEGGIE & FRUIT GARDEN

GRAIN FIELDS

STEEP CLIFFSIDE

STEEP CLIFFSIDE

STEEP CLIFFSIDE

RIVER

W

S

N

E

THE UNRULY

CHAPTER ONE

raegan

THIS CAN'T BE REAL.

Orange and yellow flames lick up high above the treetops, and thick smoke billows all around as I watch my home burn to the ground.

Are they safe?

Are there survivors?

Destiny coughs until she gags but otherwise remains quiet. She's on the other side of Sadie, who's sobbing uncontrollably next to me in the bed of Wild's truck. I would console her, but my hands are bound behind my back.

This is a nightmare.

One I can't seem to wake from.

To my left, Ronan is out cold and closest to the tailgate. Blood trickles from a blow he received to his head when he fought back. He's missing his glasses. I've never seen him so wrecked.

Tears, caused by the horrible situation I've found

myself in, or the thickening smoke, blind me even further. I want to scream at our captors for doing this to my family, but something is tied around my head, holding a sock or some other material in my mouth.

Is everyone dead?

Mya climbs into the bed of the truck and sneers at me as she sits directly across from me. If I weren't crudely tied up, I'd take a swing at her ugly face. Since I can't use my fists, I level her with a glare that promises pain and lots of it.

Voices can be heard from beyond the snapping and crackling of the fire that's quickly consuming my home with my family in it on the other side of the fence.

Is it Mom? Dad?

The voices belong to CJ and Mya's parents, Owen and Tee. Tee's carrying a small child bundled in her arms and Owen has a larger one folded over his shoulder like a sack of potatoes. He climbs into the back and settles on Mya's right while positioning the child in between them. When terrified eyes meet mine, I recognize them immediately.

Dakota.

Oh God. He's alive.

He wails at seeing me, reaching his small hand toward me, but I'm unable to help him. Mya gives him a smack on the arm, hissing something harsh and cruel that has him cowering.

I hate her.

I want to watch her suffer.

Tee shuffles in the truck bed until she's on Owen's other side. Declan clings to her but keeps his eyes on his older brother who's sobbing.

Where're Mom and Dad and Dawson?

If I weren't ripped from my bed in the middle of the night and then quickly subdued by rope, I'd just think these people were saving us from a house fire. But I've quickly put together that they're the *reason* for the fire.

Someone sobs, the sounds growing closer as they approach. Stacey, the hugely pregnant lady who wormed herself into our home, clutches her belly and holds on to her husband, Michael's arm.

Does she feel sick about what they've done to us?

I knew she was bad news, but Mom didn't listen.

I notice the blood all over Stacey's shirt that's stretched over her pregnant belly, slices going every which way like she got in a fight with a bear. Satisfaction spreads through me like a toxic infection. Seeing her blood brings me pleasure.

I want to see them all bleed.

"I'm sorry," Michael croons. "We tried. Now get up front and let's see to those wounds. You're lucky she didn't stab you in the stomach."

She.

Mom?

"I hope you die," I croak out in a raspy, smoke-choked voice around the sock, sending Stacey a blast of my hatred with my expression. I'm not even sure she can hear me.

Stacey stops and glowers at me. "She should have given him to me. At least he wouldn't have burned to death." She covers her mouth with a bloodstained hand. "What kind of mother would rather her child die a horrible death in her arms than let another mother protect him?"

Bile burns up my esophagus as her words click inside my mind. Stacey tried to take Dawson, but Mom put up a fight, refusing to give over her baby. And now, Mom and Dawson are probably dead from the fire. More tears well and spill over.

Oh God. I can't breathe!

My mother. My brother.

These people are monsters!

As the smoke grows thicker, we all start to cough more. Michael climbs into the front of the truck and starts the engine. Is he leaving? What about the rest of their people?

"Where is she?" Lisa, one of the other women from their group calls out. "Stacey, hon? Are you okay? Seth said you lost the baby."

Not her baby.

Ours.

My baby brother, Dawson.

Good for you, Mom.

"In the truck," Tee calls out. "She's in bad shape. You should look after her up there. Have Seth bring your kids to me and Owen."

Lisa disappears and then a few moments later shows

back up with five kids all varying from around Dakota's age to Destiny's. The sleepy kids find places to insert themselves between tents, gear, and the rest of the people crammed in the bed of the truck.

Logan then shows up carrying Kristen, who is either sleeping or knocked out. He puts her up front in the extended cab. I can't see around the heads and stuff piled up as to how many people they have up there.

I need to get free.

If I could just grab my knife that's hooked to my belt under my shirt, I could take some of these assholes out. Or, at the very least, cut me and my siblings free so we could run away.

No such luck.

Michael shouts something to Logan and then starts slowly moving the truck from the thick smoke that's causing everyone to cough all around me. He stops again when he's about fifty yards away.

There are still many people from their group missing, including CJ and Jace. I hope those idiots burned to death. Maybe Ryder killed them. Thoughts of my brother have more tears falling. What if he's dead too?

And where the hell is Dad?

My father would have died protecting his family.

Just like Mom.

It's hard to believe that days ago, I'd been considering a life away from my overprotective parents. Now, I long for those loud dinners where everyone talks at once and there's never a peaceful moment. I'd give anything to be grounded again so long as it meant we could all be together, safe and alive.

Ronan groans from beside me but doesn't wake. He's hurt. It'd been a blur of men in the darkness of Ronan's cabin earlier as they urged us to throw on clothes and to keep quiet. Ronan tried to fight back—to protect me, Sadie, and Destiny—but he was just one young man against several. The loud crack of a weapon against his skull plays on repeat inside my head.

Several men come running through the dark smoke, carrying bags of food and have my father's weapons slung over their shoulders. The first to come into view is CJ. A stupid boy I kissed. If I could cut out my own tongue right now to rid the remnants of him, I would.

These people are sick and rotten to the core.

Evil bastards.

"Tie it there," Logan orders, materializing next to CJ. "Make it tight. I don't want him getting loose."

Him?

Grunts can be heard nearby. Slapping of flesh like someone is getting punched over and over and over again. My heart twists violently in my chest.

Tom and Jace show up, both of them launching themselves and their gear into the truck almost simultaneously as if they rehearsed it. Tom's big foot slams down on my shin and I cry out at the sharp pain, my arms jerking reflexively.

It's then I feel it.

A loosening of my bindings.

I blink away the tears that won't stop burning down my cheeks, ignoring the throb in my leg. Tom and Jace lift kids, pulling them into their laps as they settle in the bed of the truck. We're shoved in here, packed like sardines.

CJ doesn't make eye contact as he passes by the outside of the bed and then hops up front in the cab. Logan checks the bindings on the trailer hitch and then rushes after CJ.

"Let's roll," I hear Logan say before the truck door slams.

We're leaving?

Panic swells up inside me. What about the rest of their people? Where are they? Are they just going to leave them? I manage to move my mouth enough that the material falls away and I'm able to spit out the sock.

"Ryder!" I rasp out. "Ryder!"

The smoke has done a number on my vocal cords because I can hardly get the words past my lips.

"They can't hear you," Jace says with a laugh but then starts coughing.

I wriggle my wrists behind me and tug until I feel my hand slip through the tight bindings. The truck begins to move slowly at first, as if the heavy load is too much for the vehicle to bear. I carefully look around to see if anyone's noticed my near escape. Slowly, I slide my palm to where my knife remains hooked at my side. When they took us from our beds, they told us to throw on our clothes, but little did they know, my knife stays on my belt and they were too preoccupied to notice.

Now I'll use it to stab every damn one of them.

I grip the hilt of my knife, wondering who to maim first. Mya is a selfish choice because I hate her stupid face, but Jace or Tom would subdue me before I had the chance, which means they have to be first.

The truck begins to pick up speed, but sounds can be heard from behind us. Whatever they're pulling on the rope is dragging and bouncing and making a racket. It's not until we break free from the choke of the smoke that I'm able to make out what it is, barely visible in the red glow of the taillights.

Beard.

Dark hair.

So much blood.

A rope around his neck.

Dad.

They're dragging my daddy behind the truck!

Without considering the consequences, I lunge from my squished position, over Ronan's body, and hang over the edge of the tailgate. Commotion ensues behind me. Strong hands grab my thighs, attempting to pull me back. I'm guessing it's Jace since he was closest to me. I kick out, hitting him somewhere that obviously hurts because his hold loosens.

My arms are just long enough I'm able to reach the rope that's wrapped around the trailer hitch. I hack through the rope feverishly, kicking and fighting the arms trying to pull me back. I've lost my chance to be smart about attempting an escape. All that matters is freeing my dad.

The rope isn't completely sawed through, but I've made a good effort. I've almost succeeded when a vise-like hand grips around mine, a heavy body pinning me. I recognize Jace's voice cursing as we fight. His other arm wraps around my throat in a chokehold that has stars bursting across my vision. The knife is torn from my hold and then he yanks me back into the bed of the truck, shoving the tip of my own blade against the throbbing vein in my neck.

"Stop. Fucking. Moving." Jace, though breathing heavily, laughs. "Now you have to watch."

I gape in horror as Dad continues to be dragged behind us. I didn't do enough. I wasn't quick enough. I couldn't save him.

I'm sorry, Daddy.

Snap!

The rope severs suddenly, whipping back at us like a snake. It smacks me across the chest and Jace's arm that holds me in place. It knocks the breath out of me. He howls in pain but doesn't release me. It's a long few seconds before I'm able to suck in air.

Dad is no longer behind us.

There's a chance.

He could be alive.

I could have saved him.

Jace turns us around and shoves me into Tom's

waiting arms. He's no longer holding the kids from before, having pushed them into other laps around him. Since Tom is built like redwood, he easily captures me and pins me to him, forcing me to inhale his musky body odor that somehow overpowers the scent of smoke.

I'm unable to move and my heart is slamming so hard in my chest, I fear it might explode. My entire world has been upended and destroyed. These monsters hurt my family. We trusted them, welcomed them into our home, and befriended them.

And how did they repay us?

They took everything from us—from me.

The pain of losing so much drags me into a pit of despair. Dark. Lonely. Horrible. I want to wake up tomorrow morning and it have all been a sick dream.

Something touches my hand. I follow my arm until I find a small hand curled around mine. Dakota sniffles and searches my eyes like I know how to save us.

I don't.

I can't.

"Rae," he mouths, bottom lip quivering. "I'm scared."

Yesterday, I'd have gloated about him being scared about something because he and I have always annoyed one another. Tonight is different.

"I know, Kota," I croak out, unsure if he can hear me. "Me too."

Tom, upon noticing us, plucks Dakota's hand off mine and then twists me around until my face is forced between his man boobs. I struggle but soon learn it's futile. Tom is much bigger than me. I'm not going to ever be able to beat him physically.

I'll have to be smart.

These people will pay for what they've done to us.

And more importantly, I will find a way to save what's left of my family.

CHAPTER TWO

ronan

THE THROBBING INSIDE MY SKULL IS INCESSANT and maddening.

I can't think. I can't move. I'm going to puke.

My body bounces and the back of my head hits metal. The sharp pain is enough to rouse me from my daze, forcing me to make sense of my surroundings.

Metal. Wind in my hair. Movement.

I'm in the back of a truck.

A groan slips past my lips as I attempt to crack my eyes open. There's a purplish tint to the sky, promising dawn soon. Trees whip past at a nauseating pace. I clamp my eyes shut and breathe deeply.

What's happening?

When I reopen my eyes, everything is blurry. I see people of all shapes and sizes all tucked tightly around me. Squinting, I try to focus on the person closest to me.

Freckles.

Reddish-orange hair.

Jace smirks at me and then turns his head away. My stomach twists as I begin to piece things together. I remember last night.

Falling asleep in the bed beside Raegan…

And then?

I woke up to men in our cabin. I'd thought it was Ryder and Wild playing a prank on us at first. But the voices were harsh and threatening. Noncompliance had one of them bashing me in the head. I remember the cracking of my glasses under a heavy boot.

I'm fucked without my glasses.

"Rae," I whisper, my voice raw as if someone clawed at my esophagus for hours straight. "Rae?"

Why is my throat so ravaged?

My fuzzy mind connects the smokey scent to the equation. In and out of my consciousness, I remember fire. Not a campfire. No, something big. Worse. Catastrophic.

Panic swells up inside me. Where are my parents? My siblings? What's happened?

"Dez?"

Jace nudges me hard in the ribs with his elbow. "They're passed out. Can't hear you, dude."

I go to rub my eyes but learn they're bound behind me. When I begin to struggle, Jace chuckles. Ignoring him, I squint, trying to learn where my sisters are. They were taken with me. I remember their hushed, terrified mewls.

We were kidnapped.

It's so absurd and mind-boggling, I can't begin to understand why or by whom. Was Jace kidnapped too?

The thundering inside my skull is relentless. The more I try to figure out what's going on, the worse it gets. I'm tempted to close my eyes and forget all about it.

So I do.

Sometime later, I jerk back awake.

The sun peeks over the horizon behind the trees as our vehicle rolls to a stop. So much for figuring out this nightmare. How could I fall asleep?

A wave of dizziness washes over me. Something's not right. The blow to the head fucked me up. I wonder if I have a concussion. My sisters may need me and I'm over here snoozing.

I sit up, squinting once more, to see if I can place where we are. We've driven for a while down the sole road that leads to our home but haven't made it anywhere near town yet if the never-ending forest surrounding us is anything to go by. The truck's engine shuts off and car doors open.

So many faces in this truck that all blur together.

Where are my sisters?

"Finally," Jace grunts, pushing a sleeping kid into my lap. "I need to piss."

My own bladder screams in protest, but I don't dare ask to join him. I look over the child, blowing dark hair out of his face. Not a Jamison. Definitely one of theirs. The relief is short-lived because I soon hear a small voice.

"Ronan?"

I can't see him, but he's here somewhere. How did Kota get here? Is the rest of my family here as well?

No.

If Dad or Rowdy or Ryder where here, I wouldn't be tied up in the back of this truck. Sickness curdles my gut. It takes a deep breath to keep from puking all over the kid sleeping on me.

"Ronan!"

"I'm here." My voice crackles, but I think he hears. "I'm here, Kota."

A woman's voice whispers something to him and he starts to cry. I want to free my hands so I can yank him away from her.

What the hell happened?

"Looks like this is where we abandon ship," a familiar voice grunts, slapping the side of the truck. "Best to hide the truck and get a move on."

Logan.

Unable to stop myself, I jerk my head over my shoulder, seeking him out. He'll help us.

"Logan?" I rasp out. "Help."

The tailgate whips down and I fall with it. A thud followed by crying tells me the kid who'd been thrust in my lap just got a rude awakening. Strong hands drag me off the tailgate, depositing me roughly to the ground. I moan in pain, my shoulder smarting from the impact. With my hands still bound, there was no way to brace myself for the fall. I'm lucky I didn't face-plant. The same two hands haul me back to my feet. Logan's face comes into view as he leans in.

"You'll be okay." He smiles at me. "Stick with me and you'll be fine."

Despite the friendliness in his tone, his eyes flash in a disturbing way that sends chills down my spine. I can't feel my fingers or my feet.

"I'm going to need you to stand, and soon, walk." Logan grips my chin, tilting my head to the left and then to the right. "Who did this to you?"

I blink at him in confusion. "I, uh, don't know."

CJ playfully punches him in the ribs. "You're welcome. I did what I had to do."

"You could have killed him," Logan growls, shooting his cousin a nasty glare. "Leave my things alone, CJ. You're lucky I don't break yours out of spite."

CJ mutters an apology before storming off. I nearly whimper when Logan gently runs his thumb over the goose egg on my forehead.

"You really will be fine," Logan assures me, but then his tone turns threatening. "I expect you to behave and do as you're told. You hear?"

I nod because I'm afraid of what'll happen if I don't. I can't afford to take another whack to the head. Not now. Not when I'm trying to figure out what the hell is going on around here and what's happened to my family.

Logan leaves me, barely standing on my own two feet, as he makes his way to the cab of the truck. I'm too frozen in fear to move. Not that I would run away. I could never leave Kota and whoever else is here. Something tells me it's not just the two of us.

Slowly, children, adults, and supplies are unloaded from the back of the truck. A big man I recognize as Tom carries a woman over his shoulder, arms locked around her jean-clad thighs. She bounces as he walks, dark hair flinging back and forth.

Another woman is roughly escorted over to me. It takes a second for my eyes to adjust when she's near enough. Kristen. Her face is swollen and bruised, a reminder of the asshole Logan truly is. She steps closer as though I can protect her from him. I feel like shit because I can't even protect myself.

"What happened?" I whisper, searching her blood-shot eyes for answers.

She grimaces. "I tried to warn you."

Blood turns to ice in my veins, chilling me to my soul. She'd tried and we didn't listen. These people are bad. Very, very bad.

"I can't see," I murmur. "I can't tell if my family is here or not."

Kristen slowly turns her head and I can hear her muttering under her breath. Finally, she turns back to me, her busted bottom lip jutting out. "Declan and Kota."

Declan's name is a punch to my gut.

Not just Kota, but Deck, too. Fuck.

"Is that all?" I ask, hope needling its way through me.

Her head drops and she gives it a slight shake. "Those girls too. Sadie and Destiny."

Two more proverbial kicks to my stomach.

"Fuck. Fuck. Fuck."

"They'll be good to them," Kristen says with a soft, bitter laugh. "But your other sister…"

My *other* sister.

No.

The woman Tom was carrying was Raegan.

"What about her?" I demand, fury prickling through the icy fear I've been cast in.

"They'll break her like they've broken me."

Our conversation is cut short when Logan steps behind me. I know it's him because he has this uncanny ability to make all the hairs on my arms stand on end whenever he's near. He's fucking terrifying now. I'm shocked I ever found him attractive at all.

The man is a monster.

"We try, wifey," Logan says in a cool tone, "but you've proven to be unbreakable."

She shuts down, bowing her head and trembling. Logan grips my forearm and I brace to be thrown to the ground again. To my surprise, he begins untying me.

I'll be free.

I can run and get help.

If only I could see…

As though crawling through the window of my

mind and stealing my innermost thoughts, Logan lets loose a dark laugh. "Don't think about it, pet. I need you to help carry gear. Don't make me regret taking you off your leash."

A burst of rage threatens to explode out of me, but I wisely keep my mouth shut. I don't want to give this man a reason to hurt me. I'd really be unable to help my siblings if I'm knocked unconscious again.

"I, uh, can't see well without my glasses," I choke out. "I don't know where we're going."

"Just follow the person in front of you." Logan clamps a hand on my shoulder, squeezing it. "I'm counting on you to make this easy for all of us."

I want to demand answers, but I'm not like Raegan or Ryder. I can sense danger and know well enough to step back from it when I can. Not everything is solved with punches and cruel words, especially if the person on the other side is bigger and meaner.

Logan releases his grip on me and walks away to gather more supplies from the truck. Kristen sidles closer to me. She may have been with them, but she's not one of them. It's so clear now to see she's a captive every bit as much as me and my siblings are.

"Are they okay?" I ask, my cold hand brushing against her warm one. "Can you see them all still?"

She nods and glances at me. "Raegan is asleep or something. Tom's still got her. Tee has your two little brothers in with the group of the other kids and is feeding them snacks. They seem scared but aren't hurt."

I let out a rush of breath, relieved to hear of it. "Destiny? Sadie?"

Sadie may have just come to visit, but she's one of us because she's Wild's friend. It's my duty to look after her too until we can escape this mess.

"They're okay. Both are standing by Jace and CJ."

I bite down on my bottom lip, willing the emotion to go away. Knowing my family here is safe is a relief that nearly has me in tears.

"Don't worry," I assure Kristen. "As soon as Dad and my brothers realize we're gone, they'll come for us. They'll rescue us."

Kristen tenses and takes hold of my hand. "You don't remember what happened?"

Bits. Flashes. Fragments.

"Just that we were taken from our beds and I got a whack to the head."

"Ronan…" She squeezes my hand and sighs. "They set the big house on fire. Your mom and the baby were still inside. I'm sorry."

The fire.

Flames, hot and intense. Ruining and taking and destroying.

Her words sting, just a prick at first, but then a thousand pricks stab at me all over as I digest her words, reality finally setting in. "W-What?"

No.

Please, God, no.

My chest tightens to the point I can't breathe. The

blurry trees around me spin until I lose my balance. I fall hard to the ground on my palms and knees, nipping my tongue in the process. As the metallic taste of blood floods my mouth, I try to compute her words.

Your mom and the baby were still inside.

Fire.

I'm sorry.

This can't be happening. This can't be fucking happening.

"My dad too?"

A small sigh escapes Kristen. "I'm sorry, Ronan."

"Is he…."

"Gone. He's gone."

A cry explodes out of me. It's filled with pain and agony as my heart is ripped from my chest.

These people killed my family.

Did they kill my brothers Ryder and Rowdy?

The answer is too much to bear and one I can't fathom.

They should have just killed us too.

CHAPTER THREE

ryder

'M HELPLESS AND AT A LOSS FOR WHAT TO DO.

They took them.

They took our family.

Rowdy, Wild, and Chet have been trying to contain the spread of the fire from the big house so that we don't lose more than we already have. I think Wild's more pissed about his truck being stolen than anything, which is why it's a good thing I'm not around him. If I saw him try to catch a signal on his phone one more time this morning, I was going to punch him.

Rowdy, sensing my impending meltdown, tasked me with staying with our parents and tending to their injuries, especially Dad's.

Mom, who finally got Dawson to calm down, fell asleep beside Dad in Ronan's bed. I've been working on cleaning and dressing all of Dad's wounds. He looks as though he's been chewed up and spat out. The skin all over his back and legs has been rubbed off, he has defensive knife wounds all over his hands and forearms, and his face is so swollen he can't see out of his eyes. If it weren't for his ragged breathing, I'd think he were dead.

But he's not dead.

They tried to take my father from me but were unsuccessful.

Dad groans when I tie off one of the stitches on his forearm, tugging a little too hard. The only pain medicine we have is a bottle of ibuprofen I found in Ronan's bedside table drawer. I wish I could give him more, but the big house is gone.

Everything and everyone is gone.

Even the goddamn wolf pups are gone. I haven't had an opportunity to search for them, but I'm afraid when I finally do, I'll find their discarded corpses. As soon as the fire is contained and Dad has been taken care of, we'll have to do something with all the bodies those motherfuckers left behind.

My mind tries to drift to my missing siblings, but I force it from my head. Helping Dad is the most important thing right now for me to focus on.

I'm thankful for the extra first aid kit we keep in the workshop. Too many times one of us has hurt ourselves there, so having immediate access to bandages was a necessity. I blew through most of the supplies cleaning and dressing Dad's back and legs but saved some for the more critical wounds on his hands.

He groans again when I straighten out one of his pinkies. It's swollen and misshapen. I'm not sure if it's broken or not. The main concern is all the skin miss-ing across the top knuckles. Keeping it clean and free of infection is the priority. Setting bones, if necessary, will come later.

The insidious wrath burning inside me, begging for escape, is continuous torture. I crave to rage and de-stroy something—anything—to release some of it. But now isn't the time for that shit.

Dawson whimpers in his sleep and Dad stirs. He's been unconscious since I got that rope off his neck. I can't begin to imagine what sort of pain he's in.

I spend hours caring for him until I'm nodding off while sitting up. It's not until I feel someone's hand on my shoulder that I realize I completely fell asleep. Popping my eyes open, I discover Mom standing beside me. She's changed from her bloody, burned nightclothes into something of Raegan's that was in Ronan's cabin. Dad and Dawson are both still passed out.

"Go get some sleep, honey," Mom croaks, her voice barely a whisper. "Find something to eat and drink first."

"I can stay here with Dad."

"We need you at full strength. Catch a nap."

Once I determine that my mom is capable of taking over, despite her appearing exhausted beyond belief, I give her a nod. She kisses the top of my head and then I make my way out of the cabin. There's smoke every-where, but one look in the direction of the big house and I know the fire is mostly out. I can still see the three guys with shovels and rakes working. The urge to help them is strong, but I can barely stand on my own two feet. I stumble into my own cabin and dig through my storage bins where I keep snacks and bottled water.

Two bottles and three packs of homemade beef jerky later, I'm falling face first onto my bed. The second my head hits the pillow, I'm out.

"Anything?" Chet asks Wild, eyes barely peeking open from the sofa in my cabin.

Wild stops his pacing, spears his filthy fingers through his chaotic hair, and shakes his head. "Nope. I thought if I could get a hold of Dad or find the location of the truck, we'd be able to go after them. But of fucking course I've got nothing out here." He raises his arm like he's about to throw his phone, but in the end, he growls before shoving it into his pocket.

The sun is setting outside, which means I've slept most of the day. Every bone in my body protests as I drag myself off my bed. Wild eyes the vacated mattress and then dives onto it. Since the three of them worked on the fire all morning and afternoon, they're all half dead from exhaustion. I shove my boots on and slip out of the cabin to allow them some rest.

Rowdy is sprawled out on my hammock, passed out and snoring softly. Black soot covers his arms, face, and hair. Everyone could use a dunk in the river, but going down the cliffside stairs with zero energy sounds like a feat none of us are up for.

I tiptoe off the porch and make my way toward the big house to inspect the damages. Aside from a few black logs sticking up from the rubble, it's barely recognizable that a house stood there less than twenty-four hours ago. It's just a big pile of smoking ash now. Gone.

Tears burn at my eyes, but I quickly blink them away. Now's not the time to have an emotional breakdown. I need to gather what I can for my family.

After forcing myself away from the destruction of our home, I walk over to the big drums we use to collect rainwater. Since they were plastic, the heat melted them and the water was lost. The few bottled waters we have in the cabins and other buildings on our property will have to suffice until we can haul some river water up here.

So much work.

And all I want to do is set out to find my siblings.

Scrubbing a palm over my face, I check out the root cellar. It's buried under the rubble of the house, but it's possible that some of the food down there could have survived. I mentally mark that down in my head to unearth once things have settled.

The orchard and gardens appear to be unscathed, which is good news. We can harvest what we can from there and hunt if need be. I walk across our property over to the chicken coup. The chickens flew from the pen and are pecking around in the goat pen. A quick peek inside the coup tells me all the eggs are ruined from the heat, but at least the chickens are okay.

The chickens make a lot of racket when I climb into the goat pen. It's as though they're upset about what happened. Join the fucking club. I feed both the chickens and the goat while I'm here, pleased to discover their food isn't bad. The water collection drum on the side of the goat pen is still intact, so I breathe easier knowing we have another water source, though we'll be sharing with the animals.

After taking stock of the rest of the property, I walk back over to Ronan's cabin. A sharp pain cuts deep in my chest. I miss all my siblings, but I wish for one second to see Ronan's small smile or Raegan's determined expression. Fuck, this sucks.

"Knock-knock," I murmur softly as I push in through the cabin door. "Mom?"

Mom is sitting on the bed, taking inventory of Ronan's snack box. Dawson sits beside her, unhelpfully trying to crawl through the middle of it. Dad is sleeping, barely moving.

"I see you got some rest," Mom says, briefly looking up to offer me a sad smile.

"Enough," I agree. "Everything okay?"

Her bottom lip wobbles before she bites down on it. "It will be."

Neither of us believes her.

I sigh heavily and then take the seat beside the bed. My eyes skip over Dad's abused form and over to

Dawson. His blond hair is dirty with soot and his eyes are red. Snot runs down his upper lip. Aside from that, he seems like his usual self, trying to get into everything he can.

"I feel like I should be out there looking for them," I whisper, eyes filling with unshed tears. "I'm useless right now."

Mom unscrews a bottle of water and gently holds it to Dawson's mouth. His snot goes all over the bottle. Gross. She lets him sip from the bottle before holding it up to me to offer me some. I violently shake my head to decline.

"You're not useless, Son," Mom says, using her shirt to wipe off the snot. "You're needed here right now. We have to band together until Atticus gets here."

Knowing that Uncle Atticus and Aunt Eve will be here soon is a relief. They can't get here soon enough. Not only will we have an uninjured, able-bodied man, but we'll also have supplies and a vehicle.

"But they were kidnapped, Mom. What if they hurt them?" I scrub my palm over my dirty face and let out a ragged breath. "I'm so fucking terrified."

She doesn't chide me for language, which I'm thankful for. "I'm scared too, but they have Raegan and Ronan. Those two aren't incompetent."

They're together and quite capable. It gives me hope.

"Raegan won't be happy," I say with a dark chuckle. "Her knife's gone. Maybe she'll stab them all."

We can only hope.

"Those kids are smart," Mom agrees. "They may be outnumbered, but that won't stop them. We can count on them to take care of the little ones too."

Dawson hollers and nearly knocks the water bottle out of Mom's hands. She helps him to another snotty sip that churns my stomach.

"The animals are okay," I mutter, eager to offer some good news. "The eggs are bad, but the chickens are hanging out in the goat pen."

"Where are the pups?"

My stomach twists. Now onto the bad news. "Gone. I, uh, haven't looked around for their bodies yet."

She purses her lips together and glances over at Dad. "We'll find them, Ry. And your Dad will be up and his usual self before we know it."

Her optimism is a salve to my bleeding heart. I want to believe her words with everything I have. That by the time Uncle Atticus arrives, Dad will be healed, and together we can hunt those motherfuckers down.

My boot moves and something crunches under it. I peek down to see the remnants of Ronan's glasses. Just knowing he's out there and unable to see makes me want to throw up. Reaching down, I pick up the crushed frames and hold them up. Mom lets out a pained sound when she sees them. Tears rush down her cheeks like two rivers as she begins to cry, a soul-shattering sound that threatens to kill me.

Neither I nor my baby brother is immune to her sobbing.

He starts to wail along with her while I desperately smack away the wetness on my cheek.

Those trespassers severed the Jamison family. They took a blade and cut us right down the middle. We're bleeding out, no hope for staunching the flow.

But we will heal.

And when we finally do…

Hell *will* be to pay. Vengeance *will* be served. We *will* get even.

CHAPTER FOUR

raegan

E'VE BEEN WALKING FOR HOURS WITH FEW breaks. I'm exhausted and starving. More than anything, though, I'm pissed. With each step farther into the wilderness, I question whether or not we'll be able to find our way home again.

"Can we take a break?" I ask, ignoring Tom beside me and hollering ahead to Michael, who's leading the group. "The kids are tired and my feet are killing me."

Several murmurs ripple through the group. I counted earlier when I was bored and feeling frustrated by my situation. There are twenty-three of us in total. Six of my people, including Sadie, and seventeen of them. Of their group, four of them are small children and two are teenagers. That leaves eleven able-bodied adults. Me, Sadie, and Ronan have no hope against their eleven. Thirteen if you count their teenagers.

I may not be able to take them in a fight, but I can use their kids against them.

Tee, Owen's wife, stops walking and shoots me a thankful smile.

It wasn't for you, witch.

"It'll be evening soon," Michael calls back. "I guess it's as good of a time as any to break for camp."

I glance over my shoulder to check on Ronan, but Tom's huge, stinky body blocks my view. Cringing at his nearness, I swivel back around to check on the others. Sadie is in front of CJ and Jace, who are in front of me. Destiny is close to her with Mya just ahead of them. Dakota and Declan are way up ahead with Michael and Stacey. I hate that I'm so far away from my little brothers because I can't check on their well-being from back here.

The gear I've been saddled with feels like it weighs a ton. I'm not even sure what's inside the bag I've been forced to carry. If I get an opportunity, though, I'll steal anything useful. And if I ever get close enough to Jace, I'll steal my knife back from him.

Our group disperses from our marching line as the leaders start barking out orders. Michael and his brother Owen are clearly in charge. Since Michael appears to be older, I think he's the real boss of this group.

"Start gathering tinder for the fire," Tom instructs, relieving me of my heavy backpack. "Put it over there in that clearing." He grabs hold of my shoulder, jerking me around to face him. "Don't get any funny ideas, girl."

I want to spit in his face, but he might give me one

of those crushing bear hugs and force me to smell his armpits again. Hard pass.

"Whatever," I grumble, unable to keep the bite out of my tone.

He huffs, his red, flabby cheeks wobbling. "Not sure about *him*, but *I* won't tolerate mouthiness. Remember that."

I frown at Tom, confused by his words. Rather than let him see he's rattled me, I swivel around to start looking for sticks. Ronan stands near Kristen, looking a little worse for the wear with the knot on his head and swollen eyes from crying. Logan has a palm on each of their shoulders, leaned in and speaking quietly to them. I need a moment alone with my brother so we can formulate an escape plan.

We *will* escape.

I just have to figure out how to get us all safely away from these awful people.

For now, I keep quiet and listen to conversations that might be useful to me in the future. The men are all kinds of scary, especially Logan. CJ, Jace, Tom, and Seth aren't in any leadership roles. They do as they're told when they're told. While Michael is undoubtedly in charge, with Owen backing him up, Logan—a carbon copy of his father, Michael—holds a lot of power. The women, aside from Kristen, are all just extensions of their husbands, pretending like it's not fucked up that they kidnapped us. Kristen behaves like a victim and I'm dying to pick her brain about them.

Sadie hurries over to me and shoots me a pitiful look. I feel bad for her. She's nice and was just supposed to be here for a visit. I'm sure getting kidnapped with the rest of us was not on her list of expectations. Furthermore, she's clueless about being in the wilderness. Since our trek began from the side of the road where the men hid the truck, she's screamed no less than fifty times when a bug landed on her.

"What are we going to do?" Sadie asks, voice low. "We have to get away from these freaks."

"We will," I assure her. "I need to see my baby brothers and check on them."

Someone scoffs behind me. Both me and Sadie whip around to find Mya watching us with a cruel expression twisting her features. I cringe at the thought of her hearing us. Maybe she didn't.

"They're not *your* anything anymore," Mya says in an antagonistic tone that makes my blood boil. "May as well get used to it now."

"What are you talking about?" I demand, taking the bait she's laid out for me.

She laughs scornfully. "They're Stacey's children now."

"*My* brothers?" I gape at her in disbelief. "You're insane."

"You have no idea about how much your life has changed. It's pathetic." Mya makes a pretend sad face. "Your brothers no longer belong to you."

I curl my fists up, eager to punch the stupid look

off her face, but I refrain. Barely. Getting information is more important. If I punch her, they'll tie me up again…or worse. I'm not eager to find out what else they could do.

"Explain," I demand. "You make no sense."

Sadie huffs from beside me. "You're all fucking crazy."

Mya ignores her altogether, choosing to fling her venom my way. "Dakota and Declan will be calling Stacey and Michael Mommy and Daddy soon." She laughs. "Since theirs are dead now."

I take a step forward, forgetting to remain calm, eager to knock this psycho to the ground. "They won't do it. You can't just brainwash my family like that. It won't work and you're delusional to think so."

And, if Dad survived what they did to him, he'll come for us.

"Give it time, bitch," Mya sneers. "You'll see."

Her chilling words make my stomach tighten. "What the hell does that mean?"

"It means," she says in a derisive tone, "that you'll do your wifely duties and fall into line if you value your life."

Wifely duties?

"I still don't understand," I spit out. "Make it make sense."

Mya bravely crowds me, tilting her head so she glowers up at me. The arrogance in her expression makes tendrils of unease curl in my stomach.

"You two," she says, gesturing at Sadie and then me, "will soon marry into our Higher Earth community."

I snort out a laugh that makes her nostrils flare with fury. Wait. She's actually serious? I'm not marrying one of these awful men. And what the hell is Higher Earth?

"No," I growl, pushing her hard and causing her to fall to the ground on her butt. "Over my dead body."

She pops back up to her feet and dusts off the leaves before sending me a baleful grin. "That's essentially the main theme of Higher Earth. Drop the dead weight. The others in our community were dead weight, which is why they're no longer with us. The men ended them like they ended your family." She shrugs as if murdering their own people and mine isn't that big of a deal. "If you don't comply, you'll die. If you're weak, you'll die. If you don't contribute to the betterment of our community, you'll die. End of story."

These people are insane.

"We're kids," Sadie chokes out. "This is against the law."

Mya rolls her eyes. "There is no law out here." Her gaze drifts past us. When I turn to see what she's looking at, I stiffen. "It's a shame your other brother wouldn't play nicely. I really would have preferred him."

Preferred Ryder to Ronan?

"You think you're marrying my brother?" I blurt out, unable to stop the hysterical laughter that follows. "That's not going to happen."

He doesn't like girls, dumbass.

Mya crosses her arms over her chest. "It *is*. Logan is going to train him."

"Train him how?" I demand, darting a quick glance at my brother, who stumbles over a log that he couldn't see. They've blinded him without his glasses. "Tell me!"

Mya shrugs and starts to walk away. I chase after her, shoving her again. She whips around, baring her teeth at me. "Shove me one more time and I'll have your *husband* beat you into submission."

"Tell me how he'll train him," I hiss, ignoring her threat. "And what happens to Destiny?"

My sister kneels beside a crate of supplies, slowly pulling things out. Jace hovers nearby, smiling and talking to her as though he has the power to make her laugh.

Unbelievable.

Hell no.

"It'll be more fun to watch you learn in due time." She wriggles her fingers at me before skipping off to Lisa and Tee.

"Bitch," Sadie grumbles. "We have to get the hell out of here."

Yeah, we do.

And fast.

By the time darkness has descended upon us, camp is set up. Tents surround the campfire and people are sitting on fallen logs, munching on food they stole from our house. It won't last forever, though. I wonder if they even know how to properly hunt or trap game.

Personally, I know how to make a fish trap, construct nets, and can build weapons like a bow and arrows. I'm not worried about my survival when it comes to feeding myself if push comes to shove. However, I'm not about to show these people or offer up any information. They can starve for all I care.

Ronan sits beside Kristen across the fire. I keep trying to get his attention, but he can't see me from this far away. They've strategically kept us apart. Same with my little brothers. Dakota and Declan have been treated like little princes by Stacey and Michael, far beyond my reach. I even heard Dakota laugh, which turned my stomach inside out. Luckily, Destiny and Sadie are sitting by me. Having at least one of my siblings close by brings me relief.

"You think Mom and Dad are okay?" Destiny asks, plucking at the crust of her bread. The same bread Mom was baking just yesterday. "I feel like if they were dead, I'd feel that loss in my heart."

"Of course they're fine," I lie, patting her back. "They're probably all looking for us right now. Dad will gut all these people. You'll see."

Destiny nods, her blond hair falling in her face as she keeps her head bowed. "Raegan, I'm scared. These people aren't right."

"No, they're not," I agree. "They're monsters. We

have to be careful and stay close. When the time is right, we'll leave. All six of us. I'll get us back to the main road where our family will be waiting. Soon, this will just be a bad memory."

We turn quiet when Jace approaches. His stare lingers on Destiny as he tries to catch her attention. I flip him the bird and Sadie follows suit. He grumbles before stomping off to where CJ is.

"What's wrong?" Destiny asks. "You're tense. I can tell something's wrong."

For someone who can't see, she's always so perceptive.

"Jace. He was over here trying to get friendly. If he comes too close," I threaten, "I'll maim him with this stick." I playfully poke the stick in my hands in Destiny's side, making her stifle a giggle.

"I used to think he was a nice guy," Destiny murmurs. "But he's just like them."

"They fooled us all." I toss the stick into the fire even though it'd definitely look better in Jace's eye. "They're going to pay for this."

My mind reels with all the possible ways I could hurt them. It keeps me entertained through the rest of dinner. It's not until people start retiring to tents that my heart rate kicks up. I hadn't considered sleeping arrangements until just now.

Tom rises from his log and motions for his kids, Wyatt who's around Destiny's age, and Olivia, who can't be more than six or seven. His eyes burn into me. "You're with me, kid."

Oh, hell no.

I'm not bunking with this freak like I'm in his family.

I scramble to my feet and shake my head. "No way, creep. I'm sleeping with Sadie and Destiny."

"Don't worry," a deep voice says from behind me. "He's not allowed to touch you."

Hearing CJ behind me doesn't comfort me. In fact, it has me trembling in fear. His hands are strong as he grabs my wrists, jerking them behind me. I attempt to fight him off, but Tom joins the fray, easily manhandling me into submission while CJ ties me up.

He's not allowed to touch you.

The traitor's promise is the only thing that's stopping me from losing my mind right now.

He's not allowed to touch you.

But for how long?

I don't even want to think about it.

CHAPTER FIVE

ronan

Raegan.

AEGAN.

Oh God.

The panic in her voice has me rising to my feet. I can't exactly see where she's at, but I hear a struggle happening nearby, followed by her bellowing.

I have to help her.

Stumbling toward the sound, I make my way to my sister, uncaring of the consequences. She needs me and I'll do my best to protect her. As soon as I'm near, I can tell she's being dragged away by the big man, Tom.

"Let her go!" I shout, lunging for him.

He easily shoves me back and I nearly fall into the fire. I right my feet again, surging forward. Before I can reach him, someone grabs me by my hair on the back of my head. I cry out in shock, stunned at the sudden pain on my scalp.

"That," Logan snarls from behind me, his body pressing against my backside, "is against the rules. A man never intervenes when a woman is receiving her punishment."

What?

I start to struggle, but his other strong hand grabs hold of my bicep and squeezes to the point of excruciating pain. My whole body freezes.

"Logan, you're hurting me," I croak out.

His hold on my arm lessens, but he doesn't fully let me go.

"Kristen. Bedtime. Now," Logan orders to his wife. "You too, pet."

It's the second time he's called me "pet." He got pissed when he saw what CJ had done to my forehead, telling him not to touch his "things." And now I'm sharing a tent with him? What exactly does he want with me?

I'm about to find out.

Logan roughly guides me to our destination. I frantically look around for my sisters, but before I can locate them, I'm being shoved into a decent-sized tent. I land hard on my knees, a thin sleeping bag barely breaking my fall. Pain splinters down my legs and I scramble to the corner of the tent to escape whatever punishments I may have brought on myself.

Kristen crawls into the tent but says nothing to me. She sits down and bows her head. I'm not sure what the hell is going on or what's expected of me, but I don't like it. I don't like any of this.

"I'm sorry, but he was hurting my sister—" I start but am cut off by Logan's deep, authoritative voice.

"You speak when I allow it, pet."

Logan zips the tent and walks toward me on his knees. When he unbuckles his belt, I tense. The leather slings out of his belt loops with a swooshing sound. I'm frozen in fear, unsure of what happens next. He doesn't toss away the belt and start for the button on his jeans like I think he might, instead wrapping the leather around his fist.

Just like Dad used to when we were little and would get in trouble.

Admittedly, Ryder got the belt a lot more than I did.

"Let's get this over with," Logan commands. "This can either go quickly or you can fight me every step of the way. The latter will hurt a lot worse."

This can't be happening.

I shake my head in defiance, edging against the tent wall to keep space between us. It's futile because in the next second, he pounces at me. I swing at him, hoping to knock him in the jaw and keep him away from me. Logan easily deflects the punch and slams me onto the ground. The hand with the belt smashes my chest down as he yanks at the button of my jeans. All too easily, he unzips my jeans and jerks them down my thighs.

I fight him.

Fuck, how I do.

But Logan is massive and strong. We're no match.

A panicked keening sound escapes me as he flips

me over onto my stomach. I can see Kristen in her same submissive position, not looking over at us. This is happening and there's nothing I can do about it.

He exposes my ass, much to my humiliation, and roughly gropes one cheek. In another life, hell, even a week ago, this might've been one of my darkest fantasies come to life. Not now. Now it's torture and terrifying.

His hand disappears and then the fiery lash of the belt strikes my ass.

I scream.

So loud it makes my own ears hurt.

And it doesn't stop him.

Lash after lash after lash, Logan beats me with his belt. The pain is so excruciating, I start to black out. On the rare occasions I did get spankings from Dad, it was never this hard and he usually stopped at three licks.

I stop counting after twenty.

All I can do is moan and sob as Logan takes out his anger on my ass cheeks.

This is hell. I'm in hell.

Finally, after an eternity, Logan tosses his belt down. Then, with sickeningly sweet gentleness, he tugs my boxers up over my ass. I remain unmoving but am still crying as he removes my jeans and shoes.

"You can sleep on the end tonight, pet," Logan says, voice soft and sweet like when he played me after we first met. "We don't want your bruises to get bumped in the middle of the night."

I shudder when he hooks an arm under me and

pulls me up onto my knees. My entire face is wet from tears and sweat. I'm humiliated and feel like the weakest fucking man on the planet. He nuzzles his nose against my sweat-slicked neck before kissing the flesh there. I flinch at his touch, which causes him to sigh sadly.

Fuck. Him.

"Behave and I won't have to do this to you," Logan says in a stern tone. "I'll make a good husband out of you for Mya. She'll be lucky to have you."

These people are insanely fucked-up.

Completely bonkers.

I don't respond to him because I don't want to hear the despair in my voice. Once he releases me, I quickly scramble over to the sleeping bag he said belongs to me. Not making eye contact with him or Kristen, I gingerly start to sit down but soon realize that hurts too damn bad. With a ragged sigh, I sprawl out onto the top of the sleeping bag face down so my sore ass won't hurt as much.

Sleeping isn't an option. My mind is racing with all the ways my life has been shattered. If only Ryder were here. He would destroy him for this. The last time I was in a tent, Ryder touched my cock. It was beautiful and perfect. I'd give anything to go back to that moment we had. Anything to see him for just a second.

My distracting thoughts are pushed away by the sounds of smacking. Is he whipping Kristen now too? I manage to turn my head to catch a peek at the two of them in the shadowed tent.

He's fucking her.

It's the sound of their bare skin slapping together.

She's pressed face down onto the sleeping bag as Logan savagely thrusts into her. I can't see his face in the dark with the fire light behind him, but I sense his attention on me. Quickly, I turn away, once again choosing to stare at the tent instead.

Their fucking seems to go on forever. She whimpers and mewls, none of which sound like she's enjoying it, and he grunts more frequently as he gets close to release.

"Fuck, yes," Logan hisses as the slapping sound becomes less rhythmic. "Oh, fuck that was hot."

Hot?

The man has lost his mind.

"Stay just like that, Kristen," Logan instructs. "If you don't get pregnant soon, I may just have to trade you in for someone who can. We have options now. As a councilman for our community, I can and will slough off the dead weight. The establishment and growth of the Higher Earth family depends on creating a strong foundation and feeding it with competent men and women."

What the hell is Higher Earth?

And they have options now? Like Raegan?

Sadie?

Anger simmers beneath my pain and fear, just a few bubbles that begin to grow with intensity. This whole group of nutsos are exactly who my parents tried to protect us from. We stupidly were excited to meet new people, and me and Raegan both experienced our first crushes. Little did we know they'd turn into…this. A fucking cult of creeps.

I fall asleep, dreaming of ways to kill them all.

Every last one of them.

The sounds of children giggling wake me from my slumber. I'm unable to tell if it's Dakota or Declan. I'm still straining to listen when a large hand strokes over my back.

"How are you feeling this morning?" Logan asks, voice filled with concern.

Bile creeps up my throat. I don't want to look at him or hear his voice. I certainly don't want his touch.

Recoiling, I hiss out, "Don't touch me."

He chuckles as though what I've demanded is funny. "You're understandably upset, pet, but you'll get over it."

"Ronan. My name is Ronan. Not your fucking pet."

I tense as I wait for him to lash out in anger. He chuckles again before tugging my boxers down. "Let's have a look at the damage."

Squeezing my eyes shut, I try to put my mind anywhere but here. He's gentle as he caresses my bruised flesh.

"It's going to hurt for a few days," Logan says finally. "Try not to earn any more punishments until those heal up."

I have nothing to say to him, so I clench my teeth.

With a frustrated sigh, he pulls my boxers back up and then exits the tent. It's not until I hear his voice speaking to someone outside that I finally relax.

"You okay?" Kristen asks.

Rolling over onto my side, I see her on the sleeping bag closest to the tent exit. Her face is still swollen and bruised from days ago, but she wears a soft smile. How can she be smiling right now?

"He whipped me," I choke out, barely keeping the emotion at bay. "Like an unruly child."

She scoffs, frowning. "No, he beat you with a belt because he's a sadistic monster."

Hearing her confirm what this truly was makes me feel better. She's right. I wasn't being punished. I was being abused.

"And he rapes you," I whisper. "There was nothing consensual about that."

Her teeth bite down onto her bottom lip and her brows furl together. "I'm getting used to it."

Getting used to rape?

My chest cracks open and bleeds for her. How long has she had to endure this man? How long can she continue before he breaks her?

"I want to kill him." I swallow hard. "For you. For me."

She reaches a hand across the middle sleeping bag. Needing a friend in this mess, I can't help but clutch onto it.

"My sisters," I murmur, fear stifling my voice. "They're destined for the same fate as you."

Kristen grimaces but nods. "I was camping with my boyfriend when they found me." She closes her eyes and sighs heavily. "It's what they do. They steal and kill and rape. All in some fucked-up effort to build their group of freaks."

"What happened to your boyfriend?"

"Logan stabbed Eddie in the stomach right in front of me." She sniffles and her bottom lip trembles. "Told me if I accepted Logan as my husband and let him consummate our marriage in front of Eddie, he'd give him a quick, merciful death. If I refused, Eddie could slowly bleed out as Logan raped me day in and day out however long it took him to die."

I squeeze Kristen's hand again when she starts to cry softly. "It's okay. You don't have to tell me the rest."

"No. I at least owe Eddie this. For him to be remembered as a selfless hero." She lets out a choked sob. "Eddie told me he loved me and that if I loved him I would do as Logan said. He'd rather watch me have sex with Logan on my own terms and be followed by a quick death rather than hear my screams of resistance." Another sob. "I couldn't do it. I told Logan to fuck off."

We both grow silent as I fill in the blanks.

Eddie slowly bled out and Logan brutally raped Kristen.

"Eddie kept telling me I was so brave," Kristen whispers, a steady waterfall of tears flowing. "Over and over.

How much he loved me. How fucking brave I was." She shudders, squeezing her eyes shut. "It took him three days to finally die. Three days of…"

Sick, sexual brutality.

"I wasn't brave," she whimpers. "I was scared and caused Eddie three days of pain from my selfishness." She shoots me a begging look. "I didn't know what to do. I just needed him, you know?"

"I know that. I'm sure he knew that too, Kristen." I give her hand another squeeze. "And you are brave. You've been living with a psychopath. It's not your fault."

My words seem to give her permission to break down because she does just that, spilling tears and moaning for all she's lost. We remain still, hands gripping each other's tight until she releases her emotions.

One day, we'll escape this prison.

One day, we'll make Logan fucking pay.

CHAPTER SIX

ryder

W E STILL HAVE WEAPONS.

Dad didn't just have stashes in the big house. He had them in his workshop too. Rifles, handguns, knives. Knowing we aren't completely shit out of luck lifts my mood a little.

But only a little.

Today has been stressful. It's been another full day of taking inventory of supplies, food, and whatever else we have left on the property. Those bastards took a lot of our shit and burned the rest.

Not to mention, I'm desperate to get out there to start looking for our family. Mom, though, isn't well enough to care for Dad and Dawson. She's been throwing up all morning, which is worrying. I can't leave her like this and I don't trust Chet or Wild to know what to do.

Dad is still in and out of consciousness.

I know he's in a lot of pain because he moans and

groans while he sleeps, which is most of the time. There's nothing I can do to help him. I changed his wound dressings and have forced water down his throat, but there's not much else I can do.

God, I wish everything were back to normal.

I want my siblings back.

Especially them.

Raegan and Ronan.

Even though shit was weird between the three of us, crossing lines that weren't meant to be crossed, it was still the most invigorated I've ever felt.

I'd grown strangely possessive over Ronan and got him off in our tent. The moments between us were intensely charged. Never once had I considered being with a guy until my brother.

And Raegan?

She's been a secret, twisted, fucked-up fantasy I've had for a while now. Kissing her and touching her tits had felt like heaven.

Of course those moments we all shared were wrong, but I still loved them. I'd give anything to do them over again at least once more in my lifetime. But I'd give up the idea of touching and kissing them if it meant they could come home safely.

Someone bursts through the cabin door, hollering, and scares the shit out of me. I jump to my feet, swiveling around to face the commotion.

Wild, with his ball cap on backward and a huge grin on his face, says, "They're here. Mom and Dad are here."

For a split second, I thought he'd meant my siblings. His revelation of who exactly is here is a slight blow to my sanity, but I quickly recover to follow him out of the cabin.

Uncle Atticus is the next best thing.

We need him more than ever.

Chet leads the way, with me and Wild on his tail. Rowdy materializes from behind the equipment barn to follow us out the gate. We round the corner in time to see Uncle Atticus's big RV pulling their trailer, which will be loaded down with supplies for our family. He parks it but leaves it running, rushing out the side door within seconds.

"What the fuck happened?" Uncle Atticus demands, gesturing at the husk of a home beyond the fence.

So much.

So fucking much.

Chet and Wild are both talking over each other, explaining in detail about the visitors, their stay, the drama, and then the night of the fire and kidnapping. While Wild panics about his missing truck and Chet worries over Sadie, I just hope like hell they brought better pain meds for Dad.

The RV door opens again, revealing Aunt Eve. Her long dark hair dances in the wind as she holds the hands of their three-year-old twins, Forest and Meadow. Even though one twin is a boy and the other is a girl, they both look exactly the same—dark shoulder-length hair, deep green eyes with flecks of brown, and their usual pouty expressions. They're cute, I guess, but they're sort of creepy with their unusually pale skin, dark circles under their eyes, and the way they rarely speak.

I wait for Wild to explain all over again to his mom, growing antsy with each passing second.

"Dad's in bad shape," I tell them, despair clawing at my words. "We have him in Ronan's cabin. He hasn't woken up since…"

Since he was cut loose after those motherfuckers dragged him behind the truck.

Uncle Atticus gives me a clipped nod before stalking over to the gate. Aunt Eve walks over to me, her brows pinched together in concern.

"They'll pay for this," Aunt Eve vows, brown eyes flashing with vengeance. "We'll make sure of it."

I force a smile at her. "Damn straight they will."

She releases one of the twins' hands and plucks at a longish strand of hair that hangs over my brow. "I'm going to cut this off. It looks stupid."

This time, my smile is genuine. Aunt Eve has zero filter. It reminds me a lot of Raegan, which has my smile disappearing. "Shave it off. I'm sick of it."

"After supper. Take me to your mother."

Turns out, Uncle Atticus brought a lot of stuff we needed. Each visit, they bring new clothes, shoes, and jackets or coats, depending on the season, blankets, prepackaged snacks this family goes nuts over, medicine, tools, books and games, animal feed, and sometimes equipment. He also brings replacement solar panels, bins, buckets, hoses, furniture, and whatever else he can think of. Dad and Uncle Atticus have the supply runs down to a science these days, anticipating our needs and fulfilling them.

Just being able to replenish simple things like dishes feels like a blessing. But the most important items were the medical supplies and medicine. Not long after they arrived, Uncle Atticus forced some antibiotics down Dad's throat along with some stronger pain meds. Dad even roused long enough to clutch at Uncle Atticus's shirt.

For the first time since the fire, I feel hopeful.

Now that it's dark and we have proper dinner in our bellies thanks to hot dogs they brought with them in their RV, it's time to plan how we're going to get my family back.

The twins and Dawson went down for the night, the three of them sleeping on a sleeping bag pile in Ronan's cabin. Aunt Eve has hunkered down with Mom, and both of them watch over Dad and the kids.

The rest of us sit around the firepit wearing glum expressions. Despite the house fire having been long put out, the air reeks of smoke—different than a campfire. It's nauseating because it's a constant reminder of what happened.

"We can't all leave," Uncle Atticus says. "Some of

us will need to stay back to keep the rest of the families safe."

Nods of agreement all around.

"And, sorry, Chet, but I can't let you go out there. While you and your sister are with us, you're our responsibility." Uncle Atticus shoots Chet an apologetic look. "If you're here, that's one less person to worry about."

He frowns but doesn't argue. Uncle Atticus is a huge, burly guy. Not someone you disagree with unless you're not afraid of facing down a giant.

"Rowdy," Uncle Atticus says to my brother, "I'm going to have you take the lead on this hunt. Ryder and Wild will go with you."

Rowdy's nostrils flare, but I'm the only one to notice. I know he doesn't care that I'm going, but he clearly has an issue with Wild. Their issue goes back years and one day I'll get to the bottom of it. Wild, always arrogant and sure of himself, smirks like he's God's gift to the outdoors when the truth is, he'll be a liability since his wilderness training is limited.

"You sure you didn't see my truck while you were driving?" Wild asks for the fiftieth time. "If they put one scratch on it, I'll cut their throats. All of them."

Rowdy mutters out, "Fucking idiot," under his breath.

Uncle Atticus ignores his comment. "Shit might get dirty out there. You boys do what you have to do. The safety of those kids is the most important thing. You'll bring them back home, you hear?"

We all nod, even Wild, who's mildly peeved about being blown off.

"Maybe we should drive to town and call the police," Chet offers. "They could canvas the area and shit."

Wild snorts out a laugh. "Dude, you watch too much television. You've seen the police force in our town. The police chief's a lazy dick who only cares about handing out tickets to teenagers."

"Wild," Uncle Atticus says with a groan. "Stop calling your uncle Will a dick. He's not lazy, but you're right about one thing. They don't do shit like they do it in the movies. We'll just waste time and open ourselves up to a lot of questions. The last thing either of our families need is a spotlight shone on us."

His cryptic remark has me curious, but he continues before I can mull it over.

"The sooner we can get an organized hunt going, the quicker we'll find them," he mutters. "We'll have the advantage of surprise as they won't expect it. Clearly, they think they've gotten away easily. But traveling with that many people, a huge portion of which are small children, means they'll be slow, even with their head start with the truck."

While he explains how he'll drive us in the RV tomorrow to look for the truck and then will deposit us there to begin our hunt, my mind drifts back to my siblings.

Raegan's bratty grin as she wins an argument.

Ronan's blushing cheeks as he talks about being with a man.

I miss them.

I fucking miss them.

"You boys try to get some sleep tonight. We'll get you packed and on your way first thing in the morning. Any questions?" Uncle Atticus lifts a brow. "If not head—"

His voice is cut off by a yip.

A couple of yips.

He grabs his rifle at his feet, but I'm already on mine, tearing across the yard to the closed gate. My heart is in my chest, filled with hope that maybe just maybe there's some good news tonight. When I open the gate, two wolf pups dart in, yipping in excitement.

Mage and Spirit.

They're alive and they came back.

Rowdy scoops up Spirit, showering her with hugs and kisses while I chase down Mage, who makes a bee-line over to the chicken coup to scare them with a loud yelp. I laugh as I trot after him. Little shit thinks he's boss around here. He's reminding those chickens he's back and to watch it. I scoop him up and scratch him behind the ears.

"Did you save your sister from the bad guys?" I ask, looking down at his cute, furry face. "That's a good boy."

He licks my face with his stinky beastly breath. Our

happy reunion is short-lived as I realize I wasn't able to save mine.

At least, not yet.

Tomorrow, we'll hunt those motherfuckers who took my family down.

I'll get my siblings back.

I'll be able to tease Raegan and watch her eyes ignite with stubborn fury. Maybe I'll even get to kiss her again. The thought of peeling away all of her clothes so I can explore every inch of her is exciting and something to look forward to.

And Ronan?

I'll make sure he never thinks about another man again. I can be the one he experiments with. He can put his mouth on me or mine on him. If he wants to come, I'll jerk him off.

They're mine to take care of and make happy.

We'll just keep those times a secret from our parents. I'll make sure they never find out. Life will be better than good. It'll be fucking perfect.

Soon.

So very soon.

CHAPTER SEVEN

raegan

HE'S NOT ALLOWED TO TOUCH YOU.

Somehow, CJ was right. This group is cruel and awful, but there's some sort of hierarchy and rules system in place. Tom did make me sleep in his tent with him and his two children and kept me pinned under his heavy arm all night, but he didn't touch me like I'd feared.

Having sex with Tom would be disgusting and horrible.

If they hadn't stolen us away, my first time might've even been Ryder. The two of us kissed hard and frantically. He'd touched me in ways that made my body light up like lightning striking a tree. A few more moments alone and we could have had sex.

God, I'd wanted that so bad—whatever he was willing to give me.

But now I'm stuck in this nightmare.

All day, I'd been kept away from Ronan as we

packed up our camp and trekked farther into the wilderness. His eyes were downcast, shoulders hunched. Anytime I'd try and get his attention to check on him after last night, Tom would push me along or Logan would block my view.

Logan hurt him last night.

I heard my brother's cries of pain and sorrow but was powerless to help him.

Tonight, I'm being punished. Tom made me sit by myself away from the group. Their group laughs and cuts up while my people sit quietly. It infuriates me that they treat us like possessions to do whatever it is they feel like with.

CJ approaches and sits down on the log beside me. He's one of them, a liar and a traitor, but I don't send him away with my vicious words. I'm going crazy unable to talk to anyone. Maybe I can get information out of him or gain enough trust I can escape.

As much as the thought of escape entices me, it's not that simple. I can't leave by myself. There are so many of us who need rescuing. It's overwhelming.

"Tom says he didn't touch you," CJ says, not making eye contact. "You can tell me if he did."

"He forced me to smell his deadly body odor all night, but no, he didn't touch me like that."

In fact, it wasn't horrible. Wyatt was a good big brother to Oliva, telling her knock-knock jokes to make her giggle. I'd fought off a smile or two and even heard

Tom chuckling before everyone settled in for the night. Things definitely could have gone a lot worse.

CJ turns, flashing me a conspiratorial grin that might've once been attractive to me. Not anymore. "Good. I saw you first, so I should be the one who gets to."

My lip curls up and I glower at him. "I'm not some prize to be won. I'm a person."

CJ has the wits about him to appear embarrassed. "Sorry, Raegan. I know that. I'm just trying to make you feel better. You will be married soon and even though Tom is older, I saw you first and laid claim. My uncle might have us present an argument as to who should be able to marry you, but mine is stronger. Tom already has kids, whereas I don't. Plus, you and me already have a connection." He touches my thigh and gives it a squeeze that makes me shudder. "You could help plead my case."

Unable to stand his touch any longer, I shove his hand away. "I will never marry one of you monsters. And if you try to have sex with me, know right now that it won't ever be willingly on my part. I will not be having anyone's babies."

His features darken and his eyes flicker with anger. "One of us will fuck you soon, little virgin, rest assured. It's your choice whether or not you decide to enjoy it."

"If you have to resort to stealing girls from their beds in the middle of the night, it's very doubtful I'd enjoy it even if you tried." I spit at him. "You're pathetic."

He shoves me hard off the log and I hit the earth

on my back, knocking the breath out of me. I sit up on my elbows, ready to kick him if he comes near me, but he storms off.

I pissed him off.

Good.

Maybe he'll stay the hell away from me.

From across the fire, I see Logan stand. He helps Ronan to his feet. At first, I think they're going to their tent, but then Logan guides him over to where I'm now sitting back on the log.

"Let your sister know everything is fine," Logan says when they approach, gesturing at the log beside me. "I'm going to take a piss. You have five minutes. Your treat for being good today, pet."

Pet?

I want to jump to my feet and run my fingernails down Logan's face. The way he treats Ronan sickens me. But the last time I had a fit, Ronan took a beating. It takes everything in me not to snap at Logan.

"Thanks, Logan," Ronan grunts out, gingerly sitting next to me.

As soon as Logan walks off, I grab Ronan's hand and lean into him. The tears come out of nowhere like a flash flood. I cling to him, crying enough for both of us.

"Hey, Rae," he croons, voice soft and shaky. "It's okay. I'm all right."

But he's not all right. He's hurt. Logan hurt him.

"It's all my fault," I rasp out, hiccupping through my tears. "He hurt you because of me."

"Shh. Just a few whacks with a belt. I survived. Nothing any worse than what Dad's doled out before."

I know he's lying. I know it was terrifying and painful. He never howled like that when Dad spanked him. None of us kids ever did. This was different. This was a beating.

"I'm sorry, Ro."

"Don't be sorry," he says, voice stern. "Now tell me how you are. Did he hurt you?"

"Tom, the big oaf?" I scoff at him. "No. Just tried to kill me with his stank. Plus, his kids were there too."

Having Wyatt and Oliva there has helped make sleeping beside the man not so scary.

"Good." He kisses the side of my head. "You're strong. We'll get through this. Just need to hang on."

"Until what?" I turn to look into my brother's eyes. "When will this end?"

He reaches up and brushes away the wetness on my cheek with his thumb. "When Ryder comes for us. I know he will."

I search his eyes and frown. "What if he's too late?"

"He won't be."

"But…"

"But what?"

I chew on my bottom lip, hating to speak the words. "Tom and CJ…" Sighing heavily, I shove down the terror and let anger replace it. "Apparently, they're going to compete for the chance to marry me."

Ronan scowls, reminding me a lot of Ryder in this moment.

"I don't want to have sex with either of them," I whisper, letting fear creep back in. "I've never done it and I'm scared. I wanted it to be you. In my head, it was always you."

And then it was Ryder, but I don't mention that.

His features soften. "Even when you found out I like men?"

"Still then." I swallow down a ball of emotion. "It still could be you."

He blinks at me in confusion. "But I'm—"

"You could pretend I'm someone else," I murmur, voice quivering. "Like Ryder. Just close your eyes and pretend."

Ronan's brows pinch together and he pulls his gaze away from mine. "Rae."

"Never mind," I choke out. "It was a stupid idea."

He shakes his head and pulls me to him for a hug. "It's not. I just…I don't know what to think."

"I just didn't want those monsters to take away something so special to me."

"Okay."

"Okay?"

His arm squeezes me closer to him. "If there were ever an opportunity, I would do it for you. Somehow. Some way. I could give that to you."

My heart flutters at the idea of what he's saying.

Me and Ronan.

Together in bed. Moaning and licking and writhing. Like that night I watched my parents. Ronan could say those filthy things to me. He could rub the spot between my legs that makes me see stars. I would spread my legs for him and let him push his cock inside me.

Heat floods south and my skin burns hot.

"Tonight?" I ask in a whisper.

He groans. "Rae, I said if there were ever an opportunity. I can't slip away from Logan."

"I could come to you," I offer. "Tom and his kids have to fall asleep at some point."

"It's not safe." He pulls back and cups my cheek in his hand. "Don't do anything risky."

Before we can argue any more about this subject, the sounds of footsteps cracking through the nearby forest have us hushing up. Logan returns with eyes narrowed. Ronan gives me another quick hug before rising to his feet.

"You two behaved while I was gone?" Logan asks, gaze penetrating and hard.

"No time to plan an epic escape," I grumble. "Night, Ro."

"Night, Rae."

After they leave and disappear into their tent, I listen to make sure Ronan isn't getting beat on. Since no sounds come from that direction, I slowly stand and decide I'll check on my other siblings while no one is paying me any mind.

All the little kids are sitting on a blanket with Tee,

Lisa, and Stacey. They're singing songs and laughing. As much as it pains me to see Dakota and Declan giggling, it also alleviates some of my worry. When Ronan was getting whipped, I couldn't help but fear what would happen to the others, myself included. At the very least, the boys aren't in any kind of immediate danger. That just leaves Destiny and Sadie.

They're both farther away from the fire and sitting in front of a tent. Jace and Mya sit with them. Destiny frowns, head cast down, while Sadie keeps shooting Mya disgusted looks. When Jace playfully tugs at my sister's hair and grins at her, I march toward them, ready to pry his sleazy hand away from her. Before I reach them, a man steps in front of me.

Michael.

Their fearless, insane leader.

"You're not to be walking about all by yourself," Michael says, voice gruff. "Things happen to little girls like you when they're not properly chaperoned."

I attempt to keep my expression neutral, but Michael is terrifying. Only a monster could concoct this way of life. Still, I refuse to let him see me tremble in fear. Hardening my features, I boldly stare up at him.

"My family's safety is my number one concern." My tone is sharp like a blade. It reminds me of Mom when she's pissed and laying down the law. "Excuse me."

He doesn't step aside. Instead, he grabs hold of my jaw, tilting my head from one side to the other. "I'll allow it this once, child, because you're new to our

Higher Earth ways, but I won't allow it again." His fingers bite into my flesh, making me whimper. "You will respect me and my people. Especially me because I am an elder of our community and have earned that right. Especially your husband, whomever that may be."

Or what?

I don't speak the question, but my eyes must do it for me.

His eyes flicker with something evil. "You don't want to find out. It'll make what happened to your brother seem pleasant."

"I'm too young to marry," I grit out despite his hold on me.

"Not here," he says, gaze dropping to my mouth. "You'll behave and submit to the husband who is chosen for you. They've worked hard to earn this."

Me.

To earn *me.*

"And if I don't?" I croak out, the fear lacing my words.

He grabs hold of the front of my shirt, twisting until the fabric strains in protest. I'm pulled so close I can smell the liquor on his breath. I cower, desperate to get away from his menacing glare.

"If you don't, my unruly child, I'll be forced to take another wife." He releases me completely and steps away, an ominous smile curling his lips up. "If I do, I'll break your spirit the first night you're in my tent. Just like I broke *hers.*" He gestures to where Stacey holds her pregnant belly and reads Declan a story. "You'll wor-ship me as I put baby after baby inside of you. That will be your future."

My mind reels.

Stacey was like me once?

She's part of his psycho club. I will never willingly be a part of this monster's world.

"Now be a good girl and do as you're told. Trust me when I say you're getting it easy with either Tom or CJ. Understood?"

Trembling, I give him a curt nod. "Loud and clear."

He runs his tongue over his lip and then winks be-fore sauntering over to his wife. I watch in disgust as he plunders her mouth with his, blatantly groping her breast over her shirt. When I swivel around, unable to look a second longer, I'm staring up at another giant. This one stinky, but seemingly harmless in comparison.

"Time for bed."

I don't fight Tom.

This time, I willingly join him in the tent with his kids and am secretly thankful for his presence. Anything or anyone is better than Michael. I'll do good to remem-ber that.

CHAPTER EIGHT

ronan

SHE WANTS ME TO HAVE SEX WITH HER.

My sister.

I can't fathom the idea of us together in that way, much less understand how I can make that happen for her.

Logan watches me like a hawk. It's doubtful he'll ever let me out of his sight long enough for me to fuck my sister.

Bile creeps up my throat. Are we really in this situation? Where I'm considering having sex—me, a gay man—with my sister so her first time isn't with some rapist?

Fuck.

I am.

I have to. There's no way I could let them take that from her. I just don't know how to make that happen.

My mind drifts to Mom and Dad. They're probably

both dead. Would they roll over in their graves if their children had sex?

Yes.

Mom would come back alive just so she could strangle us.

The image of Mom, pissed and hollering, is still a better one than her being burned alive. I grimace at that thought, quickly pushing it away.

Logan clears his throat, forcing my attention back on him. I shift uncomfortably, feeling the hot reminders of every single lash he gave me last night on my ass. Kristen sits beside me, once again in a docile way, eyes down and quiet. I'm unable to keep from watching Logan as he walks on his knees closer to us, the light from the lantern in his hand swaying. He sets it down and gestures at my jeans.

"Time to check your bruises, pet."

A fiery inferno swells inside my chest, but he quells it with one fierce glare. Shuddering, I do as I'm told, unfastening my jeans. I'm about to lie down when he shakes his head.

"Pull your boxers down where I can see and then I want you bent over, your face in the sleeping bag. While I check your wounds, I need to fuck my wife. We're trying for a baby. Lucky for you, I can do two things at once."

I study his hard features for a beat to see if he's joking. He's not. He's absolutely not. In the light of the lantern, I feel more exposed and on display. But since

I don't want any more lashings, I shakily obey him, resting on my knees and elbows on my sleeping bag.

"Like this," Logan grunts, firmly pushing on the middle of my back. "Keep your legs bent and your ass prone to me. Now pull down the boxers like I said."

With my face now buried in the sleeping bag, I'm able to jerk them down without too much humiliation. His warm, calloused hand whispers over my ass cheek and he grunts as though he's satisfied with what he sees.

"Don't watch, pet. What happens between a man and his wife is sacred. Understand?"

I nod because I'm not about to disagree with him when I'm at such a disadvantage.

"Kristen. Come here."

She yelps and I flinch. I can hear shuffling while they must be undressing. A piece of clothing lands on top of my head. I recognize the scent as Logan's. I want to gag and tear it away but don't dare do so.

"You're never wet for me, wifey," Logan complains. "Spit."

Kristen spits and then I hear a slick sound. She then whimpers softly. Logan groans in pleasure.

"Make me come," Logan orders. "You're going to do all the work while I check on my pet."

The steady sounds of sex can be heard. I try to drown it out, thinking of Raegan and Ryder instead. I'm immediately jerked from my happy thoughts when Logan's thumb brushes along my ass crack.

The two of them continue, their bodies slapping

together in a rhythmic cadence as Logan's hand explores both my ass cheeks. He fingers certain bad bruises, pressing into them just enough to make me lose my breath as pain lances through me. Then, as though he truly cares, he gently caresses my flesh. His hand disappears and then it returns a second later.

A wet thumb slides back down my ass crack and stops right at my hole. I fist the sleeping bag, gritting my teeth so I don't make a sound. Sweat breaks out over my flesh and my body flares with warning signals. Bracing myself, I tense, ready for an unwanted breach.

He doesn't do as expected.

His slippery thumb teases the puckered flesh. Pressing and rubbing and stroking but never actually entering me. It's embarrassing and I hate him.

So why does my dick twitch?

I'm horrified that this sicko's touch has pleasure licking its way from my balls to the tip of my cock where a bead of pre-cum forms. I'm disgusted.

Logan's chest rumbles with approval.

He likes this. He wants *me* to like this.

Never.

I hate every second of it, despite what my body is feeling.

When his fingers brush over my balls, I let out a choked sound. He lingers for a second before his thumb is back on my hole. Back and forth he teases between the two until I'm shaking all over. Sweat runs down my spine from my lower back to my neck, tickling a trail along the way. My dick is leaking all over the sleeping bag.

I need for this to stop.

Logan groans and smacks Kristen with his free hand. She cries out in pain. The slapping of flesh slows to a stop. "Lie down and keep my cum inside you. You owe me a baby, Kristen."

She shuffles away to obey him. I remain in position, willing my body to stop reacting so positively to his terrible touch.

"Your ass looks good, pet. It's healing. Now clean me off."

Clean him off?

I turn my head to the side, peeking out from under his shirt. He's on his knees, sitting back on his laurels, naked with his flaccid cock dripping.

"W-What?" I stammer, heart rate speeding up.

"You heard me."

Glancing over at Kristen, I discover she too is completely nude. She lies there, staring up at the ceiling, lost in another space far, far away from here.

"Don't look at my naked wife," Logan growls. "Do as you're told. Last warning."

I scramble onto my knees, quickly yanking up my boxers. The wetness from my leaking cum dots the front of my underwear. When I start to pull my jeans up, Logan gives me a sharp shake of his head.

"Jeans and shirt off."

Stifling a groan, I obey him, secretly thankful he let me keep my boxers on. I eye his spent cock warily.

"It's simple, pet," Logan says, voice deceptively calm. "Put your mouth on it and clean this mess off me. We do this the easy way or the hard way."

I shudder at what might be his idea of the hard way. I can do this. It's just a cock. A week ago, I'd have done a backflip with excitement at the idea of doing this. I'll just disappear to the same place Kristen went.

Somewhere safe.

Ryder.

But I can't seem to grasp onto him. This moment is too real and too terrifying to turn my back on it. I have to face this all alone.

The musky scent of a woman lingers on Logan's cock. I close my eyes and set to licking off the salty leftover cum. Their taste makes me gag. Bile races up my throat and I barely manage to keep it down. Logan chuckles and runs his fingers through my hair.

"Such an innocent little pet. Use your tongue. Suck it off. Be a good pet and I'll reward you."

I was good all day and he rewarded me with alone time with Raegan.

I can do this.

With newfound vigor, I set to clean his softened cock, going as far as licking at his red, curly pubic hairs. His scent is disgusting, but I force myself to do the job.

He groans when I pull away. "That was…good.

Kristen could learn a thing or two from you. Your mouth is so fucking eager."

I fall back onto my ass and immediately regret it when pain shocks through me. Logan chuckles at my misfortune.

"Tomorrow you can see your other sister," Logan says. "I may even let you walk with her. You really out-performed my expectations tonight."

I don't look at him but mutter out, "Thank you."

It disgusts me to have to thank him for what just happened, but I'm looking forward to seeing Destiny. Getting to check in with her to make sure she's okay.

Ryder will come for us.

This can't last forever.

Logan shuts off the light and sprawls out on his sleeping bag closest to the tent opening. I remain still, staring into the darkness much like Kristen did. Both of their breathing soon evens out beside me. The sounds of camp have died down as everyone must've gone to bed. For a brief moment, I consider sneaking out of the tent, rounding my siblings and Sadie up, and getting the fuck out of here.

What about Kristen?

And Logan wouldn't let me get far.

Then what?

More lashings with his belt? Worse?

This time, I force all thoughts of Logan away. I think of Ryder. Ryder in the creek, his dark hair slicked back with water and wearing a bright grin. The way his

T-shirt tugs over his muscular frame in a mouthwatering way. Our time in the tent together—his hands on me, making me come. His mouth on mine.

My cock doesn't need much help growing hard again. With Ryder on my mind, I slip my hand into my boxers, gripping my aching length. I don't have lube, but just tugging on it while fantasizing about my brother is enough. Pleasure zings through my every nerve ending. It only takes a few seconds of imagining Ryder's tongue where Logan's thumb was tonight to explode with a mind-numbing orgasm.

Colors light up the dark tent, all conjured from my imagination and subsequent pleasure. I allow myself a moment of relaxing bliss as the cum jets out of me, spilling all over my naked abs. My breathing is ragged and it takes several minutes for my heart rate to slow back down.

I'm soaked in cum.

Fuck.

Logan stirs, sleepily grunting about something. It has every hair on my body standing at attention. If he wakes to find me with my dick out and jizz all over me, who knows what will happen. I sure as hell am not about to find out.

I yank my boxers over my cock and then use my fingers to scoop up the cum. Quickly, I bring my hand to my mouth to lick away the evidence. It's salty and weird but doesn't taste as bad as Logan's mixed with

Kristen's smell. A couple more swipes and I clean it all away without having been caught.

I'm almost asleep when small fingers touch my arm. I jolt in surprise, my heart rate hammering again inside my chest.

"Ronan?" Kristen says in the barest of whispers.

"Yeah?"

"Don't ever let him find you doing…*that*." She sniffles. "I can't bear to lose my only friend."

What does that mean?

"Okay, sure," I say, voice squeaky with shame. "Sorry."

"He's possessive. He'll kill you."

"Got it." I pat her hand before quickly flipping onto my side, putting my back to her.

She's right. That was careless and stupid. Logan doesn't seem the type to be okay with me getting myself off. He's controlling and likes to call the shots. When you don't follow his rules, he'll punish you.

I'll be careful.

I have to be.

My life depends on it.

CHAPTER NINE

ryder

WILD IS STILL PISSED.

We found his truck earlier this morning. The trespassers—no, kidnappers— drove it off the road and into the forest as deep as they could until the front quarter panels were wedged between two thick pines. They'd stripped the vehicle of everything he'd left inside and it was scratched all to hell. Uncle Atticus is going to have to come back later with his own truck to try and tow it out of its spot. Definitely a problem for another day.

"That shit was brand-new," Wild growls, stomping through the brush and swatting at a wasp that flies too closely. "It's ruined."

He walks ahead of me and Rowdy, loaded down with his own camping gear. I shoot Rowdy an exasperated look. My brother shakes his head. Neither of us is happy with Wild's bitch fest.

We lost our fucking family and he's worried about a stupid truck.

Wild continues to gripe as he charges ahead. His dark hair has been pulled into a man bun that sits high on his head. It's shaved underneath, which gives him an edgy look. I can remember once upon a time he loathed the idea of becoming like his dad. Yet, they both have long hair they have to tie up all the time.

Rowdy, until this morning, also had the whole man bun thing going on. However, when Aunt Eve was buzzing my hair short, Rowdy stepped in after for his own cut. His haircut, cropped short on the sides but still long enough to be messy on top, makes him seem younger. A little less…wild. I want to ask him if it's because he doesn't want to have hair like Wild, but with Wild within earshot, I refrain.

I don't understand how they went from being cool one day to despising each other the next.

Wild grows quiet, stopping to cast his gaze all around. Me and Rowdy make it to him. I realize the reason why he stopped. Their obvious trail from leaving the truck has vanished. A small brook runs through the trees and the trail doesn't pick up on the other side.

"We're never going to find them," Wild grumbles. "The trail ends here."

Rowdy ignores his pessimism and prowls past him. Easily, he leaps over the water and onto the other side, his boot crushing some brush into the dirt. He takes another step and leaves his obvious footprint.

That's what we should be seeing.

Evidence of a group of people trampling the earth.

If not here, where?

Rowdy starts trekking along the bank going north while Wild waits, unmoving, arms crossed over his chest. I start south, carefully looking for anything that might look like they crossed. For a while, I walk along the creekside as it curves between massive pines that have been here forever.

When I come to a fallen tree that provides a bridge over the creek, I pause to take in the scenery around me. It's quiet aside from birds chirping and the rushing of the water over rocks. I step onto the log, testing its strength first before climbing on top. The area west has been trampled heavily and the obvious way they could have gone. I'm just turning around to go find Rowdy and Wild when something glimmers in the sunlight, catching my attention just off the east bank.

Carefully, I continue along the log past the bank to the original location the tree started at before lightning or old age made it fall. The shiny object is tiny. Squatting, I pick it up from near the tree stump.

An earring.

Raegan's earring.

My mind drifts to the past when Raegan was thirteen. She'd begged and begged for earrings like the women on some of the book covers she'd seen. When Uncle Atticus and Aunt Eve came to visit for Christmas, they brought an ear-piercing kit plus some earrings. Me and my brothers watched with slight horror as she subjected herself to stabbing holes in her ears. I'd thought she was going to cry, and her eyes were teary, until she looked my way. The determination to be brave pushed through the pain and fear.

And now her earring is on the ground.

Did it fall out or was my sister leaving me a clue?

I jerk my head back to the other side of the creek. She must've known they were trying to throw us off their trail by smashing the ground over there. It was her only way of keeping us on the right track.

We're coming, Rae.

You did well, beautiful.

"This way," I holler to Wild and Rowdy. "Hurry up!"

Minutes later, with both Rowdy and Wild following me, I traipse along the trail that's obvious again as it winds deeper into the forest. Thanks to Rae, we're going to find them.

As night falls upon us, we decide to make camp at a place they must've. We find the remnants of a long put out campfire and the ground has been cleared some for tents. Me and Wild make quick work of erecting our own tents while Rowdy starts a fire.

"I wish we didn't have to stop," I grumble as I settle beside the fire and dig through my pack for something to eat. "We'll have to travel longer hours tomorrow if we want to catch up to them."

Rowdy nudges me with his boot, shooting me a

frown. "We need our rest too. It won't do us any good to find them but not have the energy to fight them."

"Fight them?" Wild says with a grunt. "I plan on putting a bullet in every damn one of their heads. No fighting necessary."

My brother bristles at Wild's response, obviously annoyed. I can't help but agree with Wild on this, though.

The thought of taking out each and every one of those monsters is a satisfying one.

Later, when drifting off to sleep in my tent, I dream of blood and revenge, and then I dream of her.

"You're leaving." Raegan's fiery eyes burn with hurt. "You're leaving and you never planned to tell me!"

God, why is she so infuriating?

I practically spit out my next words. "I didn't have a chance."

"Liar!" She smacks me hard across the cheek, the other hand holding the knife against my throat steady as ever. "You could have told us together!"

Everything's a competition with her. But, behind her anger, I can see how devastated she is about the news. I feel that same pain a hundred percent.

I grab hold of her wrist and squeeze it. "I'm sorry."

"That's it?" Her eyes widen and her nostrils flare. "You're sorry? Aren't you even going to try to fight them on this?"

Fight them? Fight Dad? Is she insane?

"What can I do, Rae?" I hiss at her. "Dad's word is law."

"Yeah, and he's a hypocrite!"

"It's done," I mutter. "I'm sorry, but the decision has been made."

She manages to press the tip of the blade harder into my skin. It fucking hurts. Blood trickles down from where she has me at her vicious mercy.

"It's stupid," she chokes out, tears welling. "You're not going to get me pregnant! You don't even like me. You're too busy making Ronan come! You two have shut me out."

Unbelievable.

She's definitely insane if she can't see how fucking crazy she makes me.

With a growl, I flip us until my heavy body pins her much smaller one. Since she's distracted, I easily take hold of the knife and toss it away.

"I don't like you?" I bite out. "Are you fucking kidding me right now?"

She glowers up at me, refusing to let the tears actually fall. "I said what I said."

I shift my body until my aching cock is pressed against her pussy, our clothes an unwanted barrier. Her legs have parted, easily welcoming me into this forbidden position. I can feel the heat of her pussy against my dick that's harder than stone.

"I more than like you, Rae. I fucking love you. And

not in some stupid sibling way either. It's why I have to leave."

She blinks in confusion, her lips pouting out. "What?"

"I said what I said," I mimic her with a slight grin. "But it doesn't matter. We can't do this shit. It's not right. Bad things can happen to our babies."

The thought of Raegan pregnant with my baby makes my stomach twist with uncertainty. I know it's wrong but the idea of knowing I did that to her is also a turn-on. I bet she'd be hot as fuck with a swollen belly.

"Blindness is not a birth defect, dumbass," she snaps, drawing me away from the forbidden fantasy. "Lots of people are blind and that's not because they had sex with their sister. It's just a thing that happens to some people. Like being deaf. I've read lots about disabilities. It's just biology and maybe God too."

"Regardless, nothing can happen. Dad won't allow it."

She opens her mouth with an indignant response no doubt, and it's in that second I make the decision to kiss her.

Just a taste.

One tiny taste before I'm sent away from her forever. I deserve it. We both do.

She makes a sweet keening sound that has me desperate for more than a taste. I need a bite. A whole fucking meal of her.

Holy fuck.

I'm devouring my sassy sister's wicked mouth and it tastes like heaven.

It's everything I didn't know I wanted.

Her heels bruise my ass as she uses them to pull me closer. A groan of overwhelming need rattles out of my chest. Because I can't control myself, I grind against her pussy with my cock. The sounds she makes now are needy—almost begging for more.

Fuck.

I need more.

I need all of her.

"Fuck, I'll miss you," I murmur over her mouth before nipping at her bottom lip. "You taste so goddamn perfect like I dreamed of."

This is wrong.

Everything that Dad worried about.

I'm guilty as fuck and don't even care. Not now. Not in this moment.

My palm slides under her T-shirt, eagerness to feel all the soft parts of her taking over. Her ribs beneath my fingertips make her seem delicate and fragile. Like she's something I need to protect at all costs—with my life. Our tongues grow more frantic as our kiss turns ravenous.

I need more.

I need all of her.

My thumb grazes the underside of her breast over her bra. It would be so easy to continue along this wrong path that feels so right.

I have to stop before it goes too far.

Before I ruin everything because I'm horny as fuck for my sister.

"My nipple," she pleads, her breath hot against my mouth. "Touch it. Please."

So much for self-control.

How the hell am I supposed to deny her when she begs so sweetly?

Like an animal, I roughly yank her bra away from her breast, revealing her silky skin to my roving hand. She lets out a sound of pleasure as my thumb seeks out her nipple. When I pinch her nipple between my thumb and middle finger, she jolts at the touch.

I need more.

I need all of her.

My mouth waters to taste her pert nipple, but a scream cuts through my lust-filled haze.

Lifting up from her and breaking our kiss, I look down at her, momentarily confused as to whether the scream came from her or not. Her eyes are hooded and her lips puffy from our kiss.

She's beautiful.

I start to kiss her again, but then a gunshot fires.

Snapping awake, I quickly look around to reorient myself. My dick is hard, straining in my boxers, pre-cum slicking the material. My dream of her wasn't a dream at all. It was a memory of that moment we shared. So hot. So terrible because she's my sister, but so fucking good because she's Raegan.

Another gunshot.

This one not a memory, but in my reality.

I throw on clothes at record speed, grab my rifle, and bolt out of the tent, ready to take out the threat.

Except there is no threat.

Wild holds up a dead rabbit by its foot and grins at me. "I'm still a fucking awesome shot."

"Good shot? It took you two to kill that rabbit," I grumble. "Now let's just hope those fuckers are far enough away that they didn't hear the shots."

Wild's smile falls and he winces as realization kicks in. "Dammit. I didn't think—"

"You never do," Rowdy snaps. "Let's pack up and move out. We have people to find."

CHAPTER TEN

raegan

EVERY DAY IS EXACTLY THE SAME.
Wake up early, travel in silence beside Tom and his kids, break for dinner, make camp, sleep. Over and over and over. We've been at this for a whole week and I'm so tired of it. Mostly, I'm concerned since Ryder hasn't come for us yet.

Did they hurt him too?

Ronan holds out hope that Ryder will be here, but I'm beginning to doubt it. It seems what's left of my family is here with me or they would've already come. It's going to be up to us to get away from these traveling lunatics.

I can hear Mya complaining up ahead about blisters and begging to stop for the night. Usually, they walk us until just before dark, but today the sun is still shining proudly in the late afternoon. To my surprise, the group slows to a stop. With me and Tom's crew bringing up the rear, I'm not sure what's being decided up ahead.

I wonder how long we'll travel until Michael deems it safe to stop. Is his community forever nomads or will they build in a permanent location?

My mind drifts to our home and how it had been burning. I have no idea if anyone survived. I don't even know if the wolf pups lived or not. For some reason, that has my heart fissuring and my eyes stinging.

Poor Mage and Spirit.

Maybe there will be wolf karma and a grown wolf can eat Mya's face off. I'd happily watch that. The men here are terrifying, but Mya just gets on my nerves. She's a mini psychopath in the making.

I hate her.

I hate them all.

Dakota runs over to me and thrusts a strip of deer jerky in my face. Knowing it's jerky these people stole from my family's pantry makes my blood boil, but since it's my brother sharing it with me, I gift him with a smile.

"Thanks, Kota. You and Deck okay?"

Tom looms beside me, nosily listening in on our conversation, but at this point, I don't care.

"If we get sad, Momma Stacey said we can—"

A shriek escapes me and I snap at Dakota, "She is *not* your momma!"

His bottom lip pouts out and he glowers at me. "We have to call her that. Papa Michael said so or else we'll get spankins."

The thought of Michael putting his hands on my

baby brothers makes me dizzy with terror. Guilt from lashing out at Dakota who's doing his best to survive his own hell threatens to swallow me whole.

"Run along, kid," Tom grunts to Dakota, his meaty hand grabbing the back of my neck. "Don't make me tell your parents."

Dakota shrivels under Tom's hard glare but nods.

"I'm sorry, Kota," I croak out, pleading for him to forgive me for my outburst.

He throws his skinny arms around my middle for a quick hug. "Bye, Rae."

I've barely hugged him back, thankful for his quick forgiveness, before he bolts, rushing back over to where Stacey holds Declan's hand, watching me with a narrowed stare. I have the urge to give her the finger but don't want to get Dakota in trouble for my actions.

Tom's grip doesn't loosen. I want him to let me go so we can erect our tent. I ache to crawl into the safety of it, sleeping instead of facing this new reality I live in.

"Looks like we're making camp," Tom rumbles, finally releasing me. "Mind your mouth and do your chores."

An hour later, camp is set up. After a week of this, we're getting pretty good at the routine of it. I hate to think about what that means. How I've slipped into a monotony of this nightmare I'm in. Is this what happened to Stacey? Did she simply give up and go along with it to make life easier?

I may not be able to wreak the havoc I'd like to

because of fear of my siblings getting punished on my behalf, but I also don't have to make things easy.

"Everyone," Michael calls out. "Gather up for a second before we break for supper."

The crowd of monsters mixed in with my family scoots in close to hear what Michael has to say. It's strange for us to be settling in so early and I can't help the unease of the unknown that washes over me.

"Tonight is a very special night for the Higher Earth community," Michael begins, grinning wide. "As an elder and your active leader, I've made my decision on the matches."

A few of the men, mainly CJ and Jace, hoot out in appreciation. My stomach twists with nerves.

"After supper, when the little ones have gone to bed, I'll announce the couplings and we'll make things official." Michael pulls Stacey to him, his eyes twinkling with delight. "Who's ready to celebrate?"

The whole group, aside from my people, cheers happily.

I'm going to be sick.

Dinner flies by way too quickly. By the time it's fully dark, the campfire is roaring, and the alcohol is doing its part to make their people somehow more obnoxious, it's time for the dreaded coupling.

"Raegan," Michael calls out, penetrating orbs on me. "Come here."

I'm frozen in place at Tom's side, heart hammering

like a jackrabbit. From across the fire, Ronan's brows are pinched and his lips are pressed into a worried line.

"Get on with it," Tom grunts, smacking me on the butt. "Don't make him wait."

I shoot Tom a nasty glare before shakily making my way forward. When I'm close to Michael, he grabs my wrist, dragging me closer with a sharp yank.

"Ahh," I cry out, stumbling over my own feet and nearly crashing into him.

Mya starts to cackle from nearby. I swear to God, I am going to claw her eyeballs out.

"Tonight, my unruly child, you will be paired with a good man who deserves a wife and family. You'll be given a grace period to learn to obey and eventually you'll become accustomed to our ways. And if you don't, you'll be culled and removed as those before you have been. There's no room for weak, disobedient, incapable people in our community." Michael pulls me into his side with his steely arm. "Tom. CJ. I've made my decision."

I squirm against Michael, hating that I'm having to be touched by him. My frantic eyes find Ronan, who's now standing. He can't see me from this far away based on his squinting, but he's worried about me.

Don't freak out.

Don't freak out.

Ronan will get punished if you do…

"Please don't make me," I whimper, pleading with Michael. "Please."

He releases me to shove me forward. Tom and CJ both grab my arms, righting me so I don't fall to the ground. I attempt to tug from their hold, but Tom's hand is an iron grip around my bicep and CJ's bony fingers dig into my flesh.

I'm trapped.

A big, loud, embarrassing sob chokes out of me. Fat tears well and then spill down my cheeks. I don't want this. I don't want this!

"Tom," Michael booms. "Let CJ handle his wife alone."

My panicked stare finds CJ's eyes. They flash with triumph. I'm stunned stupid, unsure if I feel relieved or horrified CJ is the chosen one.

"No," I cry out. "Please."

Someone rushes forward, venom in their tone. "You can't do this!"

Ronan.

Tom releases me, and for a moment, I think they're going to let me run into my brother's safe arms, but CJ's hold tightens to the point of pain. He never releases his grip, twisting to face off with Ronan.

"It's done. She's my wife now," CJ growls. "Back the fuck off."

My heart trips over itself when Ronan takes a swing at CJ. His fist smacks into CJ's jaw, forcing him to stagger into me. I try to shake my arm free, but CJ is too strong.

"Logan," Michael snarls. "Deal with your problem now, Son."

Ronan, before he can advance on CJ again, is yanked back by his hair. Logan's furious glare burns a hole through me. He twists his fist in Ronan's hair, making my brother howl in pain. I'm helpless to do anything but stare uselessly.

"Ronan," I wail, tears running hot rivers down my cheeks. "Ronan!"

Logan forces Ronan to his knees and then onto the ground face first. He then slams his foot down on the side of Ronan's head, pinning him to the ground.

"You're hurting him!" I screech.

A hand flies out, smacking me across the cheek so hard I see stars. When I blink them away, Michael is towering over me, nostrils flaring in fury. I wilt under his terrifying glare.

"CJ, control your wife. *Now.*"

I allow CJ to jerk me away from Michael, thankful to withdraw from the fiery hatred emanating from their leader. CJ forcefully drags me over to a log and makes me sit. His arm wraps around me, locking me in, and his other hand is a vise over the top of my thigh.

I'm not going anywhere.

I've lost this fight.

"That was an unfortunate interruption," Michael growls. "And, as you can see, Logan, he's not ready to be a husband for our dear Mya. He'll need more time with you."

Logan gives a clipped nod, but his lips curl into one of satisfaction. My poor brother doesn't move from his flattened position aside from the heavy rise and fall of his back as he breathes.

"That's not fair," Mya whines. "I want a husband!"

"That's enough, sweetheart," Owen chides, pulling her to him. "Soon."

As her father comforts her, I glower at her. I'm caught between being thrilled she won't get my brother and horrified that he's going to take another punishment from Logan.

I did this.

"Tom," Michael calls out. "Your wife will be Sadie."

Sadie gasps and I freeze. She starts shaking her head frantically. Tom walks over to her, snagging her small hand in his giant one. Her eyes lock on mine. I try to convey to her that Tom isn't the worst—that he might treat her well since his kids are there too—but she doesn't find comfort in my stare. The poor girl starts crying hysterically until she collapses. Tom easily scoops her up like a sack of apples, whistles for his kids, and then the four of them disappear into my tent.

Not *my* tent anymore.

I'm ready for this night to be over with.

To crawl into my sleeping bag and sleep this living nightmare away.

"What an eventful night," Michael croons. "And now, for our last pairing."

Last pairing?

From across the fire, Destiny sits beside Jace, her head bowed and silent.

No.

"Son, I trust you'll be a good husband for sweet little Destiny?" Michael asks, grinning his way. "She seems like she's a lot more compliant than the wife your cousin is dealing with."

I attempt to stand, but CJ grips me tighter. Spluttering out my words will have to do. "She's just a kid. Please don't do this."

Jace hugs Destiny to his side. "Don't worry, Raegan. I promise I'll protect her."

Protect her?

He's who she needs protecting from!

"Now that that's settled, men, secure your wives so we can have a celebratory drink." Michael nods at CJ and then Jace. "And, Logan, make sure your problem won't continue to be a problem."

With tears continuing to stream out of my eyes, I watch as Logan takes his foot off Ronan's head and then hauls him to his feet. He's rough with him as he forces him back to his tent. Kristen hops to her feet and trots after them. Before the zipper closes behind them, CJ stands, pulling me to my feet.

"Let's go," he grunts. "Behave."

I jerk at his hold to no avail. Too easily, he drags me over to his tent. Once I'm shoved inside, he follows, removing his belt. At first, I think he's going to whip me with it.

"Don't," I warn, my voice shaking as I crab walk backward over the sleeping bags. "Please."

"Turn around," CJ orders. "Don't fight me on this."

I scream when he tackles me. Because he's a grown man, it's not difficult for him to flip me onto my stomach. He grabs both of my hands, yanking them together at the small of my back.

"Seriously, Raegan. Just fucking behave. We can be good together. Let it happen."

Let it happen?

Is he insane?

"I would rather eat bear shit than let anything willingly 'happen' between us," I spit out, heart racing in my chest. "You disgust me."

He grumbles under his breath as he uses his belt to bind my wrists together. I cry out when he squeezes them together too hard.

"Ow," I choke out. "I'm sorry. Please, not so tight."

His sigh is one of frustration as though I'm a bratty child, but he thankfully listens, loosening the belt so that I can feel my fingers again. Once he secures me, he crouches over me, nose in my hair, and inhales me. My entire body freezes as warning bells go off.

"Soon," he promises in the barest of whispers. "We'll consummate our marriage. You'll officially be mine, little virgin." He chuckles. "I'll have to come up with a new nickname, though, because little virgin won't work after tonight."

He pulls away and playfully smacks my ass over my

jeans before slipping out of the tent. I bury my face in the sleeping bag, allowing myself a moment to feel sorry for myself, sobbing until I'm hiccupping.

But after a few minutes, my breathing evens out and my heart rate slows.

I wriggle until I free one hand and then another.

These people may have taken away everything from me, but they won't take *that*. I refuse to let CJ take my virginity. I'll sneak out and check on Ronan while these assholes have their celebratory drink. Then I'll hold my brother to his promise.

I choose Ronan.

Consequences be damned.

CHAPTER ELEVEN

ronan

M Y HEAD IS THROBBING AND THE BRUISES ON my face are going to be ugly tomorrow. Blood trickles from my nose from the last dizzying punch I received. I'm alive, though, and Logan is gone.

I survived his latest attack—or punishment as he likes to call it—but I still don't know how my sisters are faring. And Kristen? Fuck. I wish she wouldn't have tried to stick up for me. The punch he slammed against her cheek completely knocked her out. Thankfully, her breathing is even. She's still with me.

Rope digs into my wrists, cutting the flesh anytime I attempt to move. Assisting Kristen is out of the question. Sneaking out to save my sisters is also not going to happen. We're all well and truly fucked.

On my knees, I shuffle over to Kristen and attempt to see her in the dimly lit tent. The last thing I saw, though blurry, of Logan before he left was his rage-filled expression as he wailed his fist into Kristen's face.

I hate him with everything in me.

Leaning in, I again make sure she's breathing. Since she's not crying or trying to speak to me, it's clear she's asleep. There's nothing I can do for her. All I can do is hope that when Logan comes back, he'll no longer be angry. Maybe he'll leave us alone tonight.

Walking on my knees again, I make my way back over to the zipper of the tent, straining to listen for any sounds. I'm clearly a masochist because if I hear my sisters screaming or fending off an attack, I'm unable to do any-fucking-thing about it.

All I hear are cheerful hollers and laughter in the distance. The monsters are celebrating their tyranny. Fury, hot and uncontrollable, swells up inside me. If only I could break through these ropes with just my anger. I attempt to do just that and the burn across my flesh is a reminder that it's not going to work.

I'm about to flop down on a sleeping bag, giving in to my despair, when a shadow creeps closer, blotting out the light from the campfire.

Logan.

Fuck.

I scramble back on my knees until I'm away from the opening, heart thundering in my chest. Is he back to beat on us some more? Fear chases away my anger, leaving me to tremble in anticipation.

Ziiiip.

The shadowy figure enters the tent and zips it back

up behind them. I stay unmoving, bracing myself for the impending attack.

"Ronan?"

Holy shit.

Relief explodes through me as I realize the soft voice belongs to Raegan. It's quickly snuffed out with worry over her being here. If Logan catches her…

"Rae," I hiss. "What are you doing here?"

She approaches and then I feel her hands on my shoulders. I'm tugged against her as she hugs me. As dangerous is this is, I can't help but bury my nose against her neck, inhaling her familiar scent. God, I've missed my sister so fucking much.

"Are you tied up?" she whispers. "Hold on. I can help."

Her warm, comforting arms leave me as she shuffles behind me. I groan with every tug as she attempts to untie me. It fucking hurts.

"I can't see," she grumbles, "and they're tied so tight. Can you feel your fingers?"

"Barely," I croak out. "I don't think we can get through them without a knife."

She sighs in frustration before settling in front of me again. "Are you okay? Did he hurt you?"

Fingertips brush over my face, gently dancing over my bruises. When she touches the drying blood under my nose, she sucks in a breath.

"I'm going to clean you up, Ro," she says, voice

cracking with emotion. "I hate these people. They're sick."

She pulls back and then she's using something—her shirt maybe—that's slightly wet, probably from her mouth, carefully cleaning the blood away. Once it's taken care of, her face nears mine. I can feel her warm breath tickling me.

"I'm so sorry. This is all my fault."

Leaning forward, I rest my forehead to hers. "None of this is your fault, Rae. It's mine for not being able to protect you all. I'm so fucking useless."

She shakes her head but remains leaned against me. "It's all on them. We'll figure it out. I promise."

I want to believe her.

Fuck, how I do.

"Did CJ, um, hurt you?" I ask, dreading the answer.

"No." She pauses. "Not yet."

Not yet.

My stomach roils with disgust.

"Rae..."

"I need you to be my first." Her voice quavers. "Please, Ronan. I'm so damn scared, but I refuse to let them take this from me. Please. I beg of you."

I press my lips to her mouth, needing her to understand I'd do anything for her. Any-fucking-thing. She surprises me by parting her lips and thrusting her tongue into my mouth. Raegan tastes familiar. Like home. Like happiness and love. Because of that, I'm unable to keep from kissing her back. With a hunger of what used to be. Nostalgia sweetening the kiss.

Her hand slides down to my lap, rubbing over my flaccid cock through the denim. The idea of my dick inside her is one I can't seem to wrap my head around. She's Raegan. My sister and a *girl*. She's not Ryder. And, in all the fantasies I had about sex, I'd imagined me being the one penetrated. Not the other way around.

How can I do this?

I'm not sure, but I'll have to figure it out and quickly.

"Are we doing this?" she whispers, vulnerability making her voice crack.

"Y-Yeah," I murmur. "Yeah, Rae, we're doing this."

She pecks my lips and then pulls away to work at unfastening my jeans. I sit up on my knees, helping her so she can drag my clothes down, freeing my limp cock.

Fuck.

What if I can't get it up for her?

"It's not hard," she says, uncertainty in her tone. "What do we do?"

I sigh in frustration. "You have to get it hard."

Her hand encircles my cock and it pulses with interest. I try not to focus on the fact Logan could come in at any second, instead on the way her soft hand strokes me up and down. It's different from the way Ryder's hand felt. His actions were practiced, whereas hers are unsure. Still feels good, though.

"Like this?" she breathes.

"Uh, yeah."

My sister works my dick until it's at half-mast before pulling away. I can hear her fumbling for her clothes. The chill of the evening settles over my dick and naked thighs as I wait for what comes next. Then her hands are on my shoulders as she straddles my thighs. My half-hard dick rubs against her pussy lips. Just like in the magazines, except that the women there were mostly bald and my sister has hair that tickles against me.

I think about the magazine…the pretty assholes those women had. I bet Raegan has a pretty asshole. My dick thickens, heat flooding south.

She reaches between us, grabbing hold of my dick, and then tries to line it up with her entrance. It's dry and the tip of my dick refuses to breach the opening.

"Get it wet, Rae, otherwise it's not going in."

Her lips brush against mine and then she slides off me. She shuffles some more before her hot breath is on my dick. I groan as it feathers over me. Okay, yeah, that feels nice. Rae's soft hand once again curls around me, but this time, her mouth joins the fray.

Holy fuck.

Her slick tongue dances over my crown as she wets my tip. A groan of surprised pleasure escapes me. That feels good. Really good. My cock swells in her grip.

"Rae," I rasp out. "Fuck."

She runs her tongue up and down along my shaft, making me dizzy with need. My hips thrust forward of their own accord, desperate for more.

I'd always imagined a man doing this very thing

to me—sucking me off until I lost my shit. Never once did I think it'd be Raegan. And yet…I can't imagine it any other way now. Her mouth is so gentle and sweet, but urgent.

We can't delay.

She needs this from me and apparently, I need it too.

"It's wet," I murmur. "It should work now."

Fuck how I want to keep letting her run her tongue all over my dick, but this isn't all about me. She climbs back up, straddling me like before. Our mouths meet for another kiss. This time, we're both breathing heavily, need coursing through both of us. She grips my dick, again guiding me to her entrance. Without being able to touch her, all I can do is hope she can figure it out on her own.

The tip of my cock slides between her pussy lips but immediately meets tight resistance. Much tighter than mine or Ryder's hand. I can't help but wonder how good it will feel to be inside her all the way.

"It's not going in," she whimpers. "I don't know what to do."

"Let me help. Hold on," I breathe against her mouth.

She tenses just as I thrust upward. A garbled cry escapes her that I quickly quiet with a soul-stealing kiss. I'm barely inside her. My cock throbs uncontrollably with need. I kiss her hard as I thrust again. This time, her body seems to accept me, and she slides all the way down my shaft. Her fingers dig painfully into my shoulders and I think she might be crying.

"Are…are you okay?" I stammer. "Am I hurting you?"

"It's…I'm fine."

I kiss her again, thrusting upward once more. Her body grips me so tightly. Everything is hot and wet. It feels so fucking good. I'm lost to the sensations of her body and the sweetness of her mouth on mine. Her pussy seems to squeeze around me and I lose it. A choked sound rattles from my chest as my nuts draw up tight. My cock pulses, sending thick ropes of cum into her body.

I've never come inside of someone before and it's everything I ever fantasized about.

Feels. So. Fucking. Good.

"Oh," Raegan mutters. "Yuck. It's messy. All that stuff gets everywhere, huh?"

"Cum." I kiss along her jaw to her throat. "Very messy."

I want to untangle my wrists so I can hold her to me forever. She may have needed something from me, but she gave me a beautiful gift as well.

"I love you," I tell her, unable to keep from suckling her neck. "Fuck, Raegan. I love you. I'm going to get us out of here."

She slips off my softening cock and redresses. Then she helps me pull my clothes back on over my dripping dick.

I wish I could have kept her impaled on my dick permanently.

"Thank you," she says, once again throwing her arms around me to kiss me wildly.

The kiss we share isn't like anything we've shared ever before. It's intimate and private. Only ours. Hot and wet and forbidden, but perfect.

"I have to leave." She sniffles. "I'm sorry."

"No, don't be. Leave. Stay safe. We'll figure this out soon."

Another peck on my lips and then she's gone. I fall down on the sleeping bag, my chest heaving and a smile on my face. That felt good and I feel like I did at least one thing to protect my little sister. At least her first time was with me as it should have been.

I'm just about to fall asleep, hours later, when Logan stumbles into the tent stinking of liquor. He shuffles past me and attempts to shake Kristen awake. I freeze, hoping he won't hurt her, not that I would be able to hit him with my numb, unusable hands that are still bound behind me.

"Fuck it," Logan grumbles.

I squeeze my eyes shut, hoping he'll just pass out. Sounds of him undressing can be heard and just when I think he's going to fall asleep, he runs his palm down the side of my thigh. My abs tighten with dread. Then he pushes me onto my stomach.

Panic alights inside me.

Roughly, he starts jerking my jeans and boxers off. He completely removes them before his palm squeezes my ass cheek. He spits and then he's on top of me.

No.

He's not about to do that.

I'm stunned, not completely sure of what's happening, and then fire burns at my hole.

"No," I cry out. "Please—"

His fist slams down between my shoulder blades, knocking the breath out of me. The fire breach turns into a full-on invasion as his thick length shoves into me, splitting me in half.

The pain is overwhelming.

I can't breathe.

I'm crying.

I'm dying.

Slap. Slap. Slap. Slap. Slap.

The abuse continues forever, the pain growing so intense, I vomit all over my sleeping bag. The acidic scent of puke plus the needy grunts coming from Logan are too much.

I black out. For how long, I'm not sure. And then I'm back to my nightmarish reality.

Slap. Slap. Slap. Slap. Slap.

I attempt to replay the moment with Raegan.

Just her and me. Just us. Her soft whimpers.

But it's not enough. He steals me from her.

Slap. Slap. Slap. Slap. Slap.

Logan is raping me.

He's fucking raping me.

Everything feels as though it's spinning, but finally, the brutality stops. I'm left half naked, messy from his

spent cum spitting out of my ravaged asshole, and sobbing uncontrollably.

It's not until I hear his snores beside me do I allow
myself to finally relax all my muscles.

I can't take this again.

We have to get the fuck out of here.

CHAPTER TWELVE

ryder

THIS IS TAKING FOREVER.

Me and my brother are good trackers, but they always seem to be too far ahead of us. We wasted a couple of days when our trail went cold again. It opened up to a huge meadow near a water source. Bears, wolves, deer, and other game trampled down the brush, leading in many different directions. All we had to go on was the general southeast route they had been taking this whole time and assume it'd continue.

We were wrong.

The trail quickly went cold and we were forced to backtrack, losing half a day by going in the wrong direction. Another several hours were spent splitting up and searching deeper for the trail to pick up again. Wild eventually found it, shooting more southwest this time. By the time he rounded us up, it was dark and traveling through the night when we barely picked up their trail seemed stupid. We couldn't afford to lose any more time, so breaking for camp was a necessity.

"We're never going to find them," I grumble, rolling Raegan's earring around between my thumb and finger. "Who's to say they're even still alive?"

My stomach roils at the thought of losing any of my siblings.

"Raegan probably already mouthed off and got herself killed," Wild agrees with a snort. "We should pack it up and head back."

Rowdy bristles at Wild's words but doesn't say anything. In fact, he hasn't said much at all this entire trip. Wild keeps saying things to rile him up, but Rowdy's not rising to the bait.

When neither of us says anything to Wild's attempt to stir the pot, he huffs and then stomps off to his tent. Me and my brother sit in silence, the crickets singing in the dark, until I'm sure Wild has finally fallen asleep.

"Hey," I mutter, elbowing Rowdy. "What's your deal with him anyway?"

Rowdy doesn't speak for a full minute before a sigh rasps out of him. "He hates me. Thinks punishing me is his job now."

I roll my eyes in the dark. "I could figure that out on my own. But why, man? What happened when you stayed with them four years ago?"

With only the moonlight shining through the trees, it's hard to make out Rowdy's shadowed expression. We'd decided against fires in case we get close to the traveling group. No more fires and no more gunshots if we want to have the element of surprise.

"I wanted to go experience life," Rowdy says, voice soft. "Back then, I'd felt trapped at home, you know? Every day was the same with the same people. Pretty boring. I'm sure you get that."

He was my age when he left us. Difference is, he chose to leave, whereas Dad was going to make me leave. Not sure that's on Dad's list of priorities anymore. I can certainly hope not.

"Sure." My lie seems obvious to me, but Rowdy relaxes and continues.

"I showed up at Uncle Atticus's. Evan, Wild's cousin, was there. It was nice to hang out with another guy—a man." He picks up a stick and snaps it in two. "Wild seemed so…young. Like a little boy and so far from who I was becoming. No offense, but he was like my little brother and I was trying to get away from all that."

All *that* being us.

Nice.

Rather than bite out a retort, I wait for him to continue.

"Evan was cool. Funny as shit. And he got me to try things. It was exactly the experience I was after."

"How does Wild come into play?" I ask, canting my head to look at him better. "He was annoyed with not being the center of attention?"

Rowdy pauses for a bit and then tosses one of his broken sticks away from us. "Something like that."

"Dude, that's all you're giving me? For fuck's sake—"

"I kissed him. Evan. We were drinking, smoking a little pot, and then we were kissing. It happened all so fast."

I'm reeling at his words. "You're gay?"

Rowdy scoffs. "I don't think so. I mean, I liked everything that happened, but when I see my future, I see a wife. It was just fun. Felt good, you know?"

We both grow silent for a couple of minutes before he starts speaking again.

"I'd heard something and assumed Wild saw us because he was different toward me after that. Pissed and refused to speak to me for a long time. I never could figure out why, though. Maybe he thought it was wrong I was kissing a guy or he was mad that it was his cousin? I have no idea, but he's been shitty toward me ever since."

"How come you came back if you were living your best life and experiencing fun shit?"

Rowdy grunts, reminding me of Dad. "I learned the hard way that life out there isn't always fun."

"When you came back, you isolated yourself," I murmur. "Did something bad happen?"

"You could say that."

"I'm sorry, man. You know you can tell me. I'm not going to judge you or anything."

He picks up another stick and starts snapping it into small pieces. Whatever happened it's something he clearly feels nervous talking about. It makes me wonder if I even want to hear what it is.

"I had sex with Evan," he blurts out. "It wasn't long after Evan got an apartment, leaving Wild's house where he was staying. I went with him. That's when all the sex stuff started."

"Oh."

"At first, it was good. Lots of blow jobs, frotting, hand jobs." He lets out a small chuckle. "I really thought I'd hit the jackpot. No responsibilities to speak of, I was getting off all the damn time, and smoking weed was relaxing. I fucking loved it."

Dread pools in the pit of my stomach. "Until you didn't?"

"Yeah. Until I didn't." He scrubs a palm over his face, leaving his hand there as if to cover his expression from me. "I was cool with everything we'd been doing. He'd mentioned me bottoming for him a time or two, but I wasn't interested. Sounded kind of painful, to be honest."

I'm not completely sure what bottoming means, but I'm not an idiot. I'm guessing penetration. Evan wanted to penetrate his ass. It makes my own asshole tighten. It does sound painful if you are on the receiving end.

"I told him no. He was pissy about it, but he seemed to get over it." He rises to his feet and paces back and forth in front of me. "One day, he got me shitfaced drunk. I don't remember much, but it happened between us. The pain was there the next day, but I figured I'd survived."

"But you said no…"

Rowdy pauses. "I guess when I was drunk, I said yes."

The whole situation makes my skin itchy. I don't like that he isn't sure.

"We started drinking more and more, which led to more fucking." He sighs heavily. "And then, I don't know, I was just bored of it."

"Evan didn't take that well?"

"Fuck no. He wanted…I don't know. A relationship? But I wasn't there for that. I still wanted to have a wife, have children, eventually come back home to be with my family. What I had with Evan was just sex and fun."

I don't speak or breathe, desperate to know the rest of the story. My quiet brother is a vault. For him to reveal this part of himself, I feel like I'm getting a glimpse inside of Rowdy's head that's never been seen before.

"Evan started throwing these parties where he invited everyone. The quality of these people was not the best, but I was meeting girls, which I liked. One girl dragged me into the bathroom and gave me a sloppy blowjob that left red lipstick all over my dick. It was hot and wild. I was back to having the best time of my life."

Now that Rowdy's lid has been lifted, all sorts of shit is spilling out of him. All I can do is intently listen, eager to know how this story plays out.

"I admitted to him later that night that I was with this girl. He was pissed, but we weren't a couple or anything. We got into a big fight, though. He nearly broke my nose in a rage. Cops got called and everything.

Luckily, it was Will, Evan's dad who responded, so neither of us got into any trouble."

"Evan seems like a total asshole," I grunt. "I've only met him a handful of times and he seemed fine then, but I've definitely changed my stance now."

"The next day, when we were both sober and everyone was gone, he begged me not to leave. Said I was his best friend. I wanted to believe him that we were cool." He sits back down beside me and lets loose a pained groan. "The next party we had, Evan stayed glued to my hip. It was annoying until he told me about a new party favor he had that would fuck me up real good. Since he scared away any potential girls who might want to have sex, I was game."

"What was it?" I ask, voice soft. "What was the party favor?"

Rowdy tenses and shoves his sleeve up. I can't see anything in the moonlight, but I stare down at where his thumb rubs the crease in his arm near his elbow. "Heroin. I didn't really know what it was, and supposedly neither did he. Like an idiot, I let one of his friends inject me with that shit." He lets out a whoosh of breath. "It turned me inside out. Drowned me in warm bliss. Took away my every worry."

"Sounds terrifying."

"At the time, no. Evan got really good at cooking the shit up himself and jabbing us both, so we no longer needed his friends. Our big parties became parties of two. Months went by where all we did was fuck and get high." He buries his face in his hands. "I didn't recognize who the fuck I even was anymore. Anytime I showed any dissatisfaction with how my life turned out, Evan would seduce me with the heroin and soon I'd be blissed the fuck out again."

"I thought Uncle Atticus was supposed to keep an eye on you. Where was he?"

"Around. But not enough. I think he thought we were typical roommates who drank a little too much."

"What made you decide you'd had enough?"

The crickets all seem to grow silent, they too anticipating what he'll say next.

"I…" He groans and tugs at his hair. "One day, I told him I didn't want his stupid drugs or him. That I was leaving. I'd had it with the bullshit. I felt trapped and controlled by Evan."

You think? Wisely, I keep my trap shut.

"He beat the fuck out of me, man. Cracked a few ribs, busted my lip, blackened both eyes. It hurt so bad. I hated him."

I seethe with fury. If I ever see Evan, I'm going to kick him in his goddamn balls repeatedly until he's throwing up.

"It was when I was begging him to let me call Uncle Atticus that he finally went too far. He fucked me and then he shot me up with heroin. So much. Too much." His voice cracks. "I almost died, Ryder. I overdosed on heroin and if it weren't for Evan's dad, Will, getting me to a hospital in time, I'd have died."

My blood runs cold at his words. "Did you tell them what he did to you?"

He shakes his head sharply. "No. Will was having to explain all over himself that I was visiting but lost my wallet. I don't have a driver's license or any form of identification. The hospital had questions and Dad always said that we're safer if people don't know anything about our family. I felt like I was pulling these people into my life—into my family's life—and now their safety was threatened too. All because of my mistakes. I just wanted to get the hell out of there."

"Evan beat the shit out of you. What did Will have to say about his own fucking son?"

"I lied," he croaks out. "I said I got jumped to protect Evan."

"He's a motherfucking bastard, Rowdy. Why would you protect him?"

He sucks in a staggered breath. "Because it's Wild's family. I didn't know what would happen. I just wanted to leave. I finally had my out."

I remember when Rowdy came home several months later. He was pale, his eyes were sunken in, and he'd lost muscle mass. His hair was limp and he was sporting some fading bruises. It looked like the town had chewed him up and spat him back out. But he was borderline mute when he came home. Dad set him up in the old cabin down by the river to give him his space. We were all told to back off so he could breathe. That he was going through some shit.

Guilt surges through me. I'd told Dad Rowdy came back fucked-up. I'd been cruel about it. Knowing what I know now, I feel like a total dick for saying that. My brother came back fucked-up because someone had tried to destroy him.

"I asked Uncle Atticus to take me home," he says quietly. "Evan was probably pissed, but I avoided him altogether and went straight back home after the hospital. I never saw or spoke to Evan again."

It seems unfair that Wild would punish him for such a small thing—the kiss he witnessed—when my brother was literally trying not to die.

"So this was never really about Wild?"

He shrugs. "No. Maybe Wild thinks so because he thinks everything is about him. But no. This shit was all me and Evan." Rowdy lets out a humorless laugh. "You know, even all these years later, I still crave the warmth of the heroin as it crawls through my veins. I hated it, but I miss it."

Thank fuck he's away from that shit.

"Anyway," Rowdy says with a grunt. "Dad and Mom or anyone aside from me and Evan knows about all that. I'd like to keep it that way. Mom might die if she knew I had sex with another man."

We both laugh, but it's a little flat.

I have the urge to tell him all about me and Ronan. That maybe he doesn't have to feel ashamed because we all fuck up. It's on the tip of my tongue, but in the end, I bite it back. I refuse to out Ronan or tell what we did without his permission. Maybe someday we can tell him together.

"Thanks for confiding in me, Rowdy. I'm sorry that happened to you. I wish I could beat that motherfucker's face in."

He clutches the back of my neck before gently squeezing it. "You're a good brother. Time for bed. We're going to get our people back and soon."

If Dad ever does truly send me away, I'll make sure I find Evan and pay him a little visit.

No one fucks with my family and goes unscathed.

No one.

CHAPTER THIRTEEN

raegan

'M SO SORE BETWEEN MY LEGS. IT BURNS—FEELS RAW. And when I went to pee, I noticed blood in my panties, which were also drenched with Ronan's cum.

So messy.

But it was Ronan. Despite the pain, I felt a connection between us that sparked to life. Something new and tantalizing. He kissed me with fire and purpose. I still remember the way his hips flexed and thrust, the need to impale me almost animalistic.

I did that.

I made Ronan feel that way.

It was wrong, though. I mean, he's my brother. We had sex. My parents' worst fears happened. I keep waiting for Mom to pop her head into my tent and yell at me.

Tears burn at my eyes.

She's not coming. She'll never be coming.

At least now, when CJ forces himself on me, I'll

know it was Ronan—my first true love—who got that special part of me. It hurt, yes, but it also felt like our souls were melding together. The intimacy between us was unlike anything I'd ever experienced before.

I lie awake in the tent, waiting for the inevitable. Just the thought of CJ inside of me when I'm so sore has me grimacing. If only I had my knife. I'd take great joy in stabbing him in the gut for trying to have sex with me.

A giggle from nearby has me sitting up. I crawl over to the tent opening, unzip it, and poke my head out. A couple of male voices can be heard beyond the tents in the woods, which means most of them have probably gone to bed. Except CJ, which is good. It would be a great opportunity to escape.

Maybe this is our only shot.

Quickly, I shove my feet back into my boots and scramble out of the tent. I scan the shadows, looking for anything to use as a weapon.

My eyes land on a stick between my tent and the one next to it—the one I'm pretty sure is Sadie's. Soft crying can be heard, which makes bile rise up my gorge. Before I can figure out what to do about it, I hear female laughter nearby. The giggling isn't coming from that tent. It's coming from the woods. I squint in the darkness, looking for the source.

Mya steps between two trees, Wyatt and Olivia with her. Before, those two kids were nice and I got along with them. Now, they both stare at me with contempt. If they're both here, does that mean Tom is forcing himself on Sadie as we speak? Terror mixed with hatred burns hot in my gut.

"You're not supposed to be out alone," Wyatt says, frowning. "Your husband will be angry."

I snarl at him. "What husband?"

I'm not married, no matter what their cultish leader says or what they believe.

He scowls at my attitude but doesn't say anything back. Mya walks up to me, a sneer on her stupid face.

"My brother wanted you so bad, but you're just a backwoods dumb bitch." She curls her lip up at me. "I hope it hurts when he fucks you."

With a growl, I shove her hard. She crashes into the tent with a shriek. Wyatt and Olivia scramble to help her back up.

"You psycho bitch!" she bellows, charging at me.

I'm ready for her and swing my fist this time. It connects with her face. The sickening crunch of bone is satisfying. She stumbles and falls to her knees, a loud sob ripping out of her lungs.

I take another step toward her, ready to beat this witch up, when Wyatt puts himself between us. He may be a few years younger, but I'm not opposed to hitting him too.

"Hey!" a deep voice calls out, trotting over to us. "What the hell is going on here?"

"Your wife," Mya chokes out, tone filled with venom, "was trying to escape."

CJ, the body behind the voice, helps his sister up.

The dying campfire illuminates the side of their unhappy faces. Seeing the blood running over Mya's lips makes me grin.

"Raegan," CJ says, attempting to inject authority into his tone. "Get back to our tent."

I refuse to move, making sure to give him the bitchiest expression I can muster.

"Watch your back," Mya snaps, swiping at the blood. "When you go to sleep, I will find you in your bed. And I'll cut your hair off. Maybe I'll blind *you* while I'm at it!"

Her words are exactly the same ones I said to her what feels like an eternity ago.

"I'll be too busy fucking my brainless, shitty *husband*," I bite back. "Nice try. I hope I broke your nose."

CJ hisses at them to go back to their tents before Michael gets involved and then hauls me to our tent. He reeks of liquor and I just now notice him swaying. Great. He's drunk and I've just reminded him about having sex with me. Fear prickles at my skin, making the hairs on my neck stand on end.

"Sit," he grumbles. "You've given me a goddamn headache. Jesus."

I plop down and cross my arms over my chest. "I'm not having sex with you."

He groans as he sheds his shirt. "Fuck off, Raegan. I've got whiskey dick anyway. Go to sleep and don't try any funny shit."

I make sure to lie down on the sleeping bag as far

away as I can get from him. Whatever whiskey dick is, I'm glad he's got it. I hope his dick falls off altogether. Lying stiff as a board, I wait for him to trick me and pounce when I least expect it. He settles on his own sleeping bag within seconds. The sounds of his heavy breathing as he falls asleep are oddly relaxing. At least I've dodged the bullet that is my "wedding night."

Once I'm sure he's asleep, I crash despite my efforts to stay awake.

Later, when it's still dark, I wake to someone pulling my hair. At first, I think it's CJ trying something funny, but then when I hear the sound of a blade cutting through hair, I panic.

"Oops," Mya whispers, tossing my ponytail at me. "Now you're even uglier, bitch."

Gaping down in the darkness, I fumble around until I feel the weight of my bundled hair. Tears well in my eyes for a brief moment before rage has me launching myself her way.

"Touch me again and I'll hurt the little one," Mya threatens. "I'll toss him in the river. Watch him drown."

I freeze, horrified at the thought of Declan being thrown in the river. "You wouldn't. Your uncle claimed him as his son."

"Accidents happen," she says with a harsh laugh. "Try me. Don't think I won't."

With those words, she slips out of the tent and disappears. I reach up to touch my hair—or lack thereof. It'd fallen into a loose ponytail at the top of my back.

She must've cut right above the ponytail holder. All my hair is gone. Chopped off by that hateful girl.

I curl up on my sleeping bag, biting back tears. I can't afford to lose it right now. Getting me and my family out of here is more important than hair. Hair grows back. Family does not.

From somewhere close, I can hear a man whispering soft words as a girl cries. I want to throw up. Poor Sadie. Tom is so…huge and disgusting. Is that why Wyatt and Olivia were with Mya? So he could rape Sadie without an audience?

I dry heave at the thought of him rutting over her. His body odor was always so nauseating, but he really felt like someone who wasn't totally bad. Maybe I was wrong. I'm apparently wrong about a lot of things.

The thought of Tom and Sadie, naked and having sex, makes for a horrible prelude to more inevitable nightmares.

I wake shivering. My legs are cold, but my neck is warm. Hot even. Ronan kisses my neck, suckling the flesh there as his hand greedily rubs my bare thigh.

Wait.

Jerking my eyes open, I notice a man halfway on top of me in the gray, early morning light, but it's not my brother.

It's CJ.

No!

His fingers tug at my panties, roughly jerking them down my thighs. Panic quickly races away as rage explodes inside me. I grab at his hair, yanking him away from my neck.

"Don't touch me, you sick piece of shit!"

He grunts, shocked at my response, and sits up to glower at me. "What the fuck, Raegan?"

I start to pull my panties back up, but he strikes, grabbing onto my hand to keep me from doing it.

"You smell like goat shit," I hiss, spittle hitting his face. "Your face is so embarrassing. I'm ashamed to have been matched with you."

I'm just barking out mean stuff, but it surprisingly strikes him. He winces at my words and frowns.

"Don't be hateful," he grunts. "You were attracted to me when we met. You can't lie."

"I felt your dick through your clothes," I continue, voice shaking with anger. "It's so small. I bet your finger would do a better job of fucking."

His face flames hot. Good to know. He doesn't like his dick being ridiculed.

"I'd rather fuck Tom," I lie. "At least his dick is big."

CJ's features contort into a furious expression. "Stop."

"Or what? You'll try to fuck me with your stick dick? I bet I'll fall asleep it'll be so boring."

He pounces on me and I cry out in surprise. I

struggle against his strong hold. His dick, though bigger than I implied, is half hard and not all that scary.

"Wow. Pathetic." I start laughing, hysterically I might add, but it does the trick. "No wonder you had to leave civilization. No woman in her right mind would want that tiny thing inside them."

A growl vibrates out of him. We struggle as he attempts to remove my panties. I scrape my fingernails along the side of his neck, relishing in the howl that escapes him.

"Your whole family is vile. Wretched human garbage. I'll kill you all in your sleep one day!"

His dick turns squishy against me, which has me laughing harder. My cruelty is working. Good, I'm more than happy to destroy him in any way I can.

"I bet Michael's dick is big and actually works," I taunt. "Maybe I'll take him up on his offer for a second wife. How humiliating would it be for you to have to turn me over to him? I'll tell everyone it's because your dick is so pitiful, and you can't even get it hard."

He roars, yanking my panties right off my body. When he sits back, wrenching my thighs apart and exposing my pussy to him, I tremble in fear. I'm about to change my tune—to be nice—just to get him to stop.

His eyes fixate on my pussy and he frowns. "Is that blood?"

Oh God. If he figures out how I got that blood, this could be bad for both me and Ronan.

"I'm starting my period," I blurt out, though it's a lie.

"It's about to start gushing. I always get these gross clots that look like pieces of my organs are coming out—"

He gags violently. "Sh-shut the fuck up!"

Snapping my thighs together, I scramble away from him, dragging the sleeping bag over my naked legs. "It smells like sewage and rotten eggs."

Another gag.

"Fuck it, I'm out." He stumbles out of the tent and crunches away.

I wait, listening, as he retches nearby. The thought of him throwing up makes me gleeful. Quickly, I snatch my underwear and jeans. I throw on my clothes and boots in record time.

Once I'm feeling safer, I crawl to the entrance of the tent and peek out. CJ glances my way, turns green, and vomits all over the ground.

My heart pumps with victory.

I won't let this worm of a man take me down without a fight.

CHAPTER FOURTEEN

ronan

PAIN ASSAULTS ME FROM EVERY DIRECTION.

As I wake to the low hum of voices outside our tent, I take stock of my injuries. My head is throbbing uncontrollably, my ass is raw and burning, and my wrists are on fire.

I crack open my eyes, carefully taking in my surroundings so as not to bring Logan's wrath upon me once more. I'm shocked to discover the tent is empty and my hands are no longer bound. With a groan, I sit up so I can inspect my wrists. Blood crusts around each one from the bindings cutting into me last night. My fingers are still stiff from not getting enough blood flow, but I can move them better this morning.

A twig snaps nearby and then someone is at the entrance of the tent. My heart hammers in my chest and my nerves come alive as I prepare myself to face off with Logan. Luckily, it's not him. Kristen pushes through the opening, arms full of several items.

"Hey," she says softly, handing me something wrapped in a hand towel. "You're probably starving."

I take her offering and peek inside. Strips of cooked meat, still warm, are piled in a mound. I'm apparently ravenous because I tear into the gamey meat, uncaring what exactly I'm eating. Based on the toughness and the small bones, I'm going to say rabbit or squirrel. Not my favorite, but I can't exactly complain. I suck all the meat off the bones, discreetly pocketing one of the larger, stronger pieces for a potential future weapon. Once I've wolfed down breakfast, Kristen hands me a bottle of water.

After I gulp down the water and am feeling marginally better, she scoots closer before taking hold of my hand. Neither of us speaks as she sets to using the supplies she brought in with her to clean the cuts on my wrists. The alcohol burns, but I welcome the jarring sensation. I need to be alert and ready for anything Logan throws my way.

Whatever happens, I can't let him bind me again. I was helpless to fight against him. If only I had my hands free, there's a good chance I could have landed a punch or something to escape his abuse. My efforts to protect my siblings are throwing me right into the bear's clutches.

I have to be smarter about this.

I have to find a way to escape.

As though reading my mind, Kristen lifts her gaze and says, "Don't."

My grunt in response has her continuing.

"You think you can escape, but trust me, it's not that easy," she murmurs. "I've tried many times and it all lands me right back in this tent. With him."

A wave of frustration swallows me whole. This can't be my life. I have to get away even if Logan kills me in the process. I refuse to be his pet forever.

"Come on," Kristen says, patting my wrist. "There's a creek nearby. Everyone is washing up."

She rises to her feet and then offers her hand to me. I shove my feet into my boots before taking her offering. A groan of pain rumbles out of me. I'm nineteen, but I feel more like ninety this morning.

I follow her out of the tent and immediately scan the camp, looking for my siblings. Everyone is a blur, but I recognize Destiny sitting beside Jace, both of them eating. She doesn't seem to be in any immediate distress, which is relieving. Near the fire, a group of kids and women are lively chatting. Raegan is nowhere to be found.

If CJ hurt her…

You'll what?

Bitterness creeps through me. I can't do shit. I'm fucking helpless. Kristen points to a pathway between two tents. I follow after her, scanning the ground for anything I could use for a weapon—something more substantial than a rabbit bone. It'd be too easy for anyone to leave a knife or a gun lying around. By the time we make it to the babbling creek, I've found nothing useful for fighting a war with an entire group of people in an effort to save myself and my family.

Kristen undresses down to her bra and panties before tiptoeing into the water. Slowly, I peel off my clothes and boots, leaving my boxers on. The water is icy cold but does wonders to bring clarity to my brain. If only I could also bring clarity to my vision.

I notice Sadie and Tom's kids Wyatt and Olivia talking quietly together, all of their teeth chattering as they wash up. She, too, doesn't seem to be traumatized from last night.

What about Raegan?

Sucking in a breath, I dip under the water, letting the chill shock me to the bone. When I emerge, my teeth also begin to chatter.

"Here," Kristen says, thrusting a bar of soap at me. "Who knows when the next chance to bathe is."

I take the bar of soap—a bar Mom made that *they* stole—and lather my body up. The scent reminds me of her. A terrible ache forms in my chest. God, I miss her. I miss them all.

They're still alive.

They have to be.

Living in a world without my parents would hurt too much. I can't imagine it and refuse to. Pushing those thoughts away, I scrub at my face, hair, and then hit my pits. Once I've rinsed away all the soap, I sink deeper into the creek to pull down my boxers. Quickly, I wash my dick and balls. Then I consider what to do about my ass.

I want him gone from me, but it's all so tender down there.

Closing my eyes and gritting my teeth, I soap up my fingers before gently running them along my ass crack. When I brush over my ravaged hole, my breaths come out ragged. The soap stings, but I wash the area anyway. If I didn't think it'd be extremely painful, I'd stick my fingers inside and clean there too just to rid myself of him. Instead, I let the rushing water do what it can.

"Hi, Ronan," a velvety voice purrs. "You're looking a little rough this morning."

Mya swims over to me, a wolfish grin on her face. Ignoring her, I look for Kristen, eager to get out of this cold ass water. Before I can escape, Mya's fingers bite into my bicep.

"You don't have to be rude," she says with a pout in her tone, plucking the soap from my hands. "You'll be my husband one day. We should be spending time together."

Tearing my stare from Kristen, I peer down at Mya, who's now inches away from me. Her eyes, though ringed in new bluish bruising, flicker with mischief. Maybe to some other guy, she'd be attractive, but to me, she's just another extension of evil in this fucked-up group.

"I'm not the only one looking a little rough this morning," I grunt, gesturing at her swollen nose and bruised face. "Did you run into a tree?"

"More like my fist!"

Raegan's voice is nearby, followed by a cackle of

laughter. My heart squeezes in my chest. She sounds like her usual self. Thank fuck.

"Cut your shit," CJ grumbles, dragging her farther down the creek with him and out of my line of vision.

"My uncle won't put up with her continued disobedience," Mya hisses, poking at my chest. "You people think you're so funny and smart. You're nothing but a commodity to be consumed and discarded when we no longer need you."

I glower at her, taking a step closer. "I wish I could have watched her hit you."

"Excuse me?" Her eyes narrow. "Maybe I should tell Logan what an asshole you're being. I'm sure he'd be up for a little more training."

I'm not sure if she means the beatings or the rape. Either way, her threat is effective. I cringe at her words before turning and swimming away from her.

When I pass by Sadie, she's glaring Mya's way. I give her shoulder a quick squeeze of support before making a mad dash to my pile of clothes. Once dressed, I shove my hand into my pocket, fingering the slender but pointy bone. It's small, but it's something. Right now, it's a sliver of hope and I cling desperately to it.

We're staying at this camp another night. Michael made the announcement over dinner. Because of the water source and plentiful game nearby, he wants to give Stacey and the small children a rest. Stacey didn't show up for dinner because her back was hurting and she didn't feel well. Because she didn't have her "pretend mom" claws in them, I actually got to spend the evening sitting with Declan and Dakota.

Both of the boys were doing remarkably well, much to my relief. Declan was extra clingy and to be truthful, I needed to just hold him. It reminded me that I couldn't let Logan break me down. My siblings are relying on me as their big brother to protect them—to get them out of this situation.

Speaking of Logan…he's still gone.

Been gone all day on a hunting and scouting mission for Michael. His absence was exactly what I needed to recover some mentally before having to face him again.

Now, it's bedtime and he hasn't come back, which is unusual. Me and Kristen have been silently playing a card game using the lantern light to pass the time, but my mind is loud and reeling with rampant thoughts.

What if this is my chance?

If he's out in the woods still hunting, I could sneak around to gather up my sisters and brothers and Sadie. Kristen could help me. Together, we can get the hell out of here.

My heart starts racing as I turn my attention from the game to the tent opening. Our boots sit close to it. All I need to do is put my boots on, unzip the tent, and go on a hunt for my people.

"This is our opportunity," I say to Kristen in the softest whisper. "Now or never."

Her wild eyes meet mine and she shakes her head fiercely. "No, Ronan. You can't. They'll catch you."

Ignoring her argument, I toss the cards down and scramble over to my boots. I can't seem to pull them on fast enough. Once they're on my feet, I unzip the tent. Casting a glance over my shoulder, I gesture for Kristen's boots.

"Come on," I hiss. "Let's go."

"Ronan—"

"Going somewhere?"

My blood turns to ice at the sound of *his* voice. Logan sticks his head into the tent, smirking at me. I force my body to remain stiff, desperate to keep the trembling at bay. I refuse to let him see my fear.

"Bathroom," I blurt out. "I was trying to get Kristen to go too, but she's afraid a bear will get her."

Logan's eyes turn to slits as he studies me. "You both can wait until morning. I'm beat."

Scooting back, I reluctantly pull my boots back off. Logan enters the tent, zipping it up behind him. His stare roves over me and then he flashes me a conspiratorial smile, followed by a wink.

My skin begins to crawl as the memories from last night flood my mind. The brutality. The pain. The utter helplessness I'd felt. Unable to stop them, tears brim on my eyelids and my Adam's apple bobs as I swallow.

Please don't do this.

His tongue darts out, running along his bottom lip as he pins me in place with his ravenous stare.

"Sorry to disappoint, pet," Logan murmurs. "But Kristen still owes me a baby. Perhaps it'll be lesson time again tomorrow."

I'm caught between feeling relieved he's not going to fuck me to horrified that it has to be Kristen. Resigned to her fate, she begins removing her bottoms, her head dipping to keep her eyes out of sight.

Logan turns off the lantern, bathing us in darkness. I pull my knees to my chest and bury my face against them. The sound of flesh slapping flesh soon fills the tent, stabbing at my eardrums. No matter how hard I try to ignore it, it continues to bore into me, reminding me of my own terrible fate last night. I suck in a ragged breath, desperately needing air in my seizing lungs.

I can't breathe.

I can't breathe.

I can't breathe.

It's not until I push my hand into my pocket and finger the bone fragment that I'm able to regulate my breathing again. Slowly, my heart rate begins to even out. The slapping of their skin increases, but each time I run my thumb over the sharp, jagged edge, I'm able to further disassociate from the situation and focus on what I need to do.

Escape.

I will escape.

We all will.

CHAPTER FIFTEEN

ryder

Another earring.

I pocket this one too, thrilled that we're definitely on the right trail. We're getting closer. I can feel it deep in my bones. Soon, I'll have them all back.

My mind still reels with Rowdy's confession a couple of nights ago. He slept with a man. Not just any man, but Wild's cousin, Evan.

Maybe there could be some acceptance in our family.

At least Rowdy would understand Ronan's desires and my complicated attraction to both males and females.

A sharp whistle ahead has me abandoning the replaying of my conversation with Rowdy. I catch up with Wild and we both trot over to the clearing near a creek where Rowdy waits. He's crouched, investigating something on the ground.

"What is it?" I ask, peering over his shoulder.

"Puke." He points at the mess that swarms with flies. "Can't be more than a couple of days old."

"We're close," Wild says, grinning at me. "Thank fuck."

Relief floods through me as I survey the abandoned camp. They didn't do as good of a job covering their tracks, which means they're getting careless. Enough time has passed that they think they've gotten away with the abduction of my family.

We're still here. Still hunting.

Getting closer and closer by the day.

The gap is nearly closed.

Thunder rumbles in the distance as I notice a breeze that smells like rain. Traveling in the rain won't be fun, but we will be able to move quicker. The sounds of thunder and rain will mask our own trek. Plus, the weather will stall the big group ahead of us. Rain is good news.

Wild wanders over a hill to where the babbling creek can be heard while Rowdy creeps around the perimeter, no doubt looking for our next direction.

Something flutters near the charred logs leftover from the fire. I find myself fixated on it and make my way over to it. At first, I think it's a small animal with dark hair. I'm trying to figure out what kind of animal has hair like this when I notice the binding around it.

The same one Raegan uses to tie her hair back.

My stomach lurches with worry. They cut her hair.

Those fuckers cut her hair. Is she okay? Did they cut anything else off?

Images of them removing her fingers or tongue molest my mind. Bile surges up my throat and I puke not far from where the last person did. I spit out the bitterness before scooping up the bundle of her hair. Bringing it to my nose, I inhale her lingering familiar scent.

Fuck.

Please, Rae, be okay.

Wild or Rowdy calls out something, their tone panicked, but I'm unable to focus on anything but the hair in my fist tickling over my skin. For as far back as I can remember, my sister has had thick, long tresses. One of my favorite things about her is the way her ponytail swishes back and forth when she walks.

It's all gone.

Just like she is.

"Dude," Wild grunts, grabbing me by my backpack and hauling me to my feet. "What part of 'bear' do you not understand?"

I follow his hand that's pointing to a grizzly pawing at the remains of something gory just beyond the trees surrounding the camp. Rowdy off to my right has his rifle pointed at the bear, motioning to where we need to go behind him. With slow, measured movements, me and Wild make our way over to Rowdy. If he has to shoot the bear and the kidnappers are close, we'll give away our element of surprise.

Fucking bear.

The bear lets out a guttural warning growl as it stands over the mound of remains. It eyes us, teeth bared and slobber running from its mouth. He's protecting his find from other would-be hunters like ourselves.

We pass Rowdy and he walks backward, keeping his weapon trained on the bear. As soon as we're out of sight and earshot, we take off in a sprint. Rowdy's footsteps can be heard behind me. None of us speak until we're safely away from the beastly threat.

I lean up against a tree, heaving for air as I scramble to grab my water bottle from my pack. After shoving the ponytail away for safekeeping, I snag my water, rinse the lingering stomach acid from my mouth, and then gulp the water down. Once I catch my breath, I meet Rowdy's concerned stare.

"Please tell me those weren't human remains," I croak out, voice shaking. "Please, Rowdy."

He gives me a sharp shake of his head. "Rabbit. I saw one of the traps they left behind."

I scrub my palm over my face and let out a heavy sigh. "Thank fuck."

Rain begins to patter on the leaves around and above us. The wind picks up and the thunder sounds nearer. I hope my siblings are clothed and warm because the rain will chill to the bone all too quickly as we slide into fall.

"There were tons of boot prints all around the creek

bed," Wild says after chugging his own water. "How close do you think they are?"

He's asking Rowdy but looking at me. Still awkward between these two. One day, they'll have to duke it out or get over it. We don't have time for their shit right now.

"Close," Rowdy says, casting his gaze along the trail they've clearly taken based on how trampled the earth is. "They're getting sloppy, not bothering to cover their tracks either."

Rowdy continues along the path, surveying snapped branches with intense scrutiny. We all fall quiet again, prowling through the woods carefully as we stalk our people. So far, we don't hear any human sounds, but we keep our ears open. Now that the stress of seeing Raegan's ponytail and avoiding the bear is over, my mind attempts to slip into a happier place.

My palm over Ronan's granite dick, rubbing him through his jeans.

The hot, needy, breathy sounds that escaped him as I brought him to ecstasy.

His slick, warm lips when I'd first brushed mine over his.

I ache to have Ronan in my arms to repeat what we did that night in the tent. Hell, I'd be happy to simply hold him. To inhale his hair and finally rest because he would be safe again.

Until Dad finds out…

Ignoring that nagging thought, I think of Raegan.

Without her long hair, what will she look like? If she were here, I'd hold her too. I'd stroke her hair and tell her she's beautiful no matter what.

If—no, *when* I get them back, I'm going to do everything in my power to heal them or make them happy. Whatever horrors they've endured will be a thing of the past. I'll make sure of it.

Wild interrupts my thoughts as he tells me all about some girl named Gigi that he slept with. Apparently, she's got the biggest tits at his school. I grunt out responses as though I'm listening, but my mind keeps drifting back to Raegan. Her tits weren't huge like those in the magazine, but they were a healthy handful. Her nipples were hard and perfect.

God, I'd wanted to fuck her on the forest floor.

I still would love to.

Until Dad finds out…

All pleasure-filled thoughts sour at the idea of Dad catching me with my hand around my brother's dick or my dick inside my sister.

He wouldn't just send me away.

He might kill me.

Despair sucks me into its void once again. I don't understand how something that feels natural and right is so wrong. Dad thinks he can send me away to find some "wife" out there, but I would be so miserable. I don't want a Gigi with big tits. I want Raegan.

Raegan, unlike Ronan, though, could get pregnant.

Something could go wrong with the baby.

It would be all my fault.

Rain pelts my head as it steadily falls, soaking me through my clothes. I run my palm over my buzzed scalp that's already growing back, letting out a frustrated sigh. Having Raegan just isn't an option. I need to quit thinking with my dick. When I find them, I need to put both Raegan and Ronan into the sibling category where they belong.

"…so, yeah, she's annoying, but sucks dick like a Hoover." Wild turns around to grin at me. "If you ever come visit, I'll invite her to go out with us. You're welcome."

Rowdy lets out a snort of derision and says, "Ryder has standards."

Wild bristles at his words.

Yeah, I have standards. *Of the sibling variety.*

"Gigi's a cheerleader," Wild explains, irritation in his voice. "They don't get better than that."

"I'm not interested," I grumble. "Sorry, man."

Wild glances at me again, eyes narrowed, before shrugging. He then regales us with another tale of his previous football season. Since neither I nor Rowdy know shit about football, we're forced to listen to him drone on about his favorite thing besides girls. This goes on for miles and to the point I'm ready to shove a pinecone in my friend's mouth to make him shut up.

Rowdy stops walking and cants his head to the left to look at something on the ground. If it's more hair,

I'm going to fucking lose it. I shove past Wild to see what Rowdy's looking at.

Shit.

It's literally shit.

A big-ass human turd.

Flies buzz around the Coke-can-sized log of shit.

"It's fresh," I mutter. "They can't be far."

"Could just be wet from the rain," Wild says, playing Devil's advocate.

"Nah," Rowdy grunts. "They're close. I can feel it. We need to break for camp."

"I'm not sleeping by a pile of shit," Wild argues, stepping away from the bomb left behind. "Fuck no."

Rowdy shoots him an irritated glare, as though he's still thirteen and an annoying kid.

"Hey," I say to my brother, ignoring Wild's outburst. "We're close. Why stop now? We should keep going."

Rowdy shakes his head. "No, man. We need to set up our tents, get dry and rest, and put a little food in our stomachs before we try to take on this group. Plus, with it raining and nightfall upon us, they'll start a fire for warmth. We can scout later by the scent of fire or even sighting it."

Though he makes a point, I'm not especially eager to give up when we're so close. But I do know we need to be strategic. Charging into their camp, just the three of us, is a bad idea. We're heavily outnumbered and won't stand a chance. No, when we find them, we need to quietly advance on them. Surprise is our best weapon.

I give my brother a nod and follow him a bit farther away from the shit pile to a small clearing just big enough for our tents. The three of us erect our shelter in record time. We devour a quick dinner of nuts and jerky before going our separate ways. Undressing down to my boxers, I slide into my sleeping bag and force myself to nap.

Tonight, we're bringing them home.

Tonight, I will finally be able to fucking breathe again.

CHAPTER SIXTEEN

raegan

THE RAIN BEATS DOWN ON OUR LITTLE CARAVAN, but Michael doesn't show any signs of stopping. If I'm shivering and can't feel my fingers, I worry about Declan and Dakota. They're too little to be trudging through this weather.

Now that most of my hair has been whacked off by that witch, the chilly air bites at the back of my neck. I wish I could punch Mya all over again.

Sadie walks beside Tom ahead of me. We haven't had a chance to speak properly since the night of the "choosing," but she's miserable. I'd been lying when I told CJ I'd rather sleep with Tom. His body odor coupled with his giant form rutting over me would make me gag to death. Luckily, CJ still believes me and gets pissy anytime I look at Tom.

At least he didn't put the moves on me last night. None of the men drank, so camp was surprisingly quiet and mild. I'd been relieved to have survived another night without CJ's touch.

Looking past Sadie, Tom, and his kids, I can see Destiny walking beside Mya. I seriously hope she's not punishing my sister because of me. From my vantage point, it appears they're just talking. Or, more accurately, Mya's running her mouth while Destiny is forced to listen.

Behind me, Jace and CJ carry on a conversation in hushed voices. I know CJ is complaining about me, but I don't care. I hope he tells Jace I think he has a puny little dick that doesn't interest me. Maybe Jace's dick is even more sad and he'll leave my sister alone. Since she hasn't been crying and doesn't seem to be distraught in any way, I don't think he's made any physical moves on her either.

It's only a matter of time, though.

I glance over my shoulder, looking back at Kristen, Ronan, and Logan, who pull up the rear. Ronan's face is bruised from the other night, but he seems in better spirits ever since I saw him at the creek. There's a fierce glint in his eyes that gives me hope that he might have a plan.

Please, God, let him have a plan.

A woman ahead cries out, followed by several female shrieks. I can only wish she got eaten by a bear. I quickly retract that thought because my baby brothers are with that group. Everyone slows to a stop.

"Stacey," Tom grunts to Sadie in explanation. "She sounds hurt."

Sadie is tense as she tries to see what's going on. It's raining, which muffles the sounds of the voices, but we don't have to wonder for too long. Owen makes his way over to us and offers a grim smile.

"She's in labor," Owen says. "We have to break for camp."

"Are you sure she's really in labor? Maybe it's just another ploy to trick a nice, trusting family that she can weasel her way into their home, so she can murder the parents and kidnap all the children," I blurt out, unable to keep the words from spilling out. "Or, yeah, maybe she's really having the baby this time."

Owen shoots me a nasty glare before turning his stare behind me. "Deal with your wife."

If I hear that phrase one more time, I'm going to throw myself into our next campfire.

CJ's firm hand clamps over my shoulder and he squeezes. "Stop being a bitch, Raegan."

"She can't help it," Mya calls out. "It's who she is."

I give her the finger and once again take satisfaction in the bruising on her face. A lump has formed on the bridge of her nose. Maybe it's permanently damaged. This makes me grin.

CJ pushes me out of the line and toward a clearing before I can say anything more to Mya. I jerk out of his grip to start picking up sticks since that's my job at each campsite. The rain has soaked everything, so finding dry kindling is a fruitless effort. Still, I'd rather do a pointless job than have CJ touch me for another second.

Stacey cries out again as the men work quickly to erect a tent for her. The campsite we've been forced to use isn't the best. I don't hear any creeks rushing by and I'd seen bear scat not far back on our trek, which means danger could be lurking. But this might be the perfect opportunity to make our escape.

As Ronan and Logan pass me, Ronan's hand reaches out for me. I take it, eager for a quick touch, only to discover him putting something into my hand. Rather than looking at it and outing him, I discreetly shove it into the pocket of my jeans.

It's small and sharp.

He was giving me a weapon of some sort.

I could kiss him for that.

The tents all go up at record speed but can't be placed in their usual circle because of the thick trees in the area. To my dismay, my tent and Sadie's are across from the rest of my other siblings. Stacey and Michael's tent is closest to mine, which is also a downfall, though it does put me closer to my little brothers. But if Michael were to see me trying to escape with them…

I can't finish that thought.

That man scares me more than anything.

"Can't get a fire started," Tom gripes as the rain starts dumping. "Fuck. Get in the tent."

Sadie and his kids scramble inside. I remain outside

of CJ's and my tent, eyes scanning the dark forest as I plot our escape.

Running away through a rainstorm with little kids sounds like a horrible idea, but I'm fresh out of options. It's our only chance.

"Inside," CJ barks, snatching my elbow and jerking me along.

I struggle in his hold for a moment just to piss him off before conceding and taking shelter in the tent. I'm soaked through every layer of clothing and shivering. I'd give anything for a fire right about now or dry clothes, but it's not happening tonight.

Tonight is only going to get rougher.

Me and Ronan will have to be strong for the kids. They'll be scared traveling at night. We'll have to scavenge for food and shelter all while running from these freaks. It won't be easy, but it's better than living with these murdering rapists forever.

CJ follows me inside and turns on a battery-powered lantern. He eyes me warily like I might bite. There's no might about it. I will if I have to. I'll bite his stupid penis right off.

I snap my teeth at him, taking delight in the way he shudders. Good. He can stay on his side of the tent where he belongs.

"It doesn't have to be this difficult, you know," CJ grumbles. "I'm a good guy."

At that, I snort out a laugh. "Keep telling yourself that."

Irritation twists his features into a scowl. He busies himself with peeling off his wet layers. My pulse quickens at the thought of him getting completely naked. I cram my hand into my wet jeans when he's not looking and pull out what Ronan gave me.

A bone.

No longer than my middle finger, but pointy on one end.

It'll do in a pinch.

Like if a would-be rapist tries to put his dick near me.

Curling my fingers around it, I sit down and watch him struggle with his soaked jeans. His white boxers have a brown stain along his ass crack. Gag. I can't believe I was ever interested in this guy.

I've done laundry plenty of times with Mom and my brothers didn't have shit stains in their underwear. CJ is just filthy scum plain and simple.

Stacey howls again, which then sets off Declan. He starts sobbing, calling for me. My heart shatters at the way he pleads for me to come get him. With stinging tears in my eyes, I bolt for the tent opening, forgetting all plans of escape just so I can provide my baby brother some comfort.

CJ grabs hold of my short hair before I can unzip the tent. "Where the hell do you think you're going?"

"I'm going to get my brother, swamp ass! Let me go!"

He shoves me aside and points a finger at me.

"Enough with the names and ridiculing. I'm this close to handing you over to—"

Ziiip!

We both jerk our attention to the person's head entering our tent. Michael's hard gaze locks on to me as he speaks to CJ. "Handing her over to whom?"

"Nothing," CJ mumbles. "What's up? Everything okay with Stacey?"

"She's in labor. I need a favor," Michael grunts. He finishes unzipping the tent and thrusts Declan at me. "Keep an eye on my boys. Can I trust you to do that, Raegan?"

His boys?

It's on the tip of my tongue to argue about whose boys they actually belong to, but my need to protect overshadows the need to retaliate in this moment.

"Of course," I rush out, quickly snatching my little brother and pulling him to me. "Hey, buddy. It's okay."

Declan starts to cry again and clings to me like he never wants to let go. Michael ushers Dakota inside next. Kota scrambles to sit beside me, leaning his head against my arm.

"It's going to be a long night," Michael grumbles before disappearing.

CJ, sitting in only his dirty underwear, gives me a sour look. Oh no, he can't rape me now because we have an audience. Poor guy. Ignoring him, I hug Dakota and Declan, whispering assurances to them. On a normal day, me and Dakota fight like the brats we are, but not this day. This is not a normal day and all our sibling rivalry is pushed aside.

We have to stick together.

I have to protect them.

Aside from being wet and miserable, I'm thrilled. I have my baby brothers with me for the first time since we set out on this horrible journey and I have a small weapon. I just need to get Ronan, Dez, and Sadie. Since Sadie is closest, I can start with her.

"Can you ask Sadie to come help?" I ask CJ, refusing to look at him in case he can see the deception on my face.

He huffs. "No. Absolutely not."

Snapping my head up, I glower at him. "I can't possibly get the boys warm and calm all by myself."

"I can help," he says, moving like he's going to come toward us.

Dakota screeches and kicks out at him, his small boot hitting him square on the chin. CJ curses but pulls back as he rubs his jaw.

"What the fuck, little dude? I was trying to help."

I scowl at CJ until he sighs heavily. "Fine."

Me and Dakota watch as CJ grumpily redresses, once again flashing his crusty underwear. Dakota lets loose a giggle.

"He shat his pants," I whisper, earning more giggles from him.

Declan buries his face against my chest, but his body moves as he giggles too. He doesn't know what he's laughing about, but at least he's cheered up enough to join in.

CJ looks us over, face marred with confusion, before heading back outside the tent. As soon as he's gone, I nudge Dakota to get him to peer up at me.

"As soon as Sadie's here, we're going to leave," I whisper. "She and I can take him. I'm going to have to carry Deck, but I will need you to run faster than you ever have. Can you do that, Kota?"

He nods, eyes wide with worry. "It's dark and rainy."

"It's our only chance of escape." I lean forward and rest my forehead against his. "We can do this."

I pull away as soon as Sadie enters the tent. She glances over both boys and then peeks at me, a frown of bewilderment on her face.

"Dakota is cold. Can you get him warm and comfort him?" I ask, hoping to convey with just my eyes that I have a plan.

Her eyes flash with understanding. "Of course. Come here, Kota."

CJ enters the tent once more. He gripes as he strips out of his wet clothes again. Dakota whispers to Sadie that CJ pooped his pants, which makes all four of us laugh at his expense.

"Deck," I say, voice light. "You're so heavy. Can you sit right here next to me?"

He protests, his whines quickly turning to tears. I shoot Sadie a panicked look.

"I have a secret to tell you," Sadie says to Declan. "We don't want poopy pants CJ to hear."

"I didn't shit my pants," CJ calls out, scowling.

We all erupt in another fit of laughter. During the commotion, I manage to slide Declan to my left between me and Sadie. Clutching the bone tight in my grip, I listen to Stacey wail in pain while watching CJ attempt to get warm.

Stacey's tent must be busy because I hear several panicked voices coming from it. I'm starting to think now or never. I wait until CJ's back is to me and his breathing evens out, which feels like an eternity. Finally, I make my move.

"Cover their eyes," I mouth to Sadie.

She nods and does as instructed. I prowl over to CJ, half the bone in my grip and the pointy half sticking out of my fist. Grabbing onto his shoulder, I pull him over onto his back. His eyes widen in surprise, but he doesn't have time to react.

I slam the bone down into the softest part of his face.

His eyeball.

The squish of it makes me gag, but I'm invested now. Before he can holler, I punch him across the face. Hard. Like I punched Wild. One of his teeth cuts into my knuckle on impact, sending sharp pain shooting up my arm. Not giving him a chance to retaliate, I grab the lantern and smash the metal bottom against his face several times until it breaks, bathing us in darkness.

"Let's go," I hiss to Sadie.

We scramble out of the tent in a rush. My heart is in my throat and my ears are ringing. CJ is still alive and making sounds of distress. Hopefully, Stacey's bellowing and the thunder will drown out the noise. Once we're out of the tent, I expect to be tackled by Michael or Logan.

There's no one around.

I stare longingly at the tents that house Dez and Ronan, but there's no way I can save them both right now. I need to get the kids and Sadie out first. Then I can come back later and rescue them.

Dakota runs fast just like he promised, his hand firmly attached to Sadie's. I dart after them, holding a crying Declan to my chest. He's only three, but he's chunky and heavy. I know my arms are going to be screaming in pain soon. Not that it'll matter. I'll carry him until my arms fall off and then I'll force him to hang on while I carry him some more.

No one yells after us or shoots.

I think we've made it!

Chick-chuck.

The sound of a shell being loaded into a shotgun stops me in my tracks.

"Where do you think you're going?" a voice snarls right after.

Whipping around, I come face-to-face with Mya. She's sopping wet and I can barely make her face out in the dark, but there's no mistaking the glint of metal pointed right at me.

"You can stop me, but the others will get away," I say calmly. "You know this isn't right. We're leaving, Mya."

She and I both glower at one another. Despite her smaller frame, she has the upper hand right now. I'm on the losing end of her shotgun. Maybe, if I had my knife or if my hands were free, I'd have a literal fighting chance, but not now. Not with Declan clinging to me.

"Please," I plead. "Just let us go. No one has to know."

She sneers at me. "Oh, everyone is about to know the second I start screaming. You think your life is bad now? Just wait until my uncle takes you from my brother. Your begging will be music to my ears."

"Hey, Mya," Dakota says from behind me. "Sadie said to call you a bitch."

Before I can process that my baby brother called this bitch a bitch, a figure charges toward us from my right. I turn my body, hoping to protect both Deck and Kota, and hear a sickening crack. A thumping sound follows after as a body hits the ground.

I'd expected to be the one to get attacked, but when I swivel back around, I discover a heavily breathing Sadie holding a thick branch as she stands over Mya's prone form.

Tearing my gaze from Sadie, I look down at Mya. She's not moving or crying. Even in the dark, I can tell her head is twisted at an odd angle against the base of a tree.

Holy shit.

Her neck is most definitely broken.

She won't be walking away because she's dead.

"Grab her gun," I hiss at Sadie. "And thanks for that."

Sadie snatches the shotgun from her lifeless grip and then takes Dakota's hand again. "Good job, buddy. We make a good team."

I'm cold and tired and scared out of my mind, but I'm also elated.

We're free.

We're finally free.

CHAPTER SEVENTEEN

ronan

"**F**UCKING HAVE THE BABY ALREADY," LOGAN complains with a huff. "Anyone else sick to death of hearing her scream?"

Me and Kristen both mumble out words of agreement, though neither of us really cares. I'm just happy to be out of the rain and attempting to dry out. My toes feel like ice cubes that might fall off at any second.

I shiver inside my sleeping bag, wondering if my siblings are warm. If we were together, we could huddle for warmth. I'd even considered snuggling close to Kristen, but who knows how Logan would react to that. Since I don't want to be near him, I shiver alone, hoping to eventually regulate my body temperature.

Another pained sound croaks in the distance. It sounds more masculine than Stacey's awful howls, but I could be mistaken. Maybe she really is in bad shape. I sit up on my elbows, listening for the sound again.

"Help!"

The voice is definitely male, not female, and older, so I breathe a sigh of relief that it can't be anyone in my family here. Something crashes nearby. Another groaned plea.

Ziiiip!

Our tent flap opens and the three of us dart our stares over to see who's joining us. A man bleeding from his eye, nose, and mouth staggers toward us like something from a fucked-up zombie novel. He's wearing nothing but a pair of boxers and is white as a sheet aside from all the blood spatter covering his naked chest.

"What the fuck?" Logan growls, sitting up and taking hold of the man. "CJ?"

My heart explodes inside my chest, slamming hard at the realization that he's injured hours after I passed Raegan a weapon. Stifling a grin, I stare at CJ's bloody face.

"S-She stabbed m-me in the f-fucking eye," CJ wails, gesturing wildly at his face. "Then she punched me. B-Broke my nose with the lantern, too."

Logan starts throwing on clothes at warp speed. Then he points a finger at me. "See to his wounds and do not fucking leave this tent." In another second, he's gone.

CJ pitifully crawls over to me like I'm his savior. I want to laugh in his face—to tell him he got what he deserved. Instead, I sit up on my knees to closely inspect his wounds. From nearby, Kristen watches wide-eyed but quiet.

"What did you get stabbed with?" I ask, voice soft. "I don't see anything."

"I d-don't fucking know," he cries out, sniffling. "I pulled it out, though. I can't see, man. She f-fucking blinded me!"

"Who?" Kristen asks.

CJ turns to hiss at her. "Who the fuck do you think? My wife!"

Raegan is not his goddamn wife no matter how many times he says it.

"Where is she now?" I demand, pulse quickening and blood rushing in my ears.

"She and Sadie and the little b-boys escaped. They're g-gone."

Thank God.

I bite down on my bottom lip so I don't grin at his words. They escaped. Raegan did it. She really did it. Now it's on me to get myself, Kristen, and Destiny out of here. This, I can do. I have to.

Kristen hands over her pack, unzipping the side that carries bandages and alcohol wipes. Since Logan regularly beats on her, it makes sense for her to carry a stash. I take out what I need before tending to CJ's wounds. His eye has swollen nearly closed, oozing with blood and some other thick substance. It looks disgusting and there's nothing I can do for it. I settle for cleaning around the eye and his face before placing a bandage over the creepy-looking thing.

"Your nose looks swollen," I murmur, pressing on

the bridge and enjoying the hiss of pain coming from him. "I don't think it's broken, though. There's going to be a nasty bump here." I press on the spot again, causing him to sob. "Sorry."

Not sorry at all, actually.

His lip is split, still bleeding like crazy. As I inspect it, I notice that half his top front tooth has broken off, leaving a sharp point that keeps poking at the cut on his lip.

Raegan permanently disfigured this fool.

Good girl.

"Got anything to stitch him up with?" I ask Kristen. "I need to do something about this lip."

She scrambles to pull out a needle and some thread.

"Is that n-needle clean?" CJ demands, panic rising in his voice. "Clean it f-first."

Biting back my irritation, I use one of the alcohol wipes to clean off the needle. Then, without consideration of his pain level, I begin sewing up his lip. He cries hard, whining unintelligible things to me as I work. When I finish, I tug the thread tight, watching his bottom lip pucker in an unnatural way, and then tie it in a knot. He starts to say something and his pointy broken tooth scrapes along the wound, causing him to cry more.

Looks painful as hell, which satisfies me to no end.

"Lie down," I say to CJ as I guide him to stretch out. "You need to calm down and get warm."

Kristen grabs Logan's sleeping bag and tosses it onto

CJ. I tuck it around him like I'm a caring doctor, but in reality, I just want him to pass out so I can make my next move. My stare meets Kristen's, and we have a silent conversation.

We're leaving.

Get dressed. Grab your bag. Let's get the fuck out.

She nods once before the both of us are throwing on our cold, wet clothes. I've barely pulled my boots on when I hear a man bellow like he's in pain. I can only hope it's Raegan jabbing Logan in the eye too.

"Hurry," I murmur to Kristen. "We need to go. Now."

If CJ lets on that he hears us making an escape, he doesn't say a word. The man continues to tremble and cry, ignoring both of us. Within minutes, she and I are both creeping out of the tent.

Stacey is still wailing in pain, but there are more voices that can be heard in the distance, lanterns bobbing near them. I grab Kristen's hand, tugging for her to follow me to Dez's tent. Fumbling around for a weapon, I locate a thick stick before unzipping the tent. When I peek inside, Jace isn't there, but Dez's blurry form is sitting up, peering my way.

"It's me," I say, crawling toward her. "Get dressed. We're leaving."

"Ronan!" She throws her arms around me, squeezing my neck. "Where's everyone else?"

"Gone. Raegan stabbed CJ. She took Sadie and the

boys with her. This is our chance to get the hell out of here."

A hysterical laugh bubbles out of her before she's dressing with incredible speed. Once she's ready, I exit the tent with her on my heels. The three of us stand near the tent in the pouring rain, considering our next option.

"She's dead," Owen hollers, anguish in his voice. "My baby girl is fucking dead!"

Holy shit.

Did Raegan kill Mya?

"We have to go. Now," I hiss, grabbing Dez's hand in mine. "Kristen, you have to lead the way. As far away from those lanterns as possible."

She starts toward the dark forest between two thick pines, the both of us following after. I may not be able to see well without my glasses, but Dez can't see anything at all. She's relying on me to get her to safety.

I have to do this.

I will do this.

"I'm scared," Dez whispers, voice shaking. "What if they catch us?"

"They won't," I promise.

I sure as hell hope I don't break that promise.

Kristen stumbles over something, causing both me and Destiny to crash into her. The three of us scramble back to our feet. The shouts and voices behind us feel louder.

They've discovered us gone.

Fuck.

I chance a look over my shoulder. Lanterns bob wildly toward us. Whipping back around, I try not to focus on them gaining on us and instead run as fast as we can. Branches slap at us and tug at our clothes, but we don't stop.

We can't stop.

"There!" a voice yells.

My skin crawls at the sound of the men drawing closer. We can't let them get to us. No way in hell. Kristen starts to stumble again, but I drop my stick to grab onto her backpack. She keeps going, but I'm left defenseless now.

Dez cries out when a branch snags her hair, nearly ripping her out of my grip. I stop long enough to untangle her before dragging her away once more. The forest lights up behind us as they close in.

This can't happen.

Please, God.

Destiny screams seconds before she's yanked from my grip. I swivel around, looking for yet another branch, only to see her being wrapped in the arms of Jace. She kicks out and bellows, clawing at him to let her go.

"Dez!" I cry out, abandoning Kristen to help my sister. "Let her go!"

Behind me, Kristen screams as someone grunts. There's a struggle, but right now my focus is on freeing my sister. I charge for Jace, tackling them both to the ground. He grunts and I'm able to loosen his grip on Destiny. From behind them, I see two male figures rushing our way to assist them.

Jace manages to scramble back to his feet, jerking my sister to him. The two men approach, backing him up. I stand in the pouring rain, panting and utterly defeated. Could I find a stick big enough to hit them with?

We can still escape.

Dez yells at Jace, elbowing him and trying to bite him.

Michael's voice joins the fray. "Get a hold of your wife, Son. Now, goddammit!"

Michael's and Owen's forms come into view, stepping past Jace and Destiny. As Dez is dragged away by Jace, her screams haunt my fucking soul.

"No!" I bellow, throwing a fist toward Michael. "You can't do this!"

My fist glances off his jaw and I end up shoving Owen to the ground in my efforts. Michael glowers at me but doesn't move to fight me. Turning to my right, I take off through the trees. I'll come back for her, for both of them. I'm nothing if they capture me again.

I don't make it very far before a strong hand grabs my arm and twists to throw me to the ground. I land with a painful smack against my side on some exposed tree roots. Groaning, I attempt to sit up on my hands and knees to escape.

A boot slams into my ribs, making me roll across the rain-soaked forest floor. Before I can defend myself, the butt of a rifle comes down against my face.

Crack!

The world spins around me as pain throbs inside my skull. A wave of nausea has me retching. My attacker looms over me, blocking the pattering of the cold rain.

"Sleep well, pet. We have much to discuss when you wake up."

Another crack of his rifle.

Everything immediately goes black.

CHAPTER EIGHTEEN

ryder

I WAKE WITH A START, MOMENTARILY CONFUSED BY my surroundings. Rain patters on my tent and the chill of the evening air burrowing into my bones reminds me that I'm camped out deep in the wilderness on a hunt for my siblings.

"Psst. Ryder."

Rubbing the sleep out of my eyes, I sit up as Rowdy enters my tent. It's too dark to make out his features, but I recognize his voice.

"What's up?" I ask, voice raspy with sleep. "Is it time?"

He grunts. "Not yet. I heard something. Get dressed."

With my heart beginning to race, I throw on my clothes within sixty seconds and am out of the tent the next minute. Wild and Rowdy stand huddled nearby, whispering. The rain is cold, drenching me once more, but I'm more interested in what they're saying since those two don't exactly directly speak to one another.

"Predator?" I ask when I approach them.

From far in the distance, I hear what sounds like crying. Definitely not a predator. The three of us tear off toward the sound without further conversation, weapons at the ready. I'm hopeful we're near the camp where my siblings are being held.

We travel for what feels like an eternity when we hear it again. Crying. Young, familiar, terrified.

"Declan," Rowdy hisses. "This way."

No longer running, we carefully prowl toward the sound of his voice. If their camp is nearby, we don't want to stumble upon it unprepared. We need to locate it, make a plan, and then extract our people via whatever means necessary.

Knowing we're so close has me feeling elated. I just want them all back safely so we can go back home and rebuild our lives.

The crying fades and we all come to a stop. I can't hear anything over the sound of my heart thundering in my ears.

Come on, Deck. Let your big brothers know where you're at.

Thunder rumbles above us, making the earth feel as though it's trembling. I'm desperately trying to see through the dark rain, looking for a campsite fire.

Nothing.

More crying.

Rowdy starts up again, slightly changing his direction. Me and Wild follow after, carefully avoiding brush that's thick and will give away our location.

"What's wrong with him?"

"He's scared and cold."

I know those voices.

"Sadie," Wild utters as I say, "Raegan."

It takes everything in me not to yell for my sister. I don't want the kidnappers to know we're close. Stealth is more important than ever.

Despite the darkness and steady rainfall, I see movement through the trees. Rowdy holds up a fist, gesturing for us to stop. The shadowy figure lumbers our way and the voices grow in volume. In the mix of their low talking, I hear Dakota asking when they can rest.

There aren't any tents that I can see or campfires.

Did they manage to escape?

Still, we don't move or speak in case they're not alone. The crunching of feet in the brush grows louder as they get closer. Then, like a flash, Rowdy darts forward.

"Sadie, shoot him!" Raegan cries out.

Sadie never gets a chance because Rowdy manhandles the shotgun out of her hand before it can go off.

"It's me, Rowdy," he whispers. "We're here."

I rush forward, eager to see my siblings. As soon as I get close to Raegan, with Declan in her arms, I yank her to me. Declan shudders between us, whimpering. My nose finds Raegan's temple and I inhale her sweet scent.

"Ryder?" Raegan chokes out. "You're really here?"

"I'm here, Rae. I'm here."

Pulling back, I kiss Declan on the head and then tug Dakota over to us. Then my gaze falls to Sadie, who's now crying in Wild's arms and…no one else.

My stomach plummets.

"Where're Destiny and Ronan?" Rowdy demands, stealing the words out of my mouth. "Where the hell are they?"

Raegan's knees buckle and if it weren't for my arm around her, she'd collapse. Her tears are my undoing. Between her hiccupping sobs and mumbling, I make out the fact that they had to leave them behind.

We have to go rescue them.

Rowdy starts swearing over and over under his breath. Then, with a ragged, resigned sigh, he says, "We have to get them dry. When we have more to go on, we'll go after them."

Wild is already guiding Sadie back the way we came, but my feet are rooted in place. Ronan and Destiny are all alone now. They'll feel abandoned. Will the kidnappers punish them for Raegan's escape?

"Rowdy," I plead. "We can't leave them alone with those fucking monsters."

He grunts, pausing to scoop Dakota up and into his arms. "I don't want to either, Ry, but we have to."

I know, deep down, he's right, but it doesn't hurt any less. None of us wants to leave them, but Declan is shaking so hard I'm worried about the little guy. This small group of escapees are cold, tired, and scared shitless.

We have to regroup.

Fuck.

"Come here, kid," I say, regret lacing my words. "I'll carry you now. Rae's probably tired."

Declan reaches for me, burying his face against my chest. I attempt to shield him from the elements as best as I can. Raegan latches onto my elbow.

Rowdy trudges after Wild, whispering things to Dakota while me, Declan, and Raegan take up the rear. Raegan is weirdly quiet, which worries me. They've been gone for so long. I can't even begin to imagine what happened during that time or what lengths she had to go through to escape.

We take the long hike back to where our tents are still set up. Sadie and Wild immediately go into his tent. I'm thankful she has him to take care of her. Rowdy comes over to stand beside me.

"Let's wait out this rain. Get them dry and warm. Rest. I'll listen out." He nods toward the tent. "I'll take this one, and you two take Declan with you."

Raegan releases me to hug Rowdy and then the three of us crawl into my tent. We're cold, wet, and miserable, but having a fire is absolutely out of the question in case the kidnappers are out looking for them.

"Get undressed," I instruct. "My sleeping bag is big

enough for the three of us, but we need body heat. We can keep Declan between us."

Raegan strips out of her wet clothes and once she's done, I pass Declan to her. I remove all my clothes and then help her take off Declan's. I climb into the sleeping bag first. She passes Declan back over to me before squeezing into the sleeping bag with us. Declan's back is cold against my chest. His body quakes wildly.

"Closer," I grunt out, sliding my hand to the small of Raegan's chilled back and pulling her so that we're smashing Declan between us.

Her breath tickles over my face. I lean closer, needing her warmth and nearness like I need air to live. I rub my palm up and down her back, attempting to bring heat into her body. Declan squirms and whimpers but eventually settles.

"Fuck, I'm so happy to see you," I murmur. "I missed you so damn much."

She sniffles, snuggling closer. Her nose brushes over mine. "Me too."

I run my palm up higher on her back and then over her shoulder. My fingers slide into her chopped hair. She stills at my touch.

"Beautiful," I breathe.

A small snort escapes her. "You can't see me."

"I don't have to. You're always beautiful."

Her small hand rakes over my ribs, sending chills down my spine. I want her hand all over me. Our feet find each other's and tangle together. I pin Declan's cold feet between my thigh and Raegan's. Under any other circumstance, I'd be thrilled to be touching all these naked parts of her. Unfortunately, we're too busy trying not to die of hypothermia.

After fifteen minutes or so, I can feel the warmth penetrating me. We all still shiver, but not as badly. Declan breathes heavily, passed out from his terrible journey. All the muscles in my body ache from trembling, but I'm finally able to relax.

Raegan's fingers slide under my armpit for the warmth there and she strokes my hair. I can hear her sniffling, not just from the cold, but as emotions overtake her. I slip my palm to her ass, giving it a reassuring squeeze.

"Hey," I croon, voice soft and comforting. "I've got you, Rae."

She nods and then her lips press to mine. "I'm afraid to ask…" Another whimper. "Dad?"

My hand roams along her spine again as I say, "He's alive. He made it. That was you who cut the rope?"

A choked sob rattles out of her, startling Declan. He starts to cry as well but quickly falls back asleep. I kiss my sister's soft, cold lips, her frozen nose, her wet lashes, her forehead. Bringing my mouth back to hers, I kiss her again, leaving our lips fused together.

"You did good," I praise, my words tickling over her mouth. "You saved our dad."

"Mom?"

"Safe. Dawson is safe too."

My hand once again settles on her ass and I rub her over her cold flesh. Comforting her is all that matters to me right now. I want to bring her happiness in any way I can.

Declan twitches in his sleep and kicks me in the dick, which smashes my balls. I groan, moving both his feet over my thigh to keep my junk safe. He squirms and grunts but finally settles. Raegan's thigh slides higher between mine. I wince, expecting another kick, but she rests her leg against my nuts.

If only there wasn't a kid between us right now…

Then I'd what?

Fuck my sister?

My twisted thoughts have no place in this tent right now. I'm supposed to protect them, not be considering how to get my sister alone to appease my horny dick.

"How is Ronan doing? Destiny?" I ask, trying to redirect my sick mind back on track. "Are they going to be okay until we can get to them?"

"I don't know."

Her response guts me. I want to kill every last one of those people. How dare they hurt my family.

"Logan has been beating Ronan," she whispers. "Dez seems okay, but Logan and Michael both are so terrifying."

My gut tightens at the thought of them overpowering my brother, who's always been more of a lover than a fighter. It's not fair. They should have taken me instead.

"We'll get them and soon we'll be home," I assure her. "How did you escape?"

She chuckles, the sound dark and vengeful. "I stabbed CJ in the eye with a bone Ronan gave me."

I squeeze her ass again. "That's my girl."

A small whimper escapes her and then her mouth is on mine again. Not just a small peck, but open and inviting. Her tongue slides over my bottom lip, eliciting a groan from me. I nip at it and then bite her bottom lip.

God, I fucking want her so damn badly.

"Rest, Rae. You've been through a helluva lot."

She sighs in resignation and pulls her lips from mine. "I'm so tired, Ry."

"Sleep, baby." I kiss her nose. "I've got you now and I'll never let go."

Her breathing evens out moments later. I inhale Declan's hair, happy to have him safely in my arms. As she sleeps, I caress her back and ass, hoping to provide her both warmth and comfort. Eventually, it lulls me into relaxing as well.

We'll get Ronan and Destiny back.

And then our family will be together again.

With that thought, I smile and crash hard.

CHAPTER NINETEEN

raegan

THEY'RE TAKING HIM FROM ME!

A whine of terror rips out of me as I desperately cling to Declan's small frame.

"Hey," a soft, familiar voice murmurs. "I'm going to get the kid some breakfast. You're safe, Rae."

I peek open my eyes to see Rowdy kneeling beside me, pulling Declan to him and wrapping him in one of his giant T-shirts. It's early, the sun barely making its presence known, but at least it isn't raining anymore. I give my brother a quick nod and then snuggle back into Ryder's warmth.

After Rowdy leaves the tent with Declan, I stare at Ryder's closed eyes and slightly parted lips. I reach up to touch them, remembering how he'd pressed kisses all over my face last night. Sliding my hand down along his neck, I take a moment to appreciate the muscular curve of his shoulder. He's so strong. I feel safe tucked away in his sleeping bag with him.

His palm that rested on my bare ass all night gently squeezes me, letting me know he's awake. I cuddle closer, fully aware of our nakedness and the way he hardens against my thigh.

Despite being awake, he doesn't open his eyes. I shift my thigh to rub against his erection, a thrill running through me when I hear him groan. His hand snakes down to the back of my thigh and then he lifts it, putting it up over his hip, away from his dick.

Disappointment courses through me. Does he not want my touch?

I'm frozen with warring feelings of humiliation and anger.

But then his hot lips are on my neck, gently peppering me with sweet pecks. His hand strays over my ass, kneading and rubbing like it's the most wonderful thing he's ever held before. My body vibrates with the need to be touched everywhere—anywhere—by Ryder.

"I'm so happy you're here," he murmurs, words hot against my throat. "So fucking happy."

His words bring a smile to my lips. Tilting my head down, I seek out his mouth with mine. He groans when I attack his lips, thrusting my tongue against his, desperate for his taste. Our kiss quickly turns frantic, our hands grabbing and roaming greedily as we attempt to consume each other. He grunts when my hand rubs over his nipple.

I gasp at the feel of his fingers spread over my ass cheek, reaching far enough to touch my crack. The air in my lungs becomes trapped as he slides his longest finger down and then barely brushes against my pussy from behind. My entire body shudders at the touch.

He doesn't enter me with his finger but teases the wetness that's forming there. Up and down he slides along the opening, his fingertip never breaching. Just rubbing and sliding. It's so hot that I crave more from him. I didn't understand the whole excitement over sex before, aside from the emotional aspect of my first time being with my brother, but now, with my other brother, I crave the penetration like my next breath. This isn't me coming to him with some agenda like I'd done with Ronan.

This feels a lot more natural.

I hike my thigh higher up his body, hoping he'll get my message. I want his curious finger inside of me, stretching me like our brother's cock did. I want him to slide in and out, letting my juices of arousal coat his fingers.

Just when I think he'll give up and move along, he pulls back slightly, eyes hooded with need and lips swollen. The hunger in his expression makes me shudder. I wonder if mine matches his. Then, with eyes locked on me, he gently pushes the tip of his finger inside me. I let out a sharp gasp, my whole body trembling. A slow grin forms on his lips, tugging up on one side.

"Feel good?"

"Yeah. More."

He pulls his finger away, causing me to groan, but

then slides it between us for better access. His slick finger slides between my pussy lips, rubbing right over the spot that feels so good. My eyes roll back and I have to bite on my bottom lip to stifle a moan.

"You like this?" he whispers. "Me, touching you here?"

I nod sharply. "Y-Yes."

He's almost lazy as he rubs a continuous circle in that pleasure-filled spot. The slow building of bliss, though, is just what I need. I ache for the release he has to offer.

So close.

I start to shake, stars sparkling in my vision. The second he sends me over the edge, I let out a moan that he quickly snuffs out with a hot, deep kiss. I shatter in his arms, losing all sense of reality as the pleasure consumes me. And then his expert finger slides into my body, slicking in and out. I ride his finger as the last of my orgasm ripples through me.

"So fucking wet," he growls, nipping at my bottom lip. "You have no idea how hot you are, Rae."

I'm drunk and dazed with lust. My body, sated from the pleasure, continues to ache for more.

"Have sex with me," I whisper, forcing my weak limbs to assist me as I slide over his body. "I want you inside of me, Ryder."

His strong hands grip my hips, digging in so hard I know I'll be bruised. I can feel his cock twitching, nestled against my pussy. A few quick maneuvers and he could be inside me.

Like Ronan was.

Guilt surges through me, chasing away my high. I have to tell Ryder what happened. If he somehow finds out on his own, he'll be hurt. And keeping it from him doesn't feel right either.

He lifts his hips a little, his dick continuing to throb and sliding against my slick pussy. It feels really good against my sensitive area that still tingles with pleasure.

"I have to tell you something," I whisper, frowning at him.

His palms slide to my ass, giving it a hard squeeze. "Anything."

I close my eyes and nibble on my lip. "Please don't be mad."

"You could say anything right now, Rae, and there's no way I could be mad at you."

Falling forward, I rest on his chest, my breasts pressing against his body, and my mouth finding his ear. "I had sex with Ronan."

A beat of silence passes and then I realize he's gone completely still.

"Ronan's gay," he whispers.

"I didn't want CJ to be my first," I say, tone slightly defensive. "Ronan gave me a gift."

"A gift?" Ryder rolls us onto our sides, his brows pinched together. "You had sex with our brother and you call it a gift?"

Hurt prickles at my heart. "You wouldn't understand. You weren't there."

He scowls, staring off behind me as though he's trying to picture it. Then he huffs angrily. "I wasn't there because I was traveling tirelessly to find you—to find you both."

"Ryder," I choke out. "You're not being fair."

"I'm jealous," he clips out. "I'm just fucking jealous."

My heart warms at his admission. Scooting closer, I press a tentative kiss on his mouth. "You and me. We can do it too. Right now. It only takes a few minutes."

"Sex only lasts a few minutes?" He grunts in irritation. "Wild says he goes for hours. Maybe you did it wrong."

I scoff at him. "Really? You're going to be an asshole? I didn't do it wrong. His dick was hard and he came. It was messy."

His eyes close and he lets out a sharp breath. "I'm sorry. I'm just stressed and feeling a little left out, is all."

"Left out? Ryder, I'm here, naked and begging for you to have sex with me. That's not exclusion, that's an invitation."

A small smile quirks his lips and then he kisses me—hot and dirty. His roaming hand once again finds my ass, squeezing it. I'm pretty sure he's going to give in until we hear Wild laugh.

Voices just outside our tent have both of us freezing. All sexual energy evaporates and I'm met with another scowl.

"Rae, we can't do this shit."

This *shit*?

My heart feels as though he's whipped it with a belt. I even flinch as though I've been struck.

"This *shit* is love, dumbass."

"I can't love you like that," he says in a pained voice. "I want to. So fucking badly, but I can't."

"Clearly, I don't understand. You just had your finger inside me."

Our voices are growing in volume. Ryder's eyes widen with panic. He covers my mouth with his palm. The leftover scent of my arousal on his finger is strong.

"If Dad were to find out," he hisses, "he'd kill me. Dad would kill me, Rae. Is that what you want?"

I grab hold of his wrist, pulling his hand away to frown at him.

"He won't kill you," I say, though my words feel hollow with uncertainty. "Dad loves you. He loves all of us."

"No." His features harden. "I can't. *We* can't."

I bite down on my bottom lip to keep it from wobbling. "I hate you."

My words strike him and his features crumple. I immediately feel like a monster for saying them. But, with tears in my eyes and emotion clogging my throat, I don't have the ability to retract them.

He leans forward, rubbing his nose against mine. "Please don't hate me, Rae. I fucking need you."

Sorrow cuts through my soul, dissecting me with

brutal precision. How can he love and need me so much but can't give me this?

Dad wouldn't kill him.

Would he?

Ryder's eyes dart back and forth, pleading with me to understand. He's breaking apart and I'm the one holding the hammer. Guilt threatens to swallow me whole.

"I don't hate you," I croak out, leaning closer to kiss his mouth. "I just don't understand why we can't have sex. It can be our secret. I won't tell anyone. I swear."

His large hand cradles my cheek and he rubs his thumb along my cheekbone like I'm precious. Fat tears well and then spill at his tenderness.

"I love you so fucking much it hurts. I would give anything to be with you like that…"

"But?"

"But I can't give my life. Not if I intend to stick around to protect you. If Dad sends me away or kills me, I can't keep you safe."

Feeling defeated, I give in to my tears and snuggle against him. He holds me as though his arms alone will fix everything. If only they could.

How does Dad expect us to be happy if we're not allowed to love how we want to?

Ryder deserves to have sex with whomever he wants. He's a good, brave man. And if I could have sex with Ronan, why can't I have sex with Ryder?

My stomach flips so hard I feel like I might be sick.

What happens if Dad finds out about me and Ronan?

Will he send him away or kill him?

The bone-deep ache that penetrates the edges of my soul physically hurts. Life is supposed to be filled with love and freaking living. Not allowing us to be together is wrong, right?

I could plead my case to Dad.

Dread consumes me. I know my father. I know both of my parents. They barely let us swim together alone. If they knew about what me and Ryder just did or how I gave my virginity to Ronan, they'd lose it.

They'd lose their minds and our family would be irrevocably shattered.

Even I'm not that selfish.

"Everything's going to be okay," Ryder assures me, voice cracking with emotion. "I'll find Ronan and Dez. We'll all go home and back to being best friends like before. Life can be normal. No one leaves and no one dies. Please tell me that's enough, Rae."

It's not.

"It's enough." My lie is bitter on my tongue. "Find them. Bring them home. It'll be enough. I promise."

I may not be selfish, but I'm a liar.

A miserable one at that.

CHAPTER TWENTY

ronan

CAN'T MOVE.

Every muscle in my body screams in pain. The throbbing in my skull is the worst. I was up all night, wondering if I was going to die. Nausea consumes me and my limbs tremble with weakness.

We almost made it.

I just knew we'd escape and meet up with Raegan. It felt so possible. So close.

Rolling to my side, I wince at the new pains that assault me along my ribs. Logan didn't hold back when he kicked me. They're tender and burning, but since I can still draw breaths easily, I'm pretty certain they're not broken.

Cracking open my eyes, I search the tent for the monster. He's not here, thank God, but Kristen is. She lies completely still, curled into a fetal position. My heart rate speeds up in fear.

Is she still alive?

Last night, after we returned to the tent, it'd been a blur of abuse. I was forced to watch him beat the shit out of Kristen while I barely managed to stay conscious. Then I was brutally woken in the middle of the night with Logan's hand holding my head against the sleeping bag while he took what he wanted from me. Again.

My ass cheeks feel sticky and not just from his cum. I'd felt the tearing. Seen the blood on his dripping dick right after. He wrecked me and left me like discarded trash. Ignored my screams and begs for mercy.

I swallow down the ball of emotion as I force myself to sit up. Losing my shit and breaking down won't help me. I need to check on Kristen and then find Destiny. I'm desperate to know she's still alive and unpunished for our attempted escape. Logan is the cruelest one here, so I'm hoping she managed to slide under the radar.

With slow, shaky movements, I pull on my still-wet clothes, shivering at the chill of them. Once my boots are on, I crawl over to Kristen.

"Hey," I croak out, voice raw from last night. "Kristen. You okay?"

A soft moan rumbles out of her. "Mmm."

Stroking her hair, I let out a ragged sigh. "You're okay. Just rest. I'll get you some food and something to drink."

I tug her sleeping bag over her limp body and kiss her temple before forcing myself to my feet. The tent spins around me. I stumble a couple of steps before steadying myself. I'm most likely concussed, but there's nothing I can do about it. Mom's not around to nurse me back to health.

Thoughts of Mom have my heart squeezing in my chest.

I miss her so damn much.

My hand trembles as I reach for the zipper of the tent opening. Stepping out and taking stock of the aftermath from last night is the last thing I want to do. Destiny may need me, though, and Kristen definitely does. I can't let them down.

With a sharp inhalation of breath, I force myself to move and exit the tent.

Outside, the air still smells like rain and the sky is overcast, but it's not storming. Fall has slipped in, bringing its icy chill along with it. Since we were forced out of our home by monsters, we didn't exactly have an opportunity to pack a bag or grab something appropriate to wear.

A campfire crackles nearby and I'm drawn to its warmth. I can hear people whispering and a few women crying. I can only hope it's not Destiny, or worse, Raegan.

What if they found her?

Bile creeps up my throat. Surely I'd have heard her if they captured her again. She got away. I just know she did.

I find Lisa and Seth sitting by the fire, feeding their three kids some breakfast. The two adults glower at me with hatred in their eyes. Though those two and their family haven't ever done anything to my siblings or me, they're guilty by association. I don't care if they're unhappy.

Ignoring them, I continue to try and make out the faces around the fire. Tom sits nearby. His kids must still be asleep because they're not with him. His features are impassive and he says nothing to me.

Where is everyone else?

A man steps out of his tent and as he approaches, I recognize him. It's Michael. He gives me a cold stare, eyeballing me up and down as though I'm not a threat to him before calling out.

"Jace," Michael barks out. "I need help with the bodies."

The bodies?

My blood turns to ice as I frantically look around. Where is my sister? Where's Destiny? Panic claws at my throat and I struggle to breathe.

Until I see a flash of golden blond hair.

Jace, holding my little sister's hand, guides her over to the fire. He then pushes on her shoulder, making her sit down beside Tom. Then he crouches down in front of her, tucking her hair behind her ear.

"Are you hungry? I can get you something to eat."

She doesn't shake or nod her head. She doesn't reply.

"Destiny," Jace says, shaking her gently. "You can't give me the cold shoulder forever."

Again, she doesn't respond.

I curl both of my hands into fists, ready to attack

him, but he stands up without another word. He cuts his eyes over to me before gesturing at her.

"Can you check on her? She doesn't seem well."

Pushing past the desire to punch him in his fucking face, I give him a curt nod before settling on Destiny's other side.

"Hey," I murmur, taking hold of her cold hand. "You okay?"

Nothing.

No squeeze of her hand, no reply, no indication she even heard me.

"Dez," I say, voice turning firmer. "What happened?"

Again, silence.

"Tom," Michael barks out. "Keep an eye on the girl. Ronan, with us."

Gritting my teeth, I bite back hateful words to him. Instead, I press a kiss to Destiny's head before rising to my feet. I'm not eager to deal with bodies, but I have to make sure Raegan isn't one of them.

Maybe Logan is.

Now that's just wishful thinking.

I follow Jace and Michael through the trees until we arrive at our destination. There are two bodies covered with blankets. Based on the swells of their breasts under the fabric, they're female. My stomach seizes painfully.

Please don't be her.

Please.

"We're not burying them, but we're moving them away from camp. Their corpses will begin to stink and we can't afford to draw in predators." Michael tugs off the blanket from the first body. "She was too young to die."

I step closer and hold in my sigh of relief. It's Mya. I'd heard Owen mourning over her last night, but now I can confirm it with my own two blurry eyes. She was such an evil bitch. I don't feel sorry about her death.

But, if she died, did Raegan die fighting her?

Another wave of nausea has me breaking out in a sweat. My mouth waters like I'm going to puke at any second.

Michael watches me with interest before turning his back to me. Then he yanks off the other blanket. The woman is drenched in blood. The coppery scent permeates the air, making me gag. For a split second, I see Raegan's face.

But it's not her.

It's Stacey.

Did Raegan kill her too?

"The baby wasn't coming out," Michael explains in an emotionless voice. "We had to do a cesarean."

It's then I notice the tiny, naked form lying unmoving on the carnage that was her stomach. The baby. Blue and lifeless.

Jace loses it first. He starts gagging and puking. Michael remains still, watching me and waiting for my response.

"D-Did you kill the baby?" I choke out, horror dripping from my words.

Michael scoffs. "The baby didn't survive the surgery. It got nicked by my hunting knife."

It got nicked.

I close my eyes, squeezing them tight so tears won't form.

Clearly entertained by my reaction, Michael says, "Grab it. I'll grab my wife. Jace can deal with his cousin."

He wants me to take the baby.

Fuck.

With a whine in my throat, I shake my head. "Please don't make me."

Michael storms over to me and snarls in my face. "Deal with it or I'll add your pretty little sister to the pile. Your people have fucked with me enough. Do not test me."

Shuddering at his threat, I turn away from him and make my way over to Stacey and the baby. Carefully, I pick up the cold baby and cradle it to my chest. Tears freely fall as I stare at the deceased child. A small incision no wider than an inch covers his upper chest where his heart is. Michael didn't nick him, he stabbed him.

He accidentally stabbed his own baby trying to bring him into this world and now shows no remorse or emotion whatsoever.

Michael is a fucking psychopath.

I start to walk away with the baby but realize we're caught on something. It takes a second to notice the umbilical cord is still attaching mother to child. More tears fall, wetting the small angel who never took his first breath.

Michael grunts before stomping over to me. He whips out his gnarly knife and then hacks through the cord. Once it's free, he scoops Stacey up and flings her over one shoulder like a sack of potatoes.

He leads the way and I follow after him. I kiss the cold forehead of the baby before letting loose a choked sob. Michael grunts but doesn't gripe at me. We walk for about fifteen minutes until we come to a small cove, the ground covered in damp fallen leaves. Jace and Michael both drop the bodies to the earth like they're trash.

I crouch beside Stacey's body and use my free hand to push away the leaves beside her. Then I lay the baby down, tucking him against her side. Michael waits while I cover his son with a mound of leaves. When I stand up and can still see a tiny foot poking out, I know I'll never forget this awful moment.

My heart aches for both mother and child.

Hopefully, they're in a better place.

Night descends on us as we all sit around the campfire, munching on more rabbit Tom and Seth killed. Kristen is awake and doing okay. My sister is another story. She hasn't spoken a word, nor does she flinch or move away when Jace hugs her to him.

Owen and his wife Tee fuss over CJ. They're both

red-eyed and teary having lost their daughter. I can't feel any sympathy for them. CJ is fucked up. His skin is pallid, he keeps throwing up, and twice he's passed out. I hope he dies too. I'll happily dump his corpse beside his cunt sister.

Logan, who finally made an appearance, and Michael have been in his tent, having heated words for hours now. I'm sure their visions of a happy little community cult have been erased. They fucked with the wrong family, that's for sure.

The five younger kids left—Tom's and Seth's children—huddle together, whispering quietly. I'm thankful my little brothers no longer have to be near them.

If only I could get Destiny and Kristen out of here.

As we sit by the fire, my mind drifts to Ryder. He's always been the tougher, stronger one. If he were here instead of me, he'd have already saved everyone on day two. Since it's me, we're still stuck here, helpless. I can't even save myself.

I hope Raegan found him or is at least well on her way back home.

Will she tell him we had sex?

The thought makes my gut sour. He won't take the news well. It's a betrayal.

My heart aches for him.

Heavy footsteps thud over to us as Michael and Logan rejoin the group.

"Tonight, Logan, Seth, and I will go hunt for the children," Michael grunts. "Split up how you need to, but I want eyes on those three runaways at all times." He makes a pointed show of gesturing to me, Kristen, and Destiny. "When we find the lost children, we'll continue our trek south. According to my map, there are some mountains there. A cave mouth we could fortify would be great. This could be where we'll settle permanently."

CJ coughs and then spits up blood. Tee hugs him to her, sobbing quietly. Owen glowers at me as if I were the one who caused all this.

They started this the second they preyed upon our family.

"Tomorrow, I will take a new wife," Michael states. "My sons have been so gracious as to offer me theirs. I'll think while we hunt and come back with my choice."

The thought of Destiny or Kristen becoming Michael's wife makes my skin crawl. He's a heartless monster.

"CJ needs to see a doctor. His eye is infected. If he doesn't get help, he'll die," Tee says shakily, trying and failing to inject firmness in her tone. "I think this is where we'll split ways."

Owen dips his head but doesn't argue with his wife. Michael stares at his brother, waiting for him to speak. When he doesn't, he calmly walks over to CJ, grabs his hair, and slices a blade along his neck.

It all happens so fast.

I gape in shock as blood spurts from CJ's neck. Tee and Owen both make strangled sounds. CJ slumps over into Tee's lap and she attempts to desperately hold his neck together. Owen jumps to his feet, a guttural growl echoing through the trees, and takes a swing for his brother.

But Michael's quicker.

Stab. Stab. Stab. Stab.

He punches his sharp knife several times into Owen's abdomen before letting him fall to the earth. Tee's eyes widen in realization, and she scrambles to escape. She barely makes it a few feet before she slams into Logan's chest. With no expression on his face, he grabs hold of her head and snaps her neck.

Holy fuck.

My heart is in my throat and I don't think I can draw a breath.

Michael killed his own brother and nephew. Logan murdered his aunt. They did this in front of everyone, even the kids. These people are sick.

The smaller children near Tom and Seth cower under Michael's cruel glare. Their whimpers are quiet as fear paralyzes them. Lisa, Seth's wife, slumps over, crashing against her husband as she passes out.

Everyone is silent with terror as Michael pins his stare on each and every one of us.

"We are building something here," Michael growls, words cold and evil. "Anyone else who thinks they're also going to give up like my brother and his family, please, speak up. I'll handle it right here and now."

No one utters a peep.

"Good. Tom, you keep an eye on Ronan and

Kristen." Michael's harsh stare locks on mine for a moment before darting over to my sister. "Jace can handle his wife. We'll be back tomorrow with the lost children and everything will be right again."

Tom is quick to get his kids moving into the tent and then he hauls both me and Kristen with him. Neither of us fights his manhandling because we're both eager to get away from their bloodthirsty leader.

Before I step inside the tent, I get the strange sensation of someone watching me. The hairs on my neck stand on end. I glance over my shoulder expecting Logan or Michael to be staring at me, but they're busy removing the bodies of their family.

Confused, I sweep my gaze over the darkened trees beyond camp. I can't see anything clearly without my glasses, but the sudden jump in my heart rate tells me that the shadow that slowly moves beyond the tents is not a tree blowing in the wind.

It's him.

Please, God, let it be my brother.

CHAPTER TWENTY-ONE

ryder

MICHAEL JUST MURDERED HIS OWN NEPHEW and brother.

I watched it happen with my own two eyes.

No remorse. No regret. Nothing.

This hateful man needs to be eradicated from this world. I'd give anything to charge forward and stab him to death.

As much as that idea entices me, I know I can't. It's not part of the plan. Me and Rowdy have one agenda: Get Ronan and Destiny out quickly and quietly. Going on a murdering rampage would feel great for about two minutes until the rest of their people quickly outnumbered the two of us. Then where would that leave us?

This morning, Raegan and Sadie gave us the lay of their campground and the sleeping arrangements. And after we made a plan to set out just the two of us, I had to watch as Wild led Raegan, Sadie, and the boys on their trek back home.

I had her for one night.

One perfect fucking night.

My mind is a storm of tumultuous thoughts. For a bit there, with Raegan's naked body pressed against mine, I'd forgotten about all the whys we shouldn't be together like that. I let my need to hold her overpower my morality. It felt good to touch and kiss her. To get her off with my fingers. Fuck, she felt amazing. Just like I imagined.

The voices near the campfire once again draw my attention. Even though Rae said Ronan and Kristen sleep in Logan's tent, it was Tom who ushered them in with his family. Destiny disappeared to the tent with Jace, though, which was where Raegan said she'd be.

Now, all we have to do is wait until they fall asleep.

Logan and Michael work on dragging the three bodies away. I want to go after them, finding Rowdy's figure about twenty feet away, but am met with a sharp shake of his head.

Right.

Focus on the mission.

Get in, get out, and run like hell.

Waiting for a good time to make our move sucks. It's unnerving. Every second that ticks by feels like we're closer to sentencing them to their death. Michael is clearly unstable and unafraid to kill his own flesh and blood. He won't think twice about hurting my family.

Michael and Logan eventually return from their body dumping expedition. Another man, Seth I think, begins to help them pack a couple of backpacks with weapons and supplies. I'd overheard Michael state they were going to hunt for Raegan, Sadie, and the boys. I'm thankful we made the decision to send them on their way back home with Wild to get them farther away from these monsters. At least they'll have a head start.

Eventually, Michael, Logan, and Seth head out in the direction me and Rowdy came from. Knowing they're already on the right track is nerve-wracking, but I have to believe Wild and Raegan will be faster. I'm glad Rowdy told me to bring my tent and gear with us rather than leaving it back at our camp. If Michael and his group would have stumbled across it, they'd have known we were out here and close. We need them to keep their guard down just long enough to grab the rest of our people.

Camp grows quiet aside from the occasional sob from one of the children. They're probably traumatized by the actions of their leader. I just hope the horror they witnessed doesn't get in our way of taking Ronan and Dez. If I'm forced to choose between one of the kidnapper's children or my family, I'll always choose my own blood.

My legs begin to cramp from my crouched position. Slowly, I rise to my feet to stretch them. Rowdy remains kneeling by his tree. I can feel his gaze on me, but he doesn't signal to me that it's time. I'm anxious and not feeling very patient as we wait for the perfect time.

Hours tick by.

Whimpers of the children soon become overpowered by the snores of one of the men in one of the tents. From what Sadie and Raegan described, it must be Tom. His snoring will work in our favor by covering any sounds we make.

The fire is nothing but a pile of glowing embers, further shadowing the camp. A cool wind blows through the trees, nipping at my ears and nose. Summer is officially gone because I haven't felt very warm in days.

My mind drifts back to Raegan. She told me she had sex with Ronan. I still can't believe it. Until I hear it from him, I don't know that I will. What they did together—without me—has me feeling not only left out, but confused.

He's gay.

So why did he sleep with our sister?

I mean, I know why. She told me. Raegan wanted to lose her virginity on her own terms. It killed her to think CJ would take that from her—and given time, he would have. What I don't get, though, is how Ronan was able to perform.

He's gay.

His dick gets hard for me. *For me.* Not women.

Jealousy rears its ugly head again. I'm mad at them both. Angry at Raegan for having Ronan do something he most likely didn't want to do. Angry at Ronan for having sex with our sister when he's supposed to be gay. Mostly, I'm angry because they're both my best friends and they did something so life-altering without me.

As quickly as the anger forms, it cools. They've been in a fucked-up situation. Who am I to judge how they handle the stress of kidnapping?

Tap. Tap. Tap.

Three soft taps of a stick against a tree trunk have me abandoning my heavy thoughts and searching the darkness for Rowdy. He motions with the stick to himself, then to the tent Destiny is in. I motion to myself and the tent Ronan is in. We both nod in understanding and rise to our feet.

This is it.

It's time to get them.

The plan is to quietly slice through their tents, locate our siblings, and extract them without carnage. As much as I'd love to cut the throats of everyone here except them, it's too risky.

Rowdy disappears to the left and I start toward the right, both of us walking the perimeter of the camp toward our destinations. I listen carefully for any sounds of Michael returning but don't hear anything as I pass one of the tents.

A stick snaps beneath my boot, causing me to freeze. My heart thuds heavily in my chest as I wait for some sort of indication I've been heard. Nothing. Good. I continue my prowl until I reach Ronan's tent. I'm unsure of the sleeping arrangements, so this part will be tricky. My best bet is to slice the tent material from top to bottom and then peek my head inside to locate them. The zipper would be too loud, but I can slowly cut the tent soundlessly.

Barely breathing, I press the tip of my knife to the top of the side of the tent. My backpack and gear are heavy on my back, making me sweat profusely despite the chilly air surrounding me. With the patience of a saint, I slowly cut through the material, wincing at any soft sound it makes.

No one comes after me, so I'm off to a good start.

When I reach the bottom, I grab hold of one side, readying myself to push my head inside. Before I get there, a hand pokes through the opening, grabbing onto my wrist. For a split second, I freeze, unsure what to do.

A face peeks out and I immediately recognize it.

Ronan.

His grin is the most wonderful thing I've ever seen. I lean my forehead to his for a moment and then I gently help him out of the tent so as not to make any noise. Once he's out and I'm ready for him to bolt with me, he jerks his hand out of mine before turning around to face the tent again.

What the hell is he doing?

He reaches inside and then pulls out a woman I recognize as Kristen. I guess we're rescuing her too. I give them both a nod and then gesture to where Rowdy is. Ronan takes Kristen's hand and follows after me. Another spike of jealousy shoots through me.

I should be holding his hand, not her.

Ignoring the bitter, green monster inside me, I make my way over to Rowdy. He has Destiny by the bicep, pulling her through the tent opening. She's almost out when suddenly she's jerked back.

Fuck.

Jace is awake.

In the moonlight, I can see his jaw muscle ticking as his hold tightens around Destiny's ankle. Rowdy makes a soft grunt as he tries to extract Destiny from Jace's grip. She's jerked again, this time completely disappearing back into the tent.

Rowdy growls and dives into the tent.

The whole tent trembles and quakes as a struggle ensues. Then I hear the wet, tearing sound of a knife piercing flesh.

Over and over and over.

I take off running in an effort to help Rowdy. By the time I reach the tent and am crouching down, I've heard that sick stabbing sound probably twenty-five times or so.

Please let Rowdy be the one doing all the stabbing.

I can't stomach the idea of losing him to that fucker, Jace.

Before I can stick my head inside, Rowdy emerges from the tent. Destiny is limp in his arms, covered in blood. He's also wearing it splattered all over his face. His feral expression meets mine and then he nods.

It's done.

We're getting the hell out of here.

He takes off at a clipped pace, carrying Destiny like she's a sleeping princess in one of the fairy tales Mom used to read to us. Rowdy's more like an avenging dark angel, dangerous but protective.

Glancing back, I notice Ronan squinting at me. That's right. He can't fucking see a thing. I grab his other hand, happy to have an excuse to touch him and soothe some of my jealousy, to guide him in the right direction. The three of us follow after Rowdy, struggling to keep up with him. For someone carrying another human, he glides through the forest like he's a soulless wraith, not a man with a size thirteen boot.

All that can be heard as we rush through the forest is our harsh breathing. Each step away from that fucked-up camp feels like one step closer to eventual freedom. We just have to get far enough away that we won't be discovered easily.

After running for about forty-five minutes, Rowdy comes to a stop. He gently sits down with Destiny in his lap before fumbling for a bottle of water. I take the break time to do the same, sharing one of my bottles with Kristen and Ronan. While they're occupied with the water, I slide the backpack off my shoulders to dig around in a pocket for a hard case. Once I locate it, I hand it to Ronan.

His eyes widen as he accepts the case. Then he flips it open and removes one of his spare pairs of glasses. He sets them on his face and then grins at me.

"Thank you," he whispers, eyes roaming over my face in appreciation.

My heart warms. I'm glad I'm the first thing he sees after this nightmare. Pride fills my chest. I grab hold of the back of his head, pulling his forehead to mine again.

"I fucking missed you."

"I missed you too."

Letting go of Ronan, I make my way over to Rowdy. He's frowning down at Destiny. She's awake but staring off into space, a vacant expression on her face. I squat beside them and reach into my pack for something to clean her face off with. Once I locate a packaged towelette, I rip it open and start to swipe the blood off her skin.

Rowdy grunts, shooting me a warning glare before snatching the towelette from me. Gently, he cleans her face, murmuring soft assurances to her. She doesn't flinch or respond.

"We need to get going again," I say to Rowdy, careful to remain out of arm's reach. He's still acting like a cornered animal protecting his young. "It's not safe."

He gives a shake of his head as if to clear it and then meets my gaze with a more human stare before nodding. I step back, allowing him his space, as he rises to his feet once more. Destiny's head lolls toward his chest and stays there. He hugs her tighter to him. It makes me glad that we sent his backpack and tent with Raegan since he's apparently going to carry Destiny the whole time.

Rowdy nods down to his back pocket. I bend over to see what he needs. As soon as I see the familiar knife hilt sticking out, I can't help but grin at him. Sure, it's covered with Jace's blood, but it's *my* knife. Well, the knife I share with Raegan. I take it from him, unable to keep the anticipation of seeing Raegan's expression when I give it back to her out of my mind, and tuck it away in my pack.

She'll be so fucking happy.

We start forward again, but Ronan stops me, his hand gripping my wrist. I turn toward him, frowning at the utter look of despair on his face.

"What is it?" I hiss, stepping closer to him as fear clutches my heart. "Are you okay?"

He swallows thickly and then lifts his chin. "Just tell me how they died."

"Who?"

"Mom and Dad and Dawson."

I reach up, swiping the tear on his cheek away with my thumb. "They're alive, Ro. Everyone is alive."

He launches himself at me for a tight hug, his entire body trembling as he breaks down with emotion. "Thank God."

"We're going to be okay. It's all going to be okay."

I believe those words a hundred percent. I hope he does too.

CHAPTER TWENTY-TWO

ronan

T HEY'RE ALIVE.
While we've traveled all day and evening through the woods, it's all I've been able to think about. My parents didn't die. My baby brother is still here on Earth.

Unlike Michael's son.

Every time I close my eyes, I see his pale, tiny foot sticking out of those leaves. That baby didn't deserve to die.

Rowdy whistles at us up ahead, motioning down. I force the previous nauseating image from my mind to trot ahead and investigate. Down a steep incline is a small meadow nearly surrounded by more hills. It's a perfect place to stop and rest for the night. We could even have a fire without being easily seen. Since my head has been throbbing continuously, I'm eager to crawl into a tent and sleep.

Ryder slides down the hill ahead of Rowdy and

holds out his arms, waiting for him to pass Destiny to him. I'm not sure how he's been able to carry her this entire time. His arms must be about to fall off. Thankfully, Kristen hasn't made me or Ryder carry her. I can barely put each foot in front of the other, much less take care of someone else.

"You go first," I tell Kristen. "I've got your hand."

She clutches onto me while reaching for Rowdy with her other. He helps her down the hill and then takes Destiny from Ryder. I gingerly start making my way down. My foot slips and I fall down onto my ass. Hard. It's jarring and painful.

Closing my eyes, I breathe through the throbbing reminder of Logan's rape, trying desperately not to break down.

I can do this.

I'm safe.

Warm hands clutch onto mine and then I'm being pulled to my feet. Rowdy's strong arm slides around my waist as he assists me the rest of the way down. I lean against him, soaking in his strength, hoping just a little bit will rub off on me.

"I've got you," Ryder rumbles. "You're okay."

It's like he knows I'm struggling with a lot more than just a fall down the hill. The pain I'm feeling, yes, is physical, but there's a whole mental aspect to it that keeps fucking with me.

What will Ryder think when I tell him about me and Raegan?

Will he hate us?

I can almost see his handsome face twisted into one of pain. It makes me sick to even think about. Maybe we can forget about everything that happened with Michael's psychopathic cult.

That would be amazing.

Forget the sex with my sister. Forget the rape. Forget the lifeless baby I was forced to bury.

"Hey," Ryder says, snapping his fingers in my face. "You're out of it. What's going on?"

His concern sends warmth coursing through me. Unable to stop myself, I pull him to me for a fierce hug. I bury my nose against his neck, inhaling his woodsy scent. He rubs his palm up and down my back, offering me the comfort I so desperately need.

I wish he could hold me like this forever.

I'm home in his arms—safe, protected, intensely loved.

All too soon, Ryder pulls away and studies me. "I'm going to get our tent set up. Just sit beside Dez and rest. We'll take care of you guys."

I give him a nod before joining my sister, who sits with her head bowed, absently rubbing at her hands that are stained with Jace's blood. Kristen gives me a sad smile before searching for some sticks to use for the campfire. Rowdy and Ryder make quick work of erecting our one and only tent. It's going to be a tight squeeze with the five of us inside.

By the time night falls, we have a nice, warm fire

going and are munching away on the food Ryder had packed in his bag. It's nice being able to actually see for a change. Knowing Ryder thought to bring my glasses with him just makes me love him a little more if that's even possible.

"You have to eat something," Rowdy urges Destiny. "Please."

He hovers over her, watching her every move—which is very little—as though she might vanish if he blinks. When she doesn't open her mouth or attempt to eat, he scrubs a palm over his face, a weary expression taking over.

"Come on. Time for bed," he says with a grunt. "You get a pass tonight, but you have to eat something in the morning."

The unspoken "or I'll force it down your throat" hangs in the air.

I shudder. Kristen looks away, shivering. Ryder frowns.

But Destiny?

She doesn't move or flinch.

He scoops her into his arms again before striding over to the unzipped tent. Kristen reaches over to tug at my sleeve, eyes pleading for me to go to the tent with her. After being with Logan for so long, I don't understand why she seems creeped out by my brother. He's harmless.

"I'm beat," I say with a grunt as I stand. "Ry, you coming?"

His narrowed eyes dart to where Kristen's hand slides inside mine. He stares a beat longer, nostrils flaring, before also standing.

He stalks ahead of us toward the tent. Kristen steps inside next with me following after. There's enough glow from the campfire that I can see the tight sleeping arrangements well. Rowdy is to the far left, Destiny tucked protectively at his side, whereas Ryder is on the far right. Since we only have the one sleeping bag, they unzipped it and spread it across the bottom of the tent for padding, but we won't have anything to cover up with tonight.

"Put the girls in the middle where it's safe," Ryder instructs.

Kristen stretches out on her side beside Destiny and I'm left with a tiny sliver of space between her and Ryder. I'm also unable to lie flat on my back and end up on my side as well. As soon as I relax, Ryder's warmth envelops me from behind and his arm hooks over me, pulling me closer into his embrace.

Snuggling with Ryder is the best thing that's happened to me in what feels like forever. His muscular body molds to mine, freely sharing his body heat. Easily, I'm able to drift to sleep with his safe hold around me.

Logan's dick presses against my ass as he snakes his palm under my shirt. Fear surges through me, cold and

numbing. I can't move. Soon, he'll rip my jeans away and push his dick inside of me. All the soreness that's been trying to heal will be reopened, making me bleed… hopefully to death.

I don't want to die.

I want to go home and be with my family.

He ruts against me again. This time, I'm unable to hold back a scream, followed by begging that will only get me beat on.

"Please don't, please don't, please don't."

"Ronan!"

A soft smack to my cheek jerks me from my nightmare. It's too dark to see him, but I feel him. It's Ryder. I'm with Ryder. I'm safe.

The feel of his erection pressing against my ass sends full-bodied shudders wracking through me. I'm trapped and suffocating. There's nowhere to go!

"Breathe," Ryder urges, stroking my cheek. "You're having a panic attack. I've got you."

"D-Don't touch me," I choke out, attempting to scramble away from him. "P-Please."

He scoots back a hair and pulls his hand back. His absence doesn't feel better, though. It's worse. But I can't stomach the idea of his dick pressing against me like Logan's did.

"I'm sorry," I whisper. "I just…I need space."

There is no space. We're wedged in too tight.

"Everything okay?" Rowdy asks from the other side of the tent, voice thick with sleep.

"Panic attack," Ryder tells him. "It's fine."

It's not fine.

My skin continues to crawl, but I ache for Ryder's closeness. It's a double-edged sword. Either way, I hurt.

Ryder twists until his back is to mine. I instantly regret driving him away. With some wriggling, I manage to turn to my other side. My arm slides around him and I hug him to me, inhaling his scent.

"This is better," I murmur. "I don't feel trapped."

He relaxes before slipping his hand over mine. It feels so natural to let him comfort me, but would he be so accommodating if he knew what I did with our sister? I'm desperate to tell him we had sex and get it off my chest. I thought I could forget or shove it from my mind, but it feels like a betrayal keeping it from him.

"Hey, Ryder," I whisper, my words tickling softly over his ear. "I have to tell you something."

My whole body trembles as I worry how he'll take the news.

"I know."

He knows?

How could he possibly know?

"Rae told me," he says, answering my unspoken questions. He turns his head slightly to where our mouths are so close. "You gave her a gift. I'd have done the same too."

Relief floods through me knowing he's not angry and understands the mental hell we went through to drive us to that point. Our fingers thread together and

I'm able to fall back asleep feeling much lighter than when I first woke up.

I wake to a hand covering my mouth. Panic claws its way up my throat, preparing to let loose a scream, but in the early dawn light, I realize it's Ryder.

Just Ryder.

He pulls his hand away and brings a finger to his lips before handing me his rifle. I take it from him and follow him out of the tent. The girls are still both asleep, but Rowdy's missing. Clearly, they heard something and we need to check it out.

What did they hear?

Is Logan here?

The panic seizes my lungs again, but I force myself to slowly breathe. It's probably just a bear or something. I can't allow Logan to terrorize me when he's not even here.

Once outside, I scan the dim forest along the top of the hills surrounding us. I don't see anything, but that doesn't mean there's no threat. Rowdy begins climbing one hill, way ahead of us. Ryder motions for me to guard the tent while he heads in a different direction.

My heart thunders in my chest, making my head throb in the same rapid cadence. I've had a nonstop headache since Logan beat the shit out of me and it's getting old. I just want every reminder of Logan to go away.

Rowdy crests his hill first and then disappears. Ryder scales his hill not too long after.

I'm alone, charged with keeping the girls safe.

Dread consumes me. I wasn't able to keep them safe before, so why in the hell does Ryder trust me to do it again? My attention jerks back and forth between the spots I'd last seen each of my brothers. Nothing. Silence.

A sound comes from the tent. I swivel around to see if Kristen or Destiny are coming out. No one exits the tent.

It's then I see the dark form standing behind it.

I blink several times to make sure I'm not hallucinating. When the shadow moves, fear paralyzes me. It charges for me with a low growl. My attempt to raise the rifle is thwarted when the beast tackles me.

The beast from my nightmares.

My rapist.

"Miss me, pet?" Logan's spittle sprays over my face as he fights me for the rifle in my hands.

I grunt, using all my strength to keep the weapon in my hands, but with a fierce show of rage, he jerks it away from me. He tosses it aside and then pins me with his larger body. I open my mouth to scream. No sound comes out because the tip of a sharp knife presses into the side of my neck.

"Hush, pet," Logan croons, grinding his hard dick

against me. "You alert the girls in that tent and I'll be forced to cut their pretty throats."

All I can do is stare up at the monster, helpless in his trap. Tears prickle at my eyes and silently spill over. He grins wide before crudely licking the side of my face. I shudder at his touch, a whimper crawling out of me.

"You taste so good when you cry." He slowly rubs his dick against me as though he's enjoying the look of pure terror on my face. "Imagine my surprise when we stumbled upon your little hiking party. I thought I'd find the other runaways, not my naughty pet and my wicked wife."

I reach out, hoping to grab hold of the rifle. He sees my efforts and thwarts them immediately, digging the knife harder into my flesh.

"Please," I beg. "Please don't hurt me."

Logan laughs, dark and nefarious. "Oh, pet, your whole life will be nothing but pain for my pleasure. Get used to it."

My other hand curls around a thin stick. It's a weapon. Not the most powerful one, but it'll do. I only have one shot. With a roar, I swing the stick toward Logan's head, shoving the stick right into his ear. The effect is immediate. He howls, falling away from me and grabbing his ear. I scramble over to the rifle while he wails. Before I reach it, he goes quiet. Swinging around, I aim the rifle at him.

Or, where he just was.

He's already across the meadow and racing up the

hill. I pull the trigger, recoiling with the kick of it. Logan jerks but keeps going, disappearing over the hill.

Another person grabs onto me and I cry out, trying to shake them off, when I realize it's Kristen.

"He's gone," I assure her, my voice raspy.

I just hope he's gone for good.

CHAPTER TWENTY-THREE

ryder

THE CRACK OF A RIFLE GOING OFF ECHOES through the trees.

Fuck.

Rowdy was right. He did hear something, which is why we're out here checking things out. I'm praying it's a bear or a mountain lion or a goddamn squirrel at this point. What I don't want it to be is people. People means the kidnappers have found us and I can't stomach what that would mean for us.

Crouching behind a tree, I scan the forest, looking for any movement. The wind rustles the leaves and makes the trees groan, sending chilly air whispering over my face, but nothing else can be seen. Slowly, I start making my way back over to the camp to check on Ronan and the girls.

From the distance, I can hear crunching through brush as though someone is running. It could be Rowdy, but the hairs prickling at the back of my neck tell me it's not. I stealthily make my way toward the sound, my knife in hand, sharp and ready.

I can't find anyone, but I do come across a trail of blood droplets dotting leaves and smeared along tree trunks. Based on the distinct boot mark in a muddy section of the ground, it's apparent it's from a human.

Double fuck.

But I only heard the one shot. My hope is that Rowdy or Ronan took care of whoever it was. It's likely the hunting group of kidnappers ran into our camp, but I'm hoping the hell not.

One shot versus three people.

That means, if that's what I'm facing here, there are two more in their group. Armed and dangerous. I'm thankful I left Ronan with a weapon to keep himself and the girls protected.

Rather than chase after the injured person who'll no doubt die if they keep losing blood, I go after the other two. The forest grows unusually quiet. All I can hear is the whistling wind and the thrumming in my ears in tune with my heartbeat. With the absence of chirping birds, it could mean there are people nearby.

A person steps to the side from behind a tree, revealing their back. Even from fifty or so yards away, I can tell he's not one of my brothers. If I had my rifle, I could raise it and shoot the man. Instead, I have to rely on the element of surprise and my knife. I've barely made it three steps when something snaps behind me.

Whirling around, I recognize Michael charging

for me. He swings his own rifle at me. Lifting my arm, I attempt to block it, but he uses enough force that it glances off my arm and still slams into the side of my head.

Thwump.

I fall heavily to the ground, desperately fighting the hammering in my skull and shrinking vision. The forest spins around me, but I manage to roll onto my back just as he launches himself at me.

"I'm going to enjoy beating you to death, you useless piece of shit," Michael snarls, slamming the butt of his rifle against my face.

My eyebrow splits from the impact. The bones in my face feel as though they've been tested, especially my brow and cheekbone.

He laughs, spittle hitting my flesh. "After I kill you, I'm going to find your missing sister and make her my new wife. I'll fuck her teenage cunt over and over until she bleeds. There'll be nothing you can do about it because you'll be dead!"

Before he can hit me again, I block my face with one arm and manage to stab him with the other. The knife punches through his jacket, finding a soft part of him, going deep to the hilt.

"You'll never touch Raegan, you sick pedophile!"

"Motherfucker," Michael grunts. "You fucking stabbed me!"

He manages to roll away from me, taking my knife with him. I stagger to my feet, desperately trying to see straight after the two hits I took to the head. Michael, now on his back, aims his rifle at my face.

Crack!

Another shot of a rifle goes off elsewhere before Michael has a chance to shoot, stalling him long enough for me to dive at him. I shove his weapon upward, narrowly missing the end of his barrel as his gun discharges. My ear, having been so close, rings from the deafening sound so close to my head. I'm damn near deaf in the other ear too as adrenaline rushes through me. Michael is saying something to me that I can't hear.

All I know is he can't win.

He can't ever have an opportunity to get Raegan in his clutches ever again. She's mine to protect and I'll do that until the last breath I ever take.

"Just fucking die," I grit out through clenched teeth.

He and I wrestle for the upper hand, both of us trying to take his rifle. I press my knee down onto my knife that still sticks out of his side. Michael bucks from the pain of it, loosening his grip on the gun. I pull the rifle from his grip, whip it around, and point it at his face. My finger hooks around the trigger as he grabs the barrel. Rather than pushing it away from him, he yanks me toward him. When I'm close, he head butts me, hitting me across the same spot on my brow his rifle did.

I abandon the rifle to use my fists instead,

slamming them into his chest over and over and over. His own fist swings around to my back, aiming right for my kidney. Grunting in pain, I grapple with his offending arm, doing my best to keep him from hitting me again.

He rolls us, landing heavily on top of me. His hands find my throat, locking around it and blocking my air supply. I swing a fist at his head, but he easily dodges it. His grin is evil as fuck as he chokes me.

This is what she'd see if he caught her.

He'd rape my sister until she was a husk who wanted to die.

Fuck. That.

Remembering the knife, I grab hold of the hilt and yank it out of his side. He grunts, but his hold on me doesn't relent. Blackness eats at my vision, but I'm relentless in slashing and stabbing whatever parts of him I can get to. Even when I think I'm going to die from lack of oxygen, I fight with all I have, my grip on the knife never waning despite how slick it becomes.

Everything goes completely dark.

Fragments of every charged moment I've had with Raegan and Ronan flicker in my mind. If I'm going to die, this is a good way to go.

A heaviness slams down on me, dragging me completely under. Warmth washes over me. I get lost in the visions, losing touch with the here and now.

I'm dying.

I'm dead.

Air sucks into my lungs, making my body jolt. I gasp like a fish on the bank, desperate for the oxygen to bring me back to life. My chest burns and my throat damn near feels crushed, but I can breathe.

I'm breathing.

I'm alive.

Blinking several times, I try to chase away the dark haze. Daylight enters my vision, blinding me. Greedy for the light, I squint, desperate to see my surroundings.

The heavy weight remains on me and my skin still feels slick and warm. Awareness trickles through me. I shove at the heaviness on me and it falls aside with a *thwump*. With the weight gone, I can breathe more freely. Slowly, I sit up on my elbows, making sense of my situation.

Michael lies on his side, eyes open and face contorted into one of rage or pain. But he's not breathing or blinking or moving. He's dead.

How?

Last I remember, he was choking the fucking life out of me.

Did Rowdy or Ronan shoot him?

Gingerly, I sit up on my ass and nudge his body with my boot. He rolls onto his back, giving me a prime view of him. His arms bear many lacerations from my slashing and the wound in his ribs is extra bloody. It's the one on his thigh that delivered his death blow. A shit ton of blood soaks his jeans and continues to leak out of him onto the forest floor.

I hit an artery.

A fatal one.

Thank fuck.

It takes a few minutes to regain my strength, but then I'm shakily standing. I take his rifle and my knife before heading back to camp. After five or ten minutes of walking, I hear something.

"Ryder!"

Rowdy's voice can be heard off to my left. I turn, searching him out despite the lingering double vision I'm having. He's standing over something or someone. When I reach him, he eyes me warily. Blood, most of which belonged to Michael, drenches my entire front.

"You should see the other guy," I croak out, words a mere rasp.

He grunts and gives a small shake of his head. "This fucker is dead too."

The body on the ground has a bullet wound through his eyeball and he too isn't moving.

Unfortunately, it's not Logan. It's the other guy, Seth. Still, two down is better than none.

"We need to check on the others," Rowdy says, gesturing for me to follow.

Our trip back to camp doesn't take long. Trying to slide down the hill to the meadow is a lot more difficult after having the shit beat out of me, but eventually

I manage with Rowdy's help. Kristen and Ronan are waiting beside the tent, wide-eyed and nervous.

"Ryder," Ronan cries out upon seeing me. "Fuck, are you okay?"

"Michael's dead," I mutter without preamble. "I'm fine."

"Seth's dead too," Rowdy chimes in.

Ronan nods, relief flickering in his eyes. "I managed a shot and hit Logan."

"I saw his blood," I say to him. "You did good. He ran off to bleed to death."

Kristen sighs heavily and then starts to cry. "Thank you. Thank you for saving us and killing those sickos."

"We need to go, though," Rowdy grunts. "If Logan did make it, I don't want to be sitting here, waiting for when he comes back. We'll hike back home at a break-neck pace. No resting unless absolutely necessary. No straight paths. Quietly and stealthily is our mission today."

It doesn't take long for us to pack up the tent and head out. Despite being covered in sticky blood, I don't take the time to try to remove it. Eventually, we'll run across a creek that I can wash up in. I'll feel a lot better when we've put more distance between us and the bodies we left behind.

For the first couple of hours as we walk, Rowdy takes the lead with a catatonic Destiny in his arms. Ronan and Kristen walk in the middle while I bring up the rear. Though he tries to keep it discreet, I don't miss the way Ronan frequently glances over his shoulder, scanning the woods for any would-be followers.

One day, we'll be far away from this mess and these memories. Then, I can make sure Ronan is happy and feels safe.

He turns around once more and nearly stumbles over the brush underfoot. I reach out, snagging his arm, and hold him steady. His dark eyes meet mine, troubled and haunted.

"You're safe," I murmur, reminding him. Tugging him to me, I press a quick peck to his cheek near his mouth before resting my forehead on his and meeting his eyes. "I've got your back. I always do."

His shoulders relax and he gives me a small smile before pulling away. "I know you do, Ry. Thank you."

Despite my words, he doesn't believe me. He continues to scan the area, jumps at anything that moves, and trembles when he doesn't think anyone is looking.

Those people fucked him up.

I'll do whatever it takes to bring the old Ronan back to me. It may take time, but I can be patient. Anything for my brother. Anything.

CHAPTER TWENTY-FOUR

raegan

WILD IS BEING NICE.

Weird.

He's extra nice to Sadie, which has me fighting a smile. Maybe he won't be such an asshole if he dates a nice girl—a friend—rather than all the dumb-sounding girlfriends he brags about all the time. Sadie has been to hell and back and has a brain inside her skull.

And she killed for me and my family.

She'll always be cool in my book.

We've been walking for days. It's tiresome and stressful, but we're all doing okay. Dakota has gone back to being his usual mouthy self. I even threatened to whip him with my belt a handful of times. I'll never admit it aloud, but I'm happy to see him behaving like usual. Maybe Michael and his group won't have traumatized him too badly.

Declan is another story.

My baby brother won't go to Wild or Sadie. He clings to me every second of every day. I can't even go to pee without him throwing a screaming fit. Considering we're trying to be quiet, it's not exactly helpful to have him hollering, which is why I now can't even take a bathroom break alone.

Luckily, this new, nice Wild helped me make a harness to carry Declan in. My arms can be free while I tote him around like a backpack.

"Holy shit," Sadie says from up ahead. "They fucked up your truck."

Wild pretends to cry as we approach his truck that's smashed between some trees. It's all scratched up and looks terrible, something I failed to notice when we abandoned it. Knowing how much he loves that big metal beast, I can't help but feel a bit sorry for him.

Sadie cracks up, laughing and making fun of Wild. This has me and the boys also joining in. So much for feeling bad for him.

"I still can't believe those assholes did this," Wild grumbles, kicking one of the flat tires. "I love this truck and it's ruined." He sighs heavily and shakes his head. "At least we're getting closer. The road is just up ahead. Another few hours maybe and we'll be there."

Knowing home is within reach, I blink back sudden tears of happiness. Mom, Dad, and Dawson are alive. Soon, I'll see all three of them. God, I miss them so much.

We stop a bit later, after we're on the road, for a

quick snack of eating our fill of blackberries growing wild. Declan's face is stained purple, but he's smiling and not crying, which is a relief.

"Are we there yet?" Dakota asks for the millionth time since we got onto the road.

Wild tousles his hair and laughs. "Dude. Does it look like we're there yet?"

As we continue to walk, the sun begins to dip in the sky. I'm not sure exactly how far from home we are, but I hope we can make it by nightfall. I do not want to spend another night in a tent with Declan glued to my chest. Everything aches, especially my feet, but I'll walk until morning if that means avoiding another campout.

I just want to be home.

What home?

Every time I close my eyes, I see the memory of the flames. They set our house on fire. There's no telling what things will look like when we get back. I don't have the heart to ask Wild.

We continue our trek even after the sun completely sets and night closes around us like a fist. It's chilly and every sound makes us jump, but we keep going.

"Come on, Kota," Wild grunts. "Up you go."

He lifts Dakota into his arms and we keep moving. One foot after the other. Hour after hour.

A low growling sound has all three of us stopping short. Sadie swings the shotgun in her hands toward the sound. I ready myself to run Declan to safety if need be and hope Wild will do the same for Dakota.

A dark figure darts toward us. Sadie fumbles with the shotgun, trying to aim it at the animal, but she's not quick enough. It pounces on me, knocking me to my ass. A shriek of terror rips from my lips until the creature starts licking my face.

Wait.

"Mage?" I say in surprise. "It's Mage!"

He's doubled in size since I last saw him. I scratch my fingers through his scruff, laughing when he then starts licking Declan's blackberry mouth.

"Well, I'll be goddamned," a male voice says. "You boys really did it."

Uncle Atticus appears from the shadows, a wide grin on his face. He pulls Wild to him for a side hug and then does the same to Sadie. I'm still getting licked to death by Mage for any hugs.

"Please tell me we're almost home," I say, waiting for Uncle Atticus to make his way over to me. "I don't think I can walk much farther."

He chuckles, offering me his hand. "You're home, kiddo. You did it."

I let him pull me to my feet. Mage circles me, tail wagging.

"Where's everyone else?" Uncle Atticus asks, looking past me. "Your brothers and sister?"

Wild grunts in response. "They're still out there. We had to get the kids away and back home. Rowdy and Ryder went back for Ronan and Destiny."

"I see," Uncle Atticus says, voice tight. "Well, enough

standing around. Let's get you kids home. You all have people missing you a whole fuck of a lot."

Another couple of minutes and we're passing by our fenced-in property. Uncle Atticus's RV sits parked nearby. The air still smells like charred wood and lingering smoke despite all the time that's passed. I'm not thrilled to see what's left of our home.

"Welcome home," I mutter as I step through the gate.

It's dark, but I can tell there's not much left of our house. I think about all the memories we had in that house—playing with my siblings, laughing at family meals, sitting by the fireplace while Dad told stories.

It's all gone.

The other buildings on our property are still standing, though. We'll rebuild. Eventually.

"Wild," Uncle Atticus says, "why don't you and Sadie head over to the RV? Momma, Chet, and the twins are there. Let's give Raegan and the boys time with their parents." He gives my shoulder a squeeze. "They're staying in Ronan's cabin."

Dakota, now free of Wild's arms, takes off running toward Ronan's place. I trot after him, eager to see my family. He bursts through the door first. The sound of my mother's yelping and then her sobs greet me as I step inside after him.

Mom has Dakota in her arms, squeezing him to her like he might disappear. Dawson, sitting on the bed, grins at me. My gaze falls to Dad, who's lying beside him, bruises and healing cuts all over his face.

They hurt him so badly.

With a choked sob of my own, I rush over to Dad. His eyes are open and pure relief shines in them at seeing me. I'm careful when I hug him because I don't know where else he's hurt. His fingers spear into my hair, gripping me tight.

"You're really alive," I say in a ragged voice. "I didn't know. Ryder said you were, but I kept seeing you dragged behind us."

"You saved me, sunshine. That's my girl."

Declan starts crying again and the weight of him on my back soon disappears. I cling to my dad, crying, finally releasing all the horrors I'd dealt with since being kidnapped. When I finally calm down, I pull back to see I've soaked his shirt. Dawson watches me with wide eyes, sucking on his thumb.

"Hey, buddy," I whisper. Then I pull away from my dad to look at Mom. "Hey, Mom."

She has both Dakota and Declan in her lap, rocking with them in her arms. Her bloodshot blue eyes are glistening with emotion. "Come here, baby."

I fall to my knees in front of her, wiggling my way between my brothers and resting my head against her chest. She bends down and kisses my hair.

"Thank you for keeping my babies safe, Raegan." She kisses me again. "You're so brave."

It takes everything in me not to start crying again.

"Where's everyone else?" Mom asks shakily. "Are they talking to Atticus?"

Wincing, I pull back, unable to meet her eyes. "They're still out there."

"Destiny?" she hisses.

I fall onto my ass and give her a wounded look. "I'm sorry, Mom. I did my best. I couldn't save them all."

As Mom breaks down sobbing, I see Dad's hand reaching for me. I crawl over to him, resting my head against the bed. He pets my hair, uttering soft assurances.

It's okay.

You're home safe.

I love you, sunshine.

I hate how hurt my father is, but I'm so happy to see him. Being back home, protected by my parents, has exhaustion taking over. My eyelids are heavy, drooping as I try to stay awake. I can hear my parents talking to each other but am too sleepy to make sense of it.

"Come on, baby," Mom whispers when the cabin is dark. "Time to get you to bed."

I'm not sure how much time has passed. I can barely open my eyes long enough to let Mom help me off my slumped position on the floor. She guides me over to the couch. When I crash onto it, she takes my boots off and then covers me with a blanket.

The cushions beneath me are soft and smell like Ronan. Knowing I've sat on this couch a million times with him, reading and just talking, warms me.

I miss him.

I miss the way we used to be.

But now there's a new way for us—where we've been with each other in the most intimate of ways. He's been inside my body. That changes things.

Will we ever go back to the easy, happy times of reading beside each other without a worry in the world?

Do I want that?

I'm not sure. What I do know is I want my brother back. I want them both back. Ronan and Ryder. The three of us having fun times where we swam together in the creek and gave each other crap.

I miss those days.

I miss them.

CHAPTER TWENTY-FIVE

ronan

HE'S DEAD.

My tormentor and rapist is dead.

I mean, he has to be, right? I shot him and stabbed him in the ear. Without proper medical treatment, he'll get an infection like CJ did, and eventually die. The whole world can take an easy breath when that happens, knowing there's one less monster lurking about.

The problem is, though, I'll never know for sure. He'll always be my living nightmare. Waiting and biding his time for the perfect chance to pounce on me, forever making me his little pet. I'll always be forced to look over my shoulder, anticipating his next move.

He's dead.

I repeat that thought over and over and over again inside my head, hoping it'll stick, indefinitely chasing away the worry and doubt. Even if he lived for some wild reason, he won't have his brother or father or uncle.

His cousins are dead too. The few people he had left at that camp wouldn't be able to take over again and it's doubtful he'd ever find his way back having not grown up in these woods like we did.

So why can't I just let it go?

Fear keeps me on edge as we make our journey. We're almost home, having long since been walking down the road that'll take us there. Everything I love and hold dear is within my grasp.

And yet, I'm not happy.

How can I be? The shit I went through plays on repeat in my mind. I remember every thrust, every punch, every cruel word so vividly. No matter how much I try to think of better things like my parents being alive or seeing Raegan again, my mind always drifts back to the pain—pain I still feel all over my body.

I'm terrified to take a shit.

Of course no one but me knows this. It's not something I can exactly admit to my brothers or the girls. Not eating much is my solution. Maybe by the time it does happen, I'll have healed completely.

What would Ryder think if he knew Logan did that to me? Would I disgust him?

I'd always hoped to have that with someone—anal sex—and now it feels like it's been irrevocably stolen from me. The thought of anyone, even someone I absolutely love and trust, inside of me has bile creeping up my throat.

I'm fucking ruined.

Ryder trots up to me, slings an arm over my shoulders, and grins. "I can see the fence. We're home, Ro. We finally did it."

His smile is radiant and contagious, but I don't feel the joy he does.

I'm lost in unfamiliar territory. A prisoner to my memories. Despair dragging down my every thought.

We walk along the fence and then enter the gate. It's late afternoon, so I get a prime view of the complete damage Logan and his people wreaked on our lives.

The big house is gone. Just a pile of charred logs, debris, and rubble. The living room rock fireplace remains, as do some of the bigger framing logs, but most everything else is unrecognizable. Chickens cluck nearby in their pen and the goat brays in greeting. Our orchards and gardens remain, as do the smaller cabins, workshop, and barn.

We'll rebuild.

We have no other choice.

I notice Sadie and Aunt Eve near the playset by the workshop with a bunch of the little kids. Chet, Wild, and Uncle Atticus are standing in the barn, working on making another water collection container like the ones attached to Ryder's and my cabins. It makes sense now that the big house is gone that we'll need to collect more water to filter for drinking and bathing.

"My God!"

Mom's voice rings out to my left and I see her walking out of the cabin with Dawson on her hip. She starts running toward us, stopping first to greet Rowdy and Destiny. Turning away, I avoid seeing Mom's grief as she comes to her own conclusion about what's wrong with her daughter. Ryder nudges me with his shoulder, but I can't look at him either.

What will she see when she looks at my face?

Will she know the horrors I've been through?

Shame has me shutting down completely. I attempt to turn off my emotions. Talking about what happened with Logan is simply not an option. I'm hopeful Kristen will keep her knowledge to herself. I'm tempted to dart past Mom without being gathered in her comforting hug but know that won't fly with her. If anything, it'll only put more of a spotlight on me, which I certainly don't want or need.

"Hey, Mom," I say, approaching her with a forced smile. "Missed you."

She lets go of Destiny's hand to pull me to her with one arm, squeezing me. Dawson babbles his usual nonsense and tries to steal my glasses. I gently pluck his hand from the frames before moving out of his reach.

"They hurt you," Mom says, voice choked and tears spilling down her cheeks. "You're bruised and cut up. Oh, honey, I'm so sorry."

Pain swells up from the center of my chest and lodges into my throat. I fight tears by rapidly blinking. Biting down on my bottom lip to keep it from wobbling, I give her a one-shouldered shrug. Her eyebrows pinch together in worry.

"I'm going to go see Dad," I mutter. "Ryder got hurt. You need to take a look at his eyebrow."

She darts her gaze to Ryder and then lands back on mine. "Visit your daddy. He's in your cabin. Then get cleaned up. We'll talk later, sweetie."

Thankful to be out of her scrutiny, I leave my group to look for my father. I open the door to find Raegan sitting in a chair near where he lies on the bed, talking softly to him.

"Ronan!" Raegan shrieks, abandoning her seat and launching herself at me. "You're home!"

I hug my sister to me, inhaling the clean scent of her hair. Her breath tickles my neck, reminding me of when she came into my tent and put her mouth on my dick to get it wet. A shudder ripples through me and I'm unsure if it's a good one or a bad one. Either way, I extract myself from her arms and then walk over to my father.

"Dad," I rasp out. "You look like hell."

Dad chuckles and reaches for me. "Feel like hell too. Some of these stab wounds were deep. Your mother has forbidden me from doing anything until I'm better healed up. Maybe now that all her babies are home, she'll have something to distract her."

Smiling, a real one now, I take the chair Raegan vacated. I hold on to Dad's hand, drawing in his strength. His searching gaze is like Mom's, but not as intense. It's filled with warmth and relief. He's just happy we're safe and back.

Dad asks me to tell him all about my journey from the beginning until now. Raegan probably already told him everything she knew—the beatings I took from Logan—but he seems to want to hear it from my point of view. I spend the next hour telling him everything except the sexual abuse I'd suffered. Not only do I not want to burden him with that, I'm not sure how he'll react to the fact it was from a man. It would only draw attention to the reason why Logan chose me as his pet in the first place.

When I'm all talked out, I excuse myself to take a shower—my first real one in what feels like weeks.

I'll get out of my dreadful funk.

Shampooed hair, clean teeth, and comfortable clothes will all work miracles in making me feel more like myself. In a few days, it'll be as if nothing ever happened.

I can do this.

I can be happy again.

It's been a few days and it's not as if nothing ever happened.

Was I really delusional enough to think that would work? That I could surround myself with the people I love and everything would all magically go back to normal?

It's not normal.

Terror, deep-seated and nagging, digs its claws in, especially at night. I've woken in a panic, screaming so loud one night it actually dragged Dad out of bed to check on me, much to my embarrassment. I can see how they all look at me, pity in their stares.

You're home now.

You're supposed to be happy.

Even Raegan and Ryder watch me warily, treating me like I'm made of glass that might break. It's too much. I hate being inspected so closely, especially when I'm barely keeping my shit together.

Kristen, probably the only person who truly understands what I'm going through, respectfully gives me my space. I'm not sure where she is or what she's doing, but I'm glad she doesn't need me. I just hope she keeps our trauma bond to herself.

This morning, I lie with my back against the wall in Ryder's cabin, curled against Ryder's side. Watching him, before the sun fully rises and the usual family chaos ensues, is my favorite part of the day. I can stare at his handsome features without guilt or shame. It's not like he'd judge me, because he wouldn't, but I still don't like him looking too deeply inside me for fear of what he might find.

A weak man.

A man who couldn't protect his siblings or himself.

A man who was raped and wasn't able to do a damn thing to stop it.

Squeezing my eyes shut, I attempt to force away the

negative thoughts that are never-ending. Resentment settles in my gut.

I just want to be fucking normal.

My siblings made it through without all this inner turmoil. Raegan and my little brothers are fine. They went through the same experience of being kidnapped and abused but are all back to their normal selves. Even Kristen is somehow managing to deal with it much better than I am. It's just me who appears to have all the issues.

And Destiny.

Okay, so maybe I'm not completely alone. She hasn't said a word to anyone, which worries my parents. I wonder if her mind is as messy as mine is. I'd almost feel okay talking to her about it, since she clearly understands, but she won't speak, so it's pointless.

The cabin door creaks open.

Panic seizes me. I dig my fingers into Ryder's arm as terror paralyzes every muscle in my body.

He's here.

He's found me.

I won't be able to fight him off. The next time he rapes me, he'll kill me.

A low, terrified moan rattles out of my throat. Ryder tenses as if ready to head into battle. Rather than attack Logan, he sighs in relief.

What?

"Mom will be mad you left their cabin, Rae," Ryder says to Logan. But it's not Logan. It's Raegan. "Come on." Then he looks over his shoulder at me and clutches my hip with his hand. "Go back to sleep, Ro, you're safe."

Ryder pats the bed beside him, gesturing for Raegan to join him, as I try to make sense of my surroundings. Raegan, dressed in one of Ryder's long shirts, tiptoes over to the bed. Ryder lifts the covers for her to slide in next to him. They start whispering and softly giggle. Meanwhile, I'm still dying from a panic attack. I close my eyes, willing it to go the fuck away.

"Kota kicks too much," Raegan complains. "I don't know why I have to share the couch with him."

Next door, they're all packed in tight while me and Ryder have his cabin to ourselves. Uncle Atticus and Aunt Eve have all their kids plus Chet and Sadie bunked up in their RV. Rowdy went back to his own cabin, taking Spirit with him.

"Destiny gets to sleep peacefully next to Mom on the bed with her and Dad. But me? I get woken up to Dawson trying to poke my eyeballs out and Declan almost always ends up sleeping on top of me if he can't find a spot in the bed with Mom and Dad. It's too crowded over there." Raegan huffs, turning on her side to face Ryder. "You have an unused couch and all this space for me. I don't understand what their problem is. Just because I'm a girl."

The sound of Raegan and Ryder whispering eventually manages to calm me down. My heart doesn't race like it did earlier and I'm no longer breaking out into cold sweats.

I'm safe.

"I overheard Mom asking Aunt Eve if she should take Destiny into town to see a doctor," Raegan murmurs. "Since she won't talk or respond to anyone."

My stomach tightens at her words. Would she make me go to town to see a doctor if she knew what Logan did? Would the doctor have to examine me? Nausea makes my mouth water uncomfortably. I don't want anyone looking at what he did to me. Ever.

They continue their soft chattering, but I can't make my ears stop ringing long enough to make sense of what they're saying. My Logan-filled thoughts have transformed into that of an evil doctor snapping on a latex glove and instructing me to bend over.

My ass clenches and I wince in pain.

Will it ever stop hurting?

The cabin door opens again sometime later, making my heart rate ratchet up again, but I relax when Mom walks in. Her blond hair is wet from a recent shower, and for once, she doesn't have Dawson glued to her hip. When she sees Raegan tucked into bed with us, her lips press into a firm line.

"Raegan," Mom barks out. "How many times do I have to tell you being alone with your brothers is inappropriate?"

Ryder winces at her words, but anger strikes my chest like the lighting of a match and then spreads quickly as it burns through my body.

"We're just talking, Mom," Raegan sasses back. "No one's getting pregnant."

Mom storms over to us, yanking the covers off us. I'm dressed in sleep pants and a shirt, but Ryder wears nothing but a pair of tight black boxers that do nothing to hide his morning wood. Raegan doesn't look much better with her shirt showing off her naked thighs. It definitely looks a lot worse than it really is.

"Get out of this bed, young lady," Mom hisses. "You of all people should know better. Have you seen your sister after what they did to her?"

Wait.

Is Mom insinuating we'd rape Raegan like Logan did to me and what I assume Jace did to Destiny?

Unbelievable.

Raegan hops out of bed, face turning bright red with anger. "You're insane, *Mother*. We're doing nothing wrong!"

Mom grips her shoulders and physically moves her to the door. "Out. Go check on your baby brother."

Raegan makes a frustrated sound before stomping out of the cabin. Ryder sits up, hands in the air as he speaks to Mom, his voice shaking, "Mom, we weren't doing anything—"

"Yet. Not yet, but keep this up and something bad will happen."

Unable to take it any longer, I let my fury fuel me. I scramble past Ryder and off the bed, body shaking with indignation. "Really, Mom?" My words are sharp like a blade. "After all the shit we've been through and you're worried about that?"

"I'm trying to protect my daughter—"

"From us?" I snap, face souring at the insinuation. "Raegan can handle herself from our rapey ways."

She deflates at my words. "You know I didn't mean it that way, Ronan. I'm sorry, but I just worry…"

"No, you're thinking the worst and being judgmental when we just need you to be understanding." I cross my arms over my chest and glower at her. "No one judges you and Dad."

Ryder makes a choked sound and Mom gapes at me. I don't back down.

"What?" Mom hisses.

"He's your dad, right? Wild told us the truth."

Her eyes grow wider than I've ever seen them before. Owlish. Young. Horrified. But I see the truth gleaming in them. "Ronan, that's enough."

"I think I can speak for Raegan and Ryder," I clip out. "Your worries are unwarranted, way off base, and, frankly, ill-timed. We're tired of your bullshit."

"Ronan!" Ryder and Mom both cry out at once.

"Whatever," I grumble. "Be mad at me for being the one to state the truth. I don't fucking care anymore." I wave a finger at Mom. "But do not accuse me or Ryder of taking advantage of Raegan. It's insulting as fuck, especially after the hell we just endured."

With those words, I storm out of the cabin.

Tears burn at my eyes as I run barefoot toward the

orchard where I can have a moment to breathe and calm down. I'm sick to my stomach. Not once have I ever disrespected my mother as I did just now. Dad will be furious.

Logan fucked up my life and I'm not sure I'll ever get it back to the way it used to be.

CHAPTER TWENTY-SIX

ryder

OUR FAMILY IS BROKEN.

I didn't know it when I set off on my journey to find my siblings, but I certainly know it now. Mom is paranoid, Dad is physically barely holding on, Destiny is a shell of the person she once was. And Ronan?

He's not well. I can't pinpoint exactly what's wrong with him, but it's there. Always brewing and simmering just below the surface. Fear flickers in his eyes when no one's looking, but anger lives there too. I still can't believe he blew up on Mom a few days ago. Everything has been so tense since then.

With each passing day, I feel Ronan slipping from my grasp. He's withdrawing to a place I don't know how to get to. Every attempt to make him smile feels like a wasted effort. All he does is sleep, sit in the orchard alone, or vacillate between scowling and fearfully jumping at every shadow.

At night, his nightmares take over.

Logan, though most likely dead, continues to torment my poor brother from deep inside his mind. He must've tortured him or beat him to the point of insanity because Ronan is just not the same.

So, yeah, our family is broken, and Ronan's the sharpest, most jagged piece.

Every time I find myself accidentally pressed against him in the middle of the night, I wake to an elbow to my face or punches to any available body part. For someone who, weeks ago, was desperate for my touch, he's now easily agitated if I do it while he sleeps.

What did Logan do?

Disgusting images tease at my mind, but I refuse to think about them. If something that bad happened, Ronan will tell me when he's ready. All I can do is protect him the best I can and respect his boundaries.

Raegan doesn't come over early in the morning anymore in case Mom wakes up and catches her. But she does slip out for an hour or two in the middle of the night. We can whisper, just the two of us, and cuddle.

Cuddling with her feels good. And *safe*. We haven't kissed anymore or touched like when we spent the night in the tent after her rescue. I've jerked off every day in the shower, though, at the memory. Jerking off is *safe*. Kissing and touching under the clothes is not.

My mind drifts to the day we made it back home and I can't help but smile. I'd stolen a moment alone with Raegan to give her something I knew she desperately wanted.

"I got you a present," I say to Raegan, motioning for my backpack that sits on the floor in my cabin. "Ready?"

She grins, eyes sparkling with delight. "What is it?"

I unzip the bag and before I can pull it out, she reaches her hand inside, too impatient to wait. When she pulls out her ponytail, she scrunches her nose and gapes at me.

"Creeper, why do you have my hair? That's not a gift! That's a weird shrine of me you're carrying around!"

I snatch the bound hair away from her and toss it back in the bag, mock scowling at her. "That's not your present. It's mine. Close your eyes."

She narrows them at me. "I don't know if I should trust you. What's next? A bag of my toenails?"

"Close. Your. Eyes." Finally, she obeys me. I pull out the knife Rowdy retrieved from Jace and set it in her waiting palms. "Now you can open them."

Her ecstatic shriek pierces my ears. She beams, overly thrilled with getting the knife back, and then practically tackles me with a bear hug.

When she pulls back, still smiling, she asks, "Are we going to talk about the hair?"

"Nope."

Having Raegan and Ronan in my life is everything to me.

I have to keep our shattered family together. It's more important than ever with Ronan so messed up. We've all gone through enough without throwing these complicated feelings that have to be hidden on top of everything.

Maybe we can all go back to the way we used to be. Raegan annoying me but providing entertainment. Ronan being my confidant and steady presence. *Safe.*

The door to the cabin silently creaks open. I can tell it's Raegan by the sound of her footsteps. She moves lightly but with purpose. Seconds after the door closes, she slips into the bed next to me. Her skin is cool from the quick run over here and I splay my hand over her bare thigh to try to warm her up.

"Ronan?" Raegan whispers.

His heavy breathing continues, undisturbed. It has both of us relaxing. Not that he can't be a part of our middle of the night conversations, but because he's finally resting, not trapped in the throes of another nightmare.

Raegan curls her body against mine, her thigh resting on mine. My arm is wrapped around her and I hug her closer. Her soft touch as she runs her fingers down the rivets between my abs has me suppressing a shiver.

I like the way her hands feel on me.

And when I'm in the shower, I imagine them going lower.

My dick twitches at the thought, but I quickly push that line of thinking away. I run my fingers up and down her arm, noticing the goose bumps there.

"Cold?" I murmur, kissing her head.

"A little."

Her fingers dance lower, playing with the hair around my belly button. I grit my teeth to keep from groaning in pleasure. It'd be wise to move her hand back up my chest, but I've been aching for her touch even though it's not just the wrong time to allow it, but just plain wrong in general.

She's. My. Sister.

"Ryder?"

"Mmm."

"I'm worried about Ro."

"Me too, baby." I wince at my word choice. "Me too."

Her lips press to my pectoral and then her tongue peeks out, teasing a wet trail over my skin. My dick, which I'd barely been keeping in check, thickens and strains against my boxers. Hopefully, she doesn't notice.

Of course Raegan misses nothing.

She dances her fingers through my happy trail before boldly running her palm over my erection through my boxers. A grunt escapes me as my cock jolts at her touch.

"You're hard," she breathes, her words hot as they tickle over my chest. "Really hard."

Heat floods through me and it takes everything in

me not to thrust up against her palm. I want her to curl her fist around my dick, fucking it hard. As soon as that thought enters my mind, I shove it away.

"Rae," I croak out. "We can't do this. Not now. Not ever."

Especially not now.

What would Ronan do if he were to wake and witness what we are doing?

"You always say the most wounding things when I'm being sweet to you," Raegan whispers, hurt in her tone. "Why can't you just let me touch you like we both want? I bet it'll be quick. Like twenty seconds tops."

I choke on a groan when her hand slides under the material, boldly taking hold of my cock. It feels too good to have her stop. Having her hand on me like this is everything I'd ever fantasized about. I throw my head back, unable to control the need coursing through me.

"It'll feel better if it's wet," she whispers. "Trust me."

I don't have a chance to process her words before she's moving down my body. She pulls my boxers down enough to free my dick and then her tongue is on me.

Her. Fucking. Tongue.

I nearly nut just then, overwhelmed with pleasure. I'm barely able to stifle a moan as her lips wrap around the head. Her mouth—her perfect fucking mouth—is hot and wet, sliding easily over my tip. I hiss, unable to keep the sound from escaping when her tongue runs down my shaft.

Up and down.

Up and down.

Holy fuck.

Once I'm slick with her saliva, she moves back up my body, settling at my side again. Her palm slowly tugs at my aching cock, slicking over the wet flesh.

It's too much.

I'm going to die.

Within seconds, just as she predicted, my cum shoots out of me without warning. It splatters all over my chest and her hand. She keeps stroking, only slowing when the twitching and spasming of my dick finally settle.

"Rae, baby," I rasp out. "That was…"

"Good?"

"Fucking amazing." I kiss her head, savoring this stolen moment. It only takes a few minutes until the guilt is back.

"It's fine, Ryder. I can feel you tensing, but it's fine."

I'm soaked in my own cum that my sister so expertly jerked out of me while my brother slept right beside me.

Nothing is fine.

"We have to clean up and you need to go back next door." I nuzzle my nose against her hair. "Please. I just… it's too hard to think straight after what we did."

She sighs heavily. "I'll go, but I'm not sorry for making you feel good."

Reaching for her, I settle my hand around the back of her neck, urging her to my mouth. I plan to give her a soft, appreciative peck on her lips, but instead end up devouring her sweet mouth.

We're both panting by the time we come up for air.

"Leave, baby, please."

This time, she doesn't sigh. She kisses me again and then she's gone.

I am so fucked.

Ronan sits at the firepit, glaring at the flames. It's chilly out tonight and he's not wearing a jacket. I saunter past where Wild and Chet are each trying to outdo the other with outlandish stories about their classmates while Sadie giggles uncontrollably. Kristen listens, a smile on her face, but doesn't join in on the laughter. Raegan, after a lot of coaxing, is finally letting Aunt Eve fix her hair from where Mya botched it. It's the perfect time to try and talk to Ronan while everyone is distracted.

"Hey," I say, settling right next to him on the bench. "You cold?"

He shrugs. "Not really."

I sit quietly, waiting to see if he'll say anything. He doesn't. Ronan silently broods, his gaze never leaving the fire. It's like he's building a fortress around him and I don't get to have a key. This isn't the Ronan I know. This guy likes being alone.

Rather than force him to talk, I sit with him without saying anything. My mind keeps drifting to the night before when Raegan gave me a handjob. I've never come so fast in my life. Despite it feeling really, really good, I can't help but obsess over the fact we did it with Ronan right next to me. He'd been blissfully unaware and the guilt of what we did keeps eating at me.

I should tell him.

He had sex with her, though under forced and unusual conditions, but it still happened. I'd been hurt when I found out. I made peace with it, though. Maybe he'll get mad and then get over it like I did. Telling him is better than carrying around this big secret when I already feel like the distance between us is stretching.

"So, I, uh," I murmur, darting my gaze over to Wild, Chet, Sadie, and Kristen from across the fire. "Can we talk?"

Ronan cuts his eyes over to me briefly. "Isn't that what we're doing?"

There's a bitterness to his tone. A warning to back off. Still, I push through because he's my brother and we don't back away when the other bares his teeth.

Don't be a pussy, man.

I suck in a sharp breath and then quickly exhale. "Something happened."

"Something happened," Ronan repeats. "Great talk."

Rolling my eyes, I nudge his shoulder and earn a small smile from him. It's not much, but it's more than I've seen in days. I'll take it.

"So, yeah, Raegan got me off." A laugh barks out of me. "Fuck, did I say that too loud?"

The group across the fire continue to cut up, unaware of our serious conversation.

"What?"

"Last night, she came over and—"

"With me in the bed?" His voice is rising and turning shrill. "What the hell is wrong with you?"

Ronan jumps to his feet and starts striding away. I snag his bicep before he can get too far. He snaps his head back to affix me with a murderous glare.

Is he pissed?

"Let go of me," he commands, attempting to pull from my hold.

Clutching tighter, I shake my head. "Come on, Ro, don't run away. Can we talk about this?"

He shrugs me off. Instead of running off, he steps closer to me, face contorting into one of rage. "No. You can fuck right off."

"Ronan, please—"

My words are cut off the second his fist slams into my face. I'm so stunned, I fall back, landing hard on my ass.

"What the actual fuck, dude," Wild exclaims. "You just punched your brother."

"Leave me the hell alone," Ronan barks out, storming off toward the cabin.

"Someone pissed in his Cheerios," Chet grumbles. "For fuck's sake."

"Ronan, wait up." Kristen follows after him, further irritating me for some reason.

Ignoring them all, I rise to my feet and stalk down the path toward the gate. Mage, the traitor, doesn't follow me. He's been too busy sneaking treats from Dad and spending all his time with them.

Right now, I'm feeling really fucking alone.

There's only one person who can help.

I nearly crash into said person as she enters through the gate. Raegan squeaks in surprise and her hair bounces from the movement. Taking hold of her hand, I tug her into the shadows behind the equipment barn. Reaching up, I finger her short, styled hair. In the moonlight, I can tell it's pretty and chic like the women in the magazines. Very womanly.

"Wow," I murmur. "This looks…you look…"

She frowns, misunderstanding and already on the defensive. "There wasn't much hair left to work with. No need to be a dick."

"No," I growl, fingers sliding into her hair. "It's beautiful. You're fucking gorgeous."

A smile tugs at her lips. "Oh. Well, start with that next time." Her smile fades the longer she studies me. "What's wrong? You're upset. Did something happen?"

Closing my eyes, I nod and lean my forehead against hers. "I told Ronan about last night."

"Ahh." She cups my cheek and tilts her head up until her breath tickles over my lips. "How did that go?"

"He punched me." I reopen my eyes to see her peering up at me in concern. "He was so angry. I think I really hurt him."

Her other hand finds my sore jaw and she tenderly touches me there despite my flinch. "Let him cool off and then we can talk to him together. It'll be okay, Ry. I promise."

Needing to taste her promise, I lean forward, capturing her lips with mine. The kiss is soft at first. Then my tongue eagerly lashes against hers. Tasting her and breathing her in is all I care about, hidden in the shadows behind the barn. I want her to kiss away all the hurt Ronan left me with.

"Ryder," she murmurs, need making her voice raspy.

I love the way my name sounds on her lips. I nip and suck it off her mouth, tasting every syllable. I crave to devour it in one gulp but yearn to also savor every drop.

My hands find her ass and I easily lift her small frame. Her legs wrap around my waist while her fingers clutch onto my neck. Turning, I pin her against the barn, thrusting my tongue into her mouth once more. The small, needy moans she's making have my dick hard as steel. Pressing against her, I grind against her pussy, loving that I can feel the heat of it through my clothes.

I could yank her jeans down and fuck her right now.

God, that's tempting.

All the reasons this is a bad idea niggle at my mind, but I'm too distracted by her mouth, her roaming fingers, her pussy. Reaching down between us, while holding her up with one hand, I fumble with the button of her jeans. She writhes in my grip, rolling her hips toward me, urging me to take what I need. I manage to tug the zipper down far enough to gain me the access required to bring her pleasure.

"Oh," she whispers as my hand pushes past her underwear, seeking the soft, wet parts of her I ache to touch. "Yessss."

I grin against her lips as my finger rubs over her clit. She arches, her whole body shuddering with just one stroke. Nipping at her bottom lip, I tease over her throbbing clit again, marveling over how hot it is to the touch. We both groan with pleasure when my finger slides inside her slick body.

Fuck, she's so tight.

I can almost imagine my dick being sucked into her heat. She's right. It wouldn't take but ten seconds inside of her before I came.

"Raegan?"

The sound of Mom's voice incredibly close has us both freezing. I slip my hand out of her panties and set her on her feet. She fumbles to quickly buckle her jeans.

I press a quick kiss to her swollen lips and then gesture in the other direction. "Go that way. I'll deal with Mom."

She gives me a nod, steals one more kiss, and then disappears. I palm my dick through my jeans, trying to calm it, and take a breath before striding over to where I can hear Mom calling for my sister.

"Boo," I tease, jumping from the shadows.

Mom smacks me in the shoulder. "Don't do that! You scared the shit out of me."

"Sorry." I grin, hoping like hell she can't see the guilt written all over my features. "What's up?"

She studies me for a beat before casting her eyes toward the gate. "You seen Raegan?"

"She was getting her hair cut. Maybe she's still in the RV with Aunt Eve."

Mom relaxes and nods. "I'll go check there. If you see her, tell her I'm looking for her. Declan is having a bit of a tantrum and wants to see her."

"Yeah, of course."

She starts to go in for a hug and I maneuver my body, offering a side hug instead. There's no way in hell my mother needs to know about the raging boner my sister just gave me.

As soon as she's gone, I let out a sharp, relieved breath. That was close. Too fucking close for comfort.

I need to be careful.

If Mom had stumbled in on me with my hand down Raegan's pants, there's no telling what she would have done.

Thoughts of Dad chasing me with a shotgun take over.

Fuck.

We can't do that shit ever again. I'm not looking to die.

CHAPTER TWENTY-SEVEN

raegan

EVER SINCE LAST NIGHT, WHEN THINGS GOT HOT and heavy behind the barn, Ryder has been avoiding me. He even slept with the door blocked to his cabin, which meant when I attempted to sneak in when everyone was asleep, I couldn't. Now, he's gone with Wild, Chet, and Sadie to the river.

I want to throttle him.

To demand to know why he keeps giving me mixed signals.

It's frustrating.

Mostly, I want to punch him for making me feel alone. Dad was able to get out of bed and sit by the fire this evening, which should have been something to celebrate, but I could barely contain the hurt of how Ryder has made me feel.

"Do we think any of the survivors will try and return?" Dad asks Uncle Atticus, wincing slightly in pain.

Uncle Atticus shrugs. "From what Rowdy told me,

there's only a handful of them left. Mostly kids. A guy named Tom and a woman who was married to one of the men Rowdy killed."

"And Logan?" Dad grits his teeth, scanning the area for Ronan and relaxing when he doesn't see him. "Is there a chance he could come back?"

I sit away from the fire, listening but not joining in on the conversation. Mom and Aunt Eve are busy with the kids, keeping them corralled and out of trouble. Destiny sits between Rowdy and Mom, head down and fixated on her lap. Kristen, an outsider to our group, does her best to fit in with Mom and Aunt Eve, though I can tell it's forced. I'm anxious to know what Uncle Atticus thinks about Logan.

"Ryder says Ronan shot him. Saw the blood trail." Uncle Atticus grunts. "He could still be out there. But, so far from his people, injured, and lost in the wilderness, the likelihood of him coming back is slim to none."

"But there's still a chance." Dad rubs at a spot on the center of his chest, frowning. "We can never be too careful."

I'd been satisfied by Ryder's statement that Logan was most likely dead. Now, I'm not so sure it makes me feel safe. Without seeing his bloody corpse, there really is no way to know. In reality, Logan is probably rotting not far from his dad. The critters are picking over his bones as we speak. Still, I don't feel at ease.

I glance over my shoulder toward the gate. It'll be dark soon. Ryder and the rest better come home before night falls. I may be mad at him, but thoughts of Logan lurking around have me spooked.

Dad and Uncle Atticus change topics, brainstorming about the next supply run, plans to rebuild the big house, and other boring stuff. I take my leave, slipping away from the group around the firepit before anyone can ask where I'm going.

I find Ronan in Ryder's cabin, sleeping on his side in the bed with his back to the wall. He's been sleeping a lot lately, which is worrying. I wish he'd talk to me. It's like the moment we were freed from our hellish prison, I lost Ronan to himself.

Closing the door behind me, I kick off my shoes and then slide into bed next to him. The bed smells heavily like Ryder. I inhale his scent as I scoot closer to Ronan. His glasses are on the bedside table. Without them, it reminds me of when we were in captivity. My heart aches for him. He went through so much abuse from Logan.

Gently, I run my finger along his jaw, studying his relaxed features. The bruises Logan gave him are beginning to fade. I wonder if the big one on his heart will be there forever. Leaning forward, I kiss his parted lips, hoping to give him comfort.

His eyes open, panic flashing briefly in them. It takes a second for him to realize it's just me and relax. I shiver when his arm wraps around me. Cuddling closer, I breathe in his familiar scent, letting it fill my lungs with the presence of him.

"Hi, sleepyhead," I say, grinning at him.

"Hi." He doesn't return my smile. "Where's Ryder?"

I bristle at his irritated tone. "Avoiding us."

"I figure he'd avoid me," Ronan grunts, "but assumed he'd want to spend every second with you. You know, since you got him off and I punched him for it."

Lifting a brow at him, I smirk. "You almost sound jealous."

The corner of his lips twitches like he might smile. "I don't know what I am, to be honest. Confused. Pissed. And, yeah, jealous, I guess." He pauses, looking away and scowling. "Maybe I feel betrayed."

I sit up on my elbow and frown at him. "Really? You and I had sex. Like you came inside of me, Ronan, and you're mad at Ryder for getting a handjob?"

His cheeks redden and he bites on his bottom lip. "I told you. I'm confused."

"Well, that makes three of us," I say with a huff. "Ryder is avoiding me now. He seems on board with doing stuff and then something will happen for him to completely retreat. Boys are complicated."

Ronan smiles for real this time. "So are girls. I'm gay but slept with you. It felt good and I'm not sure what to do about that."

We're quiet for a bit, both of us lost in our own heads. His hand finds my hip, stroking me gently there. I let out a contented sigh as I relax, resting my head on his arm.

"I'm sorry if I hurt you," I murmur. "I have all these emotions and feelings around both you and Ryder. It's like I can't control them. All I know is it makes me happy being with you. Ryder also makes me happy. It breaks my heart knowing you feel betrayed by us. It's not all Ryder's fault. You should punch me too."

He scoffs, shaking his head. "I'm not punching you. For the record, I feel like a complete ass for hitting Ryder. He didn't deserve it. My mind is a mess and I took it out on him."

"He might've deserved it a teeny bit," I tease, holding up my finger and thumb to show him how much. "The jerk's been avoiding me all day. If he doesn't cut it out, I'll give you permission to do it again."

We both smile, the tension between us finally fading.

"Do you want to talk about it?" I ask, growing serious. "About what has your mind so messy?"

A storm brews in his eyes and he shakes his head. "You already know. We were kidnapped, hurt, and had to murder our way away from those people. That would fuck anyone up."

Some of us, though, are more fucked-up than others.

Kristen, Ronan, and Destiny all seem to be haunted by the same demons. I shiver at the thought of what they must've endured. If only Ronan would tell me what happened. Then, maybe, I could help him feel better.

"I just," Ronan starts, voice hoarse, "I just sometimes feel really fucking alone."

My heart bleeds at his words. Leaning closer, I kiss

his mouth softly. "You're not alone. You have me. And Ryder when he's not being a dick. We love you and won't ever leave you."

His gaze softens as he studies me. Then his eyes close as he kisses me back, this time, shockingly with tongue. Heat floods through me, settling in my core.

"You saved me," I murmur against his lips. "Having sex with you was everything to me."

He rolls until his body presses mine into the mattress. Pulling from our needy kiss, he stares at me and smiles. "It was everything to me too. Not exactly the way I'd imagined sex, but still good because it was you."

His words have pleasure ringing through me.

"Maybe you would feel better if you could do it again," I breathe, wriggling under his much larger body. "Without fear and able to use your hands." My fingers thread through his hair. "You wouldn't feel so alone. I could help you like you helped me."

"I'm not sure I could get hard again," he says, cheeks flaming crimson. "As much as I want to."

I slip my legs out from under him, wrapping them around his waist. "You haven't even tried."

His lips find mine again, but this time he thrusts against me. I can feel his cock as it fills with blood, turning hard against me. Digging my feet into his ass and lifting my hips, I urge him to continue. He begins frantically moving his hips, grinding into me as he devours my mouth.

I want his hands all over me.

I need him inside of me again.

Last time stung and wasn't exactly as pleasurable as having Ryder's fingers inside me, but we were at a disadvantage then. Now, just the two of us, unbound and alone, we can have the freedom to explore. The chance to bring each other actual pleasure.

"Take off my jeans," I murmur, meeting his fiery stare. "Please."

He pulls back and then sets to unbuttoning them. The eager way with which he tugs at my jeans has fire burning through my veins. I help him by kicking out of them and then allow him to settle back between my legs. With just our underwear separating us, the sensations are much more heightened.

"This feels good," I breathe, tugging at his hair. "Does it feel good for you even though I'm a girl?"

He grunts, rubbing up against me. "It feels good because you're you. My best friend. My favorite sister."

His mouth finds my neck and he suckles on my flesh while he ruts against me. It drives me wild with need. I ache to fully have him again. This time will be different—better.

"Take off your shirt," I plead. "I want to touch you."

With an exasperated groan, he sits up long enough to rip away the offending fabric and then loses himself to another kiss. I greedily touch his muscular shoulders and biceps.

"I want my shirt off too," I complain. "I want to feel you."

He tears from my kiss, jerking his head to the door. "What if Mom comes in?"

"She won't," I promise. "She's knee-deep in annoying kids right now. It's just us. No one is coming."

With a grunt, he stops long enough to start yanking at my shirt. Once it's gone, I unhook my bra and he finishes tearing it away. He looks down at my naked breasts and frowns. I don't like the way he studies them like they're something foreign and strange. I want him to admire them and touch them and taste them. Ryder likes them.

Giving his head a sharp shake, he looks away from them, turning his attention to his cock. I try to hide the disappointment. He rubs his hand against his dick as though to make it hard again.

Do I disgust him?

Emotion prickles at my eyes. I'm about to stop because he's clearly no longer enjoying it, when his knuckle rubs over my clit through my underwear. I shiver at his touch.

He remains focused between us as he tugs his boxers down. His cock bounces out, lightly smacking against my pussy. The tip leaks with his cum and dots my underwear.

"Ronan," I choke out, forcing his gaze back to me. "I want you."

He gives me a clipped nod and then pulls my underwear aside with his finger. With his other hand, he grips his cock and teases my slick slit.

"Do we need to get it wet?" I ask, a hint of doubt creeping up inside me.

His hips give a small thrust and his crown disappears inside me. "You're wet, Rae. This turns you on."

That's no lie.

I just wish he'd touch my breasts. Lick them or bite them or grab them. Something.

A groan rasps past his lips as he eases into my body. He feels so huge, stretching me to my limit. Though it still burns like last time, it does feel much better. Especially when his hand curls around my neck and he dips for another kiss. The grip on my throat is gentle but claiming. I'm at his mercy now.

"You're right," he rumbles against my mouth. "I don't feel alone right now. I feel really fucking good because of you. Thank you." A manly moan of pleasure. "Oh, God, Rae…"

And then his words are lost to his animalistic, wild thrusting.

CHAPTER TWENTY-EIGHT

ronan

Fuck, she feels good.

It's just what I needed to forget.

And yet, even as I fuck my little sister, my mind drifts to Logan. The last time we did this, he came into the tent after and raped me.

My cock flags and I panic. If I can't stay hard, she'll think something's wrong with her when there's nothing wrong with her. Raegan is perfect. I love her with my entire goddamn soul.

Think of him.

Not Logan…him.

What if this were Ryder beneath me? Would he even allow me to be inside of his body like Raegan does? Would his asshole be tight like her pussy? Tighter?

I close my eyes, desperately kissing my sister but greedily thinking of my brother. As I thrust, taking her deep, I imagine Ryder's legs spread apart.

Oh fuck, that's hot.

Guilt slams into me almost immediately after that mental image. I'm here with Rae and I'm thinking of our brother's ass. I'm not here with him. I'm with her. It's *her* teeth nipping at my lips, *her* fingernails raking down my arms, *her* heels biting into my ass.

She's so much wetter than the last time we had sex. I like how easily I can slide in and out of her. I also love that I have control now. I'm not bound and unable to move. Gripping her jaw, I hold it tight, ravishing her mouth with mine.

What if Ryder were watching?

That's not mean to think about him watching while I have sex with Raegan, right?

Would he be turned on? Would he join? Would he sit close, stroking his own cock?

Holy shit, that's hot.

Raegan makes tiny squeaks like she might be enjoying this, but I'm not sure. I don't know much about girls and what they like. I've been obsessed with men for as long as I can remember. Since I'm a man, I know what I like. But, since she has different equipment, I'm not exactly sure what would make her feel really good.

Her hand slides between us and she touches her pussy. I'm fascinated, watching as she circles one particular area between the lips over and over again. She jolts and whines, her tits jiggling with her movement. When her pussy clenches around my cock and she shudders, I lose control.

Cum spurts out of me thick and endless. Every time

her pussy spasms around my dick, it seems to milk more out of me. It feels so fucking good I can't stand it. I'm unable to keep from slowly thrusting, marveling at how every nerve ending in my body is buzzing and alive.

And Raegan?

Her cheeks are flushed and she wears an expression of pure lust.

She's so beautiful.

My dick finally quits twitching, but I don't hurry out of her. I'm content to stare at her, still seated deep inside of her.

Creak.

Fear claims me as it always does when the door to the cabin opens. At first, it's fear of Logan. Then, it quickly swaps to fear of Dad. But all fear is erased when I see Ryder instead.

The door closes behind him with a soft click as he gapes at us. He rubs at his face as though to clear his head and then anger twists his features into something far from handsome.

"What the actual fuck?" Ryder snarls, shaking his head vehemently. "What the fuckity fuck?"

The fear is back. This time it involves losing my brother—my best friend. I pull out of my sister, wincing when cum slings over her belly. Ryder watches it with horrified rapt attention. Raegan is babbling. I think she's pleading with him. I don't know. I can't hear anything over the ringing in my ears.

I sit back on my knees so I can tug my boxers up

over my messy dick. As soon as I'm covered, I grab Raegan's jeans and toss them at her to cover her nakedness. Scrambling out of the bed, I start toward Ryder.

"Hey," I start, voice rough and tight. "It's not—"

He takes a step back, holding a palm up. "No. Just… no."

Frustrated, I run my fingers through my hair and shoot him a panicked look. "Ryder."

"Don't Ryder me," he snaps, glowering at me with the same betrayal I'd tried to explain to Raegan earlier. "You punched me for letting her touch me and…and…" He laughs, dark and full of disbelief. "You fucking hypocritical asshole."

I reach for him and he smacks my hand away. "Do not touch me, Ronan. Ever."

My heart shatters in my chest. "You don't mean that."

"You clearly have your hands full. I fucking mean it."

Raegan, finally dressed, rushes over to us. "Listen, Ry—"

"No." His voice becomes deceptively calm. "You two need to listen to me." He waggles a finger between the two of us, glowering at my wet boxers, and growls. "It can't happen ever again. Our family will be ripped apart. You two are dumbasses. What if I were Dad?"

A cold chill settles in my bones.

"Put some fucking clothes on, Ronan," Ryder snaps. "And pretend this shit never happened."

"It wasn't Dad," I mutter. "It was you. Can we please talk about this?"

"Talk?" Ryder chokes out. "I've been trying to get you to talk about the shit you went through, but you've cut yourself off from the rest of us." He flashes a cruel smile. "Well, apparently not *all* of us."

Turning, he starts for the door. I leap forward, grabbing at his jacket to prevent him from leaving. He looks over his shoulder at me, hurt shining bright in his eyes.

"If Dad ever finds out, you'll be lucky if all he does is send you away," Ryder whispers. "But more likely, after what happened with those people, he might put a bullet in your fucking head. I can't deal with you two."

With those words, he storms out of the cabin. My heart thunders in my chest, making me lightheaded and dizzy. I ache to go after him but don't want to fight about it either.

He's right.

If our parents knew, they'd banish me. I'm already at my wits' end feeling alone, but sending me away would be the final nail in my coffin.

Raegan rushes over to me and throws her arms around me. I stand frozen like a tall pine, unsure what to do or what to say. She rubs her arms up and down over my bare back in an attempt to comfort me, but it doesn't work.

"He's right," I choke out. "We can't."

She pulls back and shakes her head. "He's just mad. He'll come around. You'll see. We can be more careful."

Grabbing her shoulders, I push her away from me. "No, Rae. We can't. You're my sister, for fuck's sake. I'm gay. None of this makes any goddamn sense."

Her lip wobbles wildly before she bursts into tears. She smacks me with her fist against my chest. "It makes sense to me, you prick."

Even though my heart is yelling at me to pull her to me, to soothe away the pain I've caused, I can't. I'm unable to comfort her or make her feel better in any way.

"I'm destroying our family," I rasp out, hating how the tears well in my eyes. "I started this, which means I can fix this."

She sniffles and crosses her arms over her chest. "By shutting me out?"

Yes.

"We just need space. I'm sorry."

Her middle finger whips out, inches from my nose. "Fuck. You. I hate you, Ronan. I hate you so damn much right now."

I don't get to reply, not that I even have the words to, because she's already out the door. Alone, in nothing but my cum-soaked underwear, I stand, shaking uncontrollably.

What have I done?

I didn't fix it.

I made it worse.

My chest feels hollow. Like my heart cracked down the middle. Ryder took off with one half to probably throw in the river. Raegan took off with the other, no doubt stomping it with her boot. The two people I love and adore the most in this world are the ones I've hurt the most.

I'm an asshole.

I wake later to the smell of venison. Sitting up, I find Kristen sitting on the bed with a plate of food in her lap, frowning down at me.

"You're sleeping again?" she asks, eyes narrowing.

Groaning, I take the plate she's clearly brought for me and start eating, hoping to get away with not answering.

"I'm worried," she says with a sigh. "Logan really messed you up."

Bile creeps up my throat and my stomach turns at the thought of eating the food she's brought to me. Something about his name just makes me sick.

"Let's not," I grunt.

"What? Talk about that psycho rapist?"

I shoot her a warning glare. "They don't know all the shit he's done. I'd rather keep it that way."

"Oh, Ronan. You have a family who loves you. They, of all people, are the ones you talk to." She sniffles and looks away. "When Atticus goes back to town, I'm going with him."

I tense at her words. "What? Why?"

"Because I don't belong here. I didn't choose this

life like your family did. My family is still out there in civilization." Her voice cracks and she trembles. "My mom probably thinks I'm dead."

All this time, I never considered Kristen was missing the family she left behind. I feel like an even bigger asshole than before.

"I think going back to town is a good idea then," I agree with a small smile. "You seen Raegan or Ryder?"

She sits up straight and studies my face for a beat. "Raegan's been in a bitchy mood. She and your mom sort of got into it at dinner, hence why I'm here with you rather than out there."

Guilt strangles me.

This is all my fault.

"And Ryder?"

"He said he was going hunting. Took his dog and bailed. Your dad seemed worried about him but let him go." Her head tilts to the side. "Why? Did you two have a fight?"

I'm not exactly eager to admit that they're both pissed at me because I'm selfish and closed off. That I'm a confusing jumble of mixed messages and contradicting statements.

"A little bit," I admit. "Nothing we can't get over."

That's a lie.

I've fractured this family in ways that'll never be repaired.

"You need to eat and leave this cabin," Kristen says finally. "All this sleeping isn't good for you. I know your parents are worried and they're trying to give you space, but I don't think it's doing you any good."

I need all the space.

Just me and my deserved loneliness.

"Maybe tomorrow I'll feel better." I give her a one-shoulder shrug. "How are you doing? I've been a dick and should've checked on you days ago."

"I feel good. Happy." A smile tugs at her lips. "I'm looking forward to stupid things again like driving a car, going to the movies, chatting with my mom while she makes dinner. I still can't believe I'm going home."

"I'm happy for you," I say, squeezing her knee over her jeans. "You deserve to be happy."

She sits up and leans over to kiss my forehead. "So do you, Ronan. It'll be hard, but you're going to have to move past Logan's abuse. Otherwise, he'll keep you trapped in his prison of the past. He'll win. Don't let that bastard win."

"I'll try."

"That's all we can do. A little each day."

She leaves me to my thoughts and quickly cooling dinner. I don't want Logan to keep me in his wicked clutches. I'm free of him physically and I'd give anything to be free of him mentally.

I'll try.

That's all we can do. A little each day.

Easier said than done.

CHAPTER TWENTY-NINE

ryder

APPALLED. FURIOUS. SO FUCKING HURT.

My feelings are all over the place. I can't decide if I want to punch someone or curl into a ball to cry my eyes out. All of this is so damn unfair.

Why did I have to start having feelings for Raegan in the first place?

It was much better when she hated me—when we had typical sibling rivalry. My stupid dick got hard and changed everything.

And Ronan?

There was never supposed to be any of that sort of feelings for him. He's a guy. I don't even like guys. But he still managed to get inside my head and confuse my horny dick.

Dad is right.

I need to go.

I need to pack up and leave this place. The

temptation is too great and the consequences are too dire. I'm not strong enough to quit them.

Apparently, they're not strong enough to quit each other either.

I've been trying so hard to be the responsible one around here. To remind us of what could happen if we go down that slippery slope. Raegan is reckless and female, so she doesn't see it like I do. We're supposed to protect our sisters, not fuck them. Ronan knows better, but after Logan fucked with his head, he's not been the same. All his soft, tender ways have hardened. He's doing shit that's way out of character for him and, quite frankly, it's freaking me out.

I'm so stressed out.

Humiliated. Disturbed. Turned on.

Seeing Ronan with his dick buried in our sister did crazy things to me. My own dick immediately hardened at the sight. Her gorgeous tits looked so damn bitable. I'd wanted to step closer to touch them—to witness their forbidden act with my own two eyes.

The humiliation took over and quickly turned to anger.

How dare Ronan treat me like I was horrible for letting Raegan get me off? And Raegan knew how upset I was that she slept with Ronan while in captivity. She'd claimed it was a bullshit gift to save her virginity from those monsters.

It was all a lie.

They clearly couldn't keep their hands off each other

once they were safe, choosing to fuck when our parents or anyone could have burst in to see.

I saw.

They're lucky it was me.

My mind keeps spinning round and round and round. I don't know what to do with myself or how to deal with this horrendous heartache that's gutting me.

Mage whines, nudging the side of my leg. I reach down and scratch behind his ears. He's been up Dad's ass ever since he got hurt, but when I took off after catching Ronan and Raegan in the act, he somehow found me. We've been sitting on the other side of our property, leaned against the fence, sulking. I'm thankful for my wolf's presence.

"Want to go hunting?" I ask him. "It'd be good to clear our heads, huh?"

I'm an idiot talking to a damn dog.

At least the dog can't fuck me over.

He makes a huffing sound and trots toward the cliffside stairs. I follow after him. Mage races down the stairs, clumsily nearly taking a tumble. I chuckle and whistle for him to slow down. By the time I reach the bottom, I'm out of breath.

It's dark out, but the moonlight illuminates the path. Since I'm not about to go back to my cabin to retrieve my rifle, I decide taking one of Rowdy's at his place will do. It's not like he'll even be there. I'd seen him by the fire with Destiny, glued to her side as she goes through her own mental shit.

"I'm just going to have to avoid them until I leave for town," I tell Mage. "It's going to be too hard to look at them without my heart fucking breaking."

Mage stops walking ahead of me, cocking his head to the side. He's a smart little fella. Probably understands every damn word too.

"Maybe I'll go to school with Wild," I say, watching Mage turn and trot ahead. "He has sex all the time. Chet too. There's probably some nice girl there who's just waiting for me to show up."

Mage makes another huffing sound.

I try to imagine going to Wild's school. It's his last year there and then he'll go to college. It might be fun to meet new people and date.

Or it would be really fucking lonely.

Rowdy came back changed. Granted, it was because of one person—Wild's cousin Evan—but the risk of falling in with the wrong people is there. People, aside from our family and the Knoxes, have shown their true colors to me. Logan and his group were pure evil. Maybe all that exists out there are more people like them.

I shudder at that thought.

I don't want to leave my family. Not having Ronan or Raegan to joke around with or hunt with or swim with would feel so goddamn lonely.

The river rushing beside me on my walk to Rowdy's cabin is soothing. It serves as white noise, chasing away all the terrible thoughts fighting for the forefront in my mind. I'm able to turn it all off until I reach Rowdy's place.

Dad told me the story about how he and Mom lived here ages ago. I was born in this very cabin.

Though he told us that, he never did explain how he met our mother. What Wild told us makes sense—that Dad is Mom's father. Is that why we're all so fucked-up? Because we're products of incest?

Mom didn't admit it when Ronan called her out about it. She seemed shocked that he would suggest it. Maybe Wild got it wrong.

Or maybe he was right.

Maybe that's why we live out in the wilderness. Not because they're afraid of the bad people in the world, but because they wouldn't be accepted. Hell, they can't even accept the idea of me, Ronan, and Raegan lying in the same bed.

The double standard is maddening.

Our family is fucked-up.

"Here we are, Mage," I say as we approach the cabin. "Let's see what Rowdy has to eat first."

Mage happily waits by the gate for me to open it and then runs up onto Rowdy's porch, tail wagging. I let us inside and then turn on one of his lanterns. Unlike the big house and cabins up top, his house isn't set up with solar panels and lighting. It's far more rustic than my cabin. It's old too. He has to fetch water from the river and doesn't have water collection and filtration like we do. I don't know how he lives out here, always roughing it.

I find Rowdy's food storage in the crevice of the mountain that his cabin is built up against. It stays cool, so he keeps eggs and other stuff there. He has some pouches of venison jerky that I pull out to share with Mage. Once we've had our fill, I relax in a rocking chair Rowdy made with Dad.

It's peaceful here.

No asshole siblings fucking.

Grunting, I close my eyes, choosing to rest for a moment before me and Mage go on our hunt.

I fall asleep, the events of the day playing over and over in my head like a torturous, never-ending cycle.

"I almost shot you."

My eyes snap open to see Rowdy setting his .45 down on the table. Mage's tail thumps on the wood flooring, yipping happily at Spirit's presence. Some guard dog he is.

"Glad you didn't," I grumble, sitting up and stretching. "Sorry. Needed a place to lie low."

He pulls a bottle of alcohol from a cabinet. "You look like you could use a drink."

"Yeah, man." I catch the bottle he tosses at me. "Thanks."

I unscrew the bottle of tequila and take a hearty

swig, shuddering at the burn of it. Rowdy smirks before offering to take it away. Hugging it to me, I shake my head.

"I think it's going to take a lot more than one sip."

He chuckles. "One sip. Sure."

Shrugging, I take another one. This one warms my entire chest. It feels good.

"Want to talk about it?" Rowdy asks, settling on the floor beside the wolves. "I can tell something's eating you."

I scrub my palm over my face and sigh. "It's…hard to talk about."

"Like admitting what happened to me while in town with Evan? Yeah, I get that. I think you owe me your story since I gave you mine."

He has a point.

Question is, can I trust him?

"What if you hate me for it?"

His head cocks to the side, reminding me of Mage. "Unless you hurt someone I love, I don't see why I'd hate you."

"It's more like they hurt me." I frown before taking another long pull of the tequila. "So fucking badly."

"Spill it. I promise not to judge."

A heavy sigh rattles out of me. "Man, everything's such a mess."

"Ronan?"

My gaze snaps to his. "Partly. How'd you know?"

"You were fine until we got back home. Figured it had something to do with him."

I pinch the bridge of my nose and squeeze my eyes shut. "I got jealous when those people first showed up here. He liked Logan." A laugh barks out of me. "I didn't want him looking at him like that or kissing him or letting him touch him. I told him it should be me."

Jerking my eyes back open, I study Rowdy, searching for some sort of judgment. When I don't find anything but an impassive look, I continue.

"I kissed our brother, Rowdy. Got him off with my hand too."

"Do our parents know?"

"Fuck no," I growl. "They can't ever know. Mom loses her shit anytime we're alone with Raegan."

His features darken. "This is about her, too?"

"It's so messed up," I choke out. "I've been fucking around with them both. Kissing and touching. She got me off the other day and Ronan lost his shit."

To his credit, Rowdy doesn't gape at me in horror. His eyes are narrowed slits, but he listens intently, not interrupting as I keep on rambling.

"While in captivity, Ronan had sex with Raegan. Like actual penetrative sex. I was so pissed." I rub a palm over my head, noting that the hair is already growing out since Aunt Eve buzzed it. "I was jealous, Rowdy. And then…"

His brow lifts, urging me on.

"And then I walked in on them having sex today in

my cabin. I was so pissed," I hiss, tightening my hold around the tequila bottle. "What if Mom and Dad had caught them? What would have happened then?"

He sighs heavily, taking in all of my confession. Then he reaches for the bottle. I take another swig before passing it over to him.

"You're right. That shit is fucked-up."

We both laugh and then I groan. "Yeah, man, it really is. How am I supposed to stay with Ronan right now when I can't decide if I want to kiss him or kill him?"

"You can't," he says with a shake of his head. "It's too messy. Stay here. Maybe things will cool down. You know you can't let that shit continue, right? Dad will…" He trails off, head bowing. "Dad won't take it well."

A bitter laugh escapes me. "And that brings me to the rest of this fucked-up story. Wild says Dad's not just Mom's wife. He's her father. Her actual father. The age gap between them has always been huge."

He blinks several times, digesting my words. "Wild embellishes the truth. He likes to push buttons and see how far he can antagonize someone until they lose their shit."

"I know," I grunt, "but his story adds up. Don't you ever wonder how Mom and Dad ended up here in the first place? Why they don't go live on the outskirts of town with Uncle Atticus and Aunt Eve? It also makes sense why they're so paranoid about leaving Raegan alone with us."

"Their paranoia is warranted," Rowdy reminds me.

"You guys did exactly what you're accusing them of doing."

"You're supposed to be making me feel better not worse."

"I'm not a bullshitter like Wild. I'll tell you like it is." He hands the tequila back to me. "But I'm still your older brother who's going to look out for you. I will always have your back. Stay here until this all blows over." He flashes me a smirk. "Keep your dick in your pants. I'm not Ronan."

I flip him off but feel decidedly lighter. Maybe this is exactly what I need. A break from both Ronan and Raegan. At least I won't be a part of what they're doing. It won't get me into trouble and I won't have to be tormented by it day by day.

I can move past this.

I have to if I want to keep my heart and sanity intact.

CHAPTER THIRTY

raegan

THE LONELY ACHE IN MY CHEST IS HORRIBLE these days, made worse by the cold. The weather's been bleary and hasn't made it above thirty-five degrees. Because it's so cold, I'm forced to sit in the cabin all day, helping Mom with the kids.

At least Ronan and Ryder get to actually do something. For the past two months, both of them plus Dad and Rowdy have been working on rebuilding the big house. Before Uncle Atticus took off back home with his family, Sadie, Chet, and Kristen, the men all hauled away the debris leftover from the fire and were able to get the framing done.

I'd give anything to go out there with them, physically moving my body and perhaps having an actual conversation with Ryder that is more than a few grunts. Ronan's not much better, even though I see him more since he's just next door in Ryder's cabin.

When Ronan's not doing grueling work for Dad, he's sleeping. Always sleeping. Mom says he's depressed.

If only she knew the real reason why.

Two months ago, when Ryder walked in on me and Ronan having sex, everything blew up. Ryder leaving us to go live with Rowdy sent Ronan spiraling. He hasn't touched me since.

Yes, whatever happened with Logan messed with Ronan's head, but it was that event and Ryder catching us that tipped him over the edge.

I miss him.

I miss them both.

Even if they are being the biggest assholes on the planet.

Mom's retching pulls my attention from the window, where I watch movement over at the big house. She's been hugging the same bucket for a couple of weeks now. I've been around her long enough to know she's pregnant. *Again.*

They haven't officially told us, but when we're going to bed at night, I notice the way Dad palms her belly. Don't they have enough kids already?

I'm never having any damn kids.

"Mage," I gripe when his nasty fart meets my nose. "Go out there and be a real wolf like Spirit. Wolves are supposed to like the cold weather."

He rolls over on Dad's side of the bed, tongue lolling out. Ugh, he's so dumb. And huge. He's the size of a real wolf, massive and a mouthful of sharp teeth.

Luckily for us, he's a big teddy bear. A stinky big teddy bear.

Declan and Dakota giggle, both of them holding their nose. They've been practically climbing the walls since the men are all out working and Mom's preoccupied with puking. Dawson, the little angel he is, enjoys snuggling with Destiny, but even his cute voice asking her questions doesn't pull her out of her mute state.

Everyone in this family is so messed up.

There's really no fixing us.

Mom's puke smell makes my stomach turn. Being trapped in this stupid cabin with all these kids is maddening, but adding in the stench of vomit and I'm about to lose it altogether.

"I'm going to the root cellar to get Mom more ginger," I tell Destiny. "You're in charge."

Destiny doesn't reply, but I know she'll watch over them. Just because she doesn't speak doesn't mean she turned stupid.

"I want to go with Rae," Declan whines, reaching for me.

Hell no. He's so clingy. I already have to sleep with him sprawled on top of me every night.

"Rae can go quicker without helpers," Mom croaks out. "Can you come rub Mommy's back, Deck? I'll feel better."

Declan frowns but goes over to help Mom. I'm thankful she's letting me have a moment to myself. I shove my feet in my boots and yank on my coat. Once I'm outside, the crisp air fills my lungs. I breathe it in and then exhale a white cloud. My fingers are already cold and it's been thirty seconds. This winter is going to be a nasty one. I can feel it.

Luckily, Uncle Atticus will come back alone in a few weeks to bring new furniture, windows, and other supplies for the big house. The big house should be ready in time for winter. I'm desperate to have some space to myself.

If Ryder wants to continue being roomies with Rowdy, I'll just give Ronan his cabin back and take over Ryder's. I don't care what Dad says. I feel like I've earned it.

Tucking my hands into my coat pockets, I bristle against the chilly wind and start making my way along the path to the big house. They've done an impressive amount of work in a short amount of time. It's nice seeing a house again.

Spirit sees me from inside the house and sprints for me, a flash of white and fur. I squat to greet her, running my fingers along her spine.

"Hey, girl. Rowdy feeding you well?"

She licks my face.

Rowdy grunts at me through the window cutout. "She eats better than I do."

"Because you deserve it," I praise Spirit, grinning at her. "Unlike your stupid brother."

"Mage is a good boy," Rowdy says with a smirk.

"There's nothing good about his rank ass."

With another pat on Spirit's head, I rise to my feet and then head inside. Ronan is hammering nails into a pine log, his back to me. I wish he'd talk to me and stop avoiding me. I'd give anything to be able to go up to him and hug him from behind.

Ryder is in the bathroom off the living room, on his back on the floor, cursing up a storm. Dad is standing over him, grunting as he assists. Surprisingly, the bathtub was salvaged from the fire, but from the looks of it, not hooking up properly to the new pipes.

"Need help?" I ask, peeking my head around the corner.

"Yeah," Ryder grumbles, "toss a match on this stupid fucking house."

"Not funny," Dad says with an irritated grunt. "You've almost got it. Be patient."

Something slides into place and then Ryder hollers, fist pumping the air. "Got you, you bitch."

"Language around your sister," Dad bites out.

Rolling my eyes, I walk over to Dad and give him a quick hug. "I just came to get Mom some more ginger. She's puking again."

Dad gets a dopey grin on his face, which tells me all I need to know. She's definitely pregnant. I didn't even know old people could keep making babies. Seems like their innards would rot over the years. Maybe that explains why Dakota is such a brat.

"When you guys finish up here, my cabin's next," I say to Dad, smiling prettily at him. "Sound good?"

Dad's smile vanishes and he squats to help Ryder with another piece of the plumbing. "Nice try. You'll have your old room with Destiny again."

I grit my teeth and clomp off. I'll have to work on Dad another day when he's not grumpy from working on the house.

Rowdy is still working in the kitchen when I pass by him. I make my way to the pantry that we've already been using to store food. At the back of the pantry is the hatch that leads down to the root cellar that survived the fire. Before it got too cold, we were able to harvest a lot of the fruits and vegetables, most of which we've been keeping down here. There's even a good supply of eggs and jerky. As soon as I lift the hatch, the sweet, peculiar scent of something makes my stomach turn.

Gross.

Did something die in here?

Bile creeps up my throat and I gag. Holding my breath, I scamper into the root cellar, locate a piece of ginger root, and bail as quickly as I can.

"Check for dead rats in there," I tell Rowdy, pointing toward the pantry. "That's disgusting."

He scrunches his nose before sauntering over to the root cellar. I stand there, hip against the new kitchen counter he built, clutching my ginger while I wait for him to find the source. After about five minutes, he returns shrugging.

"I can't smell anything. Must be your upper lip."

I curl said lip up and deadpan, "Thanks for nothing."

His chuckle warms me. Lately, Rowdy is more of the brother from before. Maybe Ryder is rubbing off on him. I hate to admit it, but it's probably good for Rowdy to have someone staying with him so he's not so alone.

When I finally make it back to Ronan's cabin where my family has been squished in, I find Mom is no longer puking. She's sorting laundry as if she wasn't sick as a dog twenty minutes ago. Dakota and Declan are throwing a ball back and forth, narrowly missing the puke bucket. Honestly, I think Dakota is aiming for it.

Boys are gross.

"When Ronan comes back, I need you to ask him to heat some water at the firepit. I'd like to wash some clothes tonight." Mom tosses a pair of my jeans into one of the piles. "I'd like for you girls to help."

Destiny doesn't say anything. No surprise there.

I groan in frustration. Laundry is the worst. I don't like hand washing everyone's stinky underwear.

"Maybe we should teach Kota how to do laundry," I suggest. "His undies are always the dirtiest."

He sticks his tongue out at me. "That's a girl's job."

"Dakota," Mom admonishes. "Put the ball down and help me sort."

I smirk at him, satisfied he got what was coming. Mom frowns, holding a pair of my underwear. When her eyes meet mine, flickering with worry, my stomach does a tiny flip.

"What?" I bark out, uncomfortable with the look she's giving me.

She chews on her lip before blurting out, "When was your last period?"

"Ew. Why are we talking about this?" Even as I go for an annoyed reaction, I can't help the uneasiness flooding through me. "When was *your* last period?"

"I think you're smart enough to know it's been a while." Mom levels me with a warning glare. "But we're discussing you. When, Raegan?"

Honestly, I don't know.

I know I've not had one and I thought that was weird, but I tried to appreciate not having to deal with my period rather than worry about missing it and what those repercussions could mean.

Before I can answer, Mom continues, her spine straightening. "What exactly happened when you were with those people? Did they…"

Destiny flinches at her words. I feel guilty that we've somehow hurt her just by bringing up that time.

"Did they what?" I ask, voice shrill. "No. They didn't do anything to me. But, even if they did, I wouldn't want to talk about it!"

I make a pointed look toward Destiny. Mom glances over at her and softens.

"I just worry that—"

"Last month, okay?" I huff out. "Can we stop talking about this now?"

Mom's gaze narrows. "Okay, sweetie."

I deflate at her words. Usually, she puts up more of a fight during our arguments. Maybe the baby is making her feel sick again. Or maybe she finally figured out that discussing this stuff in front of Destiny isn't the best thing to do. She's already so fragile. Reminding her of what Jace did to her—or at least what I assume he did since she won't speak—is downright cruel. She, like me and Ronan, just wish we could forget everything about the kidnapping.

While Mom gets distracted with laundry and kids, I can't help but obsess over her question. When *was* my last period? I'd had it maybe three months ago. I'm not a hundred percent sure. I know I didn't have it while in captivity or since coming home.

Oh God.

I've had sex twice with my brother.

I can't be pregnant from having sex two times. That seems impossible. Mom and Dad have sex all the time, even with us sleeping in the same stupid cabin. That's why they have a million kids.

But me?

I'm not ready to have a baby. Babies are needy and

keep you trapped inside when you'd rather be any-where instead.

Definitely not pregnant.

If I were pregnant, wouldn't I be puking all the time like Mom?

The root cellar made you gag…

That was real, though. Something died in there. Rowdy just didn't care to look for the source. It wasn't me being sensitive. *It. Wasn't.*

Dread curdles my stomach and a wave of nausea follows.

Oh God. I can't be. I better freaking not be.

CHAPTER THIRTY-ONE

ronan

I T'S SO COLD IN MY CABIN.

The fireplace is no longer putting out much heat, which means I should add a few logs, but I can't be bothered to move. Buried under my quilt, shivering and feeling sorry for myself is a better place to be.

Too bad Raegan isn't here.

I'd love to cuddle with her right now. She'd also find some way to make me smile. But, not only did I wreck my relationship with Ryder, I ruined what me and Raegan had too.

I'm all alone.

I fucking hate it.

Seeing him each day as we work on the big house is torture. He's grown his hair out again. I like the way the dark hair peeks out from beneath his beanie. When the wind blows, it moves the hair that looks silky and soft. I ache to rip the beanie off his head and run my fingers through his hair.

That's not going to happen.

I can't even get him to talk to me. After what happened a couple of months ago, he moved out. It's hard to discuss things when he sleeps at Rowdy's. During the day, when we're all working, it's not like I can exactly talk about this shit in front of everyone.

It hurts not having either one of them.

I miss them both so much.

Kota is my only company and that's just at night. Since they're so crowded next door, he shares a bed with me now. The kid is a kicker and I have more than my fair share of bruises from him. It helps, though, having him here so I'm not so alone when it's dark out. Dakota can't rescue me from my nightmares, but he gives me something else to focus on. Without him, I'd go insane.

Someone knocks on the door. I groan as I peek my head out from under the quilt. My glasses are on the bedside table, so I can't see who it is. Despite the nervousness that shivers down my spine, I call out for the person to enter. If it were Logan, he wouldn't knock.

A man steps through the door, making my heart rate quicken. Ryder clears his throat, and upon my squinting, announces himself with a, "It's me."

He closes the door behind him and kicks off his boots. I track him as he grumbles about the temperature on the way to the fireplace. With his back to me, he tosses some logs onto the fire, pokes at it with the poker, and then turns to look at me.

"I've had enough of this, Ronan."

I frown at him. "Enough of what?"

"This," he grunts, waving at me on the bed. "Sleeping all the time. Slipping into a dark place where no one can find you."

"I'm right here," I mutter. "Easy to find."

He scoffs and then crawls onto the bed beside me. A thrill runs through me. Having him this close makes blood run hot through my veins. God, I've missed him.

"Not physically here," Ryder says, gesturing between us before tapping on my forehead. "In *there*, you're lost."

His words feel like a flashlight pointing at every damaged part of me I desperately try to keep hidden. He sees me no matter how much I don't want him to.

"Sure, I was pissed about you and Raegan," he grumbles, "but it's more than that with you. I've had time to cool off and wrap my head around everything. What I can't seem to figure out is you."

"What do you want from me?" I demand, voice husky.

"I want to know what happened with Logan."

Hearing Logan's name makes my skin crawl with nerves. He's the last person I want to talk about.

"Why? It doesn't matter."

Ryder yanks the covers away so that he can also get beneath them. His body is still cold from outside, but I find myself curling toward him anyway, needing his scent and touch. He places a hand on my hip. Such a simple gesture but means so much to me.

"It matters to me," he murmurs. "I can't help you unless I know."

I swallow hard, blinking back the urge to cry. "Ryder…"

He cups my cheek and meets my gaze. I shudder under his touch as his thumb rubs along my stubbly cheek. God, I've missed him. It takes everything in me not to lean forward and kiss his perfect mouth.

"I know it was bad. I know it hurt you in ways I'll never understand. I know…" He trails off, chewing on his bottom lip. "I *know*, but I need you to trust me enough to tell me."

He knows.

It's obvious, but hearing that he knows makes my stomach roil.

"I didn't want it," I rasp out. "Even though I liked him once. Even though I'm gay…or whatever I am."

He leans forward, pressing a soft kiss to my lips. It feels like a reward for speaking my truth. I ache to let it all out, eager for more of his kisses. More of his rewards.

"I'd been forced to put my mouth on him, but it wasn't horrible. I could handle that. The beatings were far worse. But the night me and Raegan…you know," I whisper, unable to meet his eyes. "He came to me after." Hot tears blur my vision and then spill out before I can stop them. "He stripped me down, Ry, and put his dick inside my ass. It was dry."

Ryder winces and swipes away my tears with his thumb.

"It hurt," I say, barely audible. "I'd bled. It was horrible. And it wasn't just that one time. The second time was more than a smear of blood. He fucking tore me up inside. I was ashamed and disgusted, but mostly worried about the irreparable damage he might've done."

His lips find mine again, gently pressing kisses on my mouth like he can soothe the sting my words left on them. "I'm so sorry, Ro. So fucking sorry."

"It took weeks to feel right," I admit through my tears. "I was afraid to shit. He fucked me up that badly."

Ryder pulls me to him in a tight embrace. With my face buried against his neck, I finally release all the emotions whipping around inside me. The sob that escapes is ragged and pained. He holds me, rubbing my back while whispering assurances.

He loves me.

He thinks I'm brave.

He says I'm perfect.

His kind words are a balm to my bleeding heart. I mentally gobble each and every one of them up, allowing myself to be held together by my brother. He doesn't care that I'm broken—a messy, sharp fragment of my former self. He loves me anyway.

As my tears dry up, a hunger settles deep in my soul. I need Ryder to understand how even when Logan had the wool pulled over my eyes, it was always him. Ryder was my first real crush. My true love I was never allowed to have. I tilt my head up to find his lips. Our kiss is gentle at first and then I'm desperate to taste every inch of his mouth. Based on his own groans and roaming hands, he's just as eager.

I missed him.

This.

Us.

"Too many clothes on," I complain between kisses. "I need to fucking feel you."

Ryder smiles against my lips and starts tugging at his jeans. We break from our kiss long enough for him to shuck out of his jeans and shirt. With both of us in just our boxers, we'll be able to feel every inch of each other.

I roll on top of him, grinding my dick against his through our underwear. He makes a sharp gasp of pleasure, his fingers bruising my shoulders. Grabbing onto his hair like I've been craving to do, I pull his head back so I can attack his neck with my mouth. He bucks his hips, moaning when I suck on the flesh near his ear.

"Fuck," Ryder murmurs. "You feel so good. I need to…"

Pulling back from him, I stare at his blown pupils and parted lips. He's so goddamn gorgeous. I rut against him, both of us hissing in pleasure as our dicks happily play together.

"More," Ryder grunts. "I need to fuck you."

His words douse the heat burning through me with an icy bucket of reality. I can't be with Ryder the way I want to because Logan ruined me. I'll never be able to let a man be inside me like that. Not only do I think my body wouldn't be able to take it, but I think my mind might break.

"Hey." Ryder holds my face with both hands, peering up at me. "I lost you. What'd I say wrong?" He winces and then mutters, "Shit."

"It's fine," I hiss out, sitting up on my knees. "Maybe you should go."

Ryder shakes his head in vehemence. He palms my dick through my boxers, squeezing just tight enough to make me groan.

"Fuck me," Ryder says, eyes hooded with lust. "Fuck me like you fucked our little sister."

My dick twitches in his grip and he smirks knowingly. I can't stop the smile that tugs at my lips.

"You'd be willing to try that?" I ask, shock in my tone. "You're not even gay."

"I'm bisexual, apparently." Ryder shrugs. "I think maybe you are too."

The idea of fucking women is gross to me, but being with Raegan was better than good. It was amazing. There's been a few nights in the past couple of months where I jerked off to the memory.

"Maybe," I agree. "But still. You want to try it after what I just told you about…" Logan. I don't have to say his name. Ryder knows.

"I know you'll be gentle," he assures me. "You'll use lube. If it hurts, you'll stop, right?"

I nod emphatically. "I won't hurt you. It'll be good for you. For us."

"I trust you then. Tell me what to do."

We spend several seconds just staring at one another. Is this really going to happen? Am I going to actually get to fuck my brother?

"Stay here," I order. "Take your boxers off."

He laughs at my hastiness to get to my end table. I pull out the lube, yank off my own underwear, and then crawl back under the covers with him. I set the lube down beside him and then move down in the bed.

"I want to make you come while I prep you," I explain. "Can I suck you off, Ryder?"

"Seriously, dude? Do you even have to ask?"

I do, actually.

Knowing he wants it means everything to me. I won't be like that monster.

Realization flickers in his eyes. "Fuck yes, Ronan. I want your mouth on my cock."

My own dick jumps at his words. I pump it with my fist a few times before letting it go. I'll get my turn. Giving him pleasure first is what's important.

"What if someone comes in?" I ask, darting my gaze to the door.

"They're all distracted with dinner," Ryder murmurs. "We have time."

Settling between his muscular, hairy thighs, I inhale his manly scent. He grunts when I grab hold of his dick, but his sounds become needy as fuck when I lick his tip.

"Holy shit, holy shit, holy shit." He runs his fingers through my hair. "Do that again."

Grinning at him, I tongue the tip of his cock and then wrap my lips around him. His salty flavor tastes good. Like something I could suck on for hours. I bob up and down his shaft a few times to get him warmed up before pulling away. He watches with a hot stare as I pop the cap on the lube and then coat my fingers.

"Still okay?"

He nods. "Yup."

"Relax. Clenching will hurt. Trust me."

I go back to sucking on his thick cock, but this time, I tease his hole with my slick fingertip. His ass cheeks clench just like I knew they would. Rather than push him before he's ready, I keep teasing his dick with my tongue, humming and licking and, at times, choking on it. My saliva is making a big mess, but he's lost in the pleasure of it and doesn't seem to give a damn.

"Ronan," he groans. "I need…I need more."

Nodding, I continue to tease his dick. This time, I slowly breach his hole. He sucks in a sharp, pained breath. I don't move any farther in case it's hurting him.

"All the way in," he begs. "Fuck my hole with your finger."

My cock is leaking with pre-cum. He's got me all twisted up and eager to fuck. At this point, if he keeps talking filthy to me, I'm going to come all over the sheets instead.

"Yesss," he hisses out as my finger pushes all the way in. "Holy fuck, yeah, right there."

I continue rubbing against the place inside of him

that seems to feel really good while giving him the best blowjob of his life. His legs have spread almost as though he's silently begging me for more.

Popping off his dick, I fixate on his closed eyes and say, "Tell me what you need."

"More. Stretch me out so I can take your cock, dammit. I want you to fuck me."

With a grin, I tease at his hole, pressing until I can get another finger inside. Then, I scissor my fingers and attempt to stretch him some. He nearly sobs with pleasure anytime I touch the sensitive place inside him. I make sure to tease him with that until he's trembling.

I start to slide a third finger in him, but he clenches around me, making a grunting sound that might mean he feels pain. Distracting him, I start sucking on his balls while fist fucking his shaft and teasing his inside button.

"I'm going to come," he growls. "My dick is about to fucking explode."

The third finger easily goes in. I twist and thrust my fingers, marveling at how his cock twitches. Cum spurts out of his dick, splattering all over his hard abs. Watching him unravel is a beautiful sight—one I'll die trying to see again. I continue to massage the good spot inside him until his dick stops squirting and just drips. His entire body relaxes into a puddle of bliss. Gently, I pull my fingers from his body and then crawl up to his mouth.

"I love you, Ryder. Will you let me love you how I've always dreamed?"

With his hot gaze boring into me, he smiles. "Yes. I want you inside of me."

This is it.

I'm going to fuck my brother.

CHAPTER THIRTY-TWO

ryder

DESPITE HAVING JUST EXPERIENCED THE BEST orgasm of my life, I'm apprehensive about what happens next.

Ronan is going to fuck me.

Me.

He's going to put his dick—and it's every bit as big as mine—inside of me. I'd thought, at one point, that three fingers were too much. It really fucking hurt there for a minute until he found a way to push a literal button inside me to cause me to detonate. His dick is going to be worse.

But watching him coat his cock with lube, giving me one of his soft, shy smiles I didn't realize I'd missed until now, has me sucking it up.

I can do this.

The tip of his cock slides against my asshole that feels tender from all the stretching. Unable to stop myself, I clench in anticipation. He doesn't shove all the way in, instead barely breaching the pucker, a frown forming on his face.

"Relax and let me in, Ryder."

His deep, raspy voice filled with so much desire and love does the trick. I exhale heavily, forcing myself to release those muscles. He inches his crown inside of me and I hiss from the intrusion. Still, he doesn't push all the way in.

"I want to kiss you," he murmurs, crawling over me. "I need to taste you."

I groan with pleasure as his lips find mine. Slowly, he presses into my body, devouring my grunts and moans. His cock is thicker than I gave him credit for, but it's slick and he's going slow enough for me to adjust to the size of him. We're both panting heavily by the time he's fully seated.

"I'm afraid to move," he chokes out. "You feel so fucking good."

I tug at his hair, pulling him to me for a deep kiss. "It only hurts a little. I like the feeling of fullness of you inside me."

His lips curl into a smile and then he kisses me slowly. The teasing way he nips at my lips and fucks my mouth with his tongue drives me insane. Testing my muscles again, I squeeze my ass around his cock.

"Fuuuuck," he hisses. "You trying to make me come?"

I grin at him. "That's kind of the point, right?"

We kiss for a little while longer, him remaining

perfectly still, with me impaled on his cock, and then he seems to lose control. His hips pull out slowly and then he thrusts back inside. Pleasure, from that wonderful place inside of me, lights up and fucking sings. With each thrust, he rubs against it, causing me to make feral sounds of need.

My fingers in his hair, tugging and tugging with each thrust, must bother him because he grabs hold of both wrists, pinning me to the bed.

Sweet Ronan is gone.

A wild, starved animal has replaced him.

I'm his prey, trapped in his hold, waiting to be eaten alive.

Fixating on the fiery way he watches me, I give in to his sudden rougher thrusting. He's fucking me now, plain and simple. All gentleness has left. I can see his desire for ultimate control—something he needs desperately.

I'm his to own in this way.

I'm perfectly okay with that.

Urging him on, despite the sting in my ass, I rumble, "Harder. Faster. Fuck, you feel good."

This seems to shred his final thread of control. He starts bucking into me like a madman, grinding on me and stabbing inside me with each animalistic thrust.

His mouth leaves mine and then finds my neck. I groan as his teeth sink into the flesh. How something can hurt and feel so good all at once is beyond me.

"Fuck your hand," he orders, breath hot against my neck. "I want you to come again."

He releases one of my hands and I bring it between us. Even though I just came, my body is eager for more. My dick twitches, thick and ready, when I wrap my hand around it. It's still slick and sticky from my last release, leaving enough lube to make the whole sensation that much better.

Another bite has me seeing stars. I start squeezing my dick each time he bites me. It's like an explosion of pleasure in every single one of my nerve endings.

Over and over and over again he pumps into me, each thrust more ragged and wild than the last. Watching him as he loses himself to this moment is the most wonderful thing I've ever witnessed. I'd never thought about having sex this way until a few months ago when I'd learned Ronan's sexual preferences, and now I can't imagine never having experienced it.

His hand locks around my jaw before he finds my mouth again with his. Teeth nip at my lips and tongue. He devours every grunt and growl and moan coming out of me. Somehow, his hand went from holding my other wrist down, to threading his fingers with mine. An overwhelming feeling of love washes over me, ultimately causing me to come.

A pleasure-filled sound belts out of me as my nuts draw up. My dick starts throbbing out my release. I can't help but squeeze my ass muscles, desperate for every dizzying pulse of pleasure. This sets Ronan off too. He cries out in ecstasy seconds before his dick thickens almost painfully inside of me and starts pumping me full of his cum. It's hot and stings the sore parts of me, but I also love it. It's as though he's claiming me as his.

I am his.

I'll always be his.

Ronan slides his still twitching dick out of my body and then collapses half on top of me. His cum runs out of my asshole like a waterfall, no doubt soaking the bed beneath me. I'm sweaty and covered in my own cum too, yet I'm not able to move. My heart continues to hammer in my chest and I long to stay in this moment for as long as I can.

Ronan, no longer fucking like a feral animal, gently runs his fingers along my collarbone, pressing soft kisses against my bruised neck. It's so sweet and soothing, I can't help but smile.

"That was amazing," I whisper, running my own fingers over his naked skin wherever I can touch him. "Thank you."

He sits up on one elbow so he can see my face, a lazy grin on his lips. "No, thank you. That was…everything." His brows knit together. "Are you okay? I didn't hurt you, did I?"

Even if he did, I wouldn't admit it.

"No. Nothing I couldn't handle."

He settles again, this time resting on my shoulder and curling himself around me. The room smells of sex and smoke from the fireplace. I love it. It's my new favorite smell.

"I didn't realize I needed this," he murmurs. "I feel… lighter."

Butterflies erupt in my chest. "Lighter means you're out of that unreachable dark hole. Lighter is good."

"Really fucking good."

"Anytime you want to sleep or go to that dark place, you find me, okay?"

He splays his hand over my pectoral, playfully teasing my nipple. "That could mean a lot of sex."

"Hey, I'm not complaining."

We both chuckle and then the air between us feels tense.

"Mom and Dad…if they find out." He shudders. "I can't think about that right now. It hurts too much."

My heart is in my throat because them knowing would be really fucked-up. They'd be more than disappointed. Banishment would be the least of our worries.

"We can't let them find out then," I murmur, hugging him tighter to me. "We'll find times to be together without anyone knowing."

"I'm going to have to tell Raegan," he says, voice soft and sad. "I can't keep this from her."

Knowing how I felt when I'd learned they'd had sex while in captivity and then caught them together once back home, I understand why he wants to tell her. It doesn't make it any easier. All these feelings and emotions between the three of us are so messy and complicated.

"Why is this so hard?" I ask, mostly to myself. "Love should be easy. Mom and Dad make it look so simple."

"It is simple," Ronan whispers. "Simple to us. Just because no one else understands it doesn't mean it's not the easiest thing in the world for us."

"How does Raegan fit into all this?"

"She just does. She's always been there and right in the middle."

I think back to the moments she and I have shared. Hot, passionate moments. Thinking about her naked tits bouncing has my dick filling with blood and hardening again. He's right. She's twisted up right here with us.

"I should probably go before anyone comes looking for me," I say with heavy regret. "I'd rather stay right here with you."

He moves his head and kisses my jaw. "We'll have more time. Go, Ryder."

With a groan, I give him a hot, dirty kiss and then slide out from under him before my unruly dick can suggest more playtime. Ronan leans on one elbow, watching me with amusement. I shake my head at him when he laughs as I attempt to wipe all the cum off my raging erection. It's a miracle when I manage to get it contained to the confines of my boxers and then locked away in my jeans. Once I'm completely dressed, I grab the discarded shirt I'd used to clean myself and toss it at him.

"I want to do this again soon," I warn him, grinning. "Just give me time to recover."

His eyebrow lifts and an evil smirk twists his lips. "I'll suck your dick until your ass is no longer sore."

My dick throbs painfully. "That was cruel," I grumble, pointing an accusing finger at him. "Really fucking cruel."

He starts cracking up with laughter, missing the leg hole of his boxers twice before he manages to get his leg through. "You're the only man I know who thinks a promised blowjob is cruel."

I flip him off, chuckling right along with him. Our easy conversation has the muscles losing their tension in my neck. He'd been so closed off to me and now it feels like we've gained so much ground. I have my brother—my best friend—back and it feels amazing.

"Night, Ronan."

He climbs out of the bed, pulls on his glasses, and then saunters over to me. All his muscles flex beautifully and on display. Heat burns through my every nerve ending. God, how I crave to go another round with him.

"Night, Ry." He curls his hand around my neck, pulling me to him for a dirty, promising kiss. My eager hands find his ass, squeezing and pulling him against my front. Both our dicks are hard, pressed against the other. "Better go before I think twice and decide to keep you trapped in my bed."

I lean my forehead against his. "Don't threaten me with a good time."

After another kiss, I finally manage to tear myself away from him. I throw on my boots and coat before slipping quietly out of the cabin. Nerves threaten to consume me as I expect to come face-to-face with Dad. No one is on the cabin porch except Mage, who watches me knowingly.

"What?" I mutter, taking off in long strides away from the cabin. "I really thought I was just going to talk to him."

Mage huffs as though he doesn't believe me.

"Not my fault it took longer than I expected."

And that I ended up getting fucked by my brother…

My mind is racing with a thousand different thoughts, going back and forth between how wonderful it was and how horrible it would be if our parents found out.

In the end, I chase away all the bad thoughts and replay every single memory of tonight over and over again. The chill of the fall air, whispering of a looming wicked winter, does nothing to cool the blazing fire running hot in my veins.

This may be wrong, but my life finally feels as though it's starting to go right.

All I had to do was quit fighting and give in.

CHAPTER THIRTY-THREE

raegan

I WOKE UP THIS MORNING SICK TO MY STOMACH. NOT just queasy, but full-on sick. I'd had to rush out of the cabin under the ruse I wanted to check on the chickens, but in reality, I'd ended up puking my guts out behind the equipment barn.

I am so screwed.

How can this be real?

I'm only seventeen. When I turn eighteen in a few months, I had these grand plans to leave the confines of my parents' strict ways—to build a cabin of my own and live by my own rules.

Was that just a stupid dream?

Why did I stupidly have sex with my brother knowing good and damn well the women in this family are quite fertile?

After getting sick, and the wave passed, I didn't go back to Ronan's stifling cabin where my family has been holed up. I'd climbed on top of the roof of the big house, testing its sturdiness, and was relieved to find my old spot with the same view. I've been sitting up here, contemplating everything while freezing my ass off.

Still better than being in the cabin with Mom.

Voices below me can be heard as the guys work tirelessly on the house. I've heard Ronan and Ryder laugh hysterically several times. Their beef is gone and I'm alone, drowning in my own despair. While I'm happy that Ronan seems to finally have climbed out of his depression this week, I feel my own self tumbling into that lonely, dark spot.

Spirit, from near the firepit, watches me, guarding me like I might slip and fall any second. She doesn't move but continues to stare at me. I'm thankful I didn't let Dad kill her and Mage all those months ago. They may be wolves, but they're the best dogs in the world. We don't deserve to have such sweet animals.

A wave of emotion stirs inside me. Hot tears well and then roll down my cool cheeks. I angrily swipe them away. Lately, all I do is cry at everything. It's dumb and I hate it.

Pregnancy hormones.

I gag just thinking about it. Bitterness remains on my tongue, reminding me that I never made it back to the cabin to brush my teeth. Eventually, I'll have to go back, but until then, I'll stay in my favorite place all by myself.

While I sit, shivering, I try to pinpoint when Ronan changed. He was sleeping all day, doing the bare minimum on the house, and then one day earlier this week it's like he woke up a new man. He joined us each night for supper, worked hard on the big house, and actually smiled. Still, though, he won't talk to me.

Or, rather, I haven't allowed myself to get close enough to him to talk.

He hurt me. They both did. Abandoned me for months, forcing me to die a slow death in the torture cabin. Literally. Declan still sleeps on me at night and head butts my boobs often to the point they're sore and hurt all the time.

I see Mom, with Dawson on her hip, round Ronan's cabin. She shields her eyes as she scans the property, no doubt looking for me.

Sorry, Mom, they're all yours today.

Remaining motionless, I pray she won't look up on the roof or that Spirit won't give me away. She walks toward the big house and disappears inside. Exhaling in relief, I relax and close my eyes. Wind nips at my exposed flesh. It helps chase away the nauseous feeling.

Now that the sickness has fully passed, I pull an apple out of my pocket and start munching on it. The sweet juices erase the bitterness from earlier. All too quickly, I devour it, wishing I'd thought to grab more.

Maybe I can live up here. All I need is a sleeping bag, some food, and maybe Hot Hands pouches Uncle Atticus brings us sometimes.

You can't do that with a big, giant belly...

Just thinking about getting huge and pregnant like

Mom always gets has me bursting into tears again. How did I let this happen? My parents have babies because they have sex. What did I think would happen when I did the same?

Stupid baby.

As soon as the thought enters my mind, guilt rushes through me. It's just a baby. Not its fault I had sex with my brother and made it.

I wonder how Ronan will feel once he learns that I'm pregnant.

Something tells me he might be happy. Another part of me worries he will shut me out again. Of course, this makes me cry some more. No wonder Mom is always so emotional when she's pregnant. It's literally out of her control. I sort of feel sorry for her now.

Sniffling, I swipe away the ongoing tears and stagger out a breath of frustration. Once Mom figures out I'm pregnant, she's going to freak out. I could lie to her and tell it was from CJ. We all know Destiny was raped by Jace. It's not a stretch to claim that as well for myself. But that feels icky. Like I'd be taking something from Ronan and that's the last thing I want to do.

I need to tell Ronan.

Confessing to him that we made a baby will help me not feel so alone. I have to believe that since he seems happier, he'll take the news well. I need him to take it well. I'm tired of feeling alone in general but more so now that I have concluded I'm pregnant.

This evening, after dinner, that's what I'll do.

I'll tell him and he'll make it all better.

With new hope trickling through me, I dry my tears one last time and climb back down.

As soon as Ronan gets up from our dinner at the fire-pit, I wait a few seconds and then follow after him. He barely makes it into Ryder's cabin that he's taken over before I rush in after him.

"Hey," I mutter, muscles coiled and tense. "What's up?"

He whirls around and flashes me a small smile. "Not much. What's up with you?"

I stiffen, wondering if he can tell. Is my face rounder? Do I smell like this morning's puke despite brushing my teeth three times? Can he see my swollen eyes from my emotional breakdown on the roof earlier today?

If he does notice any of that, he doesn't say anything. I watch woodenly as he adds logs to the fireplace. He sits down to pull off his boots and then tosses his coat over onto the sofa. Boldly, he strips out of his jeans and replaces them with his comfy sleep pants.

"Wanna talk?" he asks as he sits on the edge of the bed.

"Yes." My voice is a tiny squeak so unlike me it has him frowning in concern.

"Get comfy." He gestures to my boots and coat. "I'll keep you warm."

The cold tension freezing my muscles thaws a bit. I shakily yank off my boots and coat before moving toward the bed. He pulls back the quilt, eases under the covers, and then pats the place beside him. Needing his touch more than anything, I dive under the covers with him, throwing my arms around his middle and burying my face against his chest.

"I hate you," I remind him, tears already forming. "I love you too. I've missed you. You abandoned me and broke my heart. Why do you always shut me out?"

Hearing the sadness in my voice, he hugs me tighter and kisses the top of my head. "I'm sorry. I don't mean to and I'm going to work on that. Things are…*better*. *I'm* better."

Must be nice.

I'm falling apart.

"I've been so alone. Both of you just left me."

"I know and I'm sorry. I'll keep apologizing until you believe me, Rae."

His sincerity is believable, to which I'm thankful.

"Ronan," I say, tilting my head up so I can look at him. "There's something you need to know."

His fingers stroke my hair out of my face. It's grown some since Mya whacked it all off and I'm glad. I hated it so short but had to do the best with what I had. It's finally long enough to pull back into a ponytail.

"Tell me anything," he murmurs, gaze intense and imploring. "I'm always here for you."

His words give me faith that he's not going to run the other way. Dipping forward, he presses a sweet kiss to my forehead. I melt at the simple affection.

Here goes nothing…

"Ronan, I'm pregnant." I exhale heavily. "The baby is obviously yours."

He blinks at me, brows pinching together. "What?"

Huffing in frustration, I growl, "You came inside me. We made a baby."

Again, he blinks. Nothing tumbles past his pouty lips that were made for kissing. All he does is stare at me. Digesting my words.

"I'm slightly freaking out right now," I tell him, my voice turning shrill. "Say something before I die of a heart attack!"

His lips crash to mine, shocking the hell out of me. Relieved for the touch, I part my lips, accepting his urgent kiss. It feels like coming home kissing him like this. He tastes like Ronan. Yummy. Like my favorite treat. When he pulls back, we're both gasping for air.

"We're going to have a baby," he whispers, a grin spreading over his face. "Holy shit. Raegan, I'm so fucking happy."

My heart stutters in my chest.

"You are?"

"Yeah, I am."

Our blissful moment bursts as reality comes

crashing down on him. I watch his smile disappear, concern twisting his features.

"Dad's going to kill me." He studies me, eyes darting back and forth. "And you're my sister… What about what Mya had said?"

Birth defects.

The thought of something being wrong with this baby I didn't even want has me crying. Again. I don't want anything to happen to it. An ache forms inside my chest. I already love the thing somehow, which makes no sense.

What if it dies because it's not supposed to live because of who the parents are?

A whine rattles through me as I sob. Ronan holds me, whispering assurances neither of us believes. I'm worried about the future.

"What if something is wrong with it?" I ask, voicing my concerns.

"We'll love it anyway."

"What if it has three eyes?"

"The better to see us with."

I snort, punching him in the arm. "Not funny."

"Jokes aside, I'm mostly being serious. We'll love it anyway, Rae."

"What if Mom and Dad send us away?"

"We'll make a new home."

Leaving my super annoying family doesn't sound so fun anymore. I don't want to leave them. Not even Mom and Dakota. Who will help Mom with all the kids? Who will Declan sleep on? Who will keep Dakota in line? Will Ryder be distraught without us like when we were kidnapped?

I have so many questions and not enough answers.

Everything leads to broken hearts and a ripped apart family.

"I don't know what to do," I admit, choking on tears. "I'm scared."

"Me too, but we'll figure it out."

I stop crying eventually, but my mind keeps racing until Ronan speaks again.

"I have to tell you something, Rae. I need you to not flip your shit."

Oh great. My shit is already flipping and he hasn't even told me.

"W-What?" I demand, tensing for a fight.

He strokes my hair, intensely watching me with a look of pure love that warms me. "Me and Ryder made up."

I relax and nod. "I could tell. You're talking to each other again."

"It's more than that." His lips purse together. "We had sex."

They had sex? Like how me and Ronan had sex? How does it work for men?

"I thought you liked having sex with me," I whisper, stupid tears back again. "What's wrong with me?"

"Nothing is wrong with you," he growls and kisses my mouth. "You're fucking perfect, Rae."

"I don't understand."

"You do. You always have. The three of us share an unbreakable bond. We've been fighting it, but it's too strong." He grins at me. "Don't you understand? Our love is so strong that nothing can tear it apart."

When I think about the three of us together, happy and laughing, it's definitely the best part of my life.

"I love you," Ronan says, stroking my cheek with his thumb. "I'll always love you. I love Ryder too. The three of us can be together. And with the baby…" He beams at me. "We'll be our own little family."

My heart patters happily at his words. Perhaps we can be happy. There could be a future where the three of us can love each other and care for our baby.

It still doesn't fix the problem with Mom and Dad or being forced to leave our family.

"We have to tell Ryder," I say, biting my lip. "He'll know what to do, right?"

Ronan nods. "Ryder has always wanted to protect us. That won't ever stop. Do you trust me this will all work out?"

Even though I really don't, I nod and lie anyway. "I trust you."

CHAPTER THIRTY-FOUR

ronan

'M GOING TO BE A DAD.

Holy shit.

Something I never thought possible is going to happen.

My sister is pregnant with my baby.

Joy and disbelief keep warring with actual fear. Fear for the health of the baby, of Raegan giving birth at such a young age and away from proper medical facilities, of my parents and their reaction.

We need Ryder.

He's always been a steady presence in our lives. Safe and protective. A fierce lover who'd do anything for his family. He'll know what to do and say to have us feeling better.

Because, despite all the fear, this is a good thing. Babies are a product of love.

The cabin door opens with its usual creak, but instead of fear of Logan, I have the overwhelming feeling of relief knowing Ryder is finally here. He steps in, grinning, but it falters when he sees Raegan wrapped in my arms.

He closes the door behind him and slowly approaches, his eyebrows pinching and his lips turning down in a small frown. The panicked way with which he meets my stare solidifies the fact he's nervous about the fragility of our newly repaired relationship. I smile at him, hoping to assure him I'm not going anywhere.

"Hey," Ryder says, voice gruff as he sits on the edge of the bed. "What are you two up to?"

Raegan twists in my arms to face him. She's tense as fuck. Ryder studies her for a beat, wincing at whatever expression she gives to him. I whisper my fingers over her stomach and she relaxes.

"I told her about us," I tell my brother. "About the sex."

His face burns hot and bright red. Then he stiffens as if bracing himself for her wrath. Raegan's a hothead. We all know this. Surprising us, she reaches over and touches his arm. He turns toward us, taking her hand in his, threading their fingers together.

This is what we needed.

The three of us together like it was always supposed to be.

Together we can endure anything.

"I don't care that you two had sex," Raegan says finally, though her shaking voice contradicts her words. "I'm hurt that you both shut me out."

Ryder squeezes her hand and brings it to his mouth for a kiss. "I'm sorry. I'm so fucking sorry, Rae."

She lets out a ragged sigh as if expelling all the hurt and stress at once. "It's obvious I already forgave you two idiots."

Ryder grins at her. "Thank God. I missed you."

"If you missed me so much, take your coat and boots off so we can cuddle. You owe me lots of hugs and kisses."

I slip my hand under her shirt to feel her flat belly, wondering how big the baby is right now. I don't often care about internet access, but right now, I wish I had Wild's phone and a signal so I could research.

Ryder slips out of his coat, then yanks off his boots and jeans before climbing into bed in just his shirt and boxers. He lies on his side, staring at our sister. Then, because he owes her, he leans forward and kisses her pouty lips.

"Missed this sassy mouth," he says with a grunt.

She sighs happily, letting him stroke her hair and kiss her for several more moments. While he comforts her, I rub circles on her stomach, already smitten with this baby and the idea of my sister big and round with my child.

"We have something to tell you," Raegan finally says, her voice a mere whisper.

Ryder sits up on his elbow, casting his gaze my way before saying, "You two had sex again? I understand.

This thing will work a lot better if we keep the lines of communication open."

I snort out a laugh. "We didn't have sex again."

Frowning, Ryder turns his gaze back to Raegan. "What is it then?"

Raegan cups Ryder's cheek and whispers, "Ronan got me pregnant."

Silence falls over us, the only sounds the crackling from the fire and the squeals from our younger siblings far off at the firepit with our parents. Ryder's eyes are wide and his mouth gapes open. Raegan reaches up, pushing under his chin.

"I don't…I don't know what to say." He blinks several times before glancing at me. "How are you two so calm?"

"Calm?" Raegan barks out a laugh. "We're far from calm. We're both freaking out. We wanted to tell you because you always know what to do."

Ryder continues to blink, still reeling from our confession.

"The obvious problem is Dad is going to kill me," I say with a dark chuckle. "Or send me away."

He grunts at that. "I won't let either of those things happen." His hand leaves Raegan's hair to toy with mine. "No one's dying on my watch."

"This is why we needed to tell you," I murmur, teasing my fingers higher up Raegan's stomach. "You're a fixer. We need fixing."

Ryder flashes each of us a devilish grin. "I don't

think either of you needs fixing. I love you the way you are."

He lets go of my hair to reach between himself and Raegan. She trembles when he touches her belly, both our fingers now stroking over her.

"We'll keep you safe," Ryder promises, his mouth finding Raegan's. "I swear on my life."

As the two of them kiss, their hands becoming greedier, my dick hardens. I have numerous images that flash in my mind, all of which end with the three of us naked and touching. Reaching across Rae, I squeeze Ryder's ass cheek.

"Do you want to really make it up to Raegan?" I ask Ryder, sliding my hand under his boxers around the front to grip his dick. "You could get her off." I squeeze his cock. "I could get you off."

Ryder's eyes darken with lust. "You want that, Rae?"

"Yes," she breathes. "Touch me, Ryder."

I let go of him to slide off the bed. A quick peek past the curtains and seeing my family making s'mores lets me know we have time. Shedding my clothes, I watch as Ryder sits up to remove his shirt. His back muscles ripple with strength. He's so goddamn hot.

"Take your boxers off," I command as I saunter over to grab the lube. "Slide to the end of the bed."

Ryder shivers at my words and nods before peeling out of his underwear. Raegan watches us, eyes darting back and forth, as Ryder then starts pulling off her clothes for her. I'm back at the end of the bed, lube in hand by the time she's fully naked. Ryder groans, clearly appreciating her nudity.

Like she's a present just for him, he gently parts her thighs, exposing her pussy to him. He makes a growl of hunger before dipping down to inhale her.

"You're sniffing me," she says with a gasp. "Don't be gross."

He chuckles and then licks up her seam. "I like being gross. You taste like heaven, Rae."

Jerking my own cock a few times, I watch as Ryder continues to lick her pussy. I realize maybe it was something I should have done for her the last time we had sex. Her body writhes and jolts with every lick. She's clearly enjoying the hell out of Ryder's "gross" tactics.

Kneeling behind Ryder, I revel in his sharp gasp when my fingers trace down his crack. I lubricate my fingers to start teasing his hole and suck one of his balls into my mouth.

"Holy fuck," Ryder growls. "You drive me insane when you do that."

Raegan giggles, delighted by his words. "Now you know how it feels."

In response, he starts making a suckling sound that has her moaning. I wonder if his fingers are inside of her. Imagining what he's doing to her, I mimic him and slowly urge a finger into his asshole. Easily, I find the spongy part inside of him that he likes for me to massage. I tease it over and over while I go back and forth between his balls, giving them equal amounts of attention. My free hand finds his cock that weeps with pre-cum.

I slide another finger in and then another, boldly fucking him as I pleasure other parts of him. Based on Raegan's grunts and mewls, he's giving it to her just as good as I'm giving it to him. I love how we're all three connected in this moment. Like it was always supposed to be this way.

Our sister comes abruptly with a shout that Ryder quickly covers with his palm. The whole bed trembles as she orgasms. I grin after popping off Ryder's balls and pulling my fingers from him. Standing up, I give his ass a stinging swat that earns me a growl.

"Get a couple of pillows and put them under her," I instruct, breathless and needy for more. "I have an idea. Do you both trust me?"

"Yes," they say in unison without hesitation.

"Good."

Ryder stands up too, moving to grab the pillows. Raegan is a vision with her tits on display and pussy glistening. I love her so fucking much. He returns a moment later, gently urging her to wrap her legs around his waist so he can tuck the pillows beneath her.

"Fuck our sister while I fuck you," I murmur, roaming my hands over Ryder's back. "I want this so fucking badly for us."

Ryder shudders in anticipation. He grabs hold of his cock, lining it up against our sister's tight pussy, and pushes inside of her with a garbled sound of pleasure.

Then he leans forward, reaching for her tits. Again, I wonder if I was supposed to touch them when we had sex before. The way she keens and pants as he thumbs her nipples makes me think I really should have.

I watch his ass flex as he thrusts into her. Since he's never experienced the joy of penetration like I have, I allow him to fuck her wildly like the hungry beast he is.

"Don't come," I warn, gripping his ass and squeezing. "Not until I'm inside you."

Raegan moans when he stops pumping. "Ronan, you're so damn bossy in bed."

"Hot as fuck, right?" Ryder rasps out. "Don't worry, baby, you get to be the boss outside of bed like usual."

They start kissing again. I decide it's my turn to join. Adding more lube to my dick and his ass crack, I finally start teasing his hole with my cock. He groans against her mouth as I inch my way inside.

"Fuck," Ryder hisses. "I'm going to die right the fuck now."

Raegan giggles again, which makes him clench his ass, eliciting another moan from him.

I run my fingers up and down Ryder's back before settling on his hips. Gripping them tightly, I begin slowly fucking my brother. Once I've established a good rhythm, he no longer seems okay with waiting for further instruction. He starts thrusting opposite from my thrusts.

This is insanely hot.

I'm fucking my brother while he fucks our pregnant sister.

Nothing can ever beat this moment. Nothing.

Ryder's hands are greedily devouring Raegan as I fuck him relentlessly. I know when his fingers have found her pussy because she starts whimpering. Is he touching her just like she touched herself when we had sex? Does it feel good for her in the way Ryder likes when I massage inside him?

Tilting my hips back, I aim to press against the spongy button inside him. When I drag over it, he moans so loud I think he'll alert everyone on our property.

"Hush," I warn, smacking his ass cheek.

Raegan silences him with a sloppy kiss. I drive into him harder and harder, digging my fingers into his hips. My orgasm is building and I'm trying to hold on to make this good for him—for them both.

"Fuck," Ryder hisses. "I can't take it."

His ass clenches hard around my cock and then he's groaning out his release. Raegan must enjoy the feeling or maybe he's also taken her over the edge because she cries out in pleasure. Their combined sounds of pure ecstasy are what finally have me erupting.

Cum shoots out of me, deep inside his ass, for the first shot. I pull out, sliding along his ass crack, marveling at the way my cum continues to spurt out over his back. So much cum.

Voices nearing our cabin can be heard, which has

the three of us scrambling. I clean them up quickly and then we all dress like our asses are on fire. Raegan bolts over to the door, yanking on her boots along the way. Glancing over her shoulder, she gives us both a brilliant smile.

"I love you," she says to both of us. "I'll come back later tonight when they've gone to bed."

Later, for round two.

I can't fucking wait.

CHAPTER THIRTY-FIVE

ryder

BEING SANDWICHED BETWEEN RONAN AND Raegan is the best fucking thing ever. I'm tired as hell after our second romp in the middle of the night and revel in sleeping between them. Ronan's dick miraculously stays hard, pressed against me. Raegan's tit perfectly fits inside my palm. I love how good this feels.

I squint to check the light coming through the window. It's dark, but morning is definitely upon us. We'll have to get up soon and dressed before the whole family wakes up. But lying here a few moments longer won't hurt anything.

Ronan's hand snakes to my front, lazily stroking my cock. I groan, squeezing Raegan's tit as pleasure trembles through me.

"Sore," she mumbles sleepily. "Don't squeeze it like that."

Grinning, I go back to doing what I know she likes.

Pinching and rubbing and twisting her nipple. I like how it makes her breathy and needy. Perhaps we have time for a little fun. My asshole, though, needs a break. Ronan seems to understand this because he doesn't touch it, just continues to stroke my cock. His mouth is on my neck, sucking and licking, driving me insane with need.

I slip my palm to Raegan's stomach and caress her there before sliding the rest of the way to her pussy. She shifts her thigh aside, whining when I touch her clit. In the middle of the night, I tried gently biting it and she immediately came. I roll it between my thumb and finger, applying some intense pressure.

"Yesss," she moans. "God, you're so good at this."

I move my hips in tune with Ronan's jerking while I tease our sister to the edge of pleasure. She moves her leg farther aside, quietly urging me to touch her more. I slide a finger inside her, loving how she gasps. Just like me, there's a place inside her body that makes her come unglued with only a few strokes. I find the spot, gently rubbing firm circles over it. Dipping down, I put my mouth on her nipple, using my teeth to tease her while I fuck her with my finger.

Ronan's dick is dripping with pre-cum, sliding along my crack and continually dotting my back with the wetness. His hot breath against my neck is driving me wild.

I come with a groan, fucking hard against Ronan's fist. I'm so lost in the wonderful feeling that I don't connect the sounds and voice until it's too late.

"Ryder, your dog shit all over the cabin," Mom hollers before her eyes lock onto mine.

I'm still coming with my brother's hand around my cock while my finger is inside my sister and staring at my mom.

Fuck.

Oh God.

She stands there, her eyes wide with disbelief. The seconds drag on like multiple eternities smashed up against each other. I note Raegan's hand pulling mine away from her and Ronan sliding back. I'm left, still staring at Mom, lying in a puddle of my own cum.

"I can explain," I blurt out, already scrambling out of the bed. "Mom, I can explain."

Her eyes follow me as I fumble my way out of the bed. I can feel my cum flinging all over the place. Every inch of my skin is on fire, hot with humiliation and horror. I grab my underwear off the floor, accidentally grabbing Raegan's while I'm at it. Her eyes lock onto the girly panties in my hand and her features slowly transform from complete shock to something I've never seen before.

Angry rage bordering on hate.

I yank my boxers up and then pull on my jeans. I'm shaking my head, willing her to understand, but neither of us can speak. We're caught in a strange face-off—a calm before a motherfucking hurricane.

Once I grab my shirt and pull it over my head, I feel ready to speak to our mother. I take a step toward her and she stumbles away from me like I've got rabies, or worse yet, like I'm a predator come to eat her children alive.

"Mom," I choke out.

"No, no, no, no," she chants, shaking her head harshly. "No, no, no, no, no."

"We love each other," I blurt out in explanation. "Please, Mom—"

"GET OUT!" she bellows, waving a finger angrily at the door. "Get the fuck out!"

I'm unable to tear my gaze from hers to see how my siblings are faring. Based on their absolute silence, I'd say not well.

"Mom—"

"You've ruined our family!" Her horrible accusing glare burns into me. "Get out!"

I stuff my feet into my boots and grab my coat before trying once more. "I'm sorry—"

"So help me, Ryder, get out before I beat you!"

Under normal circumstances, the idea of my tiny mother trying to beat me would be laughable. I'm not laughing now. She believes it with every part of her being, and based on how furious she is, I believe it too. I rush past her, escaping into the frigid air that smells like snow is coming.

Racing past Ronan's cabin, I make a beeline for the gate. Mage, the little shit—literally—chases after me, barking happily. No thanks to him, he got us busted.

What does this mean for our family?

Nothing good.

Picking up speed, I run out the gate and around our property. When I make it to the cliffside stairs, I damn near fall down them as I make my descent. The whole world blurs around me and I realize it's because I'm crying. Not from the cold, but from the bone-deep ache that won't stop hurting.

I'm confused and upset and worried as fuck.

Does Mom hate me?

Will Dad kill me?

What happens to Ronan and Raegan?

I'm a coward running away, but I don't know what to do. They had faith in me, but they were wrong to. I can't protect them. I'm useless.

I make it to the last step and trip over my own feet. Hitting the ground hard on my shoulder, I let out a howl of pain. Mage pauses his running to turn around to check on me. After he licks me a few times, I manage to sit up and escape his assault. Once back on my feet, I hold my tender shoulder and start running again.

Away. Away. Away.

Soon, I find myself inside Rowdy's gate and on his porch. My chest is heaving with exertion. I fling open his door with a frustrated growl, only to be met with the sight of his .45 that's pointed right at me.

I raise my hands in defense, halting so he can see it's me and not some intruder. He slowly drops the gun to his side on the bed behind him and then puts a finger to his mouth. I follow his stare to where Destiny is curled up, sleeping, a soft blanket tucked all around her. Spirit is sleeping at her feet, her head resting on Destiny's leg.

Slowly, Rowdy eases out of the bed, fully dressed and wearing boots. He moves the gun to a table, grabs his coat, and then motions for me to follow him. Mage, having found his sister, chooses to stay inside. Once Rowdy closes the door behind him, I let out a pained groan.

"Is everyone okay?" Rowdy demands, eyes searching my face. "You look like hell."

I swipe at my wet cheeks. "No."

"Are they hurt?"

"No."

"For fuck's sake, Ry, what's going on?"

Throwing myself at him, I hug my brother, needing some sort of reassurance that I'm still loved and that my life isn't over. He's stiff at first and then awkwardly pats my back.

"They caught you?"

Pulling back, I gape at him in shock. "H-How'd you know?"

"I'm not an idiot. You and Ronan clearly made up this week. I figured maybe…I don't know, that you got walked in on or something. How pissed was Dad?"

If only it were that simple.

"Mom." I wince, remembering her disgusted, furious face filled with hatred for me. "She, uh, walked in on the three of us."

Rowdy's brows lift. "I see."

"I've never seen her so pissed," I admit with a choked sound of despair. "When Dad finds out, he's going to murder me."

Rowdy frowns. "Dad's not going to murder you."

"I had sex with two of his kids!"

He steps forward, a growl rumbling through him. "Keep it down or you'll wake Dez. She's had a helluva morning." I notice the pure exhaustion written all over his face from his bloodshot eyes, dark circles around them, and overall tired expression tugging at his features.

"Why is she here?" I ask, confusion lacing my tone. "Did you get her to talk?"

His head shakes and his own face is one filled with despondency like mine. "Not yet. Last night was terrible and this morning…she just needed privacy and comfort, neither of which she's getting right now in that cramped cabin."

"Does Mom know she's here?"

"Yes. Mom is the one who had Dad bring her to me to watch over."

I wait for him to elaborate, but his features shutter, closing off at once. Whatever is going on with Destiny is something he isn't willing to share with me right now. It's fine, though. I have bigger fish to fry.

"It gets worse," I whisper, scrubbing my palm over my face. I smell Raegan and my heart aches miserably. "So much worse."

"What's worse than getting caught having sex

with your siblings?" he asks in a dry, sarcastic tone. "Seriously. I think you're probably overreacting."

I grab hold of his jacket lapels and bring him close to me. "Rowdy, Raegan is pregnant."

His face blanches and he swallows hard. He turns his head, breaking eye contact, and frowns.

"Told you," I grouse. "It's not even my baby. It's Ronan's. Mom hates me because I was the first to speak to her, but when she finds out Ronan knocked up our sister, she's really going to freak out."

He plucks my hands from his jacket and pushes me away from him. I watch helplessly as he paces the porch, the cold air clouding with his hot breaths. A brisk wind blows hard, sending fallen leaves fluttering against us. A leaf gets caught in Rowdy's hair and he absently brushes it away before meeting my stare with grief-stricken eyes.

Great.

He hates me too.

How can loving Raegan and Ronan like I do be so horrible?

Pain digs deep into my chest, gutting me like a fucking fish. I can't breathe. My knees are weak and shaky, threatening to give out at any second. When I'm seconds from collapsing from a panic attack, Rowdy steps toward me again. He pulls me in for a hug, this time not awkward at all. He hugs me like he can hold all the shattered bits of me together. I collapse, letting him do the hard work because I'm no longer able to.

My older brother lets me cry, reminding me of when I was five and skinned my knees on the rocks while we played in the river. He was calm and his voice comforted me while he patched me up. We weren't supposed to be at the river without Mom and Dad, but we'd gone anyway. My brother protected me and made everything better.

"I've got your back," he says, clutching me tighter. "No matter what happens, I've got your back. I won't let Dad kill you. And if they try to send you away, I'll make sure to come visit you. It's not the end of the world, okay?"

I doubt it's that simple, but I ache to believe him.

"Can I stay with you again?" I ask, shuddering against the wind. "I'm tired and need a place to hide."

He pulls back and affixes me with a firm stare. "Under one condition."

A condition to living here? Since when?

I nod because it's not like I have a choice.

"Leave Destiny be. She needs the quiet. The space to just be. The last thing she needs is you drilling her with questions like Mom does."

I'm unsure why she needs space, but it's an easy thing to agree to.

"Okay," I drawl out. "I think I can handle that."

He claps me on the shoulder. "Good. Now get back inside before we both freeze our nuts off. If your dog starts farting, he's gone."

I hope you like sleeping outside, Mage…

"Deal." I bark out a harsh laugh. "You got any more of that tequila left?"

He smirks. "Hell yeah. Liquid breakfast it is."

I'm not sure what's in store for my future, but at least I have someone to lean on right now in my pit of despair. Family is everything to me, which complicates this entire shitshow.

CHAPTER THIRTY-SIX

raegan

"WHAT ARE YOU DOING?" Ronan asks, eyes wide with panic.

I finish dressing and stop to yank my boots on. "Having words with our mother."

"Seriously? Right now? Raegan, she's pissed. Let her cool off."

"She's being unreasonable," I grumble, snatching my coat from the couch. "She sent Ryder away like he's the problem here. Just stay here. I'll deal with her."

He spears his fingers through his hair as he starts pacing. "Everything is so fucked."

"No kidding."

As I start for the door, Ronan snaps out of his freak-out mode and stalks over to me. He cradles my face in his palms before pressing a soft kiss to my mouth. Then his knuckles brush over my clothes where my stomach is. It's a reminder of what I'm fighting for. This. Us. Our baby.

I give him another quick kiss and then hurry out of the cabin toward the one next door. Before I even reach the porch, I can hear my parents' raised voices. Lifting my chin and bracing myself for a war, I push into the cabin.

Mom is sitting on the edge of the bed, holding Dawson and crying. Dad is standing over her, an unreadable expression on his face. Kota and Deck both gape at Mom with wide eyes. Destiny is missing, which is strange. The cabin smells like wolf shit and it takes everything in me to remain fierce, not succumbing to gagging.

"It's not all his fault," I huff out, flinging an arm to indicate Ryder whom she just sent away. "We were all there. Why did he get the brunt of it?"

Dad's gaze pins me in place. He opens his mouth to speak, but Mom is quicker.

"We're not doing this here," she hisses. "Not in front of the children."

"We *are* your children," I cry out, voice bordering on hysteria. "Mothers don't send their kids away unless they're bad moms!"

Dad growls. "That's enough, Raegan."

Ignoring him, I waggle a finger at Mom. "Why him? Why is Ryder the problem? Do you love him less?"

Mom passes Dawson to Dad and stomps over to me. "I love all my children the same. But…what I saw…" She shudders, shaking her head. "How could you?"

"How could *I*?" I let out a dark chuckle. "Mom, I love them! What's wrong with love?"

"Everything," she cries out. "It's not the love, it's who you're loving!"

"Well, it's too late now," I say, glowering at her.

"Too late?"

I rub my stomach and shrug. "I'm pregnant."

Dad curses from behind her and Dawson starts repeating it between giggles.

"No," Mom chokes out. "You're just saying that to piss me off."

"I am and it's not Ryder's."

Both of my parents stare at me as though I've grown two heads.

"Ronan?" Mom whispers.

"We were kidnapped, Mother." Tears start welling and I hate that I can't keep the anger at the surface like I want to. "Things happened because I was scared. We all were."

She starts to full-on sob. Dad strokes her hair, body tense, as he scowls at me.

"We're going to have the baby and the three of us will be happy together—"

Mom launches at me, her palm cracking against my cheek before I can even register her quick movement.

"Do you have any idea what you've done?" she demands, tears streaming down her face. "Your baby will have problems. Birth defects. That is, *if* it even makes it that far."

Her words stab hard just as she intended.

"You can't scare me," I growl. "Not only are you a hypocrite, but you're a liar. You married your own father and had a million babies with him!" I motion at the slew of kids in the cabin. "We're all fine, Mom! Your lies about what could happen fall on deaf ears!"

Dad speaks up, his voice deceptively calm. "Where'd you hear this bullshit?"

"Wild." I cross my arms over my chest. "He said he overheard you and his dad talking about it. The cat's out of the bag. Everyone knows."

"You, child, are so clueless about how things are," Mom croaks out. "You think you know everything, but you know nothing. You're stubborn and reckless."

"I know that my baby will be fine," I state with a smirk. "Yours all turned out okay."

Declan runs over to me, clinging to my leg. I stroke his hair because I need the comfort as much as he does.

Dad sits on the bed and sets Dawson down, who immediately crawls over to Kota. Mom's tears haven't stopped. Her shoulders are hunched as if she's tired with defeat.

Good.

I'll win this round with her.

Fighting for the ones I love and my little baby is worth all this drama.

Mom lifts her gaze to meet mine and real fear shines in her eyes. I shift uncomfortably, unease making my stomach recoil.

"Raegan, sweetie," Mom says, her bottom lip wobbling. "He's not my father by blood."

Heat burns up my throat and settles on my cheeks. "What?"

"He adopted me. You kids are fine because our blood isn't…the same." Her eyes drop to my stomach and more tears spill out. "But you? Yours is the same. The child will be…"

No.

That can't be.

Images of a mutant baby with extra body parts or half a brain assault me. Is it really something that happens when you share blood?

"Aunt Eve's babies," Mom whispers. "The ones who died. They were all pregnancies from her brothers."

I take a step back, unlatching myself from Declan. My legs are shaky, forcing me to sit down on the sofa. Everything spins around me.

The babies from her brothers died.

Hurt, unlike anything I've ever felt, stabs at every angle of my heart. Something I was just starting to get excited about has been torn from me. All hope is lost.

My baby might die.

"And if the baby doesn't abort itself," Mom says softly, "we may need to go to town and…"

I search her face and then look at Dad, who won't meet my stare.

"The doctors," I breathe, chest filling with hope again. "They'll fix it. They can fix the baby."

Mom gives a sharp shake of her head. "No, Raegan. They can't."

"Then why go to town? Dad? Why won't you look at me?" I choke back a sob as I watch my father scrub a palm over his face, still unable to look at me.

"They have doctors in town who can remove the baby," Mom says finally, voice hardening. "It's called an abortion."

"Where does the baby go? Can they help it?" Hysteria is clawing at my throat once more. "Can I hold it when it comes out?"

"No." Mom swallows and swipes at a tear. "They remove it from your body, ending its existence since it's probable it won't be a viable fetus."

Ending its existence?

"You mean murder?" I ask, completely dumbfounded by her words. "You want them to murder my baby?"

I clutch my stomach, gaping in horror.

Mom sighs heavily. "It's not murder. It's an abortion. It's legal and common in town."

"No," I say with a shriek. "I will not let them kill my baby!"

"Raegan," Dad grunts, finally looking at me. "Calm down. We're going to figure this out."

"Figure this out? There's nothing to figure out! No one is killing my baby!"

Mom purses her lips and her eyes harden with determination. I know the look. It's the same one she gets when she has an idea she wants Dad to build or when she makes some sort of family decision. It's the look that means it will happen whether I like it or not.

"I won't go," I spit out, shuddering with fear and disgust. "I won't willingly allow you to do that to me."

"And what happens when it comes out all wrong?" Mom demands. "What if it has medical needs that we can't handle out here? Believe me, it's much easier to deal with the loss before you can see or hold the baby."

Mom starts toward me and I lean back against the cushions, shaking my head. "Don't touch me, murderer!"

She shivers and then retreats. "Reed, I'm going to the root cellar. Deal with this child. I need a minute."

I glower after her as she tugs on her boots and coat. She dresses Dawson as well. Then the two of them leave without another word. Declan climbs onto the couch next to me, putting his little arm around me and patting me. His sweet clinginess melts my heart. Knowing I could have a baby one day like him who might die or have problems crushes me.

"I should go back to Ronan," I say, voice hoarse from yelling.

Dad shakes his head. "No. You're exhausted and looking green around the gills. You'll stay in this cabin and get some rest. Once everyone cools off tomorrow, we can have a family discussion."

"What's there to say, Dad? Mom wants to kill my baby."

His eyes darken and he frowns harder. "You know that's not true. She's just trying to protect her children."

I touch my stomach and sniffle. "And I'm trying to protect mine."

Dad walks over to me and presses a kiss to the top of my head. "Please rest, sunshine. We can't figure this all out in one day."

The emotions crash over me in a drowning wave. I slide my body onto the couch, pulling Declan to my chest where he likes to lie. Secretly, I enjoy his comfort and warmth. I close my eyes, trying desperately not to cry.

Dad covers us with a blanket and then whispers for Kota to get his boots on.

As soon as they leave, I fall into a deep sleep that's safe from birth defects and murdering doctors. I just hope when I wake up, my reality doesn't hurt so much.

Because it does.

It really freaking hurts.

CHAPTER THIRTY-SEVEN

ronan

NOT KNOWING WHAT'S GOING ON IS THE WORST. I'm not sure what's happening with my family, but I'm falling into the deep cracks they left behind when they each stormed out of the cabin.

It's dark and cold and fucking lonely.

I could leave. I could easily walk out of this cabin and hunt either one of them down to demand to know the verdict.

Are we being banished?

When I'd listened to Mom and Raegan scream at each other next door this morning, I'd been horrified by what Mom was saying.

She wanted to take Raegan to town to abort the baby.

I'd never understood the word "triggered" until today.

Seeing Michael's tiny, dead baby thrown away like trash was seared into my mind and left a lasting mark that won't ever go away. I didn't realize it was still a gaping wound until I'd heard Raegan accusing Mom of wanting to murder the baby.

How could Mom suggest such a horrible thing?

My heart is raw since their argument. I'd wanted Raegan to come back so we could hold each other—so we could make a plan to track down Ryder and then figure the rest out.

She never came back, though.

I'd overheard Dad making her stay and rest. I'd seen Mom and Dawson, through my window, walk over to the big house. There was no sign of Ryder or anyone else for that matter.

What are they all doing next door?

It's so quiet.

The quiet isn't good for my mind. Not when it's a fucking mess. I'm worried about Ryder. Did he go to Rowdy's cabin? Did he go someplace farther? Is he safe?

Each time I close my eyes, I see him alone and afraid. I ache to go to him, but I'm rooted in this cabin. Anxiety has taken hold of my limbs, trapping me inside along with my unruly thoughts.

Grow some balls and go look for them…

I look toward my boots on the floor and then over at the closed door. The fresh air would do me some good. Just get off the bed, dress for the outdoors, and leave.

A shudder ripples through me.

What if Dad is waiting to beat me into next week for impregnating his daughter?

What if Ryder refuses to see me again like when he caught me and Raegan having sex months ago?

What if Mom has already taken Raegan to town to rid her of the baby?

I curl deeper into my blankets, burying my face. The heat of my breath makes it so that I feel as though I'm suffocating.

I'm alone.

I'm so fucking alone.

Peeling the blanket off my head, I once again stare at my boots and then the door. My gaze flies back over to the window where I'd left the curtains drawn. Snow continues to fall. It started while Mom was in the big house and got heavier long after she walked back. It'd been sticking all day. I'd watched it to pass the time and marveled over how quickly the ground became covered in it. Tonight, it's dark and I can't see anything.

I hope Ryder is somewhere safe. Surely, he'd have gone to Rowdy's for the time being. And Raegan, as far as I know, is still next door.

All this not knowing is driving me insane.

I could find out by walking next door.

Again, I drift my gaze to my boots and then the door. With a frustrated sigh, I pull the covers back over my face.

When I start to fall asleep, my thoughts are chaotic, showing me horrific images of what our baby might look like when it comes out. I even dream about Mom handing Michael a knife so he can "take care of it."

In and out of dreamland, I confuse what's real and what isn't. Several times I wake up sweating and in a panic, only to realize I'm not holding Stacey's blue baby. The dreams always tug me back, chasing away reality and giving me graphic, bold images that make me sick.

Logan keeps trying to enter my dreams, but I'm too focused on Raegan. Raegan's pregnancy. Raegan's delivery. Our baby. Ryder. My angry parents.

Eventually, Logan muscles his way into my dream. His voice whispers harshly, breath tickling over my face.

"I've missed you, pet."

I whimper and cry, wishing I could go back to the dreams with my family. Like in the past, Logan dominates me, his weight crushing me, reminding me that he'll always win.

"No," I plead, my throat brittle and dry. "Please."

His hand covers my mouth. "I love watching you beg."

Awareness trickles in. Wind blowing outside. Heat from the fireplace. The weight of another person on top of me.

Popping open my eyes, I stare down the monster from my nightmares.

But it's real.

He's real.

Oh, God, no.

His eyes are wilder than I remember and his beard has grown out, making him look scraggly. A beanie is pulled down over his eyebrows. He grins at me once he understands I've finally come to.

Logan isn't dead.

I stabbed him in the ear with a stick and shot him with my rifle, but he didn't die. He somehow survived, found his way back here, and intends to finish what he started.

Ruining me.

It was always his end goal.

His little pet to train and scold and beat until I either gave in or died fighting.

"You ran away from me," he growls, hand still clamped over my mouth. "I was very sad and disappointed."

His eyes flash with a storm of rage and violence. I flinch at the evilness staring back at me. I'm going to die. In my brother's bed. Alone.

Well, not all alone.

Logan will be here.

He slides off to my side and roams his free hand down my front. I sob behind his hand when he roughly touches my cock through my boxers. His touch doesn't arouse me. It terrifies the hell out of me.

I'm thrust to the past when he forced his way inside me.

How he ripped tender parts as he took and took and took.

I gag, knowing the fate that awaits me.

"I'm going to let go of your mouth," Logan warns,

"and if you cry or scream for help, I'll stab every god-damn one of them next door while they sleep. Their deaths will be on your hands. Is that what you want, pet? To be complicit in their murders?"

Tears silently roll down and I shake my head in vehemence. Almost everyone I love is next door. If he were to kill them all, there's no point in me living at all.

He pulls his palm from my mouth, eyes narrowed as he waits for me to make a sound. I clamp down, pressing my lips together, and squeeze my eyes shut so I don't have to see him.

"I missed your tight little hole, pet."

A sob crawls up my throat, but I swallow it down, refusing to be the reason my family dies. I can feel his calloused fingers digging into my stomach as he latches onto my boxers and pulls them down. With superior strength, he flips me onto my stomach and spits onto my ass crack. The entire bed quivers with my silent sobbing. I can hear him fumbling with his belt. The jangling of the buckle lets me know it's almost time for severe pain.

"Did you keep your hole safe for me?" he rumbles, pulling my ass cheeks apart. "Or did you let your brother fuck it?" He spits again, the wad landing on my asshole. "I watched the three of you last night through the window. Don't they know you belong to me, pet?"

His rough thumb rubs his spit over my asshole and I brace myself for the pain.

It's coming.

Inevitable and mighty.

Maybe this time I'll die from it.

An animal roars nearby.

Is it Logan? Is he eager to claim me once and for all?

The beast has entered the cabin with us. I can still hear its thunderous roaring. The icy sting of the air sweeps in, chilling my backside.

Is it a bear? A wolf? Will it eat us both?

I can only hope.

Logan's grip on my ass disappears. A thud to my left has me turning my head, peeking to see what the creature is. Logan is on his ass, jeans and boxers pulled down his thighs, staring up at the beast with absolute fear in his eyes.

Fear?

Logan isn't afraid of anything.

Maybe a grizzly.

The beast slams something down on Logan—an ax. What sort of animal carries around an ax? It thwacks into his shoulder, damn near severing his arm from his body. The horrible wail pouring into the cabin is from Logan. Pained and horrified. What a beautiful sound.

While Logan screams in agony, I watch the beast grab his foot and yank him out of view. Unable to keep my curiosity at bay, I roll onto my back to stare down the monster.

Massive. Feral. Rippling with rage. His eyes are pure malice as he stares down his prey. Not me. I'm not the prey. I'm the beast's young.

Dad.

It's my dad.

The man whom I feared might kill me for getting my sister pregnant is brutally attacking the man who raped me. Even with him being half blurry without my glasses, I'd recognize him anywhere.

"Dad," I croak out.

He's an animal right now, yanking and dragging the screaming rapist out of the cabin into the icy darkness.

I need to see.

Scrambling from the bed, I yank up my underwear, throw on my jeans and coat, and then stuff my feet into my boots. Lastly, I grab my glasses off the end table. Everything comes into sharp focus. I follow the bloody smears through the cabin, onto the porch, and into the snow. Past my cabin where my family is at, ignoring the cries of my sister and mom and little brothers.

I need to see.

Dad continues to drag the vermin, heading straight for the gate. I stumble over my feet, hurrying to follow after him. He disappears around the corner, but Logan's screaming leads the way. I continue to follow Dad, finally catching up to him. He's snarling and huffing, using his ax in one hand to clear any brush in his way while hauling his prey behind him.

He stops in front of a tree a hundred yards from our fenced-in property. His eyes dart briefly to mine before he drops the ax. With a grunt, he slams his boot into

Logan's face. Bones crunch and Logan makes a pained cry. I can't look away.

I need to see.

I need to see Logan in pain. *I need to see* his blood.

Dad's boot rears up again before slamming Logan in the center of his chest. Logan gasps for breath but doesn't catch it before Dad brings down his boot, this time, on his stomach. This causes Logan to vomit all over himself and Dad's brutal boot.

I watch in awe as Dad steps on Logan's nearly severed arm, grinding the bottom of his boot into the exposed bone, sinew, and muscle.

I don't gag or look away because *I need to see.*

Over and over, Dad brings his boot down on every part of Logan's body. He saves the rapist's now flaccid cock for last, stomping harder than anywhere before. Logan moans, his good arm trying to push Dad's boot away.

Not happening.

Dad abandons him for a moment to snap a small, thin tree in half. Only about two feet remain, the tip sharp and pointed. Then he grabs Logan, hauling him into a sitting position. Wrapping his arms around him, he picks him up and walks backward until they're over that tree.

I need to see even though this will be horrifying.

Dad pushes down with all his might on Logan's body. The scream that comes out of Logan is unlike anything I've ever heard in my life. Terrible and haunting. It's the scream of ultimate pain and looming death.

My fierce father steps away, scoops up his ax, and then points it at me. "Stay back, Son."

I realize I'd stumbled closer in my effort to watch him torture Logan. Staggering back several steps, I keep my eyes on Logan. His arm hangs by a flimsy, thin piece of muscle, showing through the hacked opening of his coat. The entire thing is twisted at an unnatural angle.

Disgusting.

Dad heaves the ax above him and brings the sharp blade down over Logan's other shoulder. This time, Logan loses the other arm completely.

He'll never be able to hit me with them ever again.

Then Dad swings the ax again, sinking it down between his thighs. I wince when I see his cock slide off the blade and land in the snow beside him. Dad continues hacking at this man, on his legs and torso, but strategically leaving his head, heart, and vital organs intact.

Satisfied with his work, Dad tosses the ax aside to study Logan's bleeding, twitching body. He's still alive in there somewhere because he makes soft groans and gurgling sounds.

He'll bleed out from the ax wounds or internal injuries, or the wild animals will feast on him tonight. Either way, Logan won't live to see another sunrise.

Dad scoops up his ax and then walks over to me, violence still gleaming in his eyes. I don't flinch away because he's not here to hurt me.

When he reaches me, he clutches the back of my head, pressing his forehead to mine.

"He will never hurt you again, my sweet boy. Fucking never."

A sob of relief escapes me. Dad pulls back and then kisses the top of my head. Then he wraps an arm around me. Together, we walk back home.

Free.

I'm finally free of that monster.

He'll never come for me ever again.

CHAPTER THIRTY-EIGHT

ryder

WAKE TO SOMEONE POUNDING ON THE DOOR. My eyes fly open and I quickly scan the dark cabin that's only lit up by the moonlight shining in the windows.

Rowdy grunts, grabbing his .45 and then prowling through the shadowed cabin toward the banging. Spirit and Mage both growl from their location on Rowdy's bed beside Destiny. I'm on the couch without a weapon, hoping the person is family, not foe.

"Fuck," Rowdy mutters before opening the door. "What the hell happened to you?"

The cabin suddenly illuminates as Rowdy turns on a lantern. A man, covered in blood, walks into the small home.

It's Dad.

He carries a bloody ax in hand and his feral gaze lands on each one of his kids before stopping at me. Fear crawls up my spine, clawing painfully into me. I'm frozen in his stare.

How did he get all that blood on him?

Ronan? Raegan? Mom?

The thought of something gruesome happening to any of them has me shivering wildly.

"I killed him." Dad's features remain pinned on me. "He's not quite dead yet, but give him another half hour or so and he'll be gone."

Rowdy frowns at Dad. "*Who* did you kill?"

I can sense the growing panic in my brother because I feel it too.

Ronan?

Our father killed Ronan because he got our sister pregnant?

This can't be happening. Not my dad. Please, God, no.

"Logan," Dad snarls with disgust. "That rapist, sick sonofabitch…"

Understanding washes over me and I fall back against the cushions, shaking with relief. He didn't kill my brother.

"He found his way back," Rowdy grunts. "Fuck."

Dad shifts on his feet, gaze settling on Rowdy for a moment. "I knew something wasn't right. I heard voices and went next door to investigate." Dad's eyes close and he shudders. "I saw him on *my fucking son* and I lost it."

Oh God.

Did he rape him again?

Is Ronan okay?

"I need to go to him," I croak out, shakily standing. "I need to—"

"Sit back down, Ryder," Dad rumbles, tired eyes

settling on me. "He's in the cabin with your mom and the kids. Safe."

My breath rushes out in a harsh swoosh.

"I just needed to come let you all know," Dad says with a grunt. "And to clean up before I go back home. The kids don't need to see me like this." His gaze darts over to Destiny. "Rowdy, do you have something I can change into?"

Destiny remains curled up on the bed. Her eyes are open, but it's not like she can see what our dad looks like at the moment, which is good. She doesn't speak, but her entire body trembles.

Dad strips down to his boxers while Rowdy heats water on the stove. Our father slumps onto the kitchen chair. I stare at him, surprised by the way his body trembles. His scars are all pink and puckered, but ultimately healed from where they stabbed him months ago, so the shaking must be from adrenaline, not exertion. Once Rowdy has the water warmed up and locates soap and a washcloth, he sets it down in front of Dad on the table. Dad quickly scrubs away all the blood while Rowdy digs around in his drawers for a change of clothes.

"Ryder," Dad says after he's pulled on the clean clothes. "Tomorrow morning, we need to talk. First light by the firepit."

I swallow hard and nod. I'd rather talk than be shunned by my family. I'm desperate to know how Ronan and Raegan are doing too.

"Does Mom hate me?" I ask in a raspy voice.

Dad scowls at me. "Your mother loves you all with the fire of a thousand suns. She's allowed to get angry and hate the choices you kids make, but she could never hate you. You can get that goddamn notion out of your head right now."

My heart aches at his words. "And you, Dad?"

He leans forward, elbows resting on his knees and fierce gaze boring into me. "Everything I have ever done for as long as I can remember has always been for my children. Always."

I stand on wobbly legs and make my way over to Dad. He rises to his feet, capturing me in a strong, comforting hug. I cling to my father, letting go of all the emotions that have been tearing me apart. As I lose it against his shoulder, he pats me and murmurs over and over, "You're a good boy, Ryder. I love you."

"Best get going," Rowdy says, shoving a plate onto my chest.

I crack open my eyes and sniff the air. Scrambled eggs. Not going to turn down breakfast in bed, that's for damn sure. I sit up and start wolfing down my meal. Destiny is sitting in bed, slowly eating her eggs. I'm still dying to ask what's up with her, but I have enough shit to deal with right now.

Before Dad left last night, he said we were having a

family discussion at the firepit. Me, Ronan, and Raegan were all expected to be there.

"I'm on kid duty with Destiny." Rowdy sucks down his coffee and then nods at our sister. "Dez, I'll be gentle when I carry you, but we need to go to Ronan's cabin now, okay?"

She doesn't respond but sets her plate aside. Mage, the idiot wolf dog, hops onto the bed to start licking the remaining eggs off her plate. Spirit makes a huffing warning sound that has Mage grumbling and pulling away.

I throw on my boots and then carry my plate over to his sink. Making myself a mug of coffee that's no longer hot, I chug it down, eager to wash away the morning breath since my toothbrush is in my cabin.

Fifteen minutes later, we're trudging up the cliffside stairs. Rowdy carries Destiny, all bundled in a quilt, mindfully stepping as to avoid the slick, icy spots along the way. Mage does slip and nearly busts his ass, which has me and Rowdy both snorting with amusement.

Despite the overall apprehension of this family discussion, I'm not panicking. Mom loves me. Dad does too. No one is going to die.

We reach the top and walk around the fence line. When we turn the corner, we see a trail of blood that leads out to where Logan must be. The wolves rush ahead to investigate. Me and Rowdy exchange a look but don't say anything so as not to upset Destiny. Once we make it through the gate, Rowdy heads left toward the cabins and I start for the firepit. No one is there yet, so I start building us a fire for our chat.

By the time I have a hot, crackling fire going, the rest of my family starts lumbering my way. Ronan and Raegan walk ahead of my parents. Raegan holds on to Ronan's arm, her head leaned against him. My chest tightens at seeing them. Fuck, I missed them.

Raegan ruffles my hair as she walks past. She and Ronan sit, with Ronan between us. Mom and Dad sit on the other side of the fire. He pulls her to him, his arm wrapping around her. The fire makes popping sounds, but none of us speak. The silence is brutal.

Raegan, the mouth of our family, can't take it any longer and she's the one to speak first.

"I'm keeping the baby. I will not abort it." Her voice cracks and she sniffles. "If something is wrong with it, I'll love it anyway."

Mom's lips press into a thin line, but surprisingly, she gives her a clipped nod. Dad leans in and kisses Mom's head.

"I'm going to help her," Ronan rasps out. "It's my child too. Whatever happens, we face it together."

Everything falls silent again. This time, I feel like it's my turn.

"I, uh, I'm not leaving." I look at Mom and then Dad, remembering that they don't hate me. I'm their son and a part of this family. "I'm going to stay here with Ronan and Raegan. For both of them and the baby. I love them and need to protect them."

Mom's eyes shine with tears and her bottom lip wobbles, but she doesn't say anything.

"If we need to go somewhere else," Raegan says, her voice shaking, "we will. We'll build our own home where the three of us can live together. It's what we want."

Dad sighs heavily and nods. "This thing between you three…" He trails off and bounces his gaze off of each of us before landing on the fire. "It may work out here, but if you ever decide to leave, it's going to be messy. In the real world. Civilization."

"I don't…" Mom's voice quavers. "I don't want the little children to see. It'll only confuse them."

"She's right," Dad agrees. "As soon as the big house is done, we'll work on building another house nearby for the three of you. Please respect our request for no displays of affection where the kids can see. In your own home, you may do as you wish."

"I'm pregnant, though," Raegan argues. "Eventually, they'll want to know where the baby came from."

Mom shakes her head. "One day, when they're older, they'll figure it out. Until then, I'd like to keep them in the dark as much as possible. They're small and will only understand you're pregnant, not how you came to be that way."

"You can't shut us out completely," I blurt out, my insecurities rising to the surface. "We need you."

Mom starts to cry and rises to her feet. I also stand and rush over to her. She hugs me, squeezing me tight.

I inhale her familiar scent, trying desperately not to lose it as well.

"You're my baby," Mom croons. "You always will be. I love you. I love all of you."

Dad joins the hug and then my siblings are there too. Everything's going to be okay.

"This way," Dad says, urging me to follow him out of the gate.

After our family discussion, Mom went back to the kids while Ronan and Raegan went to my cabin to wait for me. Me and Dad are going to deal with Logan's body.

As we make our trek, following the blood trail, relief floods through me. I wish I'd hunted him down when he found us months ago in the woods, but knowing he's gone for good now is enough to satisfy me.

I fall into step beside Dad and take in the gory sight before me. Logan's arms are completely gone and something seems to have made a feast of his organs. Intestines have been dragged away several feet from his body.

"Something got what was left of him," Dad says with a grunt. "If you ask me, it was too easy of a death."

I agree wholeheartedly.

"Where are we taking him?" I ask, fixating on the fact Logan's cock is gone. "Over the cliff and into the river?"

Dad shakes his head. "No. I don't want your brother ever running up on him. I want the corpse far away from here." He points west. "There's a drop-off a couple miles that way, beyond where we usually hunt. We can dump him there. The critters can make a meal of him and we don't have to worry about Ronan running across his bones."

I give him a nod of understanding.

"I'll grab his head, you grab his feet," Dad instructs. "Anything leftover, Mage will eat."

Knowing my disgusting wolf probably ate Logan's dick makes me gag. Dad chuckles before clutching onto Logan's head. He pulls him up and off a broken tree. When I realize that thing was in his ass, I decide maybe he did have a deserving, painful death. I take hold of what's left of Logan's legs and lift.

We walk miles in the snow, carrying the rapist's body.

And when we finally dump him in the hole, forever leaving that fucker behind, Dad wraps an arm around my shoulders and kisses my head.

"Time to go home, Son."

No sweeter words ever spoken.

I'm going home and I don't ever have to leave.

CHAPTER THIRTY-NINE

raegan

Several months later...

RONAN LIES ON HIS BACK, NOSE BURIED IN HIS book. Last time Uncle Atticus came to visit, Dad and Ryder went back with him for more supplies. Dad brought Ronan a whole stack of pregnancy books and baby books. I'd been more interested in the stretchy pants and marshmallows.

"Learning anything good?" I ask, lying on my side to watch him.

He tears his gaze from the book to smile at me. It never fails how he can get my heart to patter wildly whenever he looks at me with such love in his eyes. For me. For Ryder. For our baby.

"Just learning about teething." He tosses the book aside to touch my huge belly. "How's my bunny doing?"

"Missing his daddy," I say, covering his hand with

mine. "He's been kicking a lot, trying to get your attention."

He lifts a brow and smirks at me. "Sounds like his mama."

The baby kicks and we both laugh in excitement. I wish Ryder were here to feel him kick, but he's been working tirelessly on our house, trying to get it ready for the baby.

"How are you feeling?" Ronan asks, leaning forward to kiss me on the lips. "Craving anything? I can run to the big house and grab it."

I love how doting of a father Ronan already is and the baby isn't even here yet. He's such a caring, loving person. Our baby is lucky to have him.

"Nah." I groan, stretching my sore body. "Mom's about to pop with baby number eighty-seven. She might stab you if you try to take her marshmallows."

"I can handle Mom."

I run my fingers through his hair that's grown longer lately, curling over his brows and brushing against his glasses. "I'm craving something else right now."

Ronan's gaze darkens and he kisses me with tongue. He still sucks when it comes to pleasuring me, but he tries. His hand is gentle as he ghosts over one of my huge breasts.

"You should let Ryder teach you how to pinch my nipples," I tease, nipping at his lip. "He's not afraid to hurt me."

He takes hold of my nipple through my shirt and

twists it to the point I gasp for breath. "You like a little pain, don't you?"

In all honesty, yes.

When Ryder gets lost, fucking me like an animal when Ronan is inside him, he sometimes leaves bruises on me. He doesn't mean to. It's just that he loses all sense of control. I love it.

"One day," I murmur, reaching down to rub against Ronan's cock through his pants, "when I'm not pregnant, I'm going to let you take me like you take our brother. You don't treat him like he's made of glass."

Ronan ruts against my hand, breathing heavily. "You want me to fuck your ass, Rae?"

"With Rowdy inside my pussy," I taunt, flashing him a wicked grin. "I bet that would feel insane."

"You're a fucking tease," Ronan growls. "I could fuck you right now."

"Ryder says he doesn't mind if we do stuff while he's working on the house…"

"But?"

"But we both know it's just so much better when he's with us."

It's true. When the three of us come together in bed, it feels complete. Like our love is all tangled up just as it should be. We've had sex with each other without the third person plenty of times, and while it's good, it's just not mind-altering like it is with all three.

"Want me to massage your feet until Ryder gets back?"

"Just hold me. I'm content cuddling."

Ronan strokes my hair and then holds my stomach. The baby kicks like crazy. I thought I'd hate being pregnant, but I secretly love it. I love how now that our bunny kicks, I know he's okay in there. If ever he doesn't move, I start to worry and think the worst. Luckily, he's incredibly active, which keeps my anxiety at bay.

"Have you thought of a name for him?" I ask, closing my eyes as I try to imagine what our baby will look like. "I like the name Xavier."

Ronan groans. "That's the name of the villain in my favorite series. Xavier is a twat."

"But it's a cool name!"

"Maybe. How are you so sure it's a boy anyway?"

"Just a feeling."

"If it's a boy, I like the name Quinn. That could go good for a girl too. Just in case."

"Hmm. I'm not in love with it. Ryder might have to be the decider," I say with a huff. "We're too divided on this."

"What do you think Mom will name our newest sibling?"

"Hopefully, it's something with a different letter than R or D. I can't keep all these damn kids straight!"

We both crack up laughing. It's true, though. Mom and Dad didn't think that far outside the box when naming their army of children.

I must fall asleep while we cuddle because I wake to someone kissing my stomach. Cracking my eyes open,

I'm delighted to see Ryder's home and freshly show-ered. He's wearing nothing but his boxers and I decide it's almost as delicious of a sight as a bag of marshmal-lows. Almost.

"How's the house?" I ask, running my fingers through Ryder's hair. "Make any more progress?"

"It's officially enclosed," he says with a grin. "Next we'll insulate it and put in flooring. Fireplace works. We'll be able to move in before our little bunny arrives."

"Thought of any names?" Ronan asks, reaching for-ward to run a finger down Ryder's muscular shoulder. "We're at an impasse."

"What about Rover or Dante?" he deadpans.

I roll my eyes. "Shut up."

"I hear R and D names are all the rage."

"You're a dork, Ryder. Make your mouth useful and do other things."

His grin is devilish. "I can do that."

I stretch out, allowing him to pull my pants and un-derwear off. He shoves my shirt up over my boobs so he can stare at them. No one loves my boobs like Ryder does. His mouth trails kisses over my stomach, sweetly and almost innocently, before he moves lower. I can't see him over my belly. Hot breath tickles my pussy as he spreads my thighs.

Ronan slips off the bed and I watch him grab the supplies—lube and a towel. Ryder starts licking me, making me mewl in pleasure. The man can work all day on the house and not tire out when it comes to pleasuring me.

I track Ronan as he undresses and then kneels behind our brother. Ryder grunts against my pussy, letting me know Ronan's mouth is now on him. They let me watch once while Ronan spread our brother out on the bed and stuck his tongue in his ass. It'd been equal parts hot and just plain weird. But the blissed out way Ryder moaned and begged was enough to tell me it was more hot than weird. Hell, I almost asked for him to do the same to me after. Almost.

Ryder slides a finger inside me, rubbing at the good place inside of me while sucking on my clit. He has it down to an art, easily driving me over the edge within minutes. Tonight is no different. I'm falling over the cliff of ecstasy, my entire body shaking without warning.

Ryder curses against my pussy before pulling his finger out. Roughly, he grips my thighs and hauls me to the end of the bed. Ronan is no longer on the floor and waiting for Ryder to get into position. Seeing them both look down at me warms every dark part of my soul. I love them so much and am happy we found our way here.

I reach back for the pillows and hand them to Ryder. He swiftly stuffs them under my ass, positioning me to the right height for him. Once I'm ready, he teases my slick opening with the tip of his cock and then pushes deep inside me. I cry out, desperate to grab onto something, and settle for my boobs. Ryder's hot gaze latches onto them and he grins.

Behind him, Ronan pushes down on his back until Ryder is hovering over me, staring intently at me. His eyes roll back as Ronan enters him from behind. I love watching Ryder explode with pleasure.

The next several minutes are a blur of sweat, moans, and shared orgasms. Like always, Ronan takes care of the mess before sandwiching our brother between us.

At one time, we had to worry about people barging in, mainly our parents, but now they respect our privacy since we respect their rules of no PDA around the kids. Our time in our cabin, and soon our big home, is solely ours.

I'm curled around Ryder, my belly pressed against his side, when the baby starts kicking again. He chuckles, the vibration rumbling the whole bed.

"He's a little mean thing like you," Ryder says playfully.

I smack his hard stomach. "Hush."

Ronan finds my hand on Ryder's stomach and squeezes it. We're content to just lie there in our after-sex bliss, no one making a sound. After some time, I realize Mage isn't here.

"Where's the stinky ass?" I ask, tilting my head up to look at Ryder.

"With Dad."

"Again?" Ronan says with a laugh. "I bet Mom loves that."

"As long as he doesn't shit in her room, she's fine," Ryder replies. "Plus, Dad loves that wolf."

"The wolf he wanted to kill," I remind him.

"He sees the error of his ways."

"At least we don't have to smell his farts tonight." I sit up on my elbow, looking at my brothers. "It's actually a good thing Mage wants to sleep in the bed with them. Kind of hard to keep breeding your wife with a wolf in the way."

Ronan snorts out a laugh. "You really think that's going to stop them? Dad told me the other day they had sex when Mom was in labor with Rowdy."

"What?" I shriek. "Gross. Why would he tell you that?"

Ryder chuckles. "He told me too. I think it's some sort of war story. Or a flex."

"I swear to God if either of you tries to have sex with me when I'm having this kid, I'll gut you with my knife!"

"If you're big and pregnant, do you actually think you'd be able to catch us," Ryder teases, "much less gut us?"

I growl, narrowing my eyes at him. Both my brothers laugh at me. Assholes.

"That's it," I say, pointing in the direction of the big house. "Someone has to go get me marshmallows." I poke at Ryder. "That someone is you."

Ryder pouts. "Me? Ronan laughed too."

"Ronan has to rub my feet. You're both being punished."

Ryder climbs over me and starts throwing on clothes. He flashes me a sexy grin before walking toward the door.

"Wait," I cry out, reaching out a hand. "I need a kiss before you go."

He stalks over to me, kissing me hard and with filthy intent. "Love you, Rae. Even when you're a brat."

I bite his bottom lip. "You had to ruin it."

"You live to fight. I'm just giving you something to live for."

After he walks out to get my snack, I turn to Ronan and point at my feet. "They're not going to rub themselves."

He smirks and drops a kiss on my nose. "You're lucky I love the hell out of you, woman. You're bossy as fuck."

I playfully scowl at him until he starts rubbing my feet.

Closing my eyes, I try to imagine being any happier than I am in this moment. Pregnant, with my brother's baby, and preparing to move into a home I will share with my two favorite siblings.

Nope.

I can't see it ever getting more perfect than this.

Patting my stomach, I silently tell our little bunny that it's his job to come out safe and healthy. We've had enough heartache in our short lifetime.

The future is reserved for laughter and love.

EPILOGUE

ronan

Delivery Day...

WHY IS SHE SWEATING SO MUCH? THAT'S not normal. I didn't read about sweating in my books. There was nothing about sweating.

I jerk my gaze from my sister to where my mom sits in the corner, nursing Renna. We're in the big house in my parents' room because they have more space and supplies for childbirth.

When Mom had Renna, she bled a lot. So much that I thought Dad was going to take Ryder's truck and drive her all the way to town. But, eventually, she stopped and everything was okay.

Will it be okay with Raegan?

Dad and Ryder return from wherever it is they disappeared to wearing matching worried frowns. Normally, Raegan would have vicious words for them and demand what was wrong. Not tonight. Tonight, she's pale and sweating and whimpering.

I'm fucking terrified.

There were chapters in those books about delivering a baby at home. The books didn't gloss over the possible complications for both mother and baby. Their magical solution was to seek immediate medical care as soon as possible. Out here, that's simply not an option. Maybe we should pack her up in the truck and take her to the hospital.

Ryder frowns at me, reading my mind. "We can go if we need to. It's why we ended up getting the truck. For emergencies."

Mom shakes her head. "Raegan has made it clear she doesn't want to go to town. She's worried they'll ask questions and take the baby."

"We won't let them," Dad chimes in. "I'd like to see them fucking try."

Dad goes into the bathroom to wash up and then returns to where Raegan is lying on the bed, a sheet over her stomach and towels beneath her.

"Sunshine," Dad says, patting her knee. "I need to see how far you're dilated. Have you had any more contractions?"

Her eyes flutter and a low, pained moan that sends tears rolling down her cheeks gives us the answer. Dad waits until the moment passes before lifting the sheet. He motions for Ryder to come look.

"She's almost there," Dad says. "I'd say she's about ready to start pushing."

I squeeze Raegan's hand, hoping to give her the support she needs to do this. She's been terrified of the pain it'll cause and I'm afraid of the complications. Ryder has been the most levelheaded of the three of us, which is why he's assisting with the birth and not me.

"I think I need to push," Raegan says with a low whine. "Dad…"

He remains kneeling on the floor in front of her. "Okay, Raegan, start pushing."

Her entire face turns purple as she exerts her energy to push. I let go of her hand, helping her to grip onto the backs of her thighs. She pants heavily and then cries out, a soulful howl that breaks my heart.

She's in so much pain.

"You got this, baby," Ryder says, squatting down beside Dad.

Mom disappears to put Renna down and then returns with a wet cloth. She hands it to me and motions for Raegan's forehead. I settle it over her brow and whisper assurances to her.

"Next contraction, I want you to push again," Dad instructs. "Come on. You can do it."

The next contraction is quick to seize her. She whimpers and then bears down with all her might. The sweat continues to roll off her.

"Ahhh," she cries out and then starts to sob. "I can't do this, Daddy. I'm going to die."

I shoot Dad a panicked look, but he doesn't waver. "No, sunshine, you're going to do this because you have to. You're strong. I'm going to help you."

Another contraction. Another scream.

My anxiety is clawing away at my insides, but I don't dare let Raegan know. She needs to be brave and strong. Not just for our little bunny but for herself too.

I can't lose them.

"See that beautiful dark hair," Dad says, his face lighting up. "That's the baby's head, Ry. He's coming and he's positioned the right way."

I exhale heavily with relief. I'd read about breach babies and it was a worry of mine.

"You can do this," I murmur to Raegan. "Do this and I'll change every dirty diaper until he's eighteen."

She doesn't shoot me a nasty look or laugh at my joke. Another contraction hits her and her face turns purple once more as she screams in pain.

Ryder's face pales, but Dad is grinning.

"Another push and the head will be out," Dad says. "You're doing so good."

Seconds later, Dad exclaims that the head is out. Ryder watches wide-eyed but says nothing. Mom stands near Dad, frowning with her arms crossed. We're all scared shitless.

"Shoulders are next," Dad says with a grunt. "Smooth sailing after that."

Raegan sobs and then sucks in a deep breath before

pushing hard. There's a bit of commotion and then Dad is cursing. Panic swells up inside me.

"W-What?" I demand, unable to keep calm for Raegan's sake.

Dad glances over his shoulder at Mom. "Umbilical cord. It's around the baby's neck."

Raegan starts to cry. "I'm so tired, Daddy. I can't do it anymore. Can I go to sleep?"

"No," Mom barks out, rushing over to her other side. "No sleeping. Focus and push the baby out."

Raegan shakes her head in defiance, but Mom won't have any of it.

"Raegan," Mom hisses. "You push out this baby or you'll die. Understand me? We'll have to cut him out of you and you won't survive it. I can't lose you."

Horrible memories of Stacey's baby enter my mind. They'd had to cut into her and Michael accidentally killed it. I can't do this. I can't watch my sister and our baby die.

Raegan screams and then bears down with energy reserves somewhere inside of her.

"Shoulders are out," Dad bellows. "Ryder, get your knife."

I choke on my terror, scrambling away from my sister to see what they're about to do. Or stop them if necessary. By the time I reach where they're at, I see the baby sliding out, the cord wrapped tightly around its neck. Ryder grunts, sawing through the umbilical cord while Dad pulls the slippery baby the rest of the way out.

"He's not breathing, Dad," Ryder cries out, quickly unraveling the cord. "Fuck!"

Mom hands Ryder the aspirator and he sucks the baby's nose and mouth like she taught us.

"Still not breathing!"

I don't have time to marvel over the fact our baby is indeed a boy because I'm snapping into action. Scooping up my son, I bring him over to the rug and lay him down.

Thirty compressions with my two fingers. An inch and a half deep. At a rate of one hundred to one hundred twenty seconds a minute. Just like I learned in the baby books I obsessively consumed.

I tilt his tiny head back to open his airway and then cover his mouth and nose with my own mouth to give him two breaths, each one going for about a second. Then I watch for a rise and fall.

Nothing.

Fuck.

I repeat my actions, ignoring all the sounds around me. It's just me and my son. Focusing, I make sure I have a good seal before I blow air after the compressions. This time, I see it.

A rise. A fall. Another rise.

And then I hear the most beautiful thing.

A mewl. Then a soft cry. And then a scream.

Mom drops beside me with a blanket. I lift him up and then lay him back down on it. She swaddles him up before handing him to me. Pulling him to my chest,

I kiss his dark, fuzzy head and then I carry him over to Raegan.

"He's alive?" she croaks out. "Tell me he's okay."

"He's breathing," I assure her, grinning. "He's fucking perfect, Rae."

She starts to cry as I hand him to her. Her eyes are wide and filled with awe as she studies the little guy in her arms. Now that he can breathe, he doesn't stop hollering. I love it. He can scream forever and I won't care as long as he's healthy.

Mom steps over to help, shooing Ryder to go to Raegan's other side. My brother's grin is wide as he looks at the baby.

"Did you guys ever decide on a name?" Mom asks in a teasing voice.

"What about Cayden?" Ryder asks, cheeks blazing red. "I saw it in one of the baby books. It said it means fighter."

Raegan's lips curl into a grin. "Cayden. That's your name, little bunny. Cayden Reed Jamison."

"It's perfect." I stroke his soft head. "He's our little fighter."

The three of us stare at our fussy miniature human, completely awestruck and in love.

Dad finishes taking care of Raegan and covers her up with the blanket. She falls asleep mid-sentence, softly snoring. Ryder sniggers and lifts Cayden out of her arms.

"Go find somewhere to sit so you both can bond

with Cayden," Mom says to us. "Your dad and I will stay with her while she sleeps."

I follow Ryder out of their bedroom and into the living room. Rowdy has all the kids with him except for Renna, which means we don't have to fight off a bunch of littles who want to see the new baby. Ryder sits down on the sofa in front of the fire. I settle next to him, unable to take my eyes off my son.

Ryder leans toward me and I meet him for a quick kiss. We did it. We went to hell and back, killed monsters along the way, fell in love, and made a baby. This is our happily ever after just like in all the books me and Raegan read.

Cayden continues to cry, but Mom shows up with a bottle of formula.

"She's too exhausted to try to get her to nurse. Feed him and burp him. Later, we can try and see if he'll latch on when she's had proper rest."

Ryder passes Cayden to me and I cradle him in my arms. Once I'm settled, Ryder hands me the bottle. Our hungry baby boy latches onto the bottle nipple and greedily gulps at it like he was born to feed. We both chuckle at him.

"This doesn't feel real," I murmur. "I keep thinking I'm going to wake up and it'll all have been a cruel dream."

Ryder pinches my thigh, making me scowl at him. "You're awake. It's real. Enjoy it, Daddy."

Daddy.

Holy shit.

Cayden devours his bottle and when it's time to burp, Ryder takes him from me. I grin stupidly at my brother as he expertly burps him.

"I'm happy, Ryder. Like really, really happy."

He leans against me. "Me too, Ro."

raegan

"You can't hit Cayden," I say with a frown. "That wasn't nice, Deck."

Declan's bottom lip wobbles and then he puts his head on Cayden's leg and says, "I'm sorry, baby."

Cayden, completely oblivious to Declan's jealous swat, continues to sleep in my arms, mouth wide open just like how Ronan sleeps.

"Can I feed him?" Dakota asks, rushing over to me with another bottle.

"He seriously ate ten minutes ago. You're going to make him fat, Kota."

"You're fat!"

"You little shit," I bark as he runs off. "I'm going to get Dad's belt!"

Cayden, used to the loud people in our family, doesn't stir. Declan peeks up at me and grins. "You said shit."

My eyes widen and I scan the living room to make sure Mom isn't close by. "Shh. Our secret."

He giggles and then runs off to go play with Dakota.

I stand from the sofa and go into Destiny's bedroom where Renna's crib is set up. Renna is already down for a nap, so I lay Cayden at the other end of the crib. I close the door and then eventually find Mom in the pantry gathering ingredients for supper.

It's been a couple weeks since I had Cayden. And despite our house being mostly ready, Mom demands we continue to eat supper here every night. Since I don't have to cook, I'm not complaining.

"Can you keep an eye on your grandson while I round up your boys at the house?"

Mom's smile is so cheesy anytime I remind her she has a grandson. She waves me off. "Go get them. I'll listen out for Cayden."

I kiss her on the cheek and then find my boots. It's weird since I had Cayden. I don't find Mom so annoying. In fact, I find her incredibly helpful and understanding. She always knows just what to do whenever Cayden is upset and inconsolable.

Slipping out of the big house, I brace myself against the wind. The scent of campfire lingers in the air and makes me wonder if we can scrounge up marshmallows later for s'mores.

Our new house is on the other side of the path behind our property that leads to the cliffside stairs. The guys cleared an area, built us a home big enough for the four of us, and are in the middle of erecting a fence to go all the way around it. Their next project when it's warmer is to build a bridge across the two fences for quick, easy access to our parents' house.

For now, I have to take the long way around.

Hammering can be heard as I make my way to the front of our house. Dad, Ronan, and Ryder are all busy at work. Pride surges in my chest.

"Mom's looking for you," I tell Dad with a grin.

He looks up and tosses his hammer down. "What does she need?"

"Someone to admire her grandson with, I think."

Dad smirks as he passes me, messing up my hair along the way. I wait until he's gone to rush over to where Ronan and Ryder are standing.

"Hurry, let's run away while he's distracted," I call out loud enough for Dad to hear. "They'll take in Cayden as one of their own. They have so many kids they'll never know the difference."

"Real funny, sunshine," Dad hollers.

Sniggering, I find my way into my brothers' arms. They both hold me, keeping me warm against the biting wind. No one's watching, so we can display our affection as much as we want.

I'm not sure how long we stay, locked in a three-way embrace, but it feels too damn good to let go.

I'm never ever letting go.

The End

A NOTE FROM THE AUTHOR

Thank you so much for reading *The Unruly*! I hope you enjoyed the complicated but loving relationship of Raegan, Ronan, and Ryder! This Wild World is one that makes me super happy. I can't seem to let go of any of the characters. So what does this mean for the Wild World future?

I'd love to give Rowdy a book next. I've thrown some hints as to where that could go and with whom. I also thought it'd be fun to later do a book for Wild and give us more of a glimpse into his "sort of city" life and his family. Then, there's a lot of little kids that could grow up to have stories later too. Lots of ideas percolating inside the Webster brain!

I really appreciate you reading in this world and loving the characters as much as I do. I'll continue to write super-forbidden and taboo books from time to time so you can get your "not-safe-for-Amazon/Banned books" fix haha!

Since these books aren't allowed to be on the big retailers, any way you can share the word about them, I'm extremely grateful for. Even putting your review on Eden Books or Goodreads is helpful.

Thanks again for reading this book! And, if you're not on my newsletter, you should totally make sure you get on it so you never miss an update about my upcoming books!

Stay wild!
K Webster

WANT MORE TABOO ROMANCE?

Thank you for reading!

It's true...
Now, he's sick too.

READ HALE

ABOUT THE AUTHOR

K Webster is a *USA Today* Bestselling author. Her titles have claimed many bestseller tags in numerous categories, are translated in multiple languages, and have been adapted into audiobooks. She lives in "Tornado Alley" with her husband, two children, and her baby dog named Blue. When she's not writing, she's reading, drinking copious amounts of coffee, and researching aliens.

To see the full list of K Webster's books, visit authorkwebster.com/all-books.

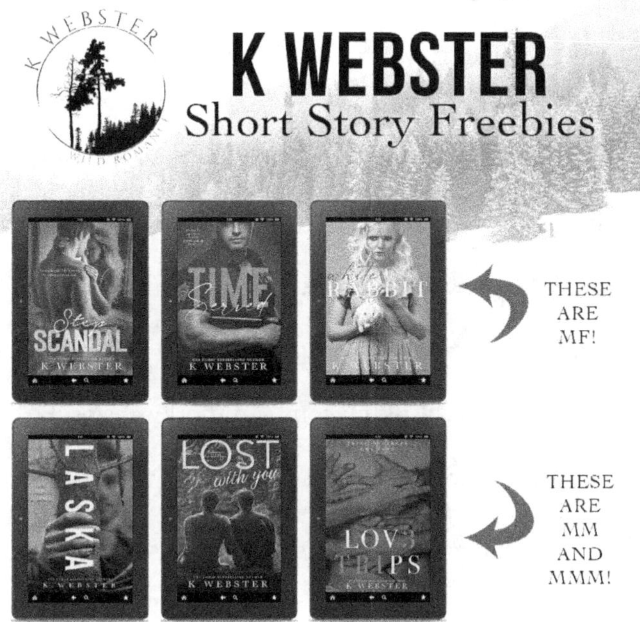

JOIN MY NEWSLETTER
at authorkwebster.com/newsletter

JOIN MY PRIVATE GROUP
at www.facebook.com/groups/krazyforkwebstersbooks

Follow K Webster here!

Facebook: www.facebook.com/authorkwebster

Readers Group:
www.facebook.com/groups/krazyforkwebstersbooks

Patreon: patreon.com/authorkwebster

Twitter: twitter.com/KristiWebster

Goodreads:
www.goodreads.com/author/show/7741564.K_Webster

Instagram: www.instagram.com/authorkwebster

BookBub: www.bookbub.com/authors/k-webster

Wattpad: www.wattpad.com/user/kwebster-wildromance

TikTok: www.tiktok.com/@authorkwebster

Pinterest: www.pinterest.com/kwebsterwildromance

LinkedIn: www.linkedin.com/in/k-webster-396b7021